Nothing Simple

LIA MILLS

PENGUIN
IRELAND

PENGUIN IRELAND

Published by the Penguin Group
Penguin Ireland, 25 St Stephen's Green, Dublin 2, Ireland
(a division of Penguin Books Ltd)
Penguin Books Ltd, 80 Strand, London WC2R ORL, England
Penguin Group (USA) Inc., 375 Hudson Street, New York, New York 10014, USA
Penguin Group (Australia), 250 Camberwell Road,
Camberwell, Victoria 3124, Australia (a division of Pearson Australia Group Pty Ltd)
Penguin Group (Canada), 10 Alcorn Avenue, Toronto, Ontario, Canada M4V 3B2
(a division of Pearson Penguin Canada Inc.)
Penguin Books India Pvt Ltd, 11 Community Centre,
Panchsheel Park, New Delhi – 110 017, India
Penguin Group (NZ), cnr Airborne and Rosedale Roads, Albany,
Auckland 1310, New Zealand (a division of Pearson New Zealand Ltd)
Penguin Books (South Africa) (Pty) Ltd, 24 Sturdee Avenue,
Rosebank 2196, South Africa

Penguin Books Ltd, Registered Offices: 80 Strand, London WC2R ORL, England

www.penguin.com

First published 2005
1

Copyright © Lia Mills, 2005

The moral right of the author has been asserted

Set in 13.5/16 pt Monotype Garamond
Typeset by Rowland Phototypesetting Ltd, Bury St Edmunds, Suffolk
Printed in Great Britain by Clays Ltd, St Ives plc

A CIP catalogue record for this book is available from the British Library

ISBN 1–844–88057–5

This is a work of fiction. Any resemblance to real persons, living or dead, is coincidental.

For Kate Cruise O'Brien

PART ONE

Leaving
(Houston, 1990)

'Did you find her?'

Dermot's voice cracks. He looks past me. His eyes dart from side to side, as if Hannah might be folded up behind me. As if I've hidden her somewhere in my clothes, or behind my back, while he was out checking the wasteground beyond the end of our street.

I'm not sure if I can speak with this tide of panic that rises in my mouth, but I don't have to. He can see that she's not here, just as I can see that she's not with him.

'I'll check her room again.' He barges down the narrow hallway to the children's rooms. The tail-end of a sentence floats behind him. '. . . wait until I get my hands on her!'

I don't go after him. We both know that Hannah won't be there. Not in the closet, or under the bunk-beds. We've already looked. We've searched the house and the back garden. We've checked the mouldy old doghouse and down behind the bush where the compost is, a rank place where Hannah, who is ten and has recently developed a loathing for bugs and creepy-crawlies, would never hide in a million years.

When Hannah stormed out of the house twenty minutes ago, there was enough rage in that ten-year-old body to carry her all the way to the coast and back. But I didn't believe for a second that she would keep going, no matter how upset she was, no matter how much conviction there'd been in her voice when she screamed, 'I *hate* you, Mom! Leave me alone!'

Hannah has always been moody, but lately things are getting out of hand. Yelling, door-slamming and hot looks have become part of our daily routine.

'Hormones,' my friend Beth suggests. She hums the theme tune from *The Twilight Zone*.

'It's because we're leaving,' I say. 'She doesn't want to go.'

'I don't blame her, Ray. I don't want you to go either.'

Hannah is furious with everyone, but with me most of all.

'But *why* do we have to go?' she wants to know.

'Hannah, you know all this. There's your dad's job, for a start.'

'Why can't he find a different one?'

'It's not that easy.'

We've lived in America for ten years, Hannah's entire life. The last seven of those have been spent in this house, in this neighbourhood on the south-western edge of Houston, Texas. This is her home, everything she knows. I don't blame her for being angry that we have to leave. But the truth is, we don't have much choice.

A recession is biting deep into this state and threatening the city. People pull up and leave every chance they get. Even in Houston, a place famous for its shifting population and the shallowness of its roots, what's happening now is remarkable. A kind of human tide. Families slip out of town in the middle of the night, defaulting on rents, on loans, on unpaid bills. There are few goodbyes, no forwarding addresses. The city is in some kind of spasm. The chill that began in the Rio Grande Valley a few winters back and killed all the fruit has spread northwards like some kind of vengeful blight. The optimism of several booms has spent itself in perky bumper stickers, a kind of state art form, urging people to DRIVE 55! ... FREEZE A YANKEE! or reminding us, as if we could forget, that TEXAS IS A STATE OF MIND.

Now reality is on its way back, with all the force of a Gulf storm behind it. Optimistic new strip-centres that sprang up one short year ago, like mushrooms after rain, have stood vacant ever since. They've lost their battle with scrub and bindweed. Spongy green shoots push their way up through seams in the concrete. Live oak and mesquite have crept back up to breathe down the necks of unused warehouses, sumac sheds its hairy fruit on fallen signs that once held property leasing information. If anyone cared to dial those phone numbers now, they would ring out.

Even Dermot's company is on the verge of bankruptcy. After years of loyalty, on both sides, we've all agreed to go our separate ways. And while his managers rack their brains for ways to cut costs and make back some of the money they've lost, Dermot has found another job, back home, in Ireland. We've sold our house. Granted, we sold it at a loss, but at least, as Dermot says, we're free to leave, we have somewhere to go, and a way of getting there. Our flight leaves the day after tomorrow.

I've seen entire houses loaded onto the back of monster flatbeds heading out of town after dark just as fast as they can go. It's the strangest traffic I've ever seen. They leave gaps behind them on suburban streets, like pulled teeth. Our son Ben, who is nearly four, is fascinated by this. He wants to know why we can't take our house with us when we leave.

'It wouldn't fit on a plane, stupid!' Hannah will take her rage out on anyone if she gets the chance.

'We've sold the house, Ben,' I said. 'You know that. The new people are moving in next week.'

Hannah's green eyes glittered. Her broad, freckled hands knotted into fists. Lately, she has closed her heart against us. Her face is a mask, her voice is flat and empty. That's on a good day. The rest of the time she sparks fights with everyone, slams doors, pulls her own hair until tears spring to her eyes. I don't know what to do. I'm not used to being at the receiving end of this kind of treatment, although God knows I probably dished it out hard enough when I was her age. I never got on with my own mother. I can't bear the thought that Hannah might feel the same way about me. I tell myself that her rage is all about the fact that we're leaving, and that she doesn't want to go.

If Jack, who's seven, could have his way, he'd probably bring this whole neighbourhood to Ireland with us, but it would be more of an exercise in logistics than anything else. He'll be happy enough wherever we are, so long as he can keep his Lego and his Erector set. Jack's two best friends have already left, part of the general exodus, and he's excited about his first journey on a plane, curious about what our new life will be like. He has devoted himself to packing as much entertainment as he can into the backpack he's allowed to carry on board. Jack's amusement comes in the form of small plastic bits and pieces that can be hooked together into an infinite number of vehicular structures and then taken apart again. The elaborate constructions that litter the carpet right now will be dismantled and crammed into a suitcase when it's time to go. Jack won't be carrying many clothes over to Ireland. I don't mind, because the clothes we wear now will be useless when we get there. We'll have to buy new ones: woollen sweaters with long sleeves and high necks. Vests. Warm socks. While we've lived here, I've grown used to going barefoot. In ten years, I haven't needed a coat.

Unlike Jack, Hannah has fought to keep every scrap of clothing she owns, including her collection of dress-up clothes, ludicrous things, all feathers and beads and diamanté bits that are bound to get wrecked on the journey. And, of course, the swimming medals that fill the corkboard I bought specially to hold them. They hang from plastic pushpins, a riot of different coloured wool and ribbons and shiny silver discs, the accumulation of five years of racing and Hannah's increasing strength and speed. 'I won't go without them!' she yells, her eyes snapping their eerie, underwater light.

'We wouldn't expect you to, Hannah.'

I've given in to Hannah more than once. I've agreed that she can take an extra bag, and I've let her cram her combs and hair ribbons in the side pocket of my own suitcase, even though she cut her rust-coloured hair razor-short this summer to make her faster in the water. I've asked my mother to look into swimming clubs for her in Ireland, but I don't hold out much hope. Not with the weather over there the way it is. Still, you never know.

Ben wants to know if there are cars in Ireland, and roads. He's looking forward to the buses, to travelling around a city by train. He's all movement, Ben. All noise and good humour. He is a big boy, nearly as tall as Jack, with broad feet and hands and a big head. It's as if he's absorbed the size and inclinations of Texas. Everything about him will be big. He already has big brown hair, like his father.

Dermot says that Ben is built like a rugby player and mentions some uncle of his who used to play for Ireland. Everyone else here says that he'll make a great linebacker some day. They make jokes comparing him to a famous American football star known as the Refrigerator. Like the Refrigerator, Ben is not exactly quick on his feet, but he's unstoppable when he puts his mind to something. But what no one takes into account is that Ben is unco-ordinated and clumsy, as if his brain hasn't quite caught up with his size. He bumps into things, trips over his feet when he runs, causes spills when he reaches across the table for the ketchup. But these disasters don't bother Ben. He dusts himself down quickly and runs off, ready for more.

Grace, who's eighteen months old, is too little to care what she brings with her, so long as it includes me and her rag doll, Bat. Bat goes everywhere with Grace, tucked into the crook of her sturdy arm, propped on the table when we eat, tucked in to bed beside her when she goes to sleep. I don't mind because up until recently it was me that Grace attached herself to with such intensity. Her ropy fingers used to knot themselves into whatever anchor they could find – clothes or hair, or even skin. For a while, I had as many bruises as Ben, all of them inflicted by his baby sister and her desperate love. Her eyes, grey like her father's and slightly un-focused, still fasten onto my face while she pours out her indignant anxieties, because even someone as young as Grace can recognize the signs of change that have invaded the little backwater where we live.

In spite of the recession, a new freeway interchange is being built right here, behind our boundary fence. In better years it was easy to ignore the proposed extension to the freeway that loops above our northern bound-ary, while it was delayed by some wrangle at City Hall. Instead of thinking about it, or even trying to stop it, we used the wide green space in the middle of the neighbourhood as if we owned it. The men got together and built a children's playground out there, set up a lightly marked soccer pitch and a baseball diamond. There are small plots of tilled earth where people grow vegetables. We thought that if we used the land well, if we ignored the proposed changes, they would go away. We thought they had forgotten about us down at City Hall. This isn't a part of town that dignitaries ever visit; it isn't even on the most recent maps. But now that the official obstacles have been removed, even though the city has run out of money, out of luck, out of steam, even though everyone is leaving, here come the diggers and the earthmovers and the vast concrete pipes to lay the new road.

'To help people leave town faster,' is Beth's opinion.

Since the work began, we've had to deal with rats and snakes and noise and dust and a constant, high-frequency rumble underfoot. When I look at the sky, I could swear those are earthquake clouds I see, although Dermot laughs at the idea, shows the children just how wrong I am on the map of the world that's pinned to the kitchen wall, where the distance between where we are now and where we will be next week seems deceptively short, the span of a single hand.

'We're miles away from any fault,' Dermot has said, more than once. 'There'll never be an earthquake here.'

'Don't tempt fate!' I know something is coming our way. I can feel it in the dead air of high summer and the shrill rolling swell of the cicadas. 'Look at Hunter,'

I say, and then wish I hadn't, because I can hardly bear to look at him myself. The dog won't let me out of his sight these days, as if he knows we're about to run out on him. He pads around the house behind me, his breath clammy on my bare heels, his black ear cocked and his white one flattened the way it is when he's worried.

'You feel like that because we're leaving,' Dermot says, always practical. 'And you're right, it's getting closer. We have a million things to do. So let's get on with it.'

Sometimes I wonder what life will be like when we go home. People will expect me to be the same as the person I used to be. But that was ten years ago. In the meantime, the children have changed me, the way they do. If you ask me, our children tame us. You'd think it would be the other way around, but no. No one ever warns you about this. You have to figure it out for yourself, like landing in a foreign country and having to learn the map, the customs, a whole new language.

I've had dreams about arriving in Dublin airport and finding the signs written in an alphabet I can't decipher. I dream about driving along the street I grew up on, but when I look for our gate, the walls crumble and fall and I'm lost downtown in some American city, where the traffic veers from lane to lane and I have no way to get my bearings on the grid.

My children will probably find the climate in Ireland unbearable. They will cry from the cold and get chilblains. People will tease them about their accents, look for things to criticize, mock the things they care about. They will have to change the way they spell words that took them so long to learn. They'll have to learn Irish. I'll have to find schools, start all over again with doctors, find a place to live. We'll start to accumulate the props of a life, the things you need, like food; the things you think you can't do without, like furniture. And if it all goes wrong and we have to move again, we'll go through exactly what we're going through now. We'll have to sell everything and start again.

2

Today, before the row with Hannah, we had a garage sale.

Our street, Station Hollow, is a balloon-shaped outcrop of Station Road. Traffic coming out of the neighbourhood, such as it is, turns right at the corner, moves away from us towards the county line. Our end of Station Road is like a backwater, forgotten by any kind of tide. No one ever turns this way unless they're visiting one of the houses down here. Or by mistake. Our house faces the wide circle of grass at the end of our street, and our tall wooden fence separates us from a tract of undeveloped land that leads down to the railway line, which marks the county line. Talk about being on the edge of town. Edges don't come much sharper than this.

Facing the open neck of our street and frowning down the length of it, is the only two-storey house in this part of the neighbourhood. A girl called Lucie, who is Hannah's best friend one day, mortal enemy the next, lives there. Lucie's mother, Marilyn, always keeps their curtains closed. A lot of people do around here. They live in semi-darkness, with wood-panelled walls and heavy furniture under slow-moving ceiling fans. It's cooler that way. You can hear the air-conditioning units run all day long.

Our house was wide open for the sale. We'd so much junk spread out on the driveway and on the grass that morning that it looked as if we lived outside. I hoped the notices we'd put up in the supermarkets and gas stations would attract a decent crowd. Dermot had been up since dawn, organising signs to point people in our direction.

Beth and her thirteen-year-old daughter, Brooke, came early to take the children out for the day, so they wouldn't have to watch while people picked through their toys and clothes, haggled over prices. She was driving them up to the lake to say goodbye to her aunt, who has a large, cool house on the waterfront.

I carried Grace out and strapped her into the booster seat in Beth's station-wagon.

'Thanks a million for doing this, Beth. I owe you.'

'Sure.'

We didn't quite look at each other. We both knew there'd be no time to repay this or any other favour. I stepped back onto the grass while the other kids piled into the car. The dog's weight was hot on my bare feet.

'Bye, Mom. Bye, Hunter!' Jack called, flapping his elbows under the weight of the towel, snorkel and flippers in his arms. Ben came over to hug me goodbye. He dropped his rubber wings and crouched down to kiss Hunter's nose. The dog licked Ben's mouth, his tail swinging like a piston.

'He wants to come too,' Ben said. 'Can he?'

'No, Ben.'

Hannah hesitated, one foot in and one foot out of the car.

'Are they taking him today?'

'Tomorrow.'

Hannah looked back once and then shoved her way into the car. '*I'm* sitting beside Brooke!' she yelled at Jack.

Beth said something soothing but indistinct in reply.

I waved at them from where I was. 'See you later!' I wished I could go with them. Dermot's face was grim.

'How did we ever accumulate all this junk?' He looked at me, accusing.

'Don't worry,' I said. 'I'm a garage-sale expert, remember?'

It was true, but this was different. This wasn't part of the general recycling of the neighbourhood. I had to watch people pick over my things, hold them up for inspection, speculate about price and value. I had to remind myself that none of it meant anything, that it was a tough market with so many people in transit and everyone broke. It was just stuff. It was all replaceable.

'Do y'all need help?' Ellen from the corner house on our side of the street appeared beside me.

Ellen is a bossy woman with an awkward manner, but she means well. Usually. She's one of those women who has allowed her hair to go grey naturally and wears it short, and the effect is striking against her olive skin, her deep brown eyes. She emphasizes the blunt haircut with thick gold jewellery: a plain collar of gold around her neck, a square bangle on her wrist. She looks strong, a no-nonsense kind of person. Sometimes I think a little nonsense would do our Ellen a lot of good.

'How you holding up, Ray?'

'Okay. Thanks.'

'You need a break, you come on over to my house. Y'hear?'

I knew I was in a bad way if even Ellen's formal kindness could make me want to weep. I nodded and went inside to bring out a box full of glasses. On the way I had to step over Hunter, who twisted around and rolled in the grass, scratching his back, showing grey splodges of colour on his belly. I stopped to rub his stomach. His tongue slid out over his teeth and he grinned at me, upside down, the black flab of his jowls wobbling.

'Lunatic,' I said.

He wagged his tail.

'Any old insult will do you, won't it? You've no pride.'

His tail wagged harder.

The phone was ringing when I got into the kitchen.

'Ray, honey? This is Lisa.'

I could tell by her voice that this was not going to be good news. Lisa Martinez had agreed to take Hunter. Her daughter, Marianna, is a schoolfriend of Hannah's and I was relieved when they offered to take the dog, not only for his sake but because Hannah agreed. We'd looked into bringing him with us, but it would have been expensive, and there are quarantine laws. Hunter is a sociable dog and it didn't seem fair to abandon him to a kennel for six months. We didn't know where we'd be living, whether we'd have a garden or not. Dermot told us that a woman he knew flew her dog over to England last year and he died in the third week of quarantine. All that, and he died anyway. 'There's no question of taking him with us,' Dermot told the children. 'It wouldn't be fair.'

They came around to the solution of 'lending' Hunter to Marianna. At least Hannah approved. As far as she's concerned, Hunter belongs to her.

We found him five years ago. Hannah clung to him so fiercely that we'd ended up keeping him, despite our reservations. Marianna had promised to write to Hannah every week, with a picture of Hunter. I doubted that she could keep that up for long, but I knew they'd take good care of him.

'I'm real sorry, Ray. Real sorry. We spent all night at the emergency room at Southwest Memorial. The baby had herself an asthma attack last night, needed oxygen and everything. The doctors say it's allergies. They say we shouldn't get a dog.'

'Oh, no!'

'I feel real bad about it. And I know it puts y'all in a spot. I didn't think, Hunter being so cute and all . . . I never thought about allergies.'

'Are you sure that's what she has?'

'That's what the doctor says.' Lisa's voice was firm. 'I can't take the risk.'

'No. No, of course you can't.' I hung up. What the hell would we do now? We'd less than two days left and we had tried the whole world before Lisa offered to take Hunter. I'd done my best to forget all about it ever since. I'd been trying to take everything about this move one step at a time, to keep it manageable, but it looked as if I was fighting a losing battle with time.

I went back out into a stifling blaze of light to find Dermot and tell him what had happened.

'Hello, Miz Graves.'

I had to shade my eyes with my hand before I recognized the tall black woman in a cotton dress as Mrs Williams, who had been Hannah's and Jack's kindergarten teacher. The woman beside her was a stranger.

'I'd like you to meet my sister, Loretta Smith. We just stopped by to say we're sorry that y'all are leaving.'

'Which Ireland are y'all headed for?' Loretta Smith leaned towards me, smiling. The sun reflected off the lenses of her glasses.

'Uh, there is only one.'

'No, ma'am. I'm sure there are two.'

'No . . . Oh, I see what you mean. We're from Dublin. The Republic. But—'

'Isn't there a war there?' Loretta Smith's even teeth were too small for her mouth.

'No.'

'Yes'm, I believe there is.'

For Mrs Williams' sake, I tried to stifle my irritation. 'It's complicated.'

'Bombing? Shootings? Killings?'

'Well, yes, but . . .'

Loretta looked over at her sister, as if to say *I told you so*. 'A war. Aren't you afraid, to take your children back to a place like that?'

I pulled myself up to my full height and stared down at her. I may have been in shorts and a sweaty T-shirt, I may have been on the run, but I was not about to be put down like that on my own driveway. 'No, ma'am,' I said, in the most deliberately Texan voice I had ever used. 'And, last time I checked, there was no shortage of shootings and killings right here in this city.'

Mrs Williams' soft, white-gloved hand landed on my arm and patted it gently. 'She meant no harm, honey,' she said. 'Don't stir yourself.'

'We-ell,' Ellen's voice boomed in my ear when the two women had gone. 'You sure did tell them a thing or two. I was mighty proud of you, Ray.'

'I have to find Dermot, Ellen. I'll be back in a minute.'

Dermot was sorting through his toolbox. He held the phase tester as if he was about to find a use for it somewhere. It had taken a long time for him to collect those tools. They'd be easy to sell. I told him about Lisa's phone call. 'What'll we do?'

Right on cue, a tall man in a stetson loomed over us. 'What y'all goin' to do with that dog? You takin' him with you?'

I shot a look at Dermot.

Up in the garage, a heavy-set woman in a pink shell-suit lifted the lid of the washing machine, leaned in to rotate the drum. Now she turned and called down to me, 'Ma'am? Is this here washer for sale?'

'Yes . . . could you wait just for a minute?'

The man in the stetson hooked his thumbs in his jeans, waiting for an answer. Ellen went off to find change for a child who had bought a stack of Hannah's old books.

'Ma'am?' The heavy-set woman insisted. Her friend raised her eyebrows, narrowed her lips, spread her feet as if settling in for a battle. Her arms were piled high with clothes, almost to her chin.

Down on the street, two teenagers twisted the remaining wing mirror of our battered old Volvo. 'Hey!' Dermot yelled.

'Ma'am? Are you selling this or not?'

'No!' I snapped.

The woman looked at her friend. I could hear something break as the friend made a big show of dropping her armful of clothes on the ground. They stepped over the mess and walked away.

'Great!' I muttered.

Ellen stepped up, shaking her head. 'I'll get it, honey.'

'Be careful, Ellen. Something broke. It might be glass,' Dermot warned, before turning his attention back to the man in the stetson.

I couldn't think straight. Everything was happening too fast and getting faster. We only had two days left and no one wanted Hunter. I knew only too well what happened to unwanted pets around here. They were lucky if animal control got to them before strung-out teenagers, or small boys, or someone, these days, who was too hungry for sentiment. And I couldn't bear the thought of putting him to sleep just because we were leaving.

'Friendly little thing.' The man watched his small son stroke Hunter's broad head. Hunter wriggled closer and pushed himself against the child, loving the attention. The boy's sister stood beside them in a pair of outsize dungarees, sucking her thumb, watching. 'Do you want money for him?'

'No. He's free to anyone who'll give him a good home.'

'Dermot, wait . . .'

'We have food and his dishes and a leash – everything you'll need.' Dermot avoided my eye.

'Can we, Dad?' The boy jumped to his feet. His eyes lit up. 'Can we really?'

The girl took her thumb out of her mouth and leaned down to pat Hunter quickly on the back. Then she folded her hand into the bib of her dungarees and looked up at her father. 'Please, Daddy?'

I went around in a daze gathering Hunter's stuff – his dish, his rubber bone, his leash. At the last minute I put a manky T-shirt of my own into the bag, and a teddy bear from the sale box of soft toys. I felt a stab of shock when I lifted Hunter onto the back of the man's pick-up and kissed his nose for the last time. He squirmed and I let him go, into the waiting arms of the quiet little boy. Hunter waved his tail at me as they drove away, but when they slowed for the corner he cocked his head and began to whine.

Jump! I wanted to shout, but they'd gone. Too late, I realized that I should have taken a telephone number.

'I have to go inside for a minute,' I told Dermot.

I locked the bathroom door, something I couldn't remember doing in the seven years we'd lived in this house. I plunged my face and hands into cold running water and avoided my own reflection in the round, scarred mirror over the sink. A hot pit had opened in my chest, but it was too late to change anything now.

I dried my hands and went back outside. I put a smile on my face and held my voice steady for the bartering, cajoling and encouraging I still had to do.

Tony from next door came over and bought Dermot's tools. He told us that Angie, his wife, was lying down. 'She have another baby,' he said. His small eyes crinkled up with delight. He held the toolbox to his chest and beamed at us. Then he swung around and walked away across the grass.

'She has had a baby? Or is about to have one?' Dermot asked.

'Must be about to have one,' I said. I hadn't even noticed that Angie was pregnant. Come to think of it, I hadn't seen her much lately. But the heat in the last few weeks had been extreme, and Angie isn't exactly the most sociable of women. We were so busy with the sale that I soon forgot about her.

I wheedled and insulted people into buying things they didn't want and in the end we shifted nearly everything. Even the Volvo that had carried us across the continent and back was towed away behind a big square sedan. I didn't pay a scrap of attention when the man handed me a twenty-dollar bill for it and said that he would strip it down for parts. Everything I was about to lose had come together when I lifted Hunter up onto that flatbed. Watching him go had ripped the heart out of me. There didn't seem to be much left to care about.

The children came home earlier than we'd expected. Hannah came running into the house, calling for the dog. 'Hunter! Hunter! Come see what I brought you!' She had a piece of driftwood in her hands, bleached to the colour of bone.

'Hunter's gone,' Dermot said.

We should have been ready for this. We should have planned what we'd say. But, like most things about our children, we were caught off-guard.

'What?'

Dermot flushed. 'He's gone, Hannah. Some people wanted him.'

'Who, Marianna?'

'No. Not Marianna.'

'Who, then?' She stopped moving.

'Some people who came to the sale.'

The children all turned to look at me. As if I might say something that could change the world, reverse the course of time.

'It's true.' Even as I said it, I knew this was the worst thing yet and that there would be no going back from it. 'I'm sorry. Lisa called. The baby is sick and they couldn't take Hunter after all, and then a family came . . .' I took a step towards Hannah, who ran behind the sofa and stood there shaking her head, warning me not to go any closer.

'They were very nice.' I caught Hannah's furious eye and stopped talking. Then I tried again. 'There were children. They loved him.'

'We loved him!' Jack flung his stuff on the ground.

'I know you did, Jack . . .'

Jack stomped out of the room and ran noisily down the hall. I could hear his bunk crash against the wall as he threw himself onto it.

'I still love him. He's my dog.' Hannah's face was a burning mask.

And then, suddenly, she was gone. The house shook from the force of the slammed front door. From the other side of it, I heard a single wail, barely human.

'I'm going after her,' I told Dermot. 'Will you talk to Jack?'

I hurried out. Ellen was getting into her car. She looked over and waved. I kept going, following Hannah, reminding myself to be calm. What I really wanted was to give vent to the burning storm inside me, to rage and spin and blow and spend myself in tears, to level this world I was about to leave.

'Hannah, wait!'

'Leave me alone!'

When I got closer to her, Hannah moved faster, breaking into a run.

'I hate you!' she screamed. 'Go away!'

She ran to the end of the street, to the live oak tree, everyone's favourite for climbing. Just beyond the tree, I could see the gap the freeway workers had made in the boundary fence that morning. On Monday they'd be back to build the solid soundproof wall that was going to close our street off from the rest of the neighbourhood, leaving us on the wrong side of everything, out there with the marsh grass and the roadworks, with only the railway track between us and the one-lane highway that leads south and west to the state prison. Someone had redrawn the city limits on a map, excluding us.

'Hannah, I can't leave you out here, don't be silly!' I moved closer, but she backed away. So I sat on the sidewalk with my back to the mailbox and waited. I listened to her crashing ascent through the sturdy lower branches of the tree, bit my lip on the usual warnings not to go too high. I knew she'd have to come down sooner or later. Hunger or tiredness or boredom would drive her back inside. I wondered if it would be easier if I wasn't sitting there, waiting for her.

In the end, I figured that pride was more likely to get in Hannah's way than anything else. So I made up my mind and got back to my feet. 'Okay, I'm going in,' I called. 'To order pizza. If you don't come in when it gets here, we won't keep you any.'

No answer.

I strolled back inside the house as if I hadn't a worry in the world and went straight to the phone.

'Where's Hannah?' Dermot asked.

'In the tree.' I placed our usual order. One large margherita pizza with extra cheese, one medium thin-crust with pepperoni and sausage, garlic bread. In a fit of extravagance I ordered a bottle of Coke as well.

'This is nuts! I'm going out there to get her down, right now!'

I went to the window to check on Hannah's position. 'Don't. She just needs time alone.'

'You let her get away with murder,' he said. 'I've a good mind to go out there and drag her in.'

'She'd never forgive you.' I strained to see Hannah's shape through the branches. She must have climbed higher than she ever had before.

It was that twilight hour where shadows thicken in the trees and the roar of the cicadas swells until you think something somewhere has to burst wide open.

'I can't see her.'

Dermot came over to look. The veins in his neck were more pronounced than usual, but I could only worry about one thing at a time. 'Right. That's enough. I'm going out there.'

I watched him stride down the drive and lope across the road, his hands deep in his pockets, his chin jutting out. I braced myself for the roaring, for Hannah's outrage and Dermot's fury while he dragged her home, making himself more fierce to cover the mortification of having to go through it all in full view of anyone who happened to be watching.

But when he started calling Hannah's name, I ran out after him, forgetting that the pizza was on its way, forgetting Jack down in his room, abandoning Ben and Grace to the television. Because I could tell, from Dermot's voice, that Hannah had gone.

3

I don't need anyone to remind me that I'm the one who took my eyes off Hannah, that I'm the one who believed that we should let her go. It doesn't matter how fast I get out there to look for her, or how soon Beth and Brooke come over when I call and howl down the phone, not making any sense at all. The single thing that I will never be able to change is that moment when I stood up, turned away from my daughter and went back inside the house.

Ellen's husband, Tyler, comes out to see what's going on. 'I'll help y'all look,' he offers, when we explain what's happened.

Out in the wasteground, we call Hannah, our voices flying up over the cicadas, over the roar of traffic from the freeway overpass. But there's no answer.

'I bet she comes back covered in poison ivy,' Dermot grumbles. 'She'll be miserable on the plane. We'll never hear the end of it.'

We beat the grass and call Hannah's name, walk around the digging equipment that has been parked near the hole in our fence, look between the dense rubber tyres, as tall as Tyler.

'I don't think she's out here,' I say.

'How do you know?' Tyler looks incongruous, dressed in a jacket, white shirt, creased grey trousers, the leather strands of his bolo looped gracefully around his neck and caught in a heavy silver and turquoise clasp. Being a determined Texan, Tyler wouldn't be seen dead in a regular necktie; there are just so many concessions he's willing to make to the corporate image of the New England insurance company that employs him. He must have been on his way in from work when he came to see what the commotion was.

'Hannah's afraid of snakes. And she knows they've been disturbed by . . .' I wave helplessly at the ruined expanse of space where we used to have ball games and street parties, where Tyler himself still grows plump courgettes and lustrous purple aubergines. Zucchini and eggplant to him. '. . . all this.' Mountains of dirt, senseless in their random size, have turned this green area into wasteground overnight.

'I thought she played out here all the time.'

'Not any more.' More's the pity, I can't help thinking. Up until a year ago, she would have been shinning up those tyres as fast as any boy. But there's not much chance that my newly fastidious Hannah, who's recently been known to lock herself into the bathroom for half an hour at a stretch, will be hidden in some mucky trench along with spiders and ants and displaced rodents. Nor is she likely to have climbed into the cabs of the earthmovers, even if they've been left unlocked. I rack my brains, trying to think. 'I'm afraid we'll scare her off, doing this.'

'Maybe she's gone back to the house already.' Dermot says it before the thought has finished forming in my own mind.

'I'll go back and check.'

'I'll stay out here with Tyler for a while.'

Hannah is not in the house. Jack is plonked in front of the television next to Brooke, whom he adores. I've had to stop Dermot from teasing him about his taste for older girls. 'We don't want him to get self-conscious about it.'

'It's true, though. Jack loves to hang out with older women.'

Grace sits on Brooke's knee, sucking her thumb and rolling the fabric of Brooke's T-shirt in the fingers of her other hand. Bat is crammed into the crook of her elbow. Ben is sprawled on the floor, his chin in his hands, legs waving around like helicopters. He's sniffling a little. I remember the fiasco with Hunter with a fresh surge of guilt, but I can't deal with it now. Beth is in the kitchen, sorting through the last oddments from the sale.

'Leave that, Beth.'

'I have to do something.'

I go back and check the bedrooms again, get on my knees and look under our bed, check out the closets, the bath, the shower stall. There's no sign of her.

Beth is still fussing in the kitchen when I get back. This time, she's cleaning my oven. I've never noticed

30

how many clocks we have before. Each one says a slightly different time. The one on the kitchen wall is a minute faster than the digital display on the oven; the red light on the TV is two minutes behind the VCR. I try to avoid checking these clashing times every few seconds, but I don't seem able to retain what they tell me. Seven thirty-five. Hannah's been gone for just over half an hour. Maybe we're overreacting. How long has she been gone again? Which clock was that? I make an effort to pull myself together.

'I'm trying to think,' I say to Beth. 'If I was Hannah, where would I go? Most likely to a friend. But she's so up and down with everyone lately.'

'Girls are like that. Best friends one minute, worst enemies the next.'

'I never was. But then, I didn't have any girlfriends when I was growing up.'

'Neither did I. I didn't need 'em. I had Curtis,' Beth says.

Brooke looks around at the sound of her father's name. Beth shakes her head. 'Fool that I was,' she says, low enough so that Brooke can't hear.

Brooke is a calm, self-possessed girl with her mother's warm face and sweet smile. She has silky brown hair that ripples down her back and all the children, even Hannah, are fascinated by it. Brooke has told Beth that she blames herself for her father's desertion, because she took so much of Beth's time and attention when she was sick. When Brooke was a toddler she developed a wasting illness that the doctors couldn't identify, no matter how many machines they hooked her up to, or how much blood they drained from her system. Beth gave up her job as a graphic designer to stay home and look after her. For a while, everyone thought that Brooke would die. But Beth refused to give up until she discovered that Brooke had a rare allergy to all forms of sugar. Most things she ate were like poison to her system. At first the doctors paid no attention to Beth. One of them even accused her of inventing her daughter's illness, just to get attention for herself. But at last she found someone who knew what she was talking about. For nearly a year, Brooke was fed intravenously. She drifted around the house like a waif, pushing her IV pole along beside her. We weren't here then, but I've seen the photographs and they'd break your heart. Little by little, they reintroduced limited kinds of food and by now Brooke can eat almost anything, so long as she's careful. She's still underweight and her skin has an unnerving, translucent look. Her features are narrow, where Beth's are broad. As if she is some elfin version of her mother.

When Brooke began to get better, Beth started painting. Her pictures are detailed and meticulous. I've seen things on Beth's canvases that you wouldn't expect to find in a formal painting, would never see on a gallery wall. Suburban gardens. Children playing. Supermarket aisles. A tray of blueberry muffins fresh from the oven and crumbling open. She pays so much attention to detail that it can take her six months to finish a single three-foot-square canvas, but when she's finished, it's like looking at a scene through glass.

'It's no wonder Beth can't make a living from her art,' Ellen says. 'It'll take her twenty years to get enough pictures together for one show.'

But I know that Ellen bought a painting from Beth just after Curtis left, and paid enough for it to cover household expenses for several months. Ellen might have a mouth like a scouring pad sometimes, but just when you're ready to slap her, she can take you by surprise.

Beth and I don't say anything for a while. I know she must be thinking about Curtis, but I'm more concerned about Hannah.

'What do you think, Brooke?' I ask.

Brooke folds her long sheet of brown hair through her hands and smooths it over her shoulder. 'I don't know,' she says. 'I saw her in a huddle with Lucie just yesterday. It looked real serious.'

'But they've gone out of town for the weekend,' Beth says. 'Marilyn and Lucie and Byron. I saw them leave. Before Hannah . . . ran off. We passed them on our way back from the lake. They waved.'

'Would she have gone to you, Brooke?' I ask.

We all stop talking.

'I'll go check the house,' Beth says.

When she's gone, I go to the phone and dial Lucie's number. Even though I don't expect an answer, I have butterflies in my stomach. I haven't spoken to Lucie's mother, Marilyn, for a while.

I'm relieved when the machine clicks in. 'Marilyn? It's Ray. We're looking for Hannah. We thought she might be with you. If you see her, could you call me? Thanks.'

I go through my address book and the lists on the wall: Hannah's class in school, the swim team. I ring everyone I can think of. No one has seen her, no one has any idea where she might be. My friends are sympathetic and offer help, but I tell them all the same thing. I know that she's all right, that she'll be back any minute, that she's just trying to give me a fright. Dermot's phrase rings in my ears.

Just wait until I get my hands on her.

As soon as I hang up from my telephone marathon, the phone rings. I snatch it up and say hello before it's even at my ear.

'Renée, is that you?'

For someone who doesn't have a maternal cell in her body, my mother has an uncanny instinct for trouble.

'Hello, Ma.' I look over at the clock, do a quick calculation. It's after half-past one in the morning over there. 'What are you doing up?'

'I couldn't sleep. It's very hot.'

I have to smile. Sylvia's idea of hot is the kind of temperature this city experiences in March.

'And the house is empty. Desmond and Jane and the

children have gone on their holidays. It's very quiet. I was thinking about all of you coming home and, well, I thought I'd phone and see how you're doing. Are you packed?'

'No, nothing like that. It's pretty chaotic.' Hannah's absence boils away at the base of my brain. If I tell Sylvia, will that make it worse? Will Hannah be more, or less, likely to come home?

I take a deep breath. 'We've lost Hannah.'

'What did you say? This is a terrible line.'

'Hannah has run away. We had a fight. She doesn't want to leave. She's hiding somewhere.'

'You'd better get out there and find her.'

'I've been . . . I came in to make some calls . . .'

'You'd better get off, now. Keep the line clear.' Sylvia breathes heavily. 'How long has she been gone? Have the police been called?'

'We'll find her, Ma. It's only been—' I check my watch again '—forty-five minutes.'

'What are you waiting for? You should call the police!'

'She's hiding somewhere, we're sure of it. She'll come home soon.'

'She could be lost. You can't be too careful.'

'A lot of people are out looking for her.'

Sylvia's voice calms. 'Mind you, let's not forget, you ran away yourself. Like mother—'

'I'm going to go, now. Like you said, we need to keep the line clear.'

*

When I hang up, I go over to look out the front window. The hole in the fence is wider. Someone, probably Dermot, has torn what's left of it down. It looks exactly the way it looked after the last big storm, except for the diggers and bulldozers, the mounds of black earth and stacks of ghostly cylinders on the other side.

Oh, Hannah, I think. *Please come home.*

Dermot comes in to see if there's any news.

'Sylvia's been on,' I say. 'She says we should call the police.'

'I was wondering about that myself.' He looks over at the clock.

'But we know she's hiding, Dermot. I'll go and check the park.'

'I've already—'

'I'll look again. I can't stay here and do nothing.'

'But she'll need you to be here when she gets home.' He comes and puts his familiar, freckled arms around me. 'That's "when", not "if".'

He presses me right into him, as if we could become one person that way, solid enough for anything. I hide my face in his neck, afraid of what anyone might read in it.

'She *will* come home. You know she will.' He makes a hoarse, strangled sound that might have been intended as a laugh. 'I bet she thinks that if she hides until the plane takes off, she'll stop us leaving.'

I pull away from him. 'She's right. That's one way to stop us going.'

He frowns in the direction of the other children. 'Don't let anyone else hear you say that.'

'Dermot, what if—'

'Stop. We'll find her. Or she'll come home, any minute now.'

'Don't yell at her when she does.'

'I won't.'

We both look at the other children. Jack is on the floor now, his thin brown legs up beside Ben's, the dirty soles of their feet waving. They kick at each other, but half-heartedly, as if they want the physical contact. Brooke has stretched out along the sofa and Grace lies across her stomach. It could be any evening in front of the TV. As if nothing is wrong.

'We'll wait another ten minutes,' Dermot said. 'If she's not back by then, we'll call them.'

Beth comes back in through the garage, shaking her head. 'She's not there. I left a note on the kitchen table, just in case.'

'What did you say?'

'Just, "No one's mad at you, honey, come on home." I said Brooke was here. I thought it might help.'

Jack stretches up to look out the window then jumps to his feet. 'Pizza guy's here!' he calls. He and Ben race to open the door.

I leave Dermot and Beth to deal with the pizza and hurry out through the hole in the fence to the wasteground. I climb up on a pipe so my voice will carry further and call to Hannah, to the freeway, to the air, in as normal a voice as I can muster.

'Hannah! The pizza's here. Come on in.'

My voice floats out and dissipates like smoke. I hear no answer, only the rise and fall of engines taking the bend of the freeway, a distant hiss of hydraulic brakes on the feeder road, insects calming from a burr to a staccato ticking, time speeding up.

I go back to the house, where the kids swarm around the table, peeling slices of pizza apart. 'I'm going to check the park.'

'I'll come with you,' Beth says. 'Brooke can stay with the kids, answer the phone . . . can't you, Brooke? But you should eat first, Ray.'

'I'm not hungry.'

'You go to the park,' Dermot said. 'I'll call the police.'

At the front door I stop dead. The sky has turned a deeper blue and the trees have darkened. A single point of silver light shines in the sky.

'The first star,' I say. 'Is it after eight already?'

'Just let me—' Beth begins.

'I'll go on.' I start walking fast. I can't bear to wait for anything now. I have to get to the park before it gets dark.

There's something eerie about a park in the dusk. I've never been able to shake off that city sense of trouble lurking in the shadows, waiting for mothers and young children to leave and take the daylight with them so that a darker force can come out to play.

The gate creaks when I push it open. The faulty spring makes the wire mesh bounce back on itself, taking me by surprise as it always does. More than one child has caught their fingers in that gate. More than one mother, struggling with the paraphernalia of children, nappy bags, picnic lunches, baby blankets, coolers, has reminded herself, up until the final snap, to lift her fingers out of the way, and still been caught out. There have been complaints, Ellen says, to the residents' association, but nothing has been done.

I climb the artificial slope to the wooden fort and look inside the base, climb the sloping ladder at the side to the den on top. There's no one in there.

I check behind the azaleas in the corner, where young teenagers come to smoke, but there's no one there either. I wish there was someone to beg a cigarette off, even though I haven't smoked since I found out I was pregnant with Hannah and Dermot and I made a pact never to smoke again.

I go and sit on one of the rubber swings and sway from side to side, remembering how we agreed about everything back then. We barely needed to discuss it.

People who knew me before I met him might well believe that I let Dermot swallow me whole – my friend Joanne got drunk one night and told me so – but it didn't feel like that. It was more like sharing a self with someone. We filled each other's gaps. Everything seemed so easy; there had been no need to think, nothing at all to think about. It was a love like a river and I plunged right into it, not stopping to ask where it would take me.

I think about what my mother said, about when I ran away from home. There's no comparison at all. I was eighteen, almost twice Hannah's age. I made it clear that I was leaving, and that I'd no intention of going back. I knew that Sylvia wouldn't care. I was sure that, if anything, she'd be relieved. As far as I was concerned I was doing both of us a favour. How could I have known that I was taking the first steps on a journey that would lead me here? I would never in a million years have foreseen myself like this, a big woman, nearing thirty, sitting on a swing in a deserted playground in Houston, Texas, trying to imagine where my angry daughter might have gone to hide from me.

PART TWO

Origins
(Ireland, 1970s)

4

By the time I was born, Sylvia had had enough of being a mother. My older brother, Barry, had already announced his intention of becoming a priest and even at ten it was obvious that Desmond, my other brother, was destined to become a solicitor, like our father. I imagine that Sylvia quite liked the prospect of a middle age nicely cushioned by a lawyer on one side and a priest on the other. It would have seemed dignified to her, and calm. And then my arrival spoiled it all. It must have been an embarrassment to find herself a mother all over again, after a ten-year gap. God only knows what the neighbours must have thought, and to Sylvia, what the neighbours thought mattered a great deal.

She told anyone who would listen that she'd thought she was finished with all that business of mess and noise and childhood illness, that she had lost her energy along with her muscle tone, that she was tired.

The list of things that made Sylvia tired was a litany I was well versed in from the time I learned to talk, when she complained that the pitch of my voice grated on her nerves and gave her a headache. 'Not *now*, Renée. I'm too tired,' was her standard response to any bid for attention. Before long, I gave up. I was well used to the guilty hush that descended on the house in the afternoons when Sylvia took to her bed in a darkened room, a cologne-soaked handkerchief pressed to her forehead. It was a relief to climb the garden wall and roam the streets and parks and beaches instead, where no one told me how to walk, or to cover my mouth with my hand when I laughed, not to get my clothes dirty.

When my father, Jack, came in from work, he shattered the silence of the house. He was a big, square-shouldered man, exactly six foot tall in his socks, who filled all the empty spaces of a room with his presence. His voice rolled out from somewhere deep in his chest in something like a growl. I always believed that voice was meant for me. A dense growth of furzy, sandy-coloured hair crowded the top of his head and his freckled wrists stuck out from the ends of his sleeves, leading to big hands, strong fingers with square tips.

As soon as Jack came in, Sylvia would beg him to take me away and keep me occupied. He would scoop me up and carry me, squealing, from room to room in search of some small present. It could be a feather or a piece of blue stone, a farthing he'd found on the street. We played hunt-the-thimble all over the house and he'd tease me with shouts of *Cold! Cold!* Or *Roasting, oh you're scalding now!* until my fingers closed around the thing he'd hidden for me. Once, after he'd been away for a cold and empty number of days, he brought me back a miniature china doll, the cool smooth porcelain overlaid with a stiff net skirt made of a gauzy fabric with golden thread.

'The gold made me think of you,' he said. He lifted my heavy hair off the back of my neck and smiled.

But I was never golden, I knew that. I was ruddy, like my father. My hair was the colour of copper, with fire at its ends. My skin was freckled and stained by the sun. My knees were scabbed, my legs and arms scratched by brambles, bark and brick, although I never noticed those cuts when they happened. I was an untidy child who'd do anything to avoid soap and water. When Sylvia caught sight of me, she used to sigh and shake her head, as if the thought of taking me in hand was too much for her. She insisted on calling me by my given name, Renée, long after everyone else had abandoned it.

The year that Desmond married his long-time girl-friend, Jane, my father died of a stroke. I was sixteen. For ten days I went to the hospital to sit with him instead of going to school. I held his hand and wiped drool from the corner of his mouth, ignoring everyone else who came and went. I tried to breathe at the same slow, uneven rate as he did, the way I used to when I was little. Every time my aching lungs clawed air into themselves ahead of his, I despised myself. I should have known that it would make no difference. He died anyway.

'What will I do now?' Sylvia asked, as if, overnight, I had become someone whose opinion was worth hear-ing. Maybe if I'd been more used to it I would have handled it better. Instead, I just stared at her.

'How am I supposed to know?'

'You could come and live with us,' Jane said, nervous.

She smoothed her hands over her sensible navy coat which no longer disguised the fact that she was pregnant.

They all looked at me.

'I don't think that's an option,' Sylvia said. 'There wouldn't be room for everyone.'

I retreated, bereft, to my room. I listened to sad music and cried in the dark with my father's smoking jacket wrapped around me. In the pockets I found the last packet of Carrolls he ever bought, along with his chrome cigarette lighter. I flicked the heavy lid up with my thumbnail, over and over, releasing the oily smell of petrol, the tarnished metal saddle. I spun the brass wheel against the flint and sparked blue flame, lit and smoked the whole packet of cigarettes, one after another. I was glad when they made me sick. I bought more to replace them. I was keeping my father's smell alive, and the feel of his arms wrapped around me when I was still small enough to be loved like that, sprawled on his knee in front of the coal fire in the front room, feeling the burr of his voice rumble deep behind his ribs, my breath rising and falling easily with every breath of his.

But I couldn't stay in my room for ever. While Sylvia pressed her scented hankie to her temples and groaned, I learned how to change plugs and fuses and how to cook. I took pride in not being like her, and found it comforting to take charge of the practical things that needed to be done. Over the next two years, I juggled household bills and stretched every penny as far as it would go. I borrowed a ladder from the neighbours to scrape the flaking plaster off the walls and then repainted the house from top to bottom. While I was at it, I cleaned out the gutters and scoured the drains. I put leather patches on the elbows of my school jumper when the wool wore out and although the nuns complained, other girls started to do it too, for effect.

But I had to draw the line somewhere. On the day that Sister John woke me up at my desk to inform the entire class that my school fees hadn't been paid for a full two years, I decided that enough was enough.

'Any other girl would be grateful.' The words slid out through Sister John's narrow mouth like cold grease. 'Another girl would be more deserving. But Renée, apparently, prefers to sleep through the opportunities we are offering.'

The room crackled and sparked around me. The radiator at the back of the room creaked and ticked the way it always had, giving out noise instead of heat. I could have sworn that no one breathed except the nun, harsh and fast, her black-winged arms hinged on her hips, waiting for me to cry.

Hardly knowing what I was doing, I stood up and walked through a narrowing tunnel to the door.

'If you walk out through the door of this classroom, you needn't ever bother coming back,' Sister John hissed after me.

'Suits me,' I said. 'You can go and fuck yourself.'

I tugged the door open on a tide of indrawn breath

from the other girls and let it slap shut behind me, the frosted glass shivering in its pane.

Sylvia groaned and pressed that rancid hankie to her brow and said she didn't know what she'd ever done to deserve an ungrateful wretch like me for a daughter.

'You should have warned me,' I said. 'How could you let me go in every day, for two whole years, and not tell me?'

'What am I supposed to do now?' Sylvia asked.

'Go and live with Desmond,' I said. 'I'm leaving.'

'Don't be ridiculous! You've no money. What will you live on?'

'I'll find something.'

'But you've no skills, no training. You're good for nothing . . .'

I didn't want to hear whatever else she might have to say. On my way out of the house, I emptied a full bottle of that vile cologne down the kitchen sink and dumped the bottle in the bin.

The boy next door, Fintan, had teased me for years with the suggestion that if I ever wanted a job, he'd pay me to get into his bed and stay there for a full hour. 'Name your price,' he jeered.

Fintan had been known as a bit of a shark on the street since he was fifteen and I was twelve. The mothers loved him because he went around in a jacket and tie and called them Missus this and Missus that, held doors open for them, told them they were looking lovely. Boys his own age made jokes about him and mimicked him behind his back, closing up all the buttons on their leather jackets and talking in a lazy drawl, sleeking their hair down flat with the palms of their hands. But they were quick enough to borrow money from him at special rates. Fintan described himself as a bit of a wheeler-dealer, a buy-and-sell merchant. He started with cigarettes and then moved to drink, passing it on to kids who were too young to buy it for themselves. Before long, everyone under twenty on our street knew where they could go for a bit of draw, or a tab of acid if they were lucky, although Fintan made a point of never touching the stuff himself.

The girls he went out with wore smart clothes and high heels, and make-up on their faces. Sometimes I could smell the arrival of a new girl in Fintan's life in a waft of fancy perfume across our shared garden wall.

When I was little, Fintan was different. I have to admit, I had a crush on him then. I used to bring him gifts of marbles, then matchbox cars, one every fortnight, until his tastes got too expensive for me to follow. He taught me to climb the trickiest trees in the monastery garden, showed me where to rob the best apples. He didn't seem to mind when I begged for rides on his bike. My favourite thing in the world in those days was to sit on his handlebars and shut my eyes while he took me flying down the hill to the harbour, speeding around the corner almost flat to the ground. And when we had to dodge the wheels of a lorry and fall into its slipstream, it never once occurred to me that we might crash. Fintan said I was a spunky kid and I'd be worth knowing when I was older. When Sylvia told me not to be stupid, that I couldn't marry my father when I grew up, I decided that Fintan would be the next best thing.

But that was before the girls with make-up and high heels appeared, before I grew breasts of my own and my legs began to stretch and curve. Before Fintan stopped smiling at me and began to leer instead, as if I wasn't the same person in my unpredictable new shape.

'What is it?' I asked. 'What's the matter?'

'You've got hooplas,' he said.

'I've got what?'

'Tits.' He pointed at my chest, stopping just short of touching me.

'I can't help it. I don't even like them.'

He laughed at me. 'You'll get to like them, wait and see. And you won't be the only one. Come and see me when you're a little older.'

And from then on, the slagging about getting into his bed for money took hold.

After I'd dropped Sylvia's expensive cologne in the bin, with enough force to hear the bottle smash, I went straight over to Fintan's house and told him that I'd come to call his bluff. I loosened my school tie, pulled my green jumper over my head and flung it through his open window into the trees.

He gaped at me. 'Are you mad?'

'I won't be wearing it again. Show me the money.'

At first he pretended not to know what I was talking about. But when I said I'd do it for a hundred quid, not a penny less, his eyes began to harden like the marbles I used to give to him, back when I thought he was great.

'A hundred quid? How do you know you're worth that much?'

'How do you know I'm not?'

I watched him count out the money and told myself that I was only dealing with unfinished business here. Given the right circumstances, I could have ended up sleeping with Fintan for nothing.

I never would have guessed that Fintan's hard edges and tough talk would turn to hunger so quickly in my hands. It was a revelation. I had a lot to think about when we lay together afterwards, his body spooned into mine, strangely likeable and easy now that all that fuss was over. I felt his breathing at my back and stirred, got out of bed.

I stepped over the crumpled heap of my discarded school uniform on my way to his wardrobe.

'What'll you do now?' Fintan asked.

I fingered my way through his hangers until I found a white cotton shirt and put it on. 'Find a place to live. How does this look?'

'Fine. You'll need a job, Ray. What can you do?'

I interrupted my progress through his hangers to take a closer look at him.

'You can't go on doing this! It's a dangerous game. And you're too . . .'

'Too what? I can do it with you, but not with anyone else, is that it?'

He looked so outraged that I wanted to laugh.

'It's not – right,' he said.

'Really?'

I felt old then, as if I saw everything through a wrinkled grey tunnel that could have been my own life or the long genetic thread that brought me back to time's beginning, all starry and bleak and cold, the music of the spheres and all that crap. I shivered and took a soft sweater, the colour of cobalt, and slipped it over my head, shaking my hair free.

'I like this one,' I said.

'God, you're hard. What's happened to you?'

'What happened to *you*?' I flung back at him, pulling on a brand new pair of his jeans.

'I have a friend—' he began, while I stuffed the tails of his shirt inside the jeans.

'And *he'd* be all right, I suppose?'

'Stop it,' Fintan said, with dignity. 'He has a club. He might give you a job, waitressing or something.'

When he told me the address of Freddie's club I had to laugh again. That street was famous for the women who came out of the shadows at night and leaned against the park railings, waiting for whatever trouble would come looking for them there.

'All right,' I said at last.

He gave me a piece of paper with a phone number on it.

'I'll give it a go. But if you tell anyone what's happened here today, Fintan – I mean anyone, ever – I'll tear your face off, do you hear me?'

'I hear you.' He had a peculiar look on his face. It might have been a smile, or else he was about to throw up. It was that look that drunks get before they vanish into oblivion or a pool of vomit, while it's still touch and go which it's going to be. I had never seen it before, but soon it would be so familiar to me that I'd know exactly when to move out of the way.

'I mean it, Fintan. Tell anyone about this and I'll rip your heart out with my bare hands.'

5

Freddie, who owned the Underground, was as tall as my father had been. Maybe even taller. When people spoke to him he twisted his neck downwards but kept his back straight, so that his head drooped while he listened. The girl who showed me round on my first night, Joanne, said he looked exactly like a lamp-post, and with his habit of dressing in charcoal suits and metallic shirts, the heavy silver chains he wore around his neck and on his wrist, I could see her point.

Freddie insisted that the girls who worked for him – me, Joanne, Dearbhall and Sally – had to wear tight satin trousers or tiny miniskirts, skimpy tops, high heels. He wanted a bit of glamour about the place, he argued when we complained about the heels, and what was wrong with that? The place needed all the help it could get.

The streets outside were grey and dismal. Tall, run-down buildings leaned against each other and blocked out the moon, while litter blew around the pavement like an incoming tide. Prostitutes leaned against the iron railings of the park and watched people come and go through the doors of the club, calling out greetings from the shadows.

Joanne told me not to worry, that the work was easy.

She advised me to think of the people who came into the club as if they were distant relatives, turning up, after years of silence, for a family party.

'Be friendly, but watch your back. Ignore any insults. Even if you like them, the chances are that you won't see most of them again for a good long while. Get the place ready for them before they arrive, offer them drinks and keep their glasses full, make sure no one's left alone for long, chat to them and clear up after they've gone.'

'What about the music?'

'Freddie is tone-deaf. He leaves it to us. Play what you like, but try to set up a mood for the punters. You know – lively if the place is slumping a little. Slow it down if they're getting out of hand.'

She showed me the turntables set up in a corner on the other side of the tiny dance floor, behind a tall bar that looked like a giant switchboard, all coloured knobs and flashing lights. There were racks of records, two turntables, headphones, a high stool to sit on. The strobe lights were controlled from back here too. I loved every minute of it, even doing stock control in the deep arches down the back, counting bottles of wine with complicated names and dates, checking them against sales receipts, noting what was popular, what we needed to push. I liked tracking down stray receipts, balancing the money in the till.

There was food too. The club was supposed to be a late-night venue for eating and dancing. When I first went to work there, there was a scary chef called Matt, who wore a white uniform but no hat on his gingery hair. Matt smoked gloomily over his newspaper in the kitchen all night long and begged us to sit and talk to him because he was bored. But when a food order came in he'd jump to his feet and crash saucepans around, making flames leap from the oil in a terrifying way as he seared steaks or spooned frozen scampi into boiling oil, rushing as if he had five thousand people to feed instead of a table for four. Steak and scampi, along with chips, represented the entire menu. Sometimes we gave people sandwiches, with a handful of Tayto crisps scattered across the top. It wasn't exactly exciting, but no one came for the food.

Sylvia was horrified when I plucked up the courage to ring her and say that I wasn't coming home.

'But – where are you living?'

'In a bedsit.' I gave her the address, but I could have sworn that she didn't bother to write it down.

'It sounds so – common. Why won't you come home?'

'It's grand. It's handy for work.'

'And what, may I ask, is "work"?'

When I said that I was a hostess in a nightclub and named the street, there was silence at the other end of the phone for a full minute.

'Hello? Sylvia? Are you there?'

'I don't remember giving you permission to call me Sylvia.'

'Come on, Ma. I've left home now.'

'I'm still your mother!' Sylvia barked. Then she lapsed into her normal, lazy voice. 'I don't know about any of this, Renée. That street has a terrible reputation!'

'It's perfectly safe.'

'But – those women!'

'They don't bother me.'

I could hear Sylvia's mouth tighten around a cigarette, the flare of a lighter. 'It's the men I'd worry about. If your father was alive . . .' She sucked in a deep breath.

But of course, he wasn't.

If Sylvia had known the half of it, she would have stopped speaking to me altogether. The Underground was barely legal. To get there, you had to walk down a narrow lane and through a tunnel-like passage, made by buildings that looked as if they might collapse any minute, into a courtyard. Seven narrow stone steps that dipped in the centre and filled with water after rain led to a perfectly ordinary black door with a peephole.

Inside, the club was all curves and angles and an uneven, stone-flagged floor. It had once been the wine cellar of a Big House. Castle Catholics had lived and danced upstairs in high-ceilinged rooms. They had entertained their rulers there. Now Freddie rented the basement and ran this joint, keeping a different tradition going. The pubs in the city were supposed to close early, and for people who didn't want to go home, the club offered an alternative. Men and women came to drink and dance and grope each other in the shadowed alcoves. When the police came to raid the place, which they did, wearily, about once a month, it gave the punters an extra thrill.

It gave them the illusion of living dangerously when the warning light flashed red and the girls flew around, sweeping bottles of wine off the tables and replacing them with minerals, while Freddie pretended to fumble with the locks at the main door, straining at the bolts and clanking the extra keys he carried on his chain for this exact purpose. When he switched the main lights on, people would blink and adjust their eyes to the sudden wash of brightness, rearrange their clothes, while Freddie let the guards in. Then everyone sat, quiet, while tall men in dark uniforms walked around and studied the dishevelled clientele, random bottles of Fanta and the occasional ageing sandwich, with sceptical eyes.

Once they'd left, all hell broke loose. People claimed that their bottles had been full, untouched, barely even *open*, for God's sake, when the girls had snatched them up and hidden them. They wanted fresh ones. Freddie ground his teeth, but what could he do?

I had no time for this. I had a good memory for detail. 'Piss off, Joe,' I told a man with political ambitions who owned half the city. 'What do you think we're running here, a charity?' I slammed his own bottle of Nuits St Georges back down on his table, in the exact spot I'd taken it from. 'If you want another bottle, pay for it.'

Joe was a pain. One time, he broke all the rules by coming in with a group of people that included his wife, a large-nosed woman who wore sunglasses perched in the wispy black nest of her hair, even though it was night-time in a Dublin basement in the middle of winter. Unfortunately for everyone, Joe's girlfriend, Caroline, turned up that night as well. I had to hide her in the kitchen for a good hour, trying to persuade her not to go out there and make a bloody great scene to show him up in front of all of them. In the end she agreed to leave by the kitchen door, into a taxi ordered by Freddie. I was half sorry, to tell the truth. I thought it would have served Joe right to be shown up like that. But Caroline was a little the worse for wear. She had a ladder in her tights and her bright red lipstick was smudged, with gashes of mascara down her cheeks. I didn't want her to make a show of herself or do anything that would give those people the right to look down their noses at her. So I suppose it turned out for the best. Joe St George, we called that man, because of the wine. We had a policy of avoiding surnames, just in case.

In the end, Matt gave himself one nasty burn too many and left. After that, Freddie decided that we might as well do the cooking too.

'I'm getting too old for this shite,' Joanne said. 'I'm twenty-two, for God's sake. One of these days I'm going to get myself a proper job.'

Joanne had worked in the club since it opened, two years earlier. But she'd had proper jobs before that and they didn't suit her either.

'You were born for this,' Freddie told her. 'You're brilliant.'

'Thanks for nothing,' she grumbled. 'Any female in this country has been bred to this kind of work. Cooking and cleaning up and entertaining the visitors, while the men count the money.'

On quiet nights, we filled each other in on where we'd come from. Joanne had grown up on a farm outside Roscrea, the only girl in a family of five. She had to fight for her share of anything in that house – food, attention, space. Because she was a girl, she got away with murder when she was a child, and with nothing when she turned into a teenager. All of a sudden she had to help her mother all the time, there was no more wandering in the fields or dreaming in the barn. When she was little, Joanne used to trail around in the mud after her father, chasing his booted legs as he crossed the yard. He usually had a switch in his hand, left it stacked at the kitchen door when he scraped off his boots, picked it up first thing when he emerged again, whistling for the dog. Sometimes, when she'd had a lot to drink, she'd turn soft and tell me what she remembered about home. Her father reading the paper in front of the fire after dinner, chuckling before he'd pass some story on to the rest of them. Riding in the cab of the tractor beside him. Bringing out kettles of tea to the men and the feel of stems puncturing her skin when they saved the hay. The dusty yellow smell of straw, like the smell of her father's hat.

But when she was old enough to notice, she realized that she was headed for a life exactly like her mother's, all laundry and butter-making and cooking for the men – including the hands. And then the dishes and making sandwiches for the next day. Shining shoes on a Saturday night. She decided it wasn't for her. So she fought for the right to do a secretarial course and as soon as she had her proficiency certificate, sixty-seven words a minute and an error rate of nil, she took off for Dublin. She told them she'd got a job in the Civil Service so they'd let her go, but it was a lie.

She soon found herself a job, but after six months in an office where her immediate superior kept trying to back her into the corner behind the filing cabinet, and then three in a typing pool where she thought she'd be better off because it was run by a woman, she decided that a job where someone looked over your shoulder and counted the number of minutes you spent in the toilet while you sneaked a cigarette was not worth having. Besides, Joanne had a problem with getting up early in the morning. So she decided to give waitressing a try, and before long Freddie recruited her for his club from the burger joint where he found her. Joanne liked the idea of a job where she could smoke and drink to her heart's content while she was working, so she took him up on his offer. And there was the small matter of her social insurance, which her current boss was deducting from her wages but which Joanne knew for a fact never made it into any government account. Freddie would pay cash. How Joanne handled her tax affairs would be her concern and no one else's from now on.

'I didn't think you'd last when you first came,' she told me one night. 'You didn't seem the type. I thought you were a bit gormless, to tell the truth. But you're all right. You'll do.'

When Joanne was out of earshot, Freddie told me that I was the best girl he'd ever had. That was before he literally had me, one morning when we'd stayed back to go over the accounts while the others went ahead to the all-night breakfast bar. I don't know what came over me. We were wild for each other for three full weeks. God only knows how any work got done. And then, overnight, Freddie lost interest.

'Don't take it personally,' Joanne advised. 'Freddie has to sleep with all of us, sooner or later. It's like a tic he has.'

'At least I didn't get pregnant.'

'What? Are you not on the pill?'

'How could I be?'

I'd gone to a GP and asked about it, but he gave me a lecture about the law and about personal continence. He advised me to go home to my mother and stay there until I got married. I squirmed when I remembered the tone of his voice, the distaste in his face when he looked at me, as if I was something nasty clinging to the underside of his shoe.

'Christ! And you accepted that?' Joanne glared at me.

'What else could I do?'

'Meet me tomorrow afternoon. We'll get you sorted.'

*

We met outside the club and Joanne set off across town, walking fast, talking faster. I could hardly keep up with her.

'Where are we going?'

'Synge Street. The family-planning clinic.'

My heart sank. I didn't relish the thought of another lecture. 'I thought I wouldn't be able to get anything.' I was out of breath, looking around, trying to memorize the streets so I could find my way there again.

'You can't buy anything. But you can go and get looked after, and then make a donation.'

'How much should I give?'

'They'll tell you, stupid.'

'But—'

Joanne whipped around a corner and I had to run to catch up with her.

'How did you find out about it? Are they in the phone book?'

Joanne stopped so suddenly that I nearly ran into her. 'Girl, the first thing you have to learn is that you'll never find anything worth knowing in a newspaper or a phone book. You have to learn to shut your mouth and pay attention to what's going on around you. Like now, for instance.'

'What?' She'd completely lost me.

'We're here, you eejit. Look.'

There was a small plaque listing opening hours on the wall of the terraced house beside us. I swallowed my nervousness and followed Joanne down the steps to the basement door.

At the clinic they gave me six months' supply of the pill, along with a warning about smoking, but no lecture. Joanne was waiting for me on the street when I got back outside.

'I thought you'd gone.'

She shrugged. 'It was too crowded in there. There was nowhere to sit.'

I looked at the paper bag in my hands, full of leaflets and slender foil sheets of tablets. 'I don't know what to say.'

She shrugged again and squinted off down the street as if she was looking at something much more fascinating than me. 'Just make sure you do the same for someone else some day.'

But for all Joanne's nonchalance, I did worry about myself, just a little. About where I might be headed. Maybe my mother and that GP were right. Maybe I was on the road to ruin and I'd end up taking my place among the women at the railings after all.

But then Dermot wandered into the club and I stopped thinking altogether.

6

Dermot came in with a crowd, but he sat in a corner of the bar by himself while his friends swarmed all over a corner under the arches, making it their own, calling noisily for a wine list and extra ashtrays.

I sighed. It was obviously going to be a long night. 'What can I get you?' I asked Dermot while I wiped a perfectly clean ashtray on the table in front of him, to avoid dealing with the group.

He didn't seem to hear me.

I was used to a lot of things in that club, but being ignored wasn't one of them. I swung my hair – a vivid, bottled red that week – away from my face and propped my matching fingernails on my hip. Joanne and I had decided on a scarlet-woman theme for the night. I wore a long red dress and Joanne had a vermilion leather miniskirt and crimson tights. The regulars had already agreed that the hair tipped the balance in my favour. But Dermot was oblivious.

'Are you all right?' I asked.

He nodded, without looking up. His face was hidden behind square, black-framed glasses. The lenses seemed quite thick. I gave him the wine list and went away.

*

During my stint at the turntables, I couldn't help watching him from where I sat. All the shadows in that corner gathered around his shadow, and they arched across the ceiling in my direction. I'd never seen anyone look quite so alone, no matter how many times the girls from his own crowd went over to him, brought him glasses of wine, tried to coax him out on the dance floor. Anyone could have told them they were wasting their time.

His friends were pretty in the controlled, well-dressed way of girls from certain schools in the suburbs. They had high voices and flicked their hair a lot, swivelled their heads to see who might be watching them. At last, the most persistent of them, a little thing with a blonde ponytail and bad legs under a corduroy midi-skirt, came over to ask me to play a request.

'For Dermot,' she simpered, throwing a misty-eyed glance in his direction.

'What's his problem?' I asked.

'He's depressed,' the girl said, self-importantly. 'We're trying to take him out of himself.' She swayed on her clunky soles, waiting for congratulations.

'It's not working,' I told her. I played the song anyway, one of those tear-jerkers that girls like that often asked for so that they could sob on someone's neck, thinking it made them interesting. The girl went over to Dermot and put her hand on his shoulder. I could have sworn he shrank and grew darker all at once.

Joanne came to take over from me and I went to check the stock behind the bar.

'Who's your man?' Harry, one of the regulars, jerked his head in Dermot's direction.

'Never seen him before,' I said. I wondered why it felt like a lie.

We were well used to strays in there, people who took up residence at the bar and followed us on to breakfast. Some of them took an interest in one or all of us, declared themselves in love and haunted the place until they found a real girlfriend somewhere else. But Dermot didn't look the type to be a hanger-on. He didn't seem to know or care where he was.

'Give us another bottle of champagne there, Ray, love,' Harry said.

Harry came in twice a week and he always bought champagne. A heavy-set man in his fifties, he had thick white hair in shocking contrast to the wrecked, reddish-purple shiny skin on one side of his face.

'Harry, I keep telling you, this stuff is half the price at an off-licence. You're mad to buy it here.'

'I'm well aware of that,' Harry said with dignity. 'It doesn't matter a bit. Sure, I get a lot more than champagne out of it.'

The man in a crumpled suit who leaned across the bar beside him waved his fat cigar at me and leered. 'And what would that be now, I wonder?'

I ignored him. The quiet *thock* of the champagne cork caught Dermot's attention and he looked around.

'Would ye like a glass?' Harry offered, turning his head so that Dermot could see the ruined side of his face.

I watched Dermot's reaction. People usually startled and then ducked their heads away from the sight of Harry's face. But later, when they thought he wasn't looking, they'd sneak glances at him, fascinated. When they spoke to him, their eyes would stay locked on his, nervous, determined not to look at anything more dangerous.

Dermot registered surprise, but he kept on looking. 'Do you mind me asking,' he said, 'what happened to your face? Is that a birthmark?'

Harry smiled at him. His scar creased and shone in an alarming way, but Dermot didn't flinch. 'I fell in a fire when I was a boy.'

'Does it hurt?'

'Not now.' Harry beamed at him. 'Give this lad a glass, there, Ray.'

When Dermot took the glass from me, my stomach clenched. The ends of his fingers were square and blunt in a way that reminded me of something. He looked straight at me for the first time. His eyes seemed unguarded behind those lenses.

'Thanks.'

The man in the suit got a glass of Harry's champagne too.

'Do I get the "more" that goes with it?' he asked.

'Give me a break!' I snapped. 'Harry, can't you control your friend?' I picked up some clean ashtrays and walked off, knowing Harry would sort that creep out. He liked to keep an eye out for us. One weekend he'd even taken me and Joanne to a solid, two-storeyed house on the banks of a river in Meath. This, it turned out, was where he lived, with his mother. Over lunch, he asked if either of us would care to go and live there with him.

'Don't you mind which one?' I asked.

'Nope,' he said. 'Either one would do.'

'And your mother, Harry?' Joanne mocked.

'My mother is a fine woman. She'd make no demands on ye.'

Our refusal didn't seem to hurt him. Afterwards, he came into the club as often as before. He covered our backs if a customer got aggressive or insistent, in a way that Freddie never bothered to do. Freddie reckoned we could look after ourselves and, most of the time, he was right.

That night went downhill very fast. The blondey girl with the ponytail, whose name turned out to be Deirdre, threw up in the toilet and made lurid, chunky splashes all over the tiled wall.

'Great,' I said. 'Just great.' I hauled the bucket and mop out of the kitchen and got to work cleaning up the smelly mess. When I came back out, Deirdre was paying Freddie for another bottle of wine.

'Don't you think it's time you went home?' I said.

'Oh no, I'll be fine now, thanks. I always feel better afterwards. Could I have a fresh glass, please?'

Joanne rolled her eyes as Deirdre began to pour drinks all round. 'Freddie, do something,' she demanded.

'Ah, relax, Jo. It's only a bit of fun.'

I went back behind the bar. 'Lovely friends you have,' I barked at Dermot.

He looked over at them and back at me. 'Barely know them.' He got to his feet and lost his balance.

'I hope you're not driving.'

'I bloody am.' His keys were on the bar between us. I snatched them up and threw them into a bucket under the cash box.

'Hey! Give them back.'

'You can barely talk, let alone drive. Sit there and I'll get you a cup of coffee.'

'Then can I've my keys?'

'Yes,' I lied.

We kept up the pretence that I'd give him back his keys after one more cup of coffee over an entire pot of the strongest coffee I had ever made. He stayed behind when his friends left.

'We're looking for my keys,' he told them.

Freddie reassured them that he was in good hands and they left, with barely a backward glance.

'Some friends,' I muttered to Joanne, but I was glad they'd gone. That blondey one was beginning to annoy me.

Dermot took his glasses off, folded his arms on the bar, put his head down and slept, oblivious to Freddie's accounting, our cleaning, the review of the night's proceedings.

'Let's go for breakfast,' Freddie said at last.

'I could eat the hind legs off a Christian Brother!' Harry agreed, with enthusiasm. Then he looked at Dermot, asleep with his head on the bar. 'What'll ye do with your man?' he asked.

Joanne looked up from filing her nails. 'We could bring him with us.'

Freddie frowned. 'He might spew.'

Joanne snorted. 'That didn't bother you before!'

'That was different. There was money involved.'

'If ye find out where he lives, I could give him a lift home.'

'Hey, you.' I poked Dermot's upper arm with my index finger. 'Wake up. It's time to go home.'

Dermot opened his eyes. He looked like a child waking in a strange house, his eyes wide and lost without their frames. I had never seen such need before. It stopped me in my tracks.

'Where do you live?'

The street he named was right behind mine.

'You don't need to drive at all!' I said. 'You could have walked. I'll walk him home,' I told the others.

'Are you sure?' Freddie looked doubtful.

'I'll come with you,' Harry offered.

'I'd be afraid for the Christian Brothers, Harry. You go on. He's harmless – and he's just around the corner from me.'

'Don't you want breakfast?' Joanne asked.

I made a face at her. 'I lost my appetite.'

Freddie propelled Dermot up the stone steps and

down the alley to the street. The working girls perked up when he appeared, but lost interest when they saw that he already had an escort.

'Good luck to you, love,' one of them called.

I waved back at her. 'See?' I told Harry. 'The girls are out. I'll be fine.'

The clean air of the morning woke Dermot up. He shook off Freddie's arm. 'I'll be all right.'

'I'm going your way anyway,' I said.

'Right, so. I'll walk you home, if you like. Make sure you're all right.'

I laughed. 'Thanks.'

'Good God.' Joanne lit a cigarette and blew smoke straight into his face. 'He's one of *those*. You'd want to watch yourself, Ray.'

When I walked Dermot home, it seemed like the most natural thing in the world to take his arm, to go inside with him, and then to make the breakfast I'd missed out on with the others.

'Don't leave me,' he said before curling up on the sofa and passing out. And even though I knew he was drunk and didn't mean it, even though I had never known Joanne to be wrong about a man before, I stayed.

'What's on your mind?' I asked, although God knows what I expected him to say, since I was naked in his bed at the time.

'I'm going to have to leave.' He put the hot crimson tip of his tongue into the hollow of my throat.

I lifted my chin, so his mouth could reach further into the angle of my jaw.

'Already?' I slid closer to him. 'But you only just got here.'

'I mean the country. I just figured it out. I'm going to have to go away, to work.'

'That's not the end of the world. Depending on where you have to go, I suppose.'

'I love it here. I don't want to leave.'

'Maybe you won't have to.'

'I've made up my mind.'

'Oh, and that's it, then? What will you do?'

At that exact moment he slid inside me.

'This,' he said, smiling.

'For the rest of your life?'

'Why not?'

Everything changed then. From one second to the next. It was one of those things that happen. Afterwards, you can point to that exact moment and say *before* and *after*. One minute my life was one thing, and the next it was another, and there was nothing to do but go along with it.

7

I had never had a friend like Dermot before. Not even Joanne, who had showed me how to make my way in the Underground. Here was someone I could lose time with, someone to help me unlock the secrets of the city and my own body. It was like being a child again, but this time I had someone to play with. Dermot seemed to know everyone, to belong everywhere. He had gone to one of those boarding schools where people grow up in a sort of geographic free-for-all, spending their Easter break in a small country town, their half-term in a coastal city. The whole country was their playground. Doors opened to Dermot everywhere we went. I went with him into sunlit gardens in the mountains, down narrow stairs into bars barely bigger than a bus. We went to champagne breakfasts and jazz brunches and I don't remember ever having to pay for anything. He thought nothing of driving out of town with no particular destination in mind. He'd pull up outside a village bar and within minutes people he knew seemed to turn up out of nowhere. We went away for weekends, to a hostel overlooking a lake and then to a house beside a churchyard full of flat stones and elegant script, where I decided I wanted to be buried when I died. It rained so hard that we stayed there for four days, reading hundred-year-old books and falling asleep in front of the fire.

'We nearly had the police out looking for you,' Joanne grumbled when we came back.

'But I was with Dermot.' How could she think I'd come to any harm, so long as I was with him?

Dermot was studying electronics. His twin obsessions were circuitry and computer programming. I told him it was no wonder his eyesight was so bad when he spent all his time figuring out symbols that were as obscure to me as ogham, or playing with tiny copper wires embedded in sheets of brightly coloured plastic. I didn't see why he had to go away to work when everyone said that computers would take over the whole world, even Ireland. But Dermot wanted to get into micro-electronics. He had visions of people carrying computers for their personal use in the pockets of their coats, wearing television sets like wristwatches. Sometimes someone would ask him a question that reawoke this dream of his and he would talk and talk for hours, not caring if they were making fun of him. I knew it was odd, but I knew he was brilliant, too, and I hated that they laughed at him. Before long, I found myself repeating Dermot's own last line of defence to Joanne.

'Ireland's not big enough. There isn't room for someone with ideas like Dermot's,' I told her.

'There's not enough money either,' Dermot said.

'If everyone leaves because times are tough,' Joanne complained, 'nothing's ever going to change. Someone's got to stick it out.'

While I was at work, Dermot studied. Most nights he came into the Underground just before closing and sat talking to Harry about boats and waterways and the price of airplane travel. He talked Freddie into updating his accounting systems and designed a program for him to do it.

'I'm glad the lad can be practical when he has to be,' Harry said. 'Ye'll be all right.'

It was all so easy that I never, not once, thought about where it was going.

'Why do you love me?' I asked one Sunday morning, the newspapers spread and rumpled around and under us on the bed, interviews with stars and politicians ripped apart, discarded and forgotten on the floor.

'Do you have to ask?' He was a parody of exhaustion, head thrown back, legs limp, while I counted his ribs with my mouth.

'I'm serious.'

'Because you will do anything, go anywhere and never once ask why. I've never known a woman like you before. You'll try anything.'

Later, when I had forgotten the question, he took it up again. 'I didn't know I was lonely until I met you,' he said into the dark.

It was exactly how I felt about him.

And I was hungry for him. My body ached when he wasn't in it. When we were apart, I felt the pain that amputees are said to feel in limbs that are no longer part of them, but I felt it everywhere. It was more than sex, I was sure of that. Sometimes a thought would slide into my mind and I'd turn to look for him and find him in the act of turning to find me, like a mirror image of myself. No one had ever made me laugh the way that he could, a deep seismic shift that began in a place so far back inside me that I couldn't name it. That laugh came rumbling out of my deepest earth and shook both of us loose.

He brought me down to meet his parents, who lived in a small Tipperary town. His father, Conall, was a solicitor, as mine had been.

'What about your mother?'

'She breeds ducks. And rabbits.'

'For people to eat?'

He laughed. 'God, no. Mum's animals are decorative. She shows them, and sells them to breeders, or as pets. She treats them like children. She'd have loved to have a full house, she says, but for some reason she couldn't have any more babies after she had me. So she took these up instead.'

'Not much of a substitute.' I felt odd going down to meet his parents. I didn't know what to expect, even though he said they would love me and I knew he loved them. The whole parent thing just seemed beyond me. I'd brought Dermot to dinner at Desmond's one night, to meet everyone. It had been a stilted, awkward night, even though Sylvia was clearly relieved to discover that Dermot had the right number of limbs and a reasonable set of table manners. She began to thaw as soon as she heard that his father was a solicitor, and melted more visibly when he named his school. The one thing she knew about it was that you needed money to go there.

Dermot's parents were comfortable, but not rich. Their house was a long, stone cottage with a slate roof. It looked as if it grew naturally from the ground, like an outcrop of rock. A luxuriant growth of ivy covered its walls and moss grew on the flagstones that led to the front door. Wild flowers burst from cracks in the garden wall. The door was already open, waiting for us, when we turned in through the gate. A tall, thin woman in jeans, with her thick grey hair in a braid, stepped out to meet us.

'So you're the one who's going to lick my boy into shape!' Pat laughed, the hoarse laugh of a heavy smoker. 'Not literally, I hope!'

'Give her five minutes to catch her breath before the onslaught, Mum!' Dermot said.

'Darling! I'm so glad to meet you at last.' Pat hugged me. 'I was beginning to wonder if you were real.'

Dermot talked to Pat easily. I could see how much he liked her and I thought that was a good sign in a man. It took me a while to get used to Pat's loud, sudden laugh, the bad jokes she told with relish. She called everyone *darling* and *sweetheart* every other sentence, but I soon gave in to these endearments once I realized that she meant them.

I fell for Conall straight away. He was a big man who wore a mustard-coloured bow-tie. The stem of a pipe stuck out of the pocket of his brown cardigan. He had thick, unruly eyebrows and eyes as clear and direct as blue water. His right wrist was encased in plaster of paris.

'You're very welcome,' he told me, taking my hand in his left one and squeezing it lightly. 'Come on in and make yourself at home.' He didn't let go of my hand as he led me inside. 'Sorry about this!' He waved the plaster at us.

'What happened?'

'He fell off a ladder,' Pat said. 'Trying to sneak a look at Charlie Farrell's niece, down for the weekend.'

'I was clearing the gutter for them,' Conall said. 'Charlie is ninety. And his niece is sixty-two.'

'Still and all,' Pat laughed.

The inside of their house was the most cluttered place I'd ever been. Every surface was piled high with books and magazines, the mantel was crowded with photographs, even the dining-room table was piled high with letters and old newspapers. Every square inch of wall space was hung with paintings, although I'd no idea whether they were valuable or not. There were a lot of hunting scenes, the type you sometimes see on place-mats, some landscapes and a few brooding pictures of the sea. Then there were portraits of grand-looking people in old-fashioned, formal clothes. 'Are these your relatives?' I asked, suddenly nervous.

'Not at all!' Pat said. 'Conall collects those. He goes around the auction houses and never comes home empty-handed. Next thing you know, we'll be hanging paintings out in the barn, with the fowl.'

The ducks were my favourite of all the animals that Pat reared. She had chickens too: big, furry-looking Silkies and tiny little bantams rioting around together. But her ducks were a breed I'd never seen before, Indian Runners. They held themselves up tall with their elongated necks stretched up straight, and ran around together in clumps, moving in unison as if they were in flight. Then one would suddenly break free and change direction. The others would spill around, confused and anxious for a second, then swerve off after him as if they had one mind. I could watch them for ever. I thought they moved like water.

Dermot had a knack of working his fingers in between the bones of my feet until they loosened and spread and I was putty in his hands. No one had ever touched my feet like that before. It seemed outrageously inti-mate, almost rude. The thought of uncovering them and putting them into his hands made me shiver, but when I did, they turned out to be a whole neglected area of delight.

'Where did you learn to do that?'

'I've always loved feet,' he said. 'They work so hard and they're badly treated. Pay them the smallest bit of attention and they give themselves to you completely.'

'Show me yours,' I said. It felt like a shocking thing to ask.

Dermot's feet were long and beautiful. His toes had

the same blunt ends as his fingers, and as soon as I saw them I knew that I would never, not ever, forget what each separate toe looked like.

'Those shoes you wear at work,' he said, stroking deep into the arch of my foot and making my flesh sing. 'They'll ruin you if you're not careful.'

I couldn't bear the sensations in my feet any longer, so I kissed him. Then there wasn't much need to say anything for a while.

Later, when I was feeling sleek and thoroughly dissolved, he told me there was a job fair coming up and that he planned to go.

'Didn't the hiring fairs go out with the ark?'

'They're back,' he said. 'The corporate version.'

That weekend Joanne brought us to a house party behind a mountain in Connemara. We were the first to arrive, but Joanne had a key to the cottage. We threw open all the windows and cooked ourselves a big fat breakfast with food we'd brought in the car. Then we climbed the mountain. We sunned ourselves on ferny rocks among the rhododendrons and looked down on the roof of a Benedictine abbey, familiar from postcards. Down on the low stone bridge, coach tours slowed to a stop and tourists got out to take photographs.

I wondered if our image would appear on some enlarged print, thousands of miles away. Would people point and ask questions and think maybe we were ghosts or creatures from the other world that was supposed to be more easily accessible from here? We climbed down a waterfall to get back before the other partygoers arrived, to make sure that we'd get the only bedroom.

Some of Joanne's friends had hitched a lift with one of those tour buses.

'Did you see us?' Dermot asked. 'Above the abbey? We waved.'

No one had.

We built a fire, doused it with petrol and set it going in the stony field below the house. Music blared out loud to indifferent sheep all night while boys played guitars and girls jumped over the flames. Time vanished. We drank from flagons of cider and smoky bottles of local brew, ate burnt sausages and the flesh of exploded potatoes and danced barefoot on the soft grass, not caring what might be hidden there. The rich smells of turf and hash deepened the air until it became a veil.

Hours later, when night peeled back the far corner of the sky and a chink of light showed through, Dermot fell into bed. Joanne and I went down to the beach with a gang of diehards. The sand was cold as silk under our swollen feet. We went to the edge of the water, let freezing salt sting the bruised skin between our toes.

'Lick your wounds, girl. There's no place like it,' Joanne said. And took off her clothes.

'What are you doing?'

'What does it look like? I'm going for a swim.'

'Don't be mad, Jo, you'll freeze to death! You can't swim alone – you'll drown!'

'Come with me, then.'

And off she went, her arms flying in graceful wheels around her head, heading for the rocks.

I set off after her, telling myself that she was mad, that I was angry, that she was a fool. At first the cold was shocking. Then it burned. First I was warm, then I was fire. I was slick and salt and the sun blazed out from the horizon and found me in its path, dappled me in crystals of pure light. Joanne passed me, laughing, on her way back. We rolled around each other like baby seals and dipped under water, headed back for the beach where the others stood, amazed.

Someone had gone to get Dermot. He wouldn't speak to me when we got out of the water. When we got back to the house, he turned on me.

'That was stupid! You could have drowned! I wouldn't even have known where you were!'

I was shivering by then. My teeth chattered off the cup where he'd poured whiskey into my tea on top of more spoons of sugar than I could count. He'd done the same for Joanne, who'd wandered off to the bedroom, towelling off her hair, the tips of her fingers blue.

Dermot built up the fire. He threw branches and twigs left over from the night before on top of the blazing turf.

'Don't burn the place down,' I said, trying to make peace.

He came over then and buried his head in my

trembling legs, his arms wrapped around my waist. 'I wouldn't have known where to look for you.'

I looked down at his brown, brown hair, brown as turf, the colour of autumn, and felt myself fall even further, a long slide, down through the fibrous roots of things, along tunnels of weeping stone, to dry caves, warm and leafless, hidden.

'I'm not going anywhere,' I said.

8

'America?' I said when Dermot first mentioned that he might work there. 'I don't know. Why not India? Africa? Tibet?'

'This is work, Ray. Be serious. It's the most likely place for me to go. Apart from Japan, and I don't talk the language.' He frowned. 'I'll have to buy a suit.' Then he looked at me. 'We'll have to get married.'

'Have to?'

'We're going to anyway, aren't we? Come on. You must have thought about it.'

'Why? Why must I have thought about it?'

'Because anything else would be stupid. And now, if we're going to America, we'll need visas.'

He came home from the job fair talking non-stop about a man he'd met who didn't even have a stand there.

'His name is J. P. Fischer. Wait till you meet him. He's a character.' Dermot threw open our wardrobe door and stood staring at the mess inside it.

'Meet him?'

'He's taking us out for dinner. Tonight.'

He turned away from the wardrobe and began to lift shirts off the arm of the chair in the corner, where most of our clothes ended up. 'Do I have any clean shirts?'

'I can't go out tonight, Dermot. I'm working.'

He stopped rummaging through our clothes. 'Cancel it. This is important.'

I tried, but there was no one to take my place and it was Friday, one of our busiest nights.

'Bring him into the club. I can meet him there. It's probably better if you're on your own with him anyway.'

J. P. Fischer was a huge hit in the Underground. He took off his stetson on the way in, but he put it carefully on the table in front of him so that it was visible all night.

'Does the hat need a glass?' I couldn't help asking.

'No thank you, sugar.' There was no trace of offence or laughter in his slow, deep voice. If he'd taken what I'd said literally, he showed no surprise.

JP was a tiny man, his skin brown and polished like a nut, his forehead ridged with lines when he laughed. Around his neck he wore a leather string looped through a silver clasp with a big turquoise stone. He told us this was called a bolo, and that it was a kind of tie, and that where he came from a lot of men wore them.

'Even for work? Would Dermot have to wear one?' I was fascinated by the ornate clasp.

'No, darlin'.' His skin glowed in the half-light of the alcove. 'I sure am glad I left my boots and spurs at the hotel. They would have been a consideration on that dance floor, for sure.' He winked at me. I wasn't sure if he was joking or not. Then he nodded at the tiny wooden rectangle in front of the sound deck. 'Not much room to move,' he drawled. 'Y'all must get up close and personal real fast.'

Joanne brought over a bottle of wine and JP gave her a tenner for a tip. I said I should be getting back to work and followed Joanne in behind the bar.

'Is that guy for real?' she asked, showing me the money.

'Dermot says he's loaded. Oil money, or something. He's from Texas.'

We watched JP lean forward to talk to Dermot, then throw his head back and laugh, exposing the brilliant clean line of a white vest under his check shirt.

The next thing, he loped over to us and asked Joanne for a dance. He put an arm around her waist and scooped her hand into his before he swept her off into something that looked like a waltz. When she came back her cheeks were pink. 'He's quite sweet,' she said, furious, and went off to the kitchen.

When things quietened down I went over to join them again.

'I hope y'all will think about what I've said,' he was saying to Dermot. 'I think this deal could be real sweet. For both of us.'

Dermot's face was as flushed as Joanne's had been. I wondered if he'd had too much to drink.

'JP here wants me to go and work for him in Texas,' he explained.

'Not just Texas, darlin'. *Dallas*, Texas. What do you say?'

All I knew about Dallas came from the TV programme, which featured big skies, big cars, big blondes, lots of money. No wonder it was popular. I looked at Dermot. 'I don't know.'

'See, Dermot here could get himself fixed up with a fancy corporate outfit like he says he wants to do. He'd get good training and all, no doubt about that, at the bottom of a mighty big heap. But if he comes to work for me – we've got ourselves a tidy little R&D outfit working on integrated circuits, just exactly what he wants – he'd be on his way to being a big old fish in a little pond in a flash.'

'R&D?'

'Research and development,' Dermot mumbled. He looked dazed.

'Y'all think about it and let me know, huh? I fly back the day after tomorrow. Good to meet you, darlin'. Now, it's time for my beauty sleep.'

Suddenly, he was gone.

Joanne said I could go, the night was winding down anyway. We headed out into streets that were slick and clean after recent rain. The black surface of the road shone with reflected light and the city seemed subdued as we passed through it.

'What do you think?' Dermot asked.

I didn't know what to think. I had never really expected this moment to come, but why not?

'What he said makes sense,' Dermot said, all in a rush. 'I might get more exposure in a big company, but I'd get to use my own initiative more, work on my own projects sooner in a small outfit like his. I don't know.'

'Looks like all our chickens are on their way home,' I said.

He nodded. 'With roosting on their empty little minds.' He did a bad imitation of JP's accent.

We walked on in silence for a while. Then I said, 'I don't just mean the job.'

'What, then?'

'I'm pregnant.'

He squeezed my hand hard. 'There, you see? We'll get married straight away.'

I looked into his face, and all I could see there was relief. As if all his decisions had been made, and the future had suddenly become clear to him. I didn't feel quite that way, but if he did, that was good enough for me.

Joanne was shocked. 'Pregnant? Married? How did that happen?'

'I forgot to take the pill a couple of times. I doubled up, but it mustn't have worked.'

'Why do you have to go so far away?'

'Dermot's got a high-tech job. It's what he wants.'

'And what do you want?'

'I hadn't thought further than ... Dermot. Don't snort like that, Jo.'

'Sometimes I want to shake you!'

Our wedding was a quiet, registry-office affair, with dinner afterwards at a local hotel. Sylvia was furious. She wanted to bring Barry home from South America, where he had a parish, to say the Mass. If Barry had been able to come we would have gone along with her, but he hadn't. His village, in Bolivia, was experiencing drought, not that we ever heard anything about it in the papers. His parishioners needed him, he said. He sent us a beautiful pair of alpaca sweaters for a wedding present, in delicate pastel patterns. In the letter he sent with them, Barry said he was sure I'd understand, and gave us his blessing.

I did, but Sylvia didn't. She thought I was headed for damnation because we weren't getting married in a church. She was furious with Barry for appearing to sanction what we were doing. It was all exhausting. I was grateful for Pat's exuberance. It swamped Sylvia and Desmond's disapproval and lifted the exhaustion of Jane's second pregnancy. It even masked Joanne's fury, Freddie's bewilderment. 'Darling, isn't this just wonderful?' Pat kept saying, to everyone she saw, including the hotel manager, the barman and the waitresses, all of whom beamed right back at her.

Within minutes of meeting her, Pat swept Sylvia off into a corner where they hid in wreaths of smoke until we were all called in to dinner.

'Don't look so worried,' Conall reassured me when he caught me looking over at them. 'I'd say those two are as thick as thieves already.'

'And what, no honeymoon?' Pat asked when we'd reached the coffee and brandy stage of the proceedings and the debris of dinner had been cleared away.

'Going to America will be enough.'

'I wonder.' Pat blew smoke out through her nostrils and arched her thick grey eyebrows. 'Don't let my boy bully you, Ray.'

'Bully? Dermot?' I was shocked. 'He wouldn't.'

Across the table, Conall was coaxing smiles from Sylvia. I was astonished to hear a sudden peal of laughter. Sylvia instantly covered her mouth with her hand, as if to take it back. 'No!' she breathed at Conall, her eyes shining.

Dermot leaned over to me. 'Rumours about the Taoiseach,' he explained. 'And his personal life.'

This was one of Sylvia's weaknesses. I wondered how Conall was smart enough to pick up on it. Sylvia loved political gossip, stories about judges. If I had told her half of what I knew about the people who came into the Underground, Sylvia would have been thrilled. But Freddie issued dire warnings about being discreet. 'Whatever stories get out, they mustn't come from us,' he said. So I kept what I knew to myself and Sylvia got her gossip from other sources.

Later, slightly drunk, I met Sylvia in the toilets fixing her make-up at the mirror.

'What do you really think about me marrying Dermot?' I asked.

Sylvia took a long appraising glance at her own reflection and then at mine. 'It's a relief, frankly. You'll be someone else's responsibility from now on.' All the wine-loosened goodwill had gone from her voice.

I opened my mouth but could think of nothing withering enough to say, so I shut it again. Behind me, I heard the torrential rush of a toilet being flushed. I looked into the glass of the mirror and saw the door of the cubicle behind me swing open. Pat emerged, tugging at her skirt. 'That's exactly how I feel!' she said briskly, stepping up to the basin beside me and winking at me in the mirror. 'Our two tearaways can look after each other now. And isn't that what it's all about?'

We spent our last weekend in Ireland with Dermot's parents. It was getting dark when we drove away from their lovely, low stone house. When I hugged Pat goodbye, I could feel her shaking, even though her eyes were dry.

'Don't worry, Pat. We'll keep in touch.'

'Sweetheart. Make sure you do.'

When it was his turn, Pat gripped Dermot's shoulders so hard that I could see her knuckles whiten under her heavy rings. 'Promise you'll write,' she said. 'Promise you'll come back.'

In the end, Conall intervened. 'Let them go, Pat.' Then he kissed me, right on the mouth. 'Good luck out there,' he said. 'Look after each other. Be kind.'

We drove away in silence. The enormity of what we were about to do flattened me down into my seat. Leaving had seemed like a game until I put my arms around the frightened hollow of Pat's grief. Dermot concentrated on the road and I watched the moon, high and full above us, clouds breaking under it like water. A pair of eyes glowed from a ditch and a fox ran across the road in front of the car, jumped over a wall and vanished.

I could hear the river turn and dive below the mountain, impatient for the sea. Cliffs of shale rose around us over heaps of gravel. We were near some sort of quarry. I'd never seen the countryside in this cold metallic light before, all black and silver, its contours sharp and gleaming. As if, knowing we were leaving, it turned a different face to us. I felt as lonely as if Dermot had left me too.

I moved closer to him, put my hand on his thigh.

'Don't do that,' he said. 'I'm concentrating.'

'Do you have to?'

He looked at me and braked hard. The car went into a skid but I made myself go on looking into his face, not at the road, not dipping stars or fractured trees.

'Jesus Christ, Ray. What the hell do you think you're doing?'

Headlights flared and there was a faint whine of rubber and displaced air as a car swerved around us. The sound of a horn subsided in the distance.

'You'll get us killed.'

'Stop the car, then.'

'I have stopped.'

'I mean properly.'

Dermot moved the car off the road, leaned against his door and looked at me. 'Now what?'

'Look how beautiful it is.' I pointed at the silvered

sky, walls of rock, dark outlines of trees. 'I want to go out there.'

He shook his head, but he followed me out of the car, into the trees and up, away from the road. Our headlights shone behind us, making a cone-shaped path in the darkness. I climbed until I found a clearing out of reach of the headlights and sat with my back to a ridged tree trunk. The moonlight was sharp and smelled of pine oil and resin. The stars were in rich clusters I wished I knew enough to name. The only light I could identify was from Venus, the planet everyone knows, the one that's never dimmed, not even by the city.

'Sit here for a minute.' I patted the ground beside me.

'The battery will go flat.' But he sat down. After a while he slid his warm arm around me.

All that cold clean light, rough wood at my back and far below us, the river, searching for the coast. I burrowed further into him, pulled him into me. 'I'm cold.'

The moon rode high above us, a full sail in the sky. I could feel stones under my hip as we rocked together against the spine of the hill, but nothing would make me move, for fear of losing him. Somewhere down there the road curved away towards the city. Headlights flared and died around us. A different kind of light flooded through me then and sent me drifting down to the cool, secret earth again, the smell of night, the blurred call of an owl.

Someone whooped through an open car window, the sound exultant and friendly.

'They can see us,' Dermot said.

'Who cares?'

But the spell, whatever it was, was broken. Stones dug into my thighs, the cold that had found its way inside my clothes was sharp and layered with damp. I couldn't remember what had driven me out of the car in the first place.

Below us, our headlights picked out threads of mist. We stood up and kissed one last time before going back. I tipped my head back, opened my mouth and breathed in deep, filling my lungs all the way to the bottom with the air of home, tasting the sky.

'Will we see the same stars over there?'

Dermot laughed. 'You can't be serious.'

He loped down the hill, energized. But he hadn't answered my question. I followed him more slowly, down into the smoky patterns of mist and air thrown up by the lights of the car.

At the airport, Sylvia wouldn't let me out of her sight.

'Why don't you go on?' I said. 'There's no point in hanging around.'

'Ah, no. I'll wait.'

When I went to buy a magazine, Sylvia was right there beside me, offering to pay for it. When I had to go to the toilet, she said she'd come with me.

I wanted to scream. Sylvia would be easier to leave in her indifferent mode. Why couldn't she be her usual spiky, selfish self?

In the cubicle, grubby and narrow and littered

with scraps of toilet paper, I tried to breathe more easily. The smell of aerosols and disinfectant didn't help. I wished this was over with, but sure enough, when I went out Sylvia was waiting for me, reapplying her lipstick for what was probably the ninety-ninth time that morning, avoiding looking at her own puffy eyes in the mirror. We'd have to play this out to the bitter end.

There was a long queue at the check-in desk. Dermot had kept a place for us near the back. We stood beside him and I leaned against his arm while Sylvia nattered about the weather and how it was ideal for flying, as if she was used to jet-setting all over the world. People nudged their cases along with their feet and the queue inched forward.

My fingers chafed under the straps of my carry-on bag. I didn't want to put it down. I'd never admit it to Dermot, but the thought of flying so far and across so much ocean made me feel queasy. Our two matching suitcases, bought for the occasion, sat square and resolute on a trolley. They could have belonged to anyone. I stared at them, trying to memorize what they looked like so that I'd recognize them when we got to the other side of the world.

At last we were through.

'We'll go on down to the gate now,' I said as calmly as I could. I didn't want Sylvia to guess that I was ready to grab Dermot's hand and run.

Sylvia's face crumpled. I put my arms around

her, something I couldn't remember doing for a very long time.

Sylvia sobbed into my shoulder. 'If this doesn't work out for you, you come straight home,' she whispered. 'I'll send you the money. No questions asked.'

And then she was gone. From behind, the slope of her shoulders struck me for the first time as thin, old. Defeated.

'She didn't say goodbye to me.' Dermot sounded shocked.

'She was upset,' I managed to say, although for a minute there it was touch and go whether what came out of my mouth would be words or shards of glass.

PART THREE

Detour

(South-western States, 1980–83)

9

In the arrivals hall at Kennedy airport, the checked-trousered tourists who'd been on our flight, the ones who had seemed so conspicuous back home, got louder as they hurried past long lines of outsiders through the special entry point for people with US passports. People of every imaginable shape and size, every possible skin tone and style of dress, poured through the barrier, surrounded us and moved on. The hall swelled with noise, a confusion of accents. I couldn't follow a single thread of conversation.

When we got to the top of the queue and handed over our passports, I smiled at the immigration officer but his expression didn't change. A black woman with a pillowed chest and jewelled glasses came out of an inner office and he whispered something to her, looking from Dermot to me and back again. Then he went inside and left the woman watching us, as if they thought we might make a run for it. The woman stared openly at my swollen body. The steep arch of her eyebrows above her glasses suggested that there was plenty she'd like to say to us if anyone would give her an opening.

My mouth went dry. Just when I was ready to scream, the immigration officer came back out, stamped our passports and handed them back to us. 'Welcome to America,' he said. Then, too late, he smiled.

We flew further south, to Dallas, into heat that wrapped itself around me like the tendrils of some carnivorous plant, pushing deep into and under my pores, making my skin prickle, clogging my lungs. It was like moving through water. Breathing was drowning. Yet all around us people walked, talked, laughed, went about their business as if nothing was out of the ordinary.

'You'll get used to it,' I was told. 'You haven't acclimated yet.'

'They mean acclimatized,' Dermot said. 'And they're probably right. Everywhere is air-conditioned.'

I knew that I'd never get used to the oppressive weight of that air, the layer of fluid collected at the base of my lungs, the sweat crusted on my skin. 'It's like another planet,' I gasped. 'We should have taken readings before coming, to see if it supports life.'

'We'll get used to it.'

'How? Grow gills?'

Dermot shrugged, irritable. We both were. The heat does that to you, no matter how laid-back and easy-going you are. 'Maybe. Maybe you should make less of a fuss?'

I'd never seen him like this. Snappy and cross, like a school teacher. His glasses kept steaming up as we went from air-conditioned buildings to the outside, or even from regular air to the stored-up heat of a parked car. I soon stopped laughing at the sight of his lenses made white by condensation, his eyebrows furrowed across the top of them.

On our first morning, we stepped out of our dark motel room into a blaze of heat and a harsh, metallic light that made my eyeballs ache. The car park shimmered, the asphalt rippled like a sea. The impression was borne out by a rhythmic, rushing sound, but instead of waves it came from cars speeding past on the freeway. I couldn't get over how many of them, or how fast. Where were they all going?

The main building was deliciously cool in contrast. Fans spun lazily over glossy green floor-to-ceiling trees that seemed to be planted in the walls. The sweat dried on my back as we walked into the sweet, sizzling air of the café. A woman with thin legs, bright blonde hair and a startling mouth, dressed like a stick of rock in broad red and white stripes, came over to show us to our table. Jody, she said her name was.

'Hi. I'm Ray. And this is—'

Dermot turned and raised his eyebrows at me.

'Nice to meet you, honey,' Jody said. 'What will y'all have this morning?'

I had to ask her to explain the menu. *Grits, hash browns, bagels; tall stack, short stack; beggarman, thief.* I stopped hearing after a while and settled for eggs and toast.

'How would you like your eggs, honey?'

Scrambled, poached, benedict . . .

'Fried, please.'

'Over-easy or sunny-side up?'

I gave up, exhausted.

Dermot intervened. 'Do you want it turned?'

I shook my head.

'Sunny-side up,' he said, and gave his own order as if he had been doing it all his life. His crisp white shirt was wilting. The ends of his hair were slightly damp. I looked at him and my stomach turned. He smiled right back at me and I knew I wouldn't be able to eat a thing. My foot came out of its sandal and crept across the floor to rest against his leg. He returned the pressure.

'It'll be all right,' he said. 'You'll see.'

Our first apartment was a corner unit in a run-down complex that emptied during the day and filled up again in the late afternoon when people sped down the ramp in their pick-ups and four-by-fours, scattering dust. A big sign outside our building said NO SOLICITORS and that made me laugh. I thought about my staid brother Desmond, and his sensible wife, Jane, and wondered why lawyers wouldn't be allowed to live here. But the letting agent looked puzzled when I asked, and explained that solicitors were door-to-door salespeople, never to be encouraged.

The people in the apartment above us had a bumper sticker on their Chevy that said HUNGRY? OUT OF WORK? EAT YOUR FOREIGN CAR!

'Don't take it personally,' Dermot said, although it was hard not to when the Chevy was parked beside our second-hand Volvo every night.

Our apartment was beside the huge dumpsters where everyone emptied their bins. Dermot complained about the smell and the health risk, but sooner or later everyone who lived in the complex had to pass our sliding doors on their way to get rid of their rubbish; I figured that watching them was as close as I was likely to get to a social life.

All my clothes were too heavy. At night I pushed the sheet away and lay sweating, naked and swollen under the fast revolving wooden blades of a ceiling fan. I kicked my shoes off every chance I got and prowled around the room in a T-shirt, my bare feet irritated by the fibre of the carpet. I felt caged. Outside was the furnace of the parking lot, its black asphalt impossible to cross, sullen air. Looking through the window I saw brightness, space, a world awash with light under an infinite sky. It looked benign, but when I stepped outside the heat unleashed itself, relentless.

I spent hours at the window staring across the empty car park, feeling more lonely and useless than I ever had in my life before. One day, a bearded old man and a skinny child with a mop of jet-black hair appeared out of nowhere. They stopped beside the dumpster and the old man lifted the child up. The next thing, the child had disappeared in amongst the garbage.

I jumped up. Had I really seen that? Was he throwing that child *away*? I went closer to the window, ready to run out there, but the old man hoisted himself up after the child, swung his legs over the lip of metal and disappeared as well.

I waited, holding my heavy belly to ease the pressure. The baby shifted inside me, trying to get comfortable.

At last the pair re-emerged. The old man slung an overstuffed black plastic bag over the side of the dumpster. It clanged when it hit the ground. Aluminium cans bounced out of it and rolled against the low kerb of the parking lot. The man jumped down and lifted his arms to the child, who jumped into them. Without once looking in my direction, although they must have seen me staring, they gathered up the spilled cans and walked away, holding hands. The awkward-shaped bag hung over the old man's shoulder.

'They must be scavengers,' Dermot said when I told him. 'Selling what they salvage.'

'Like what?'

'Cans, bottles – clothes, I suppose.' He got up to get himself another beer. 'We should keep our old cans too,' he said thoughtfully. 'For money.'

Money was tight for us. We had imagined that we'd be well off when we got to America – the numbers had sounded good on paper. Instead, we found that we had to struggle to pay for things we'd never considered before, like water and cool air. We had to buy a car and rent furniture and Dermot's salary didn't go nearly as far as we'd thought it would.

But Dermot loved his job. He came in dazed with ideas and figures and the excitement of learning new ways of doing things every day. In the mornings he hurried out with his hair still wet from the shower, a mug of coffee in his hand to drink in the car. He worked through lunch and went to meetings in the evenings where they talked strategy and projections and market share and probabilities. But when I tried to pin him down about what he actually did, it was beyond me. Dermot worked on developing programs that controlled circuitry, was as close as I ever came to understanding it. They were aiming at miniaturization all the time, making electronic gadgets smaller, more universally obtainable.

'But what's the point of having a radio in a wristwatch?' I asked him. 'How would you work the dials?' I looked at my own fingers, swollen by late pregnancy, while he tried to explain. But hormones had made me slow, and what he said made no real sense to me. All I knew was that he felt completely at home in his bizarre electronic world, while I felt as if I'd landed somewhere where the language was only a cunning imitation of anything I'd ever thought I understood.

When we brought our empty cans along to the recycling plant, I was shocked by how little money we got. It hardly seemed worth the effort.

'A measly nickel for a hundred cans. How hard do those people have to work to get what they need to live?'

'What people?'

He had forgotten already. His life was busy, real

things happened in it. His head was buzzing with ideas and information by the time he got home in the evenings. He had a Filofax and he was filling it up with the names of business contacts, colleagues. The closest I came to human contact was with the scavengers in the car park. But what really shocked me was how I watched the clock, waiting for him to come in, hungry for news of the outside world. I knew he was tired, but all I could do was pester him with questions: *What did you do, who did you see, what happened next, what happened?* I tried to stop myself, but I couldn't help it.

I was afraid that if I didn't talk to someone who knew me, I'd disappear. I rang Joanne at work, but they were busy and she couldn't hear me. The second time I tried, there was a raid and she had to hang up in the middle of a sentence.

Desperate, I rang my mother one long, hot afternoon. It was night-time over there and she had gone to bed. I could just see her in her white cotton nightie, a mug of cocoa beside the phone. I tried to imagine what it felt like to slip into cold sheets, pull blankets up around your neck.

'What kind of labour did you have with me?'

Sylvia gave a high, nervous snort of laughter down the phone. I could hear the click of her cigarette lighter and a quick suck of indrawn breath. I felt that cigarette hunger in my own throat, my stomach, under my ribs. My lungs ached for the rush of warm smoke. But I didn't dare have one – Dermot would kill me. We'd agreed that it was bad for the baby.

'I don't remember all that, Renée. It was too long ago.'

I began to talk to the baby in a non-stop stream of my own impressions – of the parking lot, the heat, the rubbish that passed my window. I didn't always know whether I spoke out loud or not, but it didn't matter.

I looked out for the old man and the boy. The boy had a wide smile, his front teeth missing, his cheeks creased in deep horizontal folds up around his eyes. I saved cans for them in a paper bag and put them outside the door when I saw them coming. We waved to each other in passing.

Somewhere over the Atlantic, I had lost myself. I became a displaced person: dependent, secondary, a wife, soon to be a mother. My passport was stamped with the information that Dermot was the 'principal alien'. Wherever he went, I'd have to go. Whatever he earned would have to support both of us. We'd joked about the fact that I'd be his accessory, that my right to be here was dependent on him. But it didn't seem funny any more. I had nothing to do, nowhere to go, no way of getting there. I thought I might die of loneliness, or boredom, or both.

Even my body changed. I grew fat and overblown, short of breath, sweaty. I had to wear clothes I'd never, not in a million years, have chosen for myself before, like the brown polyester dress with a tiny floral print that I wore every day for the last six weeks of my pregnancy. It may have been ugly, but it was light and loose. I could rinse that dress out every night and know that it would be dry enough to wear in the morning. When I looked at myself in the mirror my features were disappearing. My skin was puffy, pale. I was coming apart, and not just at the seams. Small deltas of stress appeared on my skin where it was trying to hold together.

I did nothing all day but read, watch television and drift like a ghost through deserted car parks, reading road signs and learning a new terminology. Apartment block. Parking lot. Highway. I stared at screened windows and wondered what went on behind them. I had no function except to grow a baby, feed Dermot when he came in at night, make sure he had a clean shirt in the mornings.

It was as if I had been mugged. As if some stranger had marched up to me in broad daylight and demanded that I hand over my life, my personality, my future, everything I ever was or might have thought I wanted. And I was so stunned that I simply gave it away.

These days, Dermot had to cut my toenails. When he rubbed my feet it was an absent-minded thing, comforting but not passionate.

'I'm disgusting,' I sobbed. 'You can't bear to look at me.'

'You're not disgusting, you're pregnant,' he said. 'It won't last for ever.'

*

'You've got to snap out of this,' Dermot said one evening, worried. 'It's not good for the baby.'

What about me? I wanted to wail, but I knew he was right. 'What should I do?'

'Take the car tomorrow. Get out and about. Drive around. I don't know. You'll find something.'

It was the first time I'd driven on my own in this town, or gone anywhere without Dermot. I nearly missed the turn for the supermarket. Cars and pick-ups full of busy, confident people with places to go, appointments to keep, sped past me. I wondered if I'd ever be one of them again.

I felt happier when I loaded the car with groceries and drove back to the apartment. Capable. It had all been easier than I expected. I'd negotiated the wide, brightly lit aisles full of vegetables, types of bread and brand names I didn't recognize, and opted for the safety of steak, wine, potatoes. But I'd bought American sour cream. At home, we never had sour cream like that, rich and smooth and almost, but not quite, sweet. You could practically eat it straight from the carton with a spoon.

A black pick-up truck cut in front of me while I was thinking about food. I braked hard and flashed my lights. *Idiot.* At the next set of lights I pulled into the empty middle lane. By then I was thinking about Dermot again, how patient he had been with me, and wondering whether there was any chance at all, even the remotest one, that the crampy twinges I'd started to feel were signs of the onset of labour.

When the lights changed and the traffic moved off, the black pick-up pulled up beside me, accelerated, veered in front of me and swerved back into its own lane. The driver gave me the finger. For the first time, I saw the hunting rifle slung across the gun rack in the cab.

The baby stirred and caught a nerve in my diaphragm. The sooner I got home the better. I looked around for the pick-up but couldn't see it. As I turned into our complex, I checked the mirror again and there he was, weaving from side to side, right behind me. *Oh God.*

It only struck me then that the apartment was empty, the whole complex was almost empty. And that even if I could run inside and lock the door, the driver of that truck would know where I lived.

My heart was pounding. I turned the car sharply into a gap between our complex and the one beside it, drove around the back of the buildings and pulled up behind the dumpsters. I stared into my mirror to see if the truck would appear, breathing hard. I could hear the squeal of tyres in the distance. Someone came out of the management office and shouted. I shut my eyes.

When I opened them, it was quiet. I looked around, cautious. A figure materialized out of the shadowed background of the dumpster and I yelped in fright.

It was the old man. We stared at each other through the windscreen. I could see dirt ingrained in the folds of his dark skin, holes in his loose sweater. I imagined I could see my own fear in his eyes, the fear of being seen in the wrong place by the wrong people. Slowly, I turned on the ignition, slipped the car into reverse and backed out of my hiding place. When I was in the main car park, I waved at the old man but he wasn't looking. I drove cautiously through the gap between the complexes, but there was no sign of the pick-up. I parked at the back of our building, in the visitor's slot. Just in case.

Dermot said that I should be more careful in future. As if I couldn't figure that out for myself.

'You can't react to things the way you would at home. You don't know what you're dealing with.'

'I hate it here,' I raged at him. 'I want to go home.'

'That's your hormones talking.'

'Fuck you, Dermot Graves!' I yelled, shocking both of us. In a more normal voice, I went on, 'Do you have any idea what this is like for me?'

'It will be better when the baby comes,' he said. 'You'll see.'

'And if it's not? You promised we'd go home if I hated it.'

'Ray, I'm only getting started here. It's not fair to ask me this now. Give me a chance. Please.'

When Hannah was born, I begged for an epidural and felt nothing until at last Dermot was beside me again. I struggled to sit up straighter, to get a better look at the baby, but all I could see was a mop of thick, gunky hair.

'What is it?' I asked.

'What did you want?' The doctor peered at me over his green surgical mask.

I let my head fall back against the pillows and closed my eyes. What did I want? To be alone. To crawl into some dark, earthy hole under a screen of ferns, a blanket of pine. To fall asleep.

'It's a girl,' Dermot said, his mouth up close to my ear. He helped me to sit up. The baby was over in a transparent cot under one of those big round lights and they were rubbing her with towels.

'Give her to me,' I said and my voice sounded strange. Hoarse and rough, full of silt and gravel.

The day after we brought Hannah home from the hospital, the old man and the boy came to the dumpster. Stiff, I carried her over to the window and they came closer to have a look. We smiled at each other through the glass. The old man put his lined and grimy hand up to the glass, close to Hannah. His nails were square and split, rimmed and encrusted with dirt. I tightened my grip on her fresh, soft skin and stifled the urge to pull her away.

'What are you doing?' Dermot had come into the room behind me.

'They're saying hello,' I said. But when I turned back to the window, the old man and the boy had gone.

'Are you *crazy*? Have you completely lost your mind?' Dermot's face was scarlet and his eyes were popping behind their lenses. 'Do you have any idea who those people are?' He came and took Hannah away from me. 'You've got to be careful, Ray. If you ask for trouble, you'll get it. You have more than yourself to think about now.'

Hannah began to whimper.

'You see?' Dermot demanded angrily.

'She doesn't like it when you shout.'

There were so many miraculous things about that baby, I wouldn't know where to start talking about them. I loved her sweet, milky smell and the way her eyes crossed, suddenly, in a demented squint. I loved the way she fitted right into the bend of my elbow, as if it was designed for no other reason than to support her. She gave me a reason to sit and do nothing for hours on end except play with her fingers and admire the tiny blister on her upper lip from breastfeeding. When she latched on, her eyebrows came together and her eyes crossed as if the whole universe came to a point at my breast, and she was going to take what she could from it. But most of all, she broke the silence that had come to haunt me during the day.

Her voice was music to me. She called to me in a series of sing-song notes and I called right back to her, echoing her pitch. We were like whales, beached on that sofa, making a series of soundings no one else could understand. We sang to each other for hours. I told her everything about the world that I thought she should know. When I described Pat's ducks to her, and showed her with my own body the way they'd swoop and turn in unison, she laughed out loud, her small fists flying out from her sides as if she, too, wanted to fly.

'She's not really talking,' Dermot said. 'They don't, until much later. And that's not a smile, that's wind.'

Hannah squinted and cooed at him.

'You're lucky she doesn't hold it against you, that you believe the books more than you believe in her,' I said.

'You need to get out more,' he said. 'You need adult friends.'

So I took the phone number of a local playgroup from a supermarket noticeboard, and even though I felt stupid and knew that my old self would never, not in a million years, have done such a thing, I called a total stranger to introduce myself and ask if I could join.

Sometimes I think that having Hannah was the single, irrevocable thing, that moving to another country was irrelevant. Other times I think there isn't much to choose between them as life-changing experiences go. When I crossed the park to join a group of mothers and babies for the first time, I thought I'd get sick with nerves, although I couldn't have said exactly what I was afraid of. I looked at them and saw what anyone else would see: shadows and blurred outlines that resolved themselves into women with children, if you looked hard enough. Nothing out of the ordinary. Everything as it should be. Maybe it was my own future I was afraid of. As if entering that group would be the final, irreversible step. Accepting fate. Surrendering my life to become one of them. As if that hadn't happened already, somewhere so far back that I couldn't even remember.

10

Over the next three years, we moved across the south-western states to Los Angeles and back, in a long sunlit trek over flat scrubland, dusty tracks and wide empty highways under enormous skies. We learned the architecture of roadside motels, the contours of franchises, how to recognize companies by their logos, the shape of their buildings: Pizza Hut, Taco Bell, Denny's, State Farm Insurance, Sam's Discount Warehouse, Autoparts, Target. We moved because J. P. Fischer was in search of the perfect funding arrangement, better tax breaks. When Hannah was six months old, the company opened an office in Midland, a city that stood tall against the surrounding Texas flatlands. It felt as if it was in the middle of nowhere. We had barely finished unpacking when JP asked Dermot to go to Los Angeles to supervise the installation of their latest circuitboards for a company linked with NASA. At first we lived in the city, but the smog and the drive-by shootings unnerved us, so we moved up into the foothills where it was cooler.

Everywhere we went, I found a playgroup. I pretended they were for Hannah, but really they were for me. I abandoned any trace of reticence or pride and laid myself wide open to the woman from the Welcome

Wagon, Amway sales people, the Newcomers' Club, invitations from lonely ex-pats. I took advice from sales clerks and medical receptionists and mothers I met in parks about places to live, doctors, dentists, discount food stores. I joined food co-ops and shopped in bulk with strangers in open-air markets, found my way around new towns into living rooms that varied from the palatial to the cramped, from the obsessively neat to the downright squalid. In countless different kitchens, some of them my own, I weighed out flour and cornmeal and maize, bagged all kinds of nuts, bottled syrup, divided blocks of cheese with the dedication of a drug dealer, while children played and fought, ate and spilled around my feet.

The year we crossed the San Gabriel Mountains and drove into Los Angeles had been so dry that coyotes came scavenging out of the foothills. They were so desperate that they came in the full light of day. There were rumours that they had stolen a baby from a suburban yard. Dermot laughed this story off, saying he never heard it on the news, so it couldn't have happened, but I knew better.

The house we rented in the foothills was collapsing in on itself, but it had clean air, a stone terrace in the garden. Bougainvillea, bird-of-paradise, lemons and kumquat blazed in the dry, brown grass. Despite the coyotes, and my second pregnancy, Hannah and I lived outside and wore no clothes. Hannah's eyes had settled to a vivid, jewelled green, the colour of a gecko's skin just before it sheds. Now her flame-coloured hair grew wild and tangled; her skin flushed first pink, then rose, then turned the colour of butterscotch, while the baby who would be Jack ripened inside me in the sun.

When Jack was born, women I barely knew brought gifts of food. For a whole two weeks we never knew what to expect when we peeled back the tinfoil covers from dishes I didn't recognize. Lasagne, tuna casserole, vegetable stew. The women from the playgroup came and did our laundry and entertained Hannah while Jack and I slept in the other room.

'But who are they all?' Dermot tried to read the name on a card attached to a square earthenware dish with multicoloured pasta ribbons inside in a thick tomato sauce.

I took the card from him. 'That's Marissa. She's Reuben's mother.'

'Which one is Reuben? Never mind. I can't keep up.' He looked around the immaculate kitchen. When he'd left that morning there had been clothes piled on chairs, dishes in the sink, bread and cereal scattered across the counter. 'How will we ever thank them?'

I'd already figured out that this was how we'd get by. What these women did for us, we'd do for someone else when our turn came. I'd often heard people say that American society was rootless, but as I lay in our rumpled bed with Jack's sleek, dark head nestled into me like a young seal, I let the kindness of strangers wash over us, and felt something inside me flower.

Dermot's world was different. Confident, assured, it moved along on its own track. But here, in the background, was the force that kept the world turning on its axis.

Dermot's biggest fear was that our visa wouldn't be renewed and we'd have to leave the States before we got the green card. Thousands of people worked illegally, we knew plenty of them. But the kind of corporate work that Dermot did, technical and difficult, had to be documented and in order. So we obeyed all the rules. We stayed in the country; we notified Immigration whenever we moved. J. P. Fischer had hired a lawyer to try to sort us out.

Before dawn, we stood in line with hordes of other people, most with darker skin, all with unnaturally controlled expressions that must have mirrored ours, waiting for the Immigration and Naturalization Services office to open in downtown Los Angeles. I had to steel myself for the contempt I'd come to expect when we produced the children's birth certificates, as if having them was part of a ploy to be allowed to stay.

Inside, we were put into a cramped and crowded waiting room. Jack, all of one month old, began to whimper. He was hungry. I went into the only toilet to feed him. A queue built up outside and someone banged on the door. Jack was frantic. I went back out to the waiting room and found a seat in the corner and tried to feed him there.

'Don't,' Dermot warned. 'They won't like it.'

Jack began to scream.

An armed security guard came over. 'Ma'am, I have to ask you to leave the building.'

'You're not serious!'

'You're causing a disturbance.'

'He's hungry.'

'I'm sorry, ma'am. Please go outside.' There was no expression on his face. Not sympathy, or even disapproval, nor any kind of recognition. He looked right at me, and it was as if I wasn't there.

I glared at Dermot. 'Do something.'

He stared back at me, helpless, and shrugged. 'I'll stay, in case our number is called. Leave Hannah with me.'

I carried Jack, squalling and red-faced, out into the harsh midday sun and stood on the unsheltered sidewalk where the winos sprawled against the wall under deep-brimmed hats. I turned my back on them and leaned against the wall, trying to shield Jack's head with my pulled-up shirt and hide my own breast and feeding baby from passing traffic. I tried to look nonchalant, as if I was waiting for someone. If anyone bothered me, I decided, I'd go and take my chances with the winos.

I looked around the tattered street. Weeds poked through cracks in the concrete and then wilted, as if the effort had been too much for them. Rusted vehicles sank against the sidewalks and shadowy figures kept close to the cover of dusty buildings or stood in listless groups under thirsty-looking trees. This was far from the lush palms and golden beaches where the beautiful people strolled with expensive shopping bags dangling from their arms and glossy young men played on elegant skates. Far even from our own overgrown garden and the blue air of the hills. Not for the first time, I wondered what the hell I was doing here.

At last, Dermot pushed open the door of the office and waved me back inside. 'We're next.'

I went over the answers we'd rehearsed in my mind, sure I'd forget basic facts like the date we got married, but I needn't have worried. We never got that far. The immigration official decided that our information was incomplete, there were forms missing, our case would have to be deferred. I wanted to ask what the problem was, why they couldn't let us know what forms we needed in advance, why there weren't enough seats for all the people who had to crowd in here every day, or enough toilets, or somewhere for a woman to feed a baby without having a man with a gun on his hip come to eject her from the building. But Dermot took my arm and ushered me towards the door, as if he knew what was in my mind.

'There's no point,' he said, when we were outside again. The winos waved at me and called appreciatively to Dermot. He ignored them. He looked so miserable that I felt sorry for him.

'Don't worry,' I said. 'It'll work out in the end. The lawyer said so.'

'It's moving from state to state without the paperwork that bothers me,' he said. 'I'd feel better if it was all in order.'

*

When we drove out of that neighbourhood and got onto the main freeway, I said, 'We could go home, you know.'

'No!' He slammed his open palm against the steering wheel. 'We have to get the green card first. I won't leave without it.'

'What will you do if we don't get it?'

'We will.' He gripped the wheel and accelerated into a gap in the fast lane.

'Dermot, please!' I shot a look back over my shoulder. Jack was asleep, his plump cheeks stained with tears. Hannah was staring out the window, no doubt putting herself into the travel-induced trance she was so well used to by now.

Dermot didn't slow down until a Highway Patrol car appeared on an on-ramp and joined the stream of traffic ahead of us. Then he settled to a steady fifty-five.

'I have to have it,' he said, in a calmer voice. 'This country is where I need to be, Ray. Don't you see? It's all happening here. This is cutting-edge stuff. No one at home would even understand what I do, let alone be able to use me.'

I stopped arguing.

And then the Californian funding dried up. The installation contract was completed and there was no reason for us to stay. We had to turn around and go back to Texas, this time to Houston, where JP had decided that the business climate was better. He gave all the usual reasons: tax incentives, funding, proximity to other fast-growing companies and some of the big players. I wondered if he ever stopped to think about the wear and tear on our nerves, but there seemed no point in asking. We loaded up the car and headed back to Texas.

In New Mexico, we took directions from a man with a dusty beard and black teeth who was selling watermelons at the side of the road.

'Are there any short cuts?' Dermot asked.

We were already overwhelmed by how far we had come, how far we still had to go. Distances that looked innocent on the map translated into a sky that was high and wide, endless stretches of road, space that seemed infinite. For miles all we saw were softening jet trails, solitary birds of prey hovering, the sudden fall.

The man drew lines in the dust with a stubby, nicotine-stained forefinger. His nails were cracked and black. I didn't trust him.

'I'm going to take that short cut,' Dermot said when we pulled away.

I squinted off into the scrub. 'Are you sure that's a good idea?'

Still, I was sick of being squashed into the back of the car with the children, my knees poking into the back of the passenger seat. I'd nursed a fretful Jack the whole way across New Mexico. My nipples stung. If I had to sing 'On Top Of Spaghetti' one more time, I'd scream my own head off.

But I launched into it again when Hannah asked for it, and we roared it out, tuneless and laughing. So I didn't even notice when we left the road and turned onto the unmarked track recommended by the watermelon man.

An hour later, surrounded by dust and scrub, we were all quiet.

I didn't mention the film that came to mind, one we saw before we left Ireland, where a bunch of week-enders were terrorized in the woods by locals. It was deliciously frightening. That world had seemed so remote to us then it could have been science fiction. Now look. Here we were like eejits, lost in the middle of nowhere, at the mercy of some psycho redneck who'd probably sent us out here to be picked off by predators for sport. Even without the predators, it was only a matter of time until we ran out of gas and water, or sputtered to a stop out of pure exhaustion.

The thought of water made me thirsty. There was nothing to drink in the car.

'We should have bought one of those watermelons,' I said.

Dermot pulled up in a cloud of dust. I didn't like the way the tyres slid across the ground, as if they could find nothing to grip.

'What is it?'

'You'd better get in front and read the map.'

'Are we there?' Hannah asked.

'Not yet, sweetie.' I strapped Jack back into his baby seat. When I got in beside Dermot, neither of us mentioned water, or nightfall, but we each knew what the other one was thinking. We drove for another ten minutes. I sneaked a look at the petrol gauge, hoping Dermot wouldn't notice.

'I'm thirsty,' Hannah whined from the back, but quietly.

'We'll get some water in a minute,' Dermot snapped.

'When?'

'When we find a shop.'

Hannah began to sing in her high, tuneless voice, her head turned away from Jack to look out the window.

I stared out the window too, to a horizon of scrub. High above us, a vulture with a chilling span coasted in a lazy circle. Waiting. I wondered how long he'd been there. What I couldn't get over was how empty this place was, how quickly we'd left all signs of civilization behind. At least on the road you could be sure that if you kept moving in any one direction, sooner or later you'd arrive somewhere. At least there was the chance of a passing car, or a signpost. Out here, nothing except an occasional giant cactus distinguished anything from anything else. And even if it had, the dry dust cloud thrown up by the car made it nearly impossible to see.

'Didn't we pass that yucca a while ago?' I asked, just as Dermot said, 'Do you think there's any point in going back?'

He pulled up again. We both looked openly at the petrol gauge, hovering just above empty.

'It's more than an hour since we left that road, Dermot.'

'I know.' His eyes were red-rimmed, strained from the dust and from searching for a road.

'We could go back.'

'I don't think we'd make it.'

We stared at each other. I had to look away first.

'What's that?' I blinked and leaned forward, not certain if I was seeing things. Part of the horizon had detached itself and was moving at speed across our path just a few hundred yards ahead. 'Did you see that?'

We hollered with relief. Jack, woken from his uneasy nap, began to cry.

'What is it? What is it?' Hannah bounced up and down, demanding to see.

'An eighteen-wheeler, sweetie. A big truck. Look.'

'Why is it funny?'

'It means there's a road. A real road.'

'Aren't we on a road?'

We looked at each other and burst out laughing.

Later, we held hands and watched the children sleep in the double bed of the motel room and made solemn vows to be more careful in future. What we kept reminding each other was how we had stopped just short of the main road and never even known it was there. If that truck hadn't passed at that exact moment, we might have turned around and headed back to lose ourselves for ever in the desert night.

'A car wouldn't have been big enough,' I said. 'We wouldn't have been able to see a car.'

'Nor even a pick-up.'

'We must have been mad.'

'We'll never do it again.'

In the middle of the night, I could tell by Dermot's breathing that he was as sleepless as I was.

'Remember *Deliverance*?' I whispered, across the children.

'Don't,' he whispered back. 'It was in my mind every second.'

The bed shook with our laughter, but the children slept right through until morning.

We turned east at El Paso. Remembering New Mexico, we stopped at a diner on the edge of town to stock the car with bottled water and ice.

The diner was quiet. The steel bar shone clean and the high counterstools were empty. The waitress brought us drinks, took an order for food and asked where we were headed.

'That's a long way with such cute babies,' she said. Her eyes flicked to the window, where, through the lettering ('Carl's Diner'), our battered green Volvo was the only car in the lot. The pencil line of her eyebrows arched. 'Y'all are brave,' she said.

'Or stupid,' I answered, saying what I imagined was in her mind.

Her name was Carol and it turned out that she was the owner of the diner. She'd given her no-good brother the job of doing the lettering on the window and look what happened.

'Couldn't you change it?'

Carol waved her hand in front of her face, as if batting flies. 'It makes no never-mind. Everyone round here knows who owns this diner. Everyone else is just passin' through. And we get plenty of those. Legals, illegals, aliens . . .' She laughed.

'We're legal,' Dermot said quickly.

'Hon, I never ask. Y'all are safe enough round here. You're not the type they look for, anyhow.'

I bit my lip on the dreary humiliations of hours spent in INS offices, restricted travel, moving on the whim of J. P. Fischer, unable to look for another job. The fact that I wasn't allowed to work, even if I could have afforded day-care. We began the usual round of *where-are-y'all-from?*

'Oh, I'm from around here,' Carol said. 'Born and raised. Me and my brother both.'

Her brother, Dwayne, was her biggest concern in life, she said. He had her heart broke; she was run ragged keeping track of him. Times she gave him something to do, he messed up, like with the lettering. 'That boy.' She sighed again. 'When he could be looking for a job, he spends all his time hanging out, out there in the desert. Y'all watch out for them when you're passing. If you see a no-good gang of losers with their surfboards, one of them will be my baby brother. You can count on it.'

'Surfboards? In the desert?'

'They got this notion. That one day there'll be a tidal wave. Sweeping in from one coast or the other, it makes no matter which. But they'll be ready. Oh Lord, yes. Out there with their Schlitz and their surfboards.'

*

I half-looked for Dwayne and his friends when we drove away. Wherever there were rocks, Carol had said, they would gather. So they could watch the horizon from all sides. The heat-shifting ground was disorientating. Suddenly I could see what they saw, the desert turned to ocean floor, coral scrub, tumbleweed like schools of fish, a shimmer of water in the air. I had to shake my head and concentrate on driving.

'Do you think she was winding us up?' Dermot asked after a while. So he'd been looking for them too.

'It's too crazy for that. I believed her.'

'Maybe they're looking for illegals crossing the border.'

'They have surfboards, Dermot. Not guns.'

As if he'd summoned it, the air throbbed with the sound of a helicopter. A hawk above us folded his wings and fell.

'Shit.' I checked the speedometer.

'Don't slow down,' Dermot said.

The chopper went away, but soon afterwards a patrol car appeared out of nowhere and filled the rear-view mirror. The light flashed and it made a single, tired *whoop!* I slowed and stopped.

'Keep your hands on the wheel.'

'I know!' The things I'd learned from cop shows on TV! I checked the children in the mirror. They were asleep.

I showed my licence to the officer. He asked where we were going and why. Then he asked for our permits. We had to wake the children and rummage through bags in the back to find them. We watched him carry our precious documents over to his car and get on his radio.

'This is not good,' Dermot said.

'It'll be all right,' I said, even though my heart was beating too hard for comfort. I could feel the pulse jumping in my neck when the officer walked slowly back to us.

'Sir, ma'am, I'm going to have to ask y'all to follow me.'

'Where to?' Dermot's voice came out too high. He cleared his throat.

'There's an Immigration and Naturalization Services post not far from here. Follow me in your own car. Drive slowly, please.'

'What's going on?' I asked Dermot.

'It's because our visa is under review. Those missing documents . . . but, look, remember what that woman in the diner said? We're not who they're after. They'll contact the lawyers and the company. It's going to be okay.'

He was talking to himself as much as to me. I could see how scared he was. This meant everything to Dermot. He loved his job, believed in his company. This was his future, and that meant it was mine as well. Right there in the middle of the desert, following a police car off the road to a prefab border post in the middle of nowhere, it hit me for the first time that, unless the law intervened, I was never going home.

I thought about that over the next four hours, while

we sat on plastic chairs in a narrow trailer and listened to immigration officials discuss our situation on the telephone. It turned out that the central computer was down and they had to wait for files to be checked manually, for phone calls to be made and returned between other offices. I paced around and rocked Jack on my hip to keep him quiet while Dermot read to Hannah from the same book, *Chicken Licken*, over and over again.

'Are we going to sleep here?' Hannah asked.

'I hope not, lovey.'

I thought about *Deliverance* again and tried to push the thought away. No one knew where we were. How long would it be before anyone realized we were missing? Would those people in the diner remember us? My mind began to frame headlines for the newspapers, quotes from imaginary interviews with Carol. I wondered if the surfers would be the ones to find our car, a dusty shell in the open desert.

By the time they let us go, I'd made up my mind to get my act together. This wasn't a dream from which I'd wake up back in my old home, my old life. What I had to wake up to was the fact that this, here and now, was the life I was living. What we needed was to find a place to settle down.

PART FOUR

Settling

(Houston, 1983–90)

11

The city of Houston was like a raft. Tides of people washed into it every day and clung to it until the next convulsion in their lives swept them off somewhere else. When we first got there, we were stunned all over again by the heat and humidity. The air was as murky as the swamps and rice fields the city had been built on. The roads shimmered and wavered, and the atmosphere was tense and watchful. When we weren't driving around looking for a place to live, the children and I spent all our time in the motel pool or stretched out under ceiling fans, recovering from the effort of climbing in and out of the car, strapping and unstrapping seat belts, the exhaustion of breathing.

'But how do you *think* here?' I asked Dermot.

'We have air-conditioning in the office. The computers need it.'

I drove around, with the children mutinous and sweating in the back seat, through rows and rows of strip centres with fast-food joints and autoparts warehouses, drive-thru banks and cut-price liquor stores fronting apartment complexes with 'Adult Only' banners and a discouraging assortment of pick-ups and sports cars lined up in the parking lots.

We went to parts of town recommended by Dermot's workmates. In one, the houses were tiny, with gardens the size of envelopes, and the rents were more than three times what we could afford. In the other, there were no trees, only bare squares of scorched grass, chain-link fences, no sign of children anywhere. Not a single swing, or even a bike left out to rust.

'Doesn't anybody *live* here?' I asked. 'Where do they all go during the day?'

We checked out a low-rent neighbourhood bordering a busy street close to the office. The realtor who showed us around, Shari, was enthusiastic about the convenience aspect of it, its access to the freeways. But I had seen the heavy bars on the windows of the 7–11 at the corner, the bar with no windows and *Girls! Girls! Girls!* in flashing neon at the side of the street, the pawnshop with a steel grid across the door advertising guns for sale.

In the next house, the tiny backyard was completely overgrown and full of litter inside the low chain-link fence. Shreds of plastic, crumpled cans and pieces of broken glass glittered in the sun. I wondered about fire. All the other yards on the street looked the same. Not a place for sitting out and sharing a beer with the neighbours in the evening, then.

Hannah hooked her arm around my leg and followed me around the house in that position. Jack sucked his thumb on my shoulder.

'I'm not so sure,' I said.

Shari, an older woman with vivid blonde hair and

half a pound of make-up on her face, shrugged her thin shoulders in their lime-green jacket. 'Y'all are running out of options,' she declared. 'I have one more house to show you.'

The last house she showed us had a sour smell from the minute we walked into it. I was already familiar with the panelled-walled living rooms that seemed standard around here. They made the rooms dark, but they also reduced the glare and the heat and I supposed I'd get used to them in time. But the walls in this house had an additional feature – stains marked the panelling, as if someone had thrown pots of coffee at the wall.

'What's that?' I asked.

'That there is cockroach dirt.'

I shuddered.

'You can't get away from roaches in this town,' Shari said in a bored, matter-of-fact drawl. 'Best you can do is fight to keep them under control. I guess these people lost the battle.' She chuckled without amusement, and checked her watch as if she already knew we wouldn't take the house.

'We'll call you,' I said, for courtesy's sake.

One day, I drove out under the 'Loop' freeway all the way to the city limits. The air was still and heavy and there was nobody about. The back of my neck prickled, as if some major disaster had already happened and everyone knew about it but me. I checked the children behind me. Hannah's thick rusty hair was damp with sweat and her cheeks had two bright-red patches on them. She drummed her fingers on her knees and stared through her window, bored out of her mind. Jack was asleep, but his hair too, what there was of it, was plastered to his head in a damp black frizz.

We had reached a green place bordered by live oaks. Acres of long grass spread away to the south, shining like a sea. I could see mud-brown peaks behind a high fence in the distance.

I pulled over and checked my map. I was barely inside the city limits, and the area I was looking at wasn't marked. I drove back to the motel thoughtfully, registering how far away that place was, how long it took us to get back.

That night I dragged Dermot out there, half expecting that the place would have vanished in the meantime. But it was there, all right. We found the entrance, where a faded cardboard sign, scarred with bullet holes, announced that the area was called the Plains.

'As if the whole place wasn't as flat as a pancake,' Dermot said.

Our first impressions of the neighbourhood weren't good. The entrance was alarming in itself, but inside it seemed seedy and run down. Weeds pushed their way up through cracks in uneven slabs of pavement. Tree roots played havoc with the grass.

We were in a maze of interconnecting streets, empty of cars, the windows blank. I could have sworn that we were being watched. We turned back just as the sun went down and the giant arc-lights on the freeway overpass came on. The place was lit by an artificial glow.

'Does that mean it never gets dark here?'

Just then, people appeared out of nowhere, as if by a trick of the light. It was like Samhain, when the boundaries between the worlds are meant to soften, except that this was far more modern and material. Garage doors opened, revealing workbenches and washing machines. Bikes and Big Wheels spilled out onto driveways. We passed two men jogging and I saw a group of women gossiping on a street corner while their small children swung from the branches of a tree.

When we passed the swimming pool, boom-boxes blared music that stabbed me with nostalgia.

'Led Zeppelin,' Dermot murmured, approving.

I looked at a group of teenagers with their hormones on display, their perfect teeth. They were about five years younger than me, yet they seemed like a different species.

A woman came out of the pool area and ushered two small children swathed in towels into the back of a station-wagon.

'I want to go in there,' Hannah said, perking up in the back seat.

'We'll swim back at the motel,' Dermot said.

On the way back, Hannah chattered about things she'd seen, things I had missed altogether. A wooden fort in the playground. A big blue slide at the pool.

'I liked it,' I said, as we turned into the motel parking lot. I didn't mean *like*, exactly. But it was the first place we'd come across where I could see that some kind of life might be possible.

Every city has small pockets that are overlooked by anyone who doesn't live there. The Plains was that kind of place. It was a small outgrowth of the city, it didn't lead to anywhere else, there was nothing remarkable about it except that the street plan was confusing. If you didn't know your way around, you could easily get lost. There was nothing to say whether people who lived there were on their way up or on their way down. If anything, there were signs of both. If you looked closely at the wood trim of some of the houses, you could see that it was beginning to rot, that the fences were not in the best state of repair. The pavements were uneven, as if some seismic disturbance was going on out of sight, or it could have been the burgeoning roots of some of the larger trees, refusing to stay underground. The place had an atmosphere of clinging on – perched as it was at the edge of town, with the freeway looping over its northern corner – and of keeping its head down. No one paid too much attention to newcomers, as if it was rude to ask too many questions. There was no neon, no advertising; no shops, even, of any kind.

'That's a disadvantage,' Dermot pointed out. 'You'll have to drive me to work and take the car if you need to go out for anything.'

But set against the pool, the trees, all that open space around it and the tiny elementary school, I figured it was a small price to pay. Whoever had designed this area had some kind of sense of humour, I figured. Prairie Drive led into Buffalo, which led in turn to Lariat Loop. We laughed out loud at Sheriff Street, a cul-de-sac in the shape of a star, with a solemn, square house in each point.

Way at the back, at the southernmost edge of the neighbourhood, almost over the county line, we found a small cul-de-sac called Station Hollow, a balloon-shaped street off the wide main road that led out to the old rice fields, the railway line and a one-lane, dusty highway. Station Road was wide enough to suggest that a much bigger road was planned for its future, but we had already fallen into the local habit of dismissing those signs. Instead, we saw space, children riding bikes, a tyre-swing hanging from a tree.

Tucked into the back of the Hollow, in a wedge-shaped corner plot, we found a 'For Rent' sign anchored to a mailbox outside a tiny house with a steep roof and tall, narrow windows. A live oak tree with strong, no-nonsense branches held pride of place in the grassy area at the end of the street. The roots of the tree made ridges in the grass.

'Do you think we could afford it?' I asked, not caring in the least what it was like inside.

It turned out that the house was full of light. It was small, right enough, but it was open-plan, so that the whole living area was spread out under a sloped high ceiling, with french doors leading out to a tangled garden screened by trees and a tall wooden fence. A kitchen ran the length of the house from front to back, divided from a living area by a high, vinyl breakfast counter. There was a fireplace in the centre of the room, with a brick chimney stretching up to the wooden rafters. A narrow hall led away to three cramped bedrooms and a narrow bathroom, but when I saw the living space and Dermot's smile, I knew we'd take it.

In the back garden, the grass was luxuriant and glossy. St Augustine, I would find out later. An overgrown trellis shaded a patio area with a rusty-looking barbeque. Hannah ran around and screamed, waving her arms like windmills, letting off steam. Jack squirmed in my arms, as if he wanted to join her.

On our second day in the house, Dermot took the car to work. I collapsed the empty moving cartons and stored them out in the garage, except for the one the kids were playing with. Hannah lifted Jack in and out, closed and opened the flaps. He didn't seem to mind the dark. She dragged him around the kitchen floor on his blanket, and he didn't complain.

At last, they both went for a nap. The heat had wiped us all out. Outside, the high-pitched rattle of cicadas swelled until I was sure they'd burst, but they kept on going. The only movement on the street was the faint ripple of tarmac at the end of the road where it shone like water, but I knew that was an illusion. I wondered where everyone went to hide from the heat and from that shrill, tremulous sound.

I sat in the rocking chair and creaked listlessly backwards and forwards under the fan in my loose shorts. Then, bored, I wandered over to the front window and looked out, wondering what to do with myself. The street was still and empty. The driveways were bare, the windows blank. Time stretched out ahead of me, as pointless and empty as what I saw from my window.

I shook myself. *Don't give in to this.*

I made a cup of tea and brought it to the counter, near the window. Then I hauled out the phone book and the map and started to read through the entries for local pre-schools, clinics, doctors, making lists as I went along. I'd take charge of this, the way I always had. I'd make it a campaign. I would familiarize myself with this place and, what's more, I wouldn't be shifted from it. Not easily. From the other places we'd looked at in this town, I knew that we had nowhere else to go. I called a few places and asked them to send out information. At least I'd have post to look forward to.

The sound of a car moving slowly down the drive made me look up. Maybe Dermot had decided to come home early. But the engine had a deeper rumble, unfamiliar.

A low-slung, heavy black car slid slowly, cautiously, past the window towards the garage. In reverse. I stood there frozen, the phone propped between my cheek and my ear, and stared at four complete strangers.

I knew I was looking at nothing but trouble. For a split second, my eyes locked with the empty, pale-blue eyes of the front-seat passenger and my whole body went cold. His loose vest billowed over a muscled tattoo on a deeply tanned arm. A darker, scarred face leaned across him and ducked towards the glass, as if to see into the house better. To see me. The other passengers were vague shadows in the back, but I'd already seen more than enough.

The phone slipped from my shoulder. I broke eye contact with the tattooed man and scrabbled to get it back, my heart racing. Stupidly, I lifted the phone and shook it at them, yelling, 'Go away! Go away!'

The engine roared and the car took off. The tyres screeched as the car skidded back onto the street and accelerated onto Station Road, then sped off into the distance.

I had to dial Dermot's number three times, my fingers shook so hard.

'What is it?' I could tell by his voice that someone else was in the room with him.

'These men – the driveway.'

'What men?'

'I don't know. Four men. In a car. I think they wanted to break in.'

Dermot sighed. 'They could have been visiting some-one and got the wrong house.'

'They didn't look the type for visiting.'

'What did they look like, then?'

'Terrifying.' I knew that I sounded childish, but I couldn't help it. 'Will you come home?'

I strained to hear the children. The open space of the living room loomed behind me and I turned to press my back to the wall, like a child myself, afraid of the dark.

'We're busy. They've gone, haven't they?'

'They might come back.'

He laughed at me. 'I bet you scared them off. What did you do?'

'I, uh, yelled. I shook the phone at them.' I began to laugh myself.

'They must have thought it was a gun! You'll be okay. Ring me if they come back.'

I was never more glad to hear the children wake up than I was that afternoon. I badly needed the company.

'Why didn't you come home, earlier?' I asked Dermot later. He was reading a technical manual at the table, his dinner half eaten in front of him. He looked up and I could see his eyes struggle to focus on me, as if he was travelling a long distance and had to adjust to a different light.

I slammed the pot I was drying down on the counter-top, harder than I'd meant to. We both jumped a little.

'What's this, now?' He looked wary. 'I had a meeting . . .'

'I'm talking about when I rang you. Those men were really creepy, Dermot. I was scared. What if they'd come back? What should I have said to them? "Hang on out there a minute, lads. My husband will be here to sort you out, just as soon as he comes out of his meeting"?'

'Come on, Ray. Don't exaggerate.'

I lifted up the pot and slammed it down again, on purpose this time. 'You weren't here! You didn't see them!'

And, as fast as my temper had risen, it ebbed away. That was the problem, right there. Dermot didn't believe me. Not because he thought I was lying, but because he hadn't been here. Just like I could listen to him talk about work, but the only thing I understood was office politics. When it came to the finer points of circuitry and signal processing, he might as well have been talking to me in Japanese for all I understood. He just didn't get it. I might as well hate Jack for having bitten me that morning, when I knew he was teething; or Hannah for coming awake, screaming for me, from a nightmare.

'Forget it,' I said.

He looked helpless and rumpled. 'I'm sorry,' he said. 'It doesn't matter.'

But that night I lay awake and listened to the hum of air-conditioners all around me, and thought about the men I'd seen that afternoon, and the pick-up truck that had chased me into the apartment car park in Dallas three years before. Seemed like this was some kind of Texas welcome, a reminder that whether you went out or stayed in you'd better keep your wits about you.

I began to wonder if the signs of neighbourhood life we had seen earlier had been an illusion. The only movement that I saw during the day was a classic station-wagon with wood trim that came and went from the driveway of the two-storeyed house on the main road, just across from our street. A tall woman with long black hair who always dressed in vivid colours and an olive-skinned girl of about Hannah's age would carry bags of shopping into the house and then vanish. Whenever I was ready to go over and say hello, the car was gone, or else there was no answer to my knock. The child assumed mythical status for Hannah, who referred to her as 'my friend' before they ever met.

On the fifth morning, I went to the mailbox and took out a pile of information on local schools and playgroups. On my way back inside, I saw the station-wagon pull into the driveway and brown paper bags being lifted out of the boot. I waved. The woman waved back, then went into the house.

I hesitated. It was early. Hannah and Jack were still asleep. I decided to risk running up the road to say hello.

I had barely rung the doorbell when all the things that could go wrong began to play themselves out in my mind. Fire, intruders, a random accident. I could even be reported for leaving my children in the house on their own. I stood on the other woman's doorstep and looked back at the deceptively calm exterior of my own house and wished I'd waited. I could hear the drone of a hoover coming from upstairs, deep inside the house. She probably wouldn't even hear the bell.

I was halfway down the path when the door opened, just a crack. I looked down into a pair of expressionless brown eyes.

'Hi, I'm Ray – we've just moved in over there?' I pointed back down the street towards our house. 'Is your mother here?'

The child nodded.

'Could I see her?'

For a split second, it occurred to me that this child might close the door in my face.

'What's your name?' I asked.

'Lucie.'

'Never mind, Lucie. I'll come back later.'

'Wait,' Lucie said, and vanished, leaving the door wide open. I was embarrassed to find myself looking through a marble-tiled hall with pots of plants grouped in a corner to a deep room with a champagne-coloured carpet, walnut furniture, a brick fireplace not unlike my own, except that mine was bare and this one was laden with healthy-looking plants.

'Mom.' Lucie's whine competed with the drone of the hoover. 'Mom!'

'Not now, Lucie!' The woman's voice was sharp and cold, brittle with dislike.

'But, Mom . . .'

'I said NOT NOW!' There was a crash, as if the hoover had collided with a piece of furniture. 'Goddam it! Now look what you made me do!'

The hoover resumed its irritable track across the floor. That woman was never going to come to the door, and it didn't look as if Lucie was coming back either. I pulled the door shut, ran back across the road to my own house, and went to check on the children.

Hannah lay on her back, her arm flung up across the pillow. She was sweating, despite the wide arc of the ceiling fan. Jack was on his stomach, his bottom stuck up into the air in an exaggerated hump, his thumb in his mouth. I hoped they would never hear anything in my voice to match what I'd heard that morning.

The next day I answered my own front door to Lucie and her mother. Lucie wore a white cotton dress, her smooth black hair gathered in a red velvet bow at her neck. Her mother wore a bright canary-yellow shift that flared against her pale skin.

'Oh – hi.' I shifted Jack's sticky weight on my hip. 'Come on in.'

The woman stayed where she was, out in the light. I had to squint against the sun to see her. 'Well, hi there. I just wanted to welcome y'all to the neighbourhood. My name is Marilyn and this is Lucie. We live over—'

'I know. I came over—'

Marilyn's smile showed the most perfect teeth I had ever seen, but it was quick and left no trace of itself on her even features. 'We're not easy to catch at home.' She laughed, an oddly grating sound. 'Do you care for muffins? We brought you these.'

Hannah sidled up beside me and leaned against my leg, peering shyly at the strangers.

'Thanks – please come in. Here's Hannah.'

'Say howdy, Lucie.'

'Hi.' Lucie scowled. She tugged at her mother's skirt. 'That's her, Mom!'

'Lucie, what's got into you? Where are your manners?' Marilyn's eyes flashed to mine and away again.

'That lady. In our hall, 'member?' Lucie's eyes were as fixed and wide as a china doll's.

I felt myself flush. 'I came over to introduce myself. I knocked. Lucie opened the door – you didn't hear – I went away again.' Even to my own ears, I sounded deranged.

'We don't allow Lucie to open the door to strangers.'

I could think of nothing to say that wouldn't get someone into trouble. Jack was restless on my hip. I switched him to the other one, glad of the distraction.

'Well, we'd best be on our way,' Marilyn said. 'We have an appointment.'

They walked away.

Hannah went to the window and craned to see Lucie through the glass. 'Where's my friend?' she asked.

'She had to go, sweetie. You can play with her some other time.'

That first weekend, the silence of the neighbourhood cracked open into the roar of lawnmowers, of cars and pick-ups going out and coming back, groceries being unloaded, the sound of sprinklers on lawns and hoses spraying cars. Everyone seemed friendly, but busy, set on their own tracks.

We found the nearest library and checked out books on gardening. Before Dermot had finished reading the first chapter, he went out to hire a tiller so that we could make a vegetable garden, even though it was late in the season. 'No time to lose,' he said.

We bought sunflower seeds to plant for the children, and other, edible plants recommended by the book. Beans and okra and zucchini, two types of lettuce. The earth felt strange in my hands. Dry and brittle, it soaked up gallons of water before it turned to a loamy paste. Everything that moved through it, worms, creepy-crawlies, beetles, were bigger than any I'd ever seen before. I soon found out why. Things grew quickly in that soil. Only days after we'd planted our seeds, the first shoots appeared above the ground. I felt triumphant, and it struck me that if we cared for this garden, we stood a reasonable chance of being here for the harvest.

Not long afterwards, I was out in the garden with the children. The sky was a vaulted blue cushion above us. I turned the soil and pulled weeds, still amazed by how quickly everything grew. Hannah helped, up to her elbows in muck, while Jack kicked on his blanket.

I closed my eyes and, just for a second, imagined I could feel the rotation of the earth. If I anchored myself deeply enough in this dirt, if I plunged my hands right into the soft centre of where I was, I wouldn't fall off.

'Look, Mommie!' Hannah had unearthed a glistening earthworm. Fat and segmented, it writhed on the tines of her fork, a slimy red-brown mass.

'Easy, Hannah, you'll hurt it.' I pulled the worm free and put it back in the dirt.

After that, Hannah rescued pillbugs and earthworms

and carried them solemnly over to the corner of the garden, out of reach of my fork, until the sun rose so high that there was no shade.

The phone was ringing when we got inside. Hannah snatched it up. 'Daddy! A worm! And I . . . Oh. Okay.'

I rubbed her hair. 'You can tell him all about it when he comes home. She wanted to tell you something,' I said into the phone, but Dermot interrupted me.

'Have you heard the news? There's a hurricane coming.'

'What should I do?'

'Make sure we have supplies.'

'Like what?'

'Water, batteries. That kind of thing. Turn on the TV.'

I sat on the floor with the children and looked at the weather map with its new, threatening overlay of storm clouds. The ominous cyclonic sweep of those clouds was clear, a large untidy blot on the Gulf of Mexico. The winds were already past tropical-storm force and, at eighty miles per hour, well into hurricane category. The weatherman showed several courses the storm might take and talked about probable landfall. Everything he said was in percentages. There was a seventy-five per cent chance that the storm would land on the coast just south of the city within the next three hours and rampage across the flat intervening land, with nothing to stop it or slow it down. With a thrill of shock, I realized that ours would be one of the first streets to feel the brunt of it.

'In case of flooding,' the presenter said, 'residents should look for higher ground.'

'What higher ground?' I said, out loud. Where the hell were we supposed to find higher ground? Up on the overpass? A band of text across the bottom of the screen advised us to stay tuned for details.

At the supermarket, the usual embarrassing plenty of the fresh fruit and vegetable section had gone. I put a handful of bruised bananas into the trolley and went on. There was no bread. The canned goods section had been cleaned out. I put a few packets of cookies into the trolley and Hannah began to whine to open them right there and then.

'We've got to save them, Hannah.'

'I'm hungry NOW!'

At the battery shelf, a man scooped the last packages into his basket, regardless of size. He avoided my eye as he hurried away.

I turned onto the drinks aisle. An elderly black woman moved slowly along, leaning across the top of her empty trolley as if it was a zimmer frame. Ahead of her, I could see two containers of water on an otherwise empty shelf. I moved past the woman and had a hand each on the last two bottles of water when I saw what I was doing.

'I'm sorry. Did you want one of these?'

'No thank you, honey. You go right ahead.'

Her wide smile made me feel worse. 'Are you sure?' I couldn't help looking into her trolley to see what she had managed to find. She'd done better than me. A handful of cans, a jar of peanut butter, two rolls of insulating tape. I'd forgotten tape.

'I came out earlier,' the woman said. 'I got what I need. I'm just getting me some air before the storm comes down.'

At the checkout, I asked about batteries.

'If they're not on the shelf, we don't have 'em any more, ma'am. Y'all are late. We're closing soon.'

I counted out the money. Behind me, the elderly woman leaned further across her trolley. 'They had batteries at the 7–11 an hour ago, honey. You should try there.'

'Thank you.'

The atmosphere in the 7–11 was more frenzied. They had not only batteries, but candles and – at the checkout – can-openers and torches. I was aghast at all I had forgotten. I spent every penny I had and hurried home to the television. The storm had increased in strength and speed, and the chances of landfall near the city within the next two hours had gone up to ninety-five per cent.

Outside, the clouds looked no different. Everything seemed normal, as sleepy and impenetrable as ever. But what did I know of normal in this place? I wished I knew an actual person, anyone, besides my children, to talk to. I wanted to ask how real the danger was, how bad the storm might get, what I should do if it broke before Dermot got home.

12

Dermot arrived just as I finished taping up the windows. Pioneer woman. The bath and several saucepans were full of water and I had piled pillows and duvets in the inner hall, just in case.

'Aren't you impressed?'

'Are you sure this isn't overkill?'

'It kept us busy. Hannah helped.'

'Let's hope we don't need it all.'

The rain, when it fell, was unbelievable. It was like a drum beating on our roof. The wind whipped around the house and shook it, looking for a way in. The screens shivered and a weird electric whine filled the air. The window frames rattled and I was sure I could feel gusts of air rip through the house. Outside, the trees flung their branches around in a frenzy, bent right over to the ground, snapped back as if they would turn inside out, upside down, fly away any second. Before long, the power went. We lit fat candles on saucers and set tea-lights out on the counter and told stories until the power came back.

Then we watched the progress of the storm on television as it inched across the city. Its forward motion was slow, despite its force. It vented its energy in a churning, inner motion. After a while, the power died again, and we went into the cave we'd made in the hall. I was sure that worry alone would keep me awake, never mind the violence of the storm, but I was the first to fall asleep. It was like being a child again, listening to the wind and rain and the foghorns, the sensation of safety and warmth that used to send me burrowing deeper under my eiderdown, glad of the roof over my head, the solidity of my bed.

When I woke up, I could tell the night was over, even in the tunnel of the hall. I could hear neither wind nor rain. The house was still standing. We'd made it. I climbed over the others and went out to the kitchen. Outside, there was total devastation. Our fence had collapsed on both sides and the sapling pear tree was upside down across the vegetable patch. I could see into the neighbours' gardens, in much the same state as ours. The back fence flapped open, showing glimpses of the acres of scrub leading down to the railway line. Everywhere there were broken branches, slates blown off roofs. One mature tree had split in half.

Out front, the street was full of water. A small lake stretched from halfway down our drive to the driveway of the house opposite ours. It was just as well that Dermot had managed to park the Volvo in the garage. Not everyone was so lucky. On the main road a car was half submerged, only its windows above the level of this odd, sudden tide. Tree limbs had fallen randomly across cars, other trees, fences, road and water. I could see glimpses of back gardens where fences leaned out at odd angles or had fallen. But the storm was clearly over, the sky a washed blue.

'Lookie!' Hannah sang out beside me. She was out the door before I could stop her, dancing in the water. I picked Jack up and followed her out to stand on what was left of our driveway.

'It's warm!' Hannah called. She started to splash me, giggling.

'Come and see this!' Dermot called.

We trooped inside again to sit, awed, in front of the television. We were lucky to have power. Most of the city was without it. We looked at boats blown onto roofs down by the ocean, houses collapsing into the encroaching sea, roads wiped out. Then the cameras shifted downtown, where the freeways had filled with water. People raced speedboats up and down a straight stretch of road where traffic usually slowed to a crawl. One man water-skied under familiar roadsigns. He waved at the cameras, grinning.

'I can't believe it,' Dermot said. 'I drive along that road every day. There has to be ten feet of water in that underpass.'

But it looked benign and festive. Hannah ran outside again and I waded after her, leaving Jack with Dermot this time. Jack sucked his thumb and stared at the screen as if he was as impressed by all the damage as we were. Hannah splashed around, laughing. Our next-door neighbour came around the corner from the main road, walking up close to the houses, where the water was shallow. I knew from his mailbox that his name was Bill Hillman. 'Hi!' I waved at him. 'We made it through the night!' I felt giddy and reckless, as if we had come through some initiation.

Hannah stumbled and fell under water. I reached down and hauled her out, spluttering and coughing.

'Y'all should be more careful,' Bill said.

'I'm right here.'

'The water is the least of it. The tops have come off most all the drains.' He pointed back in the direction he had come from. 'I seen snakes down there earlier.'

I gripped Hannah's hand and pulled her away from the flood. 'I didn't know.'

Bill shook his head. 'Y'all should be more careful.'

When Hannah began to burn and shake, I knew at once that the water had caused it. While Dermot was out helping clean up the neighbourhood and making plans to rebuild fences, I sat with Hannah and sponged her face, held her while she shivered. I tried to calm her down when she began to vomit, the thing she hated most in the world. 'Mommie, make it stop,' she whimpered, her hot face burning my bare arm.

I thought about horrible tropical illnesses while I sponged her down. Typhoid. Malaria. Could we get those here? It was hot enough, surely. As soon as the water subsided I got into the car and took Hannah to the doctor through heavy, but manageable, floods.

The doctor said there was nothing to do but wait for the fever to pass. Yes, she agreed, it probably was the water that had made Hannah sick. But we'd been lucky. It could have been worse. Just across the railroad tracks, two ten-year-olds had been swept away and drowned in a makeshift boat. A whole family had died, trapped in their car in a flash flood.

'There are people who go down to the beach when the storms start,' she said. 'They try to ride the rising waves. They shout into the wind.'

'I saw them on TV. It's stupid,' I agreed. Then I blushed, because I saw that she was talking about me. I had assumed that I knew what I was dealing with, but I hadn't had a clue. Because the water on our street was calm and warm, I'd assumed it was benign, but it was lethal. I had a lot to learn, and a few rolls of masking tape or a bath full of fresh water wouldn't get me very far.

After the insurance assessors had been to inspect the damage, everyone came together to rebuild fencing and repair screens and windows. People I had never seen before turned up on our driveway to claim a drink from the cooler we had stocked with beer and Dr Pepper, or to drink my tea. In return, they lent us hammers and nails, tape and wire, tools we hadn't had time to amass for ourselves.

Bill's wife, Norma, came and sat in our kitchen and we watched Bill and Dermot nail down slates on their roof while Hannah drew squiggly lines on her colouring book at the kitchen table and Jack slept on my knee.

'Look, Mommie!' Hannah tugged my arm, to get my attention. 'Look at my picture!'

'That's lovely, Hannah. Is it a road?'

'No, silly. It's a tree. On the ground. It's broken.'

'Clever girl. Draw another one.'

'At least the boat is safe,' Norma went on. 'It would have broke Bill's heart if that thing had been lost.'

They kept their boat in Galveston, and every weekend they went down there, which was why they hadn't got around to inviting us in for a barbeque yet, she said. I didn't see when they ever would. They left their house at six o'clock every morning to go to work, and they were in bed by nine o'clock every night. 'See, we're pooped by then,' Norma said.

Norma was a pretty, soft-spoken woman. I had to pay close attention to catch what she was saying. Her hair was a mass of fluffy brown curls framing a carefully made-up face, wide blue eyes. When I first saw her, I thought she was much younger than I now began to suspect she really was.

'You're lucky,' I said. 'A boat!'

Norma made a pouting shape with her mouth. 'Boats make me sick, honey.'

'Then, how . . . ?'

'Draw a boat, Mommie!'

I took the crayon Hannah gave me and drew a shaky canoe in the corner of her page, my other hand holding Jack, while Norma went on talking.

'I take me some dramamine before we go and keep right on taking it until we git back.'

'Is that healthy?'

Norma shrugged. 'What would be real unhealthy would be to send my man out there on his own every weekend.' She shook her head. 'No, ma'am. I couldn't do that.'

I was about to answer when an empty ladder fell across the open space in front of the window. Hannah shrieked and jumped down from her chair. Jack woke up, flinging his hands out to the side, the way he still did sometimes. His eyes came slowly to a focus and found my face. I dropped the crayon and lifted him to my shoulder and followed Hannah to the window, but I couldn't see the men. Norma's roof was empty.

'Did you hear anything?' Norma said.

We went outside. A ladder lay the length of Norma's garden. A hollow groan rose from the grass, somewhere around the corner.

'Oh my God,' I said. 'Where is he?' Jack hiccuped into my neck.

'Daddy!' Hannah called. Her face was screwed up and scarlet, the way it went just before a tantrum.

The men appeared from where they'd been hiding at the side of the house, laughing. 'Gotcha!' Bill said, just before Hannah started to cry.

'You big eejit,' I said to Dermot. 'Look at the state Hannah's in.'

But she was already over the fright. She laughed and clung to Dermot like a monkey, scrambling up his side and ending up on his shoulders.

'Let's have us a cook-out,' Bill said.

Norma and I set up a barbeque while the men fixed the cracked and loosened slates on our roof. We loaded Bill's trailer with shattered patio furniture and broken flower pots from all the gardens on the street and they took it off to the city dump. That night we dragged our living-room furniture out onto our driveway and had a dinner party right there in the open. A quiet man called Stephen, who lived in the corner house, came out to join us and so did Carla, the small, plump woman from the house across the road from us, with her son Eddie, a gangly boy with wire-framed glasses and kinked, close-cropped black hair. Before long, Beth and Curtis, the couple who shared a back fence with Stephen, even though they lived on the main road, came along with their pale daughter, Brooke, and a case of beer.

'Welcome to the neighbourhood,' Beth said, handing me a can.

I liked Beth straight away. She was barefoot in a pair of paint-spattered dungarees and a loose T-shirt. She had a square chin, prominent cheekbones and slightly slanted brown eyes under hair cropped shorter than any I had seen on a woman since I had come to live here. There was something about her that said that she was capable and sturdy, that what you saw was what you were likely to get.

'Howdy.' Beth's husband, Curtis, was muscled and brown. He wore a loose vest and a pair of running shorts and had the best pair of legs I'd ever seen on a man. I'd already seen him a few times, out running in the wasteground, when I took the kids to the park. 'Welcome.'

Beth laughed up at him. She only came up to his shoulder. 'My husband is a man of few words,' she said. 'Pay attention, girl, or you might miss something.'

Even Lucie came over from the main road with her dad, Byron, a tall thin man with white hair framing a young face. 'Marilyn has a headache,' he said. 'It's the pressure in the air. She's lying down.'

There was something surreal about the atmosphere. Lanterns burned all over the neighbourhood. We heard laughter, cans popping open, children playing. Bugs fizzed out against mosquito-guards. I felt a wary stir of happiness. Maybe here, at last, in this spontaneous, watery gathering of people, I'd be able to make a home.

But the street still felt strangely empty during the day. Beth worked through the daylight hours in a studio they'd built at the back of their house. She claimed never to feel time passing and, right enough, I often saw her tearing down the street, driving much too fast, because she'd suddenly remembered some appointment she was late for. She told me to call in on her whenever I wanted, but I felt bad about disturbing her at work. Curtis was often home as well, and that made me feel awkward about going over there. He was a carpenter, and worked odd hours all over the city.

Marilyn and Lucie came and went with shopping bags at all hours of the day and night, always looking busy and purposeful. Carla, a nursing assistant, worked long shifts at Memorial Hospital. And even though Stephen was friendly enough, he was so quiet that I wouldn't have noticed if he went out of town for a month.

Joanne rang one afternoon. 'You'll never guess what's happened! I bought a car!'

'That's great, Joanne.' I bent down to extricate Jack from the corner he'd rolled into, behind the armchair. 'Hang on a minute . . . come on, Jack, up you come.' I tugged the electric wire out of his grasp and braced myself for the wails as I lifted him up. 'What were you saying, Joanne?'

Her impatience gusted down the phone line. 'I said, and they broke the window! Shattered it!'

'Who did? Why?'

'Aren't you listening? I got a bumper sticker that said "If you don't agree with abortion, don't have one." And some fucker smashed the back window of my car!'

'No!'

'Are you talking to me or to Jack?'

'You.'

'Sometimes I can't tell the difference.'

'I don't know why she bothers phoning if she's going to be like that,' I said to Dermot later. 'She just doesn't know what it's like. But isn't that bad, about her car?'

'What did she expect? It's not a thing that people feel neutral about.'

'But still.' I felt disloyal. I should have known better

than to criticize Joanne to Dermot. 'Sometimes I feel as if she's the only person who remembers me the way I used to be,' I said.

'What are you talking about? I remember you. You're not so different.'

'I was thinner, then.'

'I like you the way you are now. Come here,' he said. 'And I'll show you.'

13

We settled in to our new lives. Hannah made friends with Lucie. Lucie's mother, Marilyn, was the same age as me but she had a formal manner. She always wore colourful dresses, with matching ribbons threaded through her jet-black hair emphasizing the creamy pallor of her skin. We talked on the street a couple of times while the girls played in the tree; we met at the pool. One day I brought Lucie to the pool with us and after that Marilyn invited us over to her house. I showed up with the children at three o'clock, the time she'd said. Something about her told me that it wouldn't do to be 'tardy', as she put it.

'Where's Lucie?' Hannah asked, as soon as we were inside.

'Lucie can't be with us. But there are chocolate-chip cookies on the table.' Marilyn smoothed her sundress, the colour of burnt orange. I wondered where she got her clothes. I'd never seen colours like that at K-Mart or Marshalls, or anything near as soft as the materials she wore. They must have cost a fortune.

The kitchen table was piled high with fresh cookies the size of plates, large nuggets of chocolate and brightly coloured candy visible through the dough.

'Wow!' Hannah said, awed.

'Are you expecting other people?' I was confused now. First Lucie wasn't here. Now this.

Marilyn smiled, pleased. 'Just us. There's a movie set up for you, Hannah,' she said.

'Mommie!' Hannah tugged at my shorts.

'Will Lucie be back soon?' I asked.

'Maybe.' Marilyn looked vague.

'Lucie can come over to our house later, Hannah. Or tomorrow.'

Marilyn switched on the television in the playroom and Hannah settled in front of it, on a piece of plastic sheeting that Marilyn had spread on the carpet, and pulled Jack onto her lap. I looked around nervously to see if there was anything breakable within reach, but he settled comfortably enough into her lap, and began to munch his way through a soggy mass of cracker.

'There,' Marilyn beamed at me. 'Everyone's settled. Come on over here.'

We sat in a more formal part of the room, with winged chairs and an expensive rug spread in front of the fireplace, with its arrangement of silk flowers in the grate. A glass-fronted cabinet showed a collection of china figurines, gleaming and polished.

I knew I should say something. 'That's quite a collection.'

For the next twenty minutes or so, without a break, Marilyn told me the story of the different figures, where she'd bought them, what they reminded her of. At last, I had to interrupt.

'I'm sorry, Marilyn, but could I use your bathroom?'

She bit her lip, as if she wanted to say no.

'I could go home, if you like.'

'No, no. Let me think – I'm painting the guest bathroom. You'll have to go upstairs.'

'That's okay.'

Marilyn shot a glance at the children, stretched out in front of the television. 'I'll show you.'

'I'm sure I'll find it.'

But Marilyn was on her feet already. I followed her up the stairs, trying to shake the feeling that Marilyn suspected me of spying, or stealing. An open door showed a family room with no windows.

'That's where we stayed during the hurricane.'

Marilyn led me down the landing. Just as I pushed the door to the bathroom open, I heard something rustle behind the wall.

I looked back at Marilyn. 'Do you have a cat?'

'No, ma'am.' Marilyn looked cross.

I heard the rustle again, then the sound of something falling and a short, sharp shriek. Marilyn stepped up to the door and yanked it open. I stared in at Lucie, kneeling in a large closet under a rack of clothes. She blinked in the light and her red-rimmed eyes burned right into mine.

'What . . . ?' I looked from Lucie to Marilyn, confused.

'You stay right there, young lady,' Marilyn barked and shut the door again. She looked at me. 'She was bad. She's in confinement.'

'In the dark?'

Marilyn folded her arms and lifted her chin. 'The bathroom is in there.'

When I came out, Marilyn was waiting. She ushered me back down the corridor. 'I'll let Lucie out when you've gone. Her punishment is that she stays there while the children are in the house.'

'Then we'll leave now.'

We went back downstairs in silence.

'More coffee?' Marilyn asked.

'No. Thank you.' I gathered up my children despite their protests.

'The children could stay till the end of the movie,' Marilyn said in a voice like honey.

'No, we'll go now.'

I ignored Hannah's indignant 'Mom!' I took her wrist and pulled her after me, Jack dangling from my arm.

At the front door, Marilyn stopped me. 'Lucie was out of control,' she said. 'This is how we punish her. It's the thing that works with her. It's what she's used to.'

'It seems harsh to me.'

'It never did me any harm when I was a child.'

'It's your own business,' I said. 'But I don't want it to be any longer because of us.' I hesitated. 'Thanks for the coffee.'

'You're welcome.' Marilyn was all white teeth and glossy red lips. As we left, she bent to the canna lilies in her flower-bed and twisted the dying heads from the group nearest the door, in no hurry to go up and let Lucie out. She was still there, waving and calling out greetings to a neighbour I couldn't see, when we got to our own porch. I herded Hannah inside.

'I want the movie,' Hannah complained, stamping her foot. 'Why did we have to come home?'

'It was time. We'll rent the movie at the weekend.'

'I want to watch it NOW.'

'Well, you can't.'

Hannah tilted her head back and began to scream, until I was tempted to take a leaf out of Marilyn's book and put her in a cupboard. The only problem was, there was no possible way to make Hannah stay there. She would be out and yelling even louder in five seconds flat.

The heat was unbelievable. It was like a person we had to learn to live with, no matter how exhausting or infuriating they became. There was no point in complaining; we just had to develop strategies for coping with it.

If you left fruit out of the fridge, you'd see it begin to pucker and wilt within an hour. You could almost watch the fur develop on the skin of a peach or a nectarine as it softened. Any food that wasn't canned or dry had to go straight into the fridge, and many's the time I felt like climbing right in there after it and closing the door behind me. Cold drinks were a necessity, not a luxury, and we bought ice by the five-pound bag. It was like living inside a greenhouse. There was a permanent sense of damp and uncontrolled growth.

The first time I saw a proper Houston cockroach, I

squealed. I couldn't help it. I'd never seen anything so revolting. It was a good two inches long, shiny and black, with curved feelers, hinged legs. I smashed it with my shoe, but while I watched, it stirred and heaved itself away.

I bought Roach Motels by the dozen and poured boiling water down the drains every night to keep them at bay. It made no difference. 'Those things walk through walls, honey,' Norma said. 'You need an exterminator.'

Randy's name was stitched onto the pocket of his blue company shirt. He was a big blonde man, fair-skinned. He wore an Astros cap over heavy, reddish eyebrows. Once a month he came to the house and generated ammoniac fumes that sent us out for a couple of hours while they dispersed. He soon became my guide on practical matters like hardware and fencing. He admired our vegetable garden as it took shape and the next thing I knew he was dropping round cuttings from his own garden whenever he was working in the neighbourhood.

'The exterminator brings you plants?' Dermot asked when he came home one evening and found me staking jasmine to the side of the house.

'Why not?'

'No reason. It just seems – odd. To be killing stuff one minute and planting it the next.'

That first winter there was a cold snap. Out of the blue, temperatures plummeted and our water pipes froze and burst. The cold was all the more severe because we weren't ready for it. We didn't have the right clothes, and our house was designed to reduce heat, not conserve it.

Up until then I had thought the fireplace in our living room was decorative. Now, we all got together and organized a delivery of firewood. Half a rainforest was dropped at the end of our street in the form of logs. It took three hours with everyone working together to divide it up. Even Tyler showed up, and he and Stephen worked more than their fair share, not having the distractions of children. Carla's son Eddie did his bit too, struggling under weights that were too big for any eight-year-old, let alone someone as scrawny as he was. But he refused to listen when we advised him to slow down, so we let him get on with it. Hannah helped, and I did what I could with Jack strapped into a baby-carrier. Norma made real egg-nog, with rum in it, to keep us all going.

When our firewood was all stacked in the garage, the kids and I turned the living room into a tent. We pinned sleeping bags and baby blankets up over the windows and doors to make draught excluders. We lit a big fire and kept it going for ten days, the duration of the cold spell. We heaped our duvets in front of the fire and stayed there as we huddled close together for warmth. Every day I meant to put this makeshift bed away but we didn't get around to it. Whatever routines we had begun to establish disappeared, but I didn't care. Routine is overrated, if you ask me. I pitied Dermot, who had to go out to work every day. The children and I stayed in and pretended we were hibernating. We made the occasional dash for supplies, but the rest of the time we stayed in the firelight, and told stories and sang songs, drank hot chocolate. I felt a weight of sadness for home.

On one of those cold mornings, Dermot called us as soon as he got to work. 'Are you up yet? Look out the window!'

It was snowing. I woke the children and dragged them outside, afraid they'd miss it. There was the lightest dusting of snow on the ground. We gathered it up onto a tray and I showed them how to make the biggest snowman that we could from what we had. It turned out to be a fairly pathetic specimen, not more than six inches tall. Jack tried to grab hold of it. He was at that stage where everything had to be tested in his mouth before he could be sure what it was. I lifted it out of his reach. Already, the snow was melting from the grass. It had never stuck to the concrete.

Hannah's heavy eyebrows came together in a ruddy V. 'What do we do with it, Mommie?'

'We'll put it in the freezer and show Daddy when he gets home.' Dermot was the one person who'd appreciate this tiny figure, for sure.

'I'd never have expected snow around here,' I said to Norma.

'Honey, the one thing you should know to expect in Texas is the thing you least expect,' she said.

By the time the warmer air came, I was glad of it.

We took the blankets down from the windows, folded them away and got ready for spring.

Whenever I took the little-used back road out of the neighbourhood, beside the ghosts of rice fields and across the railway line onto the broad highway, I felt as if I was moving through a dream. I could hear the heat, a low insect hum, and see it in the shivering air as well as feel it in the weight of my own hair on my neck, the flush of colour on my skin. My arm, hanging out over the open window of the driver's door, could still take me by surprise with its dense freckles spread over deeply tanned skin. When I was a child, I used to burn unevenly in the sun. My nose and shoulders peeled, my shins went bright red. My skin was winter-pale and delicate. Now it was tougher, my arms and legs were brown even in winter. My feet had grown a full size, but whether from my two pregnancies or from the freedom of being barefoot or in sandals all the time, I couldn't say.

Beyond the city limits, the roads were badly surfaced. Wooden shacks with rotting porches squatted low and crooked into the ground; broken chairs and old sofas with ripped upholstery lay open to the sun, their stuffing spilling out. They could have been growing out of the ground or sinking back into it. From time to time a magnetic sign propped at the side of the road advertised random services. There was a tarot reader called *Divine*, then *Carol's Hair Parlor*, along with *Git Y'all's Tyres Changed Here*. For a fortnight I puzzled over a sign that said *Repeat!* Until its author fixed it. Of course, they meant 'repent'. Once, on a more personal note, I read: *Annie, git yr gun* and wondered about Annie for a long time afterwards.

Just beyond the ice-house there was an old fruit market once a week, where Mexicans and people from the Valley sold oranges and squash from the backs of trucks, coarse-grain rice in brown paper sacks.

'Are you sure this stuff is safe?' Dermot asked. 'Have the bags been used before?'

'It's cheap,' I said.

Ellen and Norma echoed Dermot's warnings about the cleanliness of the food. 'Y'all can't be too careful, Ray.'

I liked the market because the sounds and smells down there were different, nothing was pre-packaged. Gaudy piñatas hung from gaily painted poles alongside sombreros and ponchos. The people were brown-skinned and loud and wore wide-brimmed hats in the sun. Cheerful music crackled through cheap radios. I could smell onions and cilantro cooking in the open air. I bought fresh-baked tortillas and enchiladas and frosted bottles of beer with Spanish names.

Hannah and Jack grew like weeds, sturdy and wiry and in sudden bursts. Jack soon developed an obsession with dismantling things that made me have to keep a close eye on him. His favourite thing was to unpack all the cans from the pantry and stack them in piles around the kitchen floor, or to pile up saucepans into giddy towers. One day I found him heading straight for an electrical socket, screwdriver in hand and an expression of sheer determination on his face.

'He knew what it was for!' Dermot beamed at Jack, picked him up and threw him up into the air. 'Jack the genius. Look at you!'

Jack squealed and wriggled so hard that Dermot almost missed catching him on the way back down.

'There's a pair of you in it,' I said.

Hannah was more physical. She loved to run, and from the day we gave her her first tricycle, she had a lust for speed. She cycled around the circle of grass at the end of our street endlessly, going faster and faster. I don't know how she didn't make herself dizzy. Dermot soon picked up a habit of driving unnecessarily past the house on his way home and making this loop a couple of times before pulling up at the kerb. The children never got tired of this. If they were in the car, they'd urge him to do it again and again. 'Just one more time, Daddy!' they'd squeal, exaggerating the way their bodies fell as the car turned.

Lucie became a regular fixture in our front yard. I couldn't warm to her, even though I wanted to. It had something to do with the way Hannah came in from playing with her, angry and rude. Or maybe it was because of the way Lucie managed to avoid meeting my eye. The harder I tried to make eye contact with her, the more her features flattened out and pasted themselves into a mask, like putty, her eyes sinking into themselves in a glassy stare. But her manners were faultless. In her high, irritating voice, she said yes ma'am and no ma'am and please and thank you until I itched to slap her.

I told myself not to resent the way Lucie told Hannah, out of the side of her mouth, 'Go ask your mom if we can have cookies,' or 'Go ask your mom if she'll take us to the playground,' instead of asking me straight out. It's hard to like a child who won't meet your eye, who convinces your own children to swop their newest toys for broken ones, who leaves your house with your daughter's clothes on her back. 'I said she could,' Hannah said. 'It's for a swop.'

In the end, I got used to having Lucie around, to the way that Hannah prefaced every second sentence with 'Lucie says . . .' and just plain 'Lucie'.

It got easier when other girls came to play with them. Laila was the first, an easy-going, plump child with coffee-coloured skin and the most startling eyes I'd ever seen. They were almost yellow. Laila was slow-moving and languid, but her mother, Shulamit, was slim, brisk and efficient. You'd never think, to look at her, that she had two daughters, Laila and her older sister, Riza.

Our garage became a playroom. We threw the doors open early in the mornings and left them like that all day. Norma asked if I wasn't worried about attracting burglars, but I said the whole point was to show there was someone home. Ellen pointed out that I had a lot of work on my hands, clearing everything back inside at the end of the day. She asked if it wouldn't be easier to keep the riding toys inside, along with Jack's pull-toys and blocks. I knew she objected to the street being converted into another messy playroom, but what could I do? I'd go mad if I stayed inside my own four walls.

Other mothers came and sat in the wicker chairs I'd bought at a garage sale and kept out on the porch. We drank Diet Coke, Dr Pepper and iced tea while we watched the kids play. Hannah soon set up a game like a chariot race. On any given day you'd be likely to find a combination of Big Wheels and tricycles making manic loops around the grass, imitating Dermot on his way home from work.

'Quite the little clubhouse you have going there,' Ellen said one day.

'It just happened,' I was feeling defensive.

'Don't get me wrong, honey. I admire y'all's patience. But, personally? – I couldn't abide to have all those folks coming and going in my yard all day long.'

'It's not like that.'

'Watch that they don't take advantage of y'all.'

Dermot said the same thing. 'What happens if some kid falls out of our tree?'

'I don't know. We pick her up, give her a band-aid?'

'I'm serious, Ray. What if we get sued?'

'Don't be mad.'

Stephen said that Dermot had a point. 'Friends of mine had people round for dinner. They all drank too much and the wife did a little cabaret turn on the table. She fell off and broke her leg in three places. Then she sued them and won.'

'For the injury?'

'For giving her too much to drink. They had to sell their house.'

'Can you imagine someone doing that in Ireland?' I asked Dermot, but he was frowning. 'Come on, Dermot. Nothing like that is going to happen to us.'

'You don't know,' he said, gloomy.

Time passed. Even though I was happy enough, I sometimes felt as if I was living someone else's life. When the children called me 'Mom', it made me feel that I wasn't quite a real mother and that I lived in a not quite real place, because it sounded so unfamiliar. When I looked out onto the empty street under its wide blue sky, stepped out in my bare feet into blazing heat, felt the crunch of St Augustine grass under my toes, it seemed artificial, too strong, too glossy. Barely grass at all, more like an artificial fibre. The vivid colours of the neighbours' gardens, the gleam of well-loved cars, the hum of air-conditioning units, was a little too co-ordinated to be true. Even the birds seemed staged, the way the grackles stood around in bizarre little groups with their heads thrown back, beaks pointing at the sky, the dart of hummingbirds. The squirrels that undulated along the wooden fence at the back of the house looked endearing, but Ellen warned me they were vicious and riddled with disease.

'What kind of disease?' I asked. I was ready for a fight, because I expected one of Ellen's anti-dirt crusades.

'Rabies.'

There wasn't much I could say to that.

14

'Julian Birkamp's wife says you're to call her,' Dermot said one day when he came in, late, from work. He took a business card out of his pocket and put it beside the phone. There was a number written on the back in violet ink.

'Which one is Julian again?'

'The new vice-president.' J. P. Fischer had joined forces with another R&D outfit and the company had doubled in size overnight. I was still trying to get used to all the new names.

'What does she want?'

'She's Welsh. They live quite near here – but inside the Loop. There's some group of women that meets for coffee once a month.' He went to the fridge for a beer. 'She'd like you to go along.'

'Have you met her?'

'She came into the Lariat today after work.'

'So that's where you were.'

'We finished off a meeting with a drink.'

'What's she like?'

Dermot snapped the can of beer open. 'She seems nice enough. What's for dinner?'

Before long the card was buried in the mountain of

bills and junk mail beside the phone. In the end, it was Diane who called me.

'I met your husband the other day,' she said, her voice smooth and rich, not at all the accent I'd have expected. 'I know you haven't been here long. There's a group of us who get together for coffee every now and then. Would you like to come?'

'I don't know.' I watched Jack and Hannah squabble over Lego pieces. 'I have two kids.'

'Well. I have children too. We're very informal.'

When I arrived at Diane's house, I was taken aback by its solidity. It was one of those newly built, baronial-style mansions, with barely an arm's length between them, in a development called Lakeview Heights. The streets were as flat as every other street in Houston, and the only water in sight was a sad-looking pond at the entrance gates with a listless fountain in the centre. A police car slowed down to check me out when I pulled up outside Diane's house. I saw them register the children and decide I wasn't a threat to anyone, before they drove on.

Inside, Diane's furniture was co-ordinated in a folksy style: heavy, reddish wood with fat red-and-white checked cushions on the chairs, rounded legs resting on terracotta-tiled floors. Photographs of Diane, her two daughters and a man with a deeply lined fore-head were clustered in solid silver frames on a pristine mantelpiece. Over the mantelpiece hung a real painting of the same group of people in heavy oils.

Plates of thinly cut sandwiches and expensive biscuits were arranged on the coffee table. An actual pot of tea rested on a silver tray beside cups and saucers of fine china. A group of women in linen trousers and cotton skirts, blouses and gold jewellery sat around in groups, talking comfortably.

I felt awkward in my shorts and T-shirt. I was aware of every stain on Jack's shirt, the dirt encrusted in his fingernails.

'These are the Oylers,' Diane said, waving her slender wrist around to include the other women. 'That's the Olive Oylers, not the football team.'

I smiled. Jack made a dive from my hip towards the biscuits. When I tried to steer him away, the nappy bag slid off my shoulder and nearly demolished the china. Flustered, I apologized.

A fat grey cat with a round face and yellow eyes padded across the carpet. Jack's eyes lit up and his fingers flexed. 'Cat!' he roared.

'Be careful, Jack.' I gripped him more tightly.

'Oh, don't worry about Tabitha. She's been de-clawed. She can't hurt you.'

'No paws?' Hannah stared in horror.

The cat undulated past us. 'She does have paws, Hannah,' I said. 'See? But her nails have been taken out.'

'Ouch.'

'It doesn't hurt them,' Diane said.

'How does she climb trees?' I asked.

'She can't. That's the point. She's an inside cat. Every-one does it. Don't they, Lorna?'

Lorna was an older woman, with leathery brown skin. Her mouth was narrow and turned down into heavily scored lines of discontent.

'It saves the furniture,' a small, cheerful-looking woman said. She smiled at me. 'Isn't that just precious? Hi. I'm Jilly. I'm from London.'

Jack climbed off my hip and tried to follow the cat out of the room. I held him back, wishing more than anything that I'd stayed at home.

'Come outside and meet my little girls, Hannah,' Diane said.

I followed them outside with Jack. Diane's garden was as formal and patterned as her furniture. Purple and scarlet flowers spilled from baskets hanging around the patio, where dark-leaved trees were set into giant wooden barrels. She had a real lawn, raised beds marked off by railroad ties, flowers and shrubs with luscious, vivid flowers.

'It's lovely,' I said.

'Do you have a garden?'

I thought about the brash yellow trumpets of flowers coming out of the heads of zucchini, the flaring red of snapping beans, the overgrown heads of sunflowers, the children's excitement as they watched the stalks shoot up until they broke eventually under their own weight. 'Nothing like this.'

Diane's eight-year-old identical twins, Emily and Sara, were sitting at a miniature picnic table in matching cotton frocks and mary-jane sandals, decanting Coke from a large bottle into doll-size cups and saucers. Their blonde hair shone in the sun.

Diane urged Hannah to go and join them. Jack looked doubtful but then one of the girls came and took his hand. 'I'm Emily,' she purred, in a mock grown-up voice. 'What's your name?'

I expected him to scowl or pull away, but to my amazement he went coy instead. 'Jack.' He took her outstretched hand.

'They'll be fine,' Diane said. 'Come on back inside.'

I looked through her deep, sparkling windows at the well-dressed women grouped around her stylish coffee table. 'Who are they all?'

'Oil-industry wives, most of them. They know each other from every godforsaken spot on the ex-pat circuit. They're friendly. We have good parties. It's a change from the bible-bashers, anyhow.' She touched my arm, apologetic. 'Have I offended you? I'm sorry. I forgot you're Irish.'

What did that have to do with anything? 'Not at all.'

'Julian's parents are very religious. First Baptist.' She looked like a little girl as she hooked her smooth hair behind her ears and went into the house ahead of me.

Diane's house was not designed for children. It seemed more suited to this gathering of bored women who complained, the whole time I was there, about the climate, the shops, the roads, the lack of decent tea, how hard it was to keep a garden, the shortcomings of the schools. They reminisced about other places they had lived – Jordan, Riyadh, Saudi, the UAE, Venezuela. They remembered drivers, cooks and nannies, currency devaluations and unspoilt beaches. Houses with high ceilings, marble floors, deep stone verandahs. Clubs with green lawns and long, gin-soaked afternoons. Gold and silver bought in souks.

'Fiesta doesn't quite compare,' Diane sighed at last and they all came back to where the conversation started: the shortcomings of Texas.

'How do you like it, Ray?' someone asked.

'What's not to like?' Jilly demanded. 'The light? The space? The heat?'

'The heat,' I murmured. 'Definitely, the heat.'

'I love it.' Jilly stretched her arms above her head and all but purred. She looked like a self-satisfied kitten. 'Don't you feel like you live in a greenhouse, that you'll blossom and sprout outrageous leaves while you're here?'

Lorna snorted. 'Give me air-conditioning any day. And seasons.'

Vivienne, from Connecticut, gave a great big gusty sigh. 'Ah, seasons! Where I come from, we certainly have those.'

'There are seasons here too,' Jilly said. 'You just have to pay attention. We might not get the leaves, but we get the grasses.'

'And the wildflowers,' I said. 'We saw them when we drove here from LA. I've never seen anything like them.' It was true, but I'd almost forgotten them until

188

now. Indian paintbrush like bursts of flame, and masses of bluebonnets spread around us like an inland sea.

'Are none of you from Houston?' I asked.

Gina, a smooth-skinned woman from Dallas, smiled at me. 'Native Houstonians are hard to find, honey.'

I went over to sit near Jilly. I tried to guess how old she was. Mid-forties, maybe, but she still wore henna in her hair. 'Did you know Diane in England?' I asked.

Jilly laughed. 'We lived in Chelsea at the same time, but I didn't know her then. You could say we were at opposite ends of the social scale. During the day, I worked in the kinds of shops where Diane bought her clothes, and at night I danced in the chorus line of shows that Diane and her friends went to see.'

'You're a dancer?'

'Not any more. I'm married to a Houstonian.' She made a face in Gina's direction. 'We travel a lot, so I can't have a regular job. I don't come to these gatherings often, either. But I produce a charity show, once a year, in aid of Memorial Hospital. You could help out if you like . . . although it looks as if you have your hands full.'

One of Diane's daughters came in, staggering under Jack's weight. Jack clung to her neck, roaring.

'He fell,' the girl said. 'But he's not bleeding.'

When Jack was calm again, I left.

'Will you come next month?' Diane asked. 'It's at Lorna's.'

Lorna flashed an empty smile at me. 'But, of course, my house is not exactly baby-proof.'

'I don't think I can,' I said. 'But thanks for asking.'

Diane followed us out to the car and helped to put Jack, who didn't want to leave, into his seat.

'Maybe I'll drop in on you, then?' she said. 'In Houston terms, we're practically neighbours.'

'You should have seen them, Joanne,' I said into the phone. 'They were like another species. They complained about their maids, for God's sake. D'you know who they reminded me of? D'you remember Joe St George's wife?'

'The one who wore sunglasses in the dark?'

'Exactly.'

Then she told me about her latest job, managing a city-centre restaurant where politicians went for lunch. A friend of Freddie's owned it. 'Don't you ever miss working, Ray?'

'I do work. I just don't get paid for it.'

I was surprised when Diane turned up a few days later with her lovely, indistinguishable daughters and a bottle of chilled white wine. She looked around the chaotic playroom that our living room had become, with its half-built towers and scattered second-hand toys, and smiled.

We drank the wine while the children unpacked my kitchen cupboards and set up a play supermarket throughout the house.

'Don't you mind?' Diane asked.

'Not if it keeps them happy.'

Diane's eyebrows made exaggerated arches. 'How lovely,' she says. 'How relaxed you are.'

'She means I'm a slob,' I told Dermot later.

'Why don't you like her? She seems nice enough to me.'

I had a run-in with Ellen that spring when she blocked up a hole in her eaves to stop some martins nesting there. But there were already babies inside. I could hear their desperate cheeps. The parents wheeled around the sealed-up hole, shrieking their distress. I stamped around underneath them and begged Ellen to think again, while Jack slept through the commotion in the stroller.

'There are babies in there, for God's sake!'

She peered at me in genuine confusion. 'Ray, honey, they are just dumb creatures. They carry disease.'

'How can you ignore that sound?'

'It won't last long, honey. Why don't you go inside and git you some earplugs if it bothers you so?'

Then Tyler came home and settled it. 'They'll stink up the house if they die in there,' he said when Ellen explained why I was red-faced and yelling on their lawn. He hauled the ladder out of their garage and unblocked the hole. I couldn't look at Ellen. I turned and stepped over the miniature picket fence she'd just installed. Six-inch stumps of the kind of wood you might use to kill a vampire, painted white, lined the edge of her lawn. She'd seen it in an article in *House Beautiful* and thought it was the most stylish thing imaginable.

I was shaking when I grabbed the stroller and pushed Jack away from there.

'You go, girl!' I saw Curtis's bronzed arm hooked over the half-open window of his truck before I saw his face.

'You scared me! Did you hear all that?'

'Sure did.'

'Why didn't you come over and back me up?'

'Seems like you did fine all by yourself.'

'Is Beth home?' I badly needed to let off steam.

''Fraid not. She's taken Brooke for her check-up.'

'Is everything all right?' I kept forgetting that Brooke had been so ill once. I knew Beth still worried about her, even though the doctors said she was perfectly healthy now.

'Sure is. It's a routine visit.' He fired up his engine. 'Catch you later,' he drawled. 'If you see Beth when she comes back, tell her I've gone to the gym.'

'That man is obsessed,' Beth said. 'He never used to be this way until Brooke got sick. All that research we did into diet and stuff turned him into a health nut. Look.' She showed me their wedding photo. Beth looked as if she was tucked into Curtis's armpit, as usual. But he was thinner, his shoulders narrower. 'That suit was two sizes too big for him.' Beth sighed. 'We had to borrow it from my brother. Curtis was puny then. He was more fun, too.'

One Friday evening, Marilyn came knocking on my door. It had been a day of dense air, so heavy I was sure I'd be able to see it take shape any minute. I could barely stay on my feet.

'Have a drink with me,' I surprised both of us by saying.

'Okay.'

I opened the box of wine that was chilling in the fridge, waiting for the weekend. We sat out on the porch and watched the girls climb the tree at the end of the street. Jack rode his Big Wheel around our two chairs, singing to himself.

'I was at the medical centre,' Marilyn said suddenly. 'I have a lump. In my breast. I have to have a biopsy on Monday. Could you take Lucie for me? It might be overnight. Byron will be out of town, on a buying trip.'

'Of course. I'm sorry, Marilyn.'

'Don't be.' Marilyn stared off in Lucie's direction, but she seemed to be looking further than that. 'My mother died of this, you know. When I was Lucie's age. I've always known it would happen. Things repeat themselves.'

'They don't have to.'

'Don't they?' Marilyn's voice was flat. She looked quickly at me, then away again. 'I wonder about you. Seems like you think you can make things be a certain way, just by making up your mind to it.'

Her eyes came to a focus on Lucie and Hannah at the base of the live oak tree, balancing on its raised roots. 'My daddy was a good man, but he didn't hardly know what to do with me. When I was out of control he used to lock me in the toolshed. I hated it in there.

There were spiders. Roaches. Rust and oil and smells.'
She shuddered. 'It was nasty. One night he forgot to
let me out. In the morning I was so stiff—'

'He left you there all night?'

'Sure did. I tell you, I was as good as gold after
that.'

'I bet you were.'

Marilyn drained her glass, got to her feet. Her accent
slipped into a new cadence. 'I just wanted you to know.
That deal with Lucie, in the closet? She's warm in there.
She knows she's safe. And I ain't never left her in there
overnight.'

'I don't—'

'Like I said. I just want you to know. I love my
daughter. Remember that.'

'I never thought any different.'

'Well. You remember.'

She called to Lucie and they went off across the
street, hand in hand. I had never felt so small in all
my life.

Marilyn's biopsy turned out negative. She came to collect Lucie after all, beaming with relief, a bottle of
champagne under her arm. When it was finished, I
opened a case of beer and by the time we'd finished
that, I felt as if I'd known Marilyn for ever. I could
see the dusty, flat town where Marilyn grew up, the
single-lane highway, the Dairy Queen where she got
her first job. There was no money, and throughout one
summer Marilyn wore her Dairy Queen outfit every-

where she went, pretending not to hear the jokes and catcalls.

She left the first chance she got, and went to work for a mail-order company in the Midwest. I could just imagine this girl, broke and lonely, studying pictures of perfect lives, matching furniture, wide smiles, outfits with matching accessories. I began to understand the importance of order in Marilyn's life.

'Is that where you met Byron?'

'It sure is. He came to work as a trainee buyer and I never looked at another man from there on in.' She raised her glass all of a sudden. 'I don't like most people. But I like you. I knew we'd be friends the minute we met.'

I laughed. 'It took me a bit longer.'

Marilyn's face went out of focus and came back together again.

'I'm sorry,' I said. 'There's me with my foot in my mouth again.'

Overnight, all the constraint between us seemed to vanish. We dropped in and out of each other's houses, borrowed items we ran out of, looked after each other's children. I didn't think about the faultlines. Marilyn was there, the first person I could call on and that was that.

Dermot didn't like her.

'You take the friends you're given,' I said. 'You don't understand. We need each other.'

'There are plenty of other people around.'

'Not during the day, Dermot. You don't know what it's like. And Hannah loves Lucie.'

We found Hunter that summer. He was in a black plastic sack that had been left out for the bin men, the only survivor in a litter of four mixed-breed puppies. The driver turned off the engine and got out of his cab to look. He opened the bag and there was Hunter, squealing, scrambling to get away from his suffocated siblings. I just happened to be out at our mailbox and the sound of Hunter's squeal got to me, somewhere too deep to ignore, the way my own babies' cries could stop me in my tracks across a crowded mall, even when no one else could hear them.

The bag had been on the kerb at the corner, outside Ellen's house. I took the shivering puppy in the crook of my arm, marched right up to Ellen's front door and banged on it.

'Do you know anything about this?'

'Why, no,' Ellen drawled, pulling back, wrinkling her nose. She squinted out past me at the halted refuse truck, the group of men standing with their muscled arms folded, their caps tipped low over their dark eyes, watching her.

When I explained, Ellen protested: 'But Ray, honey, I don't have a dog. How could I have puppies?'

I went back to the waiting men. 'They must have been dumped,' I said. 'But I don't know who would do it.'

'We seen it before,' the driver nodded.

I looked into the maw of the truck and shivered. The smell was earthy and dark and poisoned all at once. Slimy rings of rotting vegetables and shredded cardboard, scraps of fabric and diaper and unidentifiable balls of compacted rubbish were caught in the giant rusted teeth that ground everything to slime. I looked at the puppy, rank enough himself, but warm and soft under my hand. I imagined the terror of being caught in the dark with his dead siblings. The noise. The movement. Those iron jaws closing.

'How could anyone . . . ?'

'You'd be surprised what people do, ma'am. This here ain't nothing at all.' The man who'd spoken was a small black man with neat silver hair and wide nostrils. He wore worn leather gloves. I could just imagine him sitting on his porch after work, easing out his hands before cracking open a cold can and sighing, getting ready to tell his family the stories he'd unearthed in his day.

The puppy nibbled the tops of my fingers. His teeth were surprisingly sharp. I moved my hand out of reach and frowned at him, thinking.

'We'd best move on,' the driver said.

They all looked at me, waiting for me to decide what would happen next. Ellen leaned on her doorframe and folded her arms, one hip jutting out. At that exact moment, Hannah came running out of our open front door.

'What?' she said. 'What is it?' As soon as she saw Hunter, she scooped him out of my arms. 'The darling,' she said. She lifted him up to her face and buried her nose in his filthy coat.

'Hannah, don't . . .' I wanted to warn her about germs, about trauma and terror, but it was too late. She had already skipped back over to the house to show Jack.

'I'd better go and clean him up,' I said. 'Before someone gets poisoned.'

'Does that mean you'll keep him, ma'am?'

'I suppose it does.'

The driver started the engine and the others jumped onto the running boards, saluting me as they turned the corner onto the main road.

'You'll be sorry,' Ellen warned, from her porch. 'You mind. Those things may be cute as buttons, but they carry disease and I don't know what-all.'

I had an uneasy feeling that Dermot would agree with her. But Dermot was away on a training course. I avoided mentioning Hunter on the phone to him, in case he said to get rid of him straight away. I told Joanne, instead.

'Great. Something else for you to look after.'

Joanne was in a foul mood lately. She was having an affair with a married man called Tom, and she spent a lot of nights sitting at home, waiting to see if he'd turn up. She drank while she was waiting and then, when she couldn't stand it any more, she rang me for company. By then, most people in Ireland were asleep.

'Where's Dermot, anyway?'

'Silicon Valley. At a seminar.'

'Are you sure? He's hardly ever at home, our Dermot, is he?'

'That's a shitty thing to say.'

'I'm sorry, Ray. I didn't mean—'

'Just because you're having an affair doesn't mean everyone's at it. Dermot's not like that.'

'I said I'm sorry. I've had too much to drink.'

By the time Dermot came back, three days later, Hunter was too established in our lives to shift. Besides, who could turn away a puppy with a history like his? I didn't tell Dermot what Joanne had said about him, but he knew about her affair with Tom.

'Why does she put up with it?' he said. 'Joanne's a smart woman. She deserves better.'

'She says she loves him.' We were in bed. I felt his chest rise and fall under my head and knew how lucky I was. 'I wonder about Tom's wife,' I said. 'Does she know? I think I'd know.' I propped myself up to look at Dermot more closely. 'Would I?'

'There's nothing to know.'

'You'd tell me, wouldn't you? If there was anyone else? Promise.'

He laughed and kissed me. 'There's no one else. I promise.'

15

I didn't know why Diane turned up at my house from time to time, or why she invited me round to hers. We had nothing in common. When I look back on it now, we mostly talked about the children and about BBC programmes that were recycled on public television – including, to my embarrassment, *The Irish RM*. Diane thought it was hilarious. Dermot and I quite liked it too, but in an uneasy kind of way. I certainly didn't want the likes of Diane and her rich-bitch mafia chortling over Irish stupidity as shown by the BBC, thank you very much.

Not that I disliked her, exactly. It was just that we had nothing in common, so far as I could see. If we'd met under any other circumstances, I don't know that we'd have spent more than five minutes in each other's company, and that went for her as much as it did for me. She was obsessively neat, and always dressed in matching colours: navy bermuda shorts, with a navy polo shirt and sometimes even a little navy-and-white striped cardigan around her shoulders. Or beige. Diane was very fond of beige. It drained all the colour from her skin, so that her small bright-red mouth managed to seem both prim and indecent at the same time.

But Hannah loved the twins, and so did Jack, so I

went over there if only to give them a change of scene, to give us all a break from each other and from the sweat and disorder of our daily lives.

The second time I went to visit Diane, I noticed a police car cruising slowly around her block. I could have sworn it was the same one that I'd seen on the first occasion, so I mentioned it to her when I went in. 'I wouldn't have thought this was the kind of place where you'd get much trouble.'

'We don't.'

'But – the police are here a lot.'

'Oh, that.' She laughed in her neat little way. 'That's our patrol. You know, if they see any vehicle that's out of place, or any unlikely characters hanging around . . .'

I looked back at the Volvo. Dermot had finally got his own car and I had it every day now. Diane saw my look and smiled. 'Don't worry. I gave them your registration number,' she said.

I had to wonder if she'd given them a description of me as well. Overweight; unruly hair; bare legs in baggy shorts and sandals; T-shirts usually stained on the left shoulder from baby drool; children loud and generally dressed in faded garage-sale couture.

We sat in her orderly kitchen. It was late afternoon, later than usual. Hannah and the twins were bossing Jack around somewhere in the depths of the house. Diane had opened a bottle of good white wine and poured us each a generous glass over ice. The idea was that you drank the wine fast, before the ice could melt. This was a new one on me, but I was willing to try it, even though I'd have preferred a beer. We clinked our glasses together and drank thirstily.

Diane crunched her ice between perfect teeth. With teeth like those, she could have been American but in fact it was her husband, Julian, who belonged here. He came from new money, Diane had told me, smiling a little, to see how I would take it. I still hadn't met him. Like Dermot, he often worked late.

'I think they're all obsessed,' Diane said, tucking her fine hair behind her ears. 'Maybe that's what it takes. But, if they make it, they'll make it big. Dermot must have told you that.'

'Only a million times.'

It was all right for her. We were still struggling to get by on the money Dermot earned. Where other companies might give a regular raise in salary, JP and his board believed in giving out stock options instead. Dermot insisted these were worth gold. 'We could be rich when they mature,' he said.

'They don't buy shoes,' I said, more sharply than I'd meant to. I couldn't keep Jack in shoes at that time. His feet seemed to grow a full size every week. I had to juggle the bills to keep things going, trying to remember which utility I'd not paid the last time, to try to spread the debt. If I let it go too long, we got cut off.

'Oh look,' Diane said, her accent more clipped and bored than usual. 'Here's Julian.'

We watched through the window as Julian climbed out of his shining black Corvette and swung his lightweight jacket over his shoulder. His clothes looked cool, well-pressed. But his hair was a riotous tangle of black and burst out from everywhere. As he came closer, I thought I saw it erupt from between the buttons of his shirt. His sleeves were rolled up and his forearms were dark, crowded with hair. Diane had hinted to me that his temper was volatile, that he was a hard man to live with. She'd told me already that I was lucky Dermot was so relaxed, that Julian expected his house to be perfect, his children to be well dressed and neat. She said our house felt more like a home to her, but I wasn't sure I believed her. Why did she need to comment on it at all?

Whatever else he might be, Julian Birkamp was not, by any stretch of the imagination, an attractive man.

He came in and nodded to us. 'Where are the children?' he asked.

'In the den. Watching videos. This is Ray.'

He grunted, without looking at me. Instead, he leafed through a pile of letters on the bar and pulled one out.

'Dermot's wife,' Diane went on.

Julian looked at me briefly and nodded again. He let the other letters fall back onto the bar in a jumbled heap and walked on through the room and out the other side, studying the envelope in his hand.

Diane got up and rearranged the mail.

'I hate him,' she said.

'Sorry?'

'Julian,' Diane said. 'I hate him.' She looked at

me from under her wispy blonde fringe and laughed. 'Sometimes. Come on, let's have another drink.'

Dermot said that Julian was a hard person to know, but he had a lot of power. He looked aggressive, but he never so much as raised his voice, at work anyway. He only spoke if he had something to say, but they had all learned to respect that. What he said, according to Dermot, was usually worth listening to.

'I think he bullies Diane,' I said.

'What makes you think that?'

I didn't know. She'd never said as much, but she hinted at it often enough in half-finished sentences. Her fragile pallor made Julian look like a wild man. He could have used the small bones of her fingers for toothpicks. Where she was polished, he sprang hair. Her clothes were self-effacing, sensible, nun-like. And then, suddenly, she would turn around and say something absolutely direct, like that remark about her own husband, and laugh, showing her fine teeth. I didn't know what to make of her.

Before Dermot's parents arrived for their long-overdue holiday, I painted their bedroom, bought fresh sheets, put flowers on their dresser.

'You don't have to do all this, you know,' Dermot protested.

'I want to.'

At the airport Pat and Conall looked unfamiliar, like cartoon explorers, in shorts and matching checked shirts, ankle socks and hiking boots. Pat grinned, self-conscious. 'Do we look like we're going on safari? We weren't sure what to wear.'

Conall blushed. 'I haven't seen my own legs for twenty years,' he said. 'I feel like a boy scout.'

'You look gorgeous, darling.' Pat nudged him. 'Your legs are better than mine!'

It turned out that they had been reading up about Texas for weeks, planning their holiday down to the last detail. They knew more about this state than I did. They wanted to drive out to the hill country, visit the Alamo. They had come supplied with high-factor sunscreen and antihistamine cream, insect repellent.

'It really is hot.' Pat fanned herself with her wide-brimmed hat. 'I may look strange but I'm sure as hell glad not to be in a twin-set.'

They swept the children up in a tide of affection, as if they had known them every day of their lives. They declared that Hunter was the cleverest dog they'd ever met. Conall entertained Jack for a full half hour pulling coins from behind his ear or hiding a pen up one sleeve and then pulling it out of the other. Then they suddenly announced that they were exhausted. When I went into their room to see if they wanted water or extra towels, they were already asleep, side by side, flat on their backs, snoring. They hadn't even taken off their clothes.

We went on massive excursions, to the beach, to NASA, to the state park where the alligators were. Pat and Conall took photos of each other beside warning signs. ALLIGATORS! DO NOT FEED OR APPROACH! Driving out of there at twilight, we saw deer, squirrels, armadillos. 'Those are the strangest-looking creatures I've ever seen!' Pat exclaimed. She made me stop the car for more photographs. We went to eat at a roadside shack Dermot knew about, built over a faux pond, with alligator steaks on the menu. Conall insisted that we all try them, even the children. 'You've got to be adventurous!' he roared. 'Try anything once!'

Pat and Conall hired a car so they could get around independently. They'd made a list of all the strangely named places they wanted to visit. They brought back stories of encounters with other tourists, or parking attendants, short-order cooks, waitresses. Their prize trophy was a photograph of themselves in front of a sign that read BUG TUSSLE, TEXAS. POP. 15. In Waxahachie, they took photographs of the lewd carvings on the courthouse, where an artist had recorded his lust for a town official's daughter and was run out of town for his pains. There, they met an Irishwoman who came up to them as soon as she heard their accents.

'That was a sad woman,' Conall said. 'Been here thirty-five years. And still calls Ireland "home".'

'Does anyone actually come from here?' Pat said. 'Everyone seems to come from somewhere else.'

'I'm from here,' Hannah interrupted. 'From Texas, anyways.'

'No, you're not, Hannah,' Dermot smiled. 'Not really. You know you're not.'

Later that night, when the children were asleep, Pat

asked if we ever thought about going home. 'We miss you.' Her voice was soft. 'And those darling children.'

'When we get the green card we'll be able to come for holidays,' Dermot said.

'But, to live? Don't you miss it?'

All the time, I thought.

But Dermot shook his head. 'The people, maybe. Like yourselves. But we're too busy, most of the time. And we have each other.' His fingers found mine and curled around them. 'And look, here you are.'

'But don't you ever think about coming back?' she insisted, ignoring Conall's sudden fit of coughing.

'We have to wait and see what happens, Pat.' I leaned into the conversation. 'But we're here indefinitely. There's no point in agonizing over it.'

'Indefinitely? Your father is retiring,' she said to Dermot. 'We're none of us getting any younger.' I'd never heard her sound so sharp before.

'Then you'll have more time to come over here,' Dermot said, as smooth as butter.

'What are you going to do with yourselves, when you've retired?' I asked Conall.

He winked at me. 'Raise ducks with my wife,' he said. 'Don't mind her. There's more money than you'd think in ducks.'

The highlight of their stay was the 4th of July picnic J. P. Fischer laid on for employees and their families that year. JP had decided on a rodeo theme and he had hired out a farm for the day. There were horses and wide-horned cattle and even a camel for the kids to ride; there was a genuine cowboy, who demonstrated the art of lassoing. We all tried our hands at that, but only Dermot rode the mechanical bull. For the kids, there was face-painting and a clown, and in the evening there was a barbeque, which we ate at long wooden tables under a wide, clear sky. Later, we sat back and watched the fireworks. Hannah's face shone in the weird-coloured light they shed, but Jack buried his face in my side.

Pat stroked his head. 'Someone's had enough, I think. Time to go home.' She caught my eye, but I looked away.

Hannah started school that year, and so did Lucie. They became inseparable. One Saturday, Marilyn came striding over from the main road.

'Byron's away for the weekend. Can I borrow your kids?'

'Both of them? Be my guest. What for?'

'I've grounded Lucie for a week. Now I have to entertain her.' She winked, lowered her voice. 'And you can catch up with that gorgeous husband of yours.'

'What's the point of grounding someone and then laying on entertainment for her?' Dermot asked.

'Who cares? The kids are gone. We have a couple of hours to do whatever we like.'

One thing led to another and before long we were in bed, skin on skin, taking our time.

'Remind me why we don't do this more often?'

Dermot breathed into my neck, under my hair, around the whorls of my ear.

There was a knock on the front door.

'Ignore it,' Dermot said, gripping my arm.

The knock came again, louder. I lifted my head. 'That's Marilyn's knock. She knows we're here. Besides, there might be something wrong . . .'

Dermot groaned and fell back on the pillows while I pulled on a T-shirt and shorts and padded barefoot down the hall.

'Sorry,' Marilyn said, before the door was fully open. 'I need to borrow your VCR. Mine has died and the kids are all lined up waiting for the movie.' She stopped talking and nudged me. 'Well. So you took my advice.'

'What?'

'You two are something. I'll go ask Beth. Or Ellen.'

'Come on in and get the VCR, Marilyn.'

Dermot came up behind me, fully dressed. 'I'll give you a hand.'

He ended up carrying the VCR over to Marilyn's and on the way back he fell into conversation with Stephen. I watched from the window and then went in to start making dinner. I knew that as soon as the video was over Jack would want to come home. So much for passion on a suburban afternoon.

'How do you think she knew?' I asked when Dermot came back.

'Slut,' he said, affectionately. 'Your T-shirt is inside out.'

16

We were making cookies, up to our elbows in flour and sugar, when the phone rang.

'Leave it, Hannah,' I called out. Too late. Hannah could never resist a ringing telephone, no matter what she was doing or how sticky her fingers were.

'It's for you, Momma.'

'Who is it?'

'A lady.'

'Ask her to hang on a sec.'

Hannah breathed heavily into the phone. I held my fingers under the tap and tried to scrape off the dough. When I'd done the best I could, I patted my hands dry and reached for the phone. 'Hello?'

Hannah went back to the table. A row broke out at once when she snatched the star-shaped cookie-cutter out of Jack's hand.

'Hey!' he roared and snatched it back.

'I had it first!' Hannah's face was puce with rage.

Hunter, who'd been asleep under the table, woke up and began to bark, his tail wagging.

'You went away!' Jack's fingers clamped like hooks around the cutter.

She punched his shoulder. 'Give it back! Give it back!'

'Hannah, stop! Give it to me, Jack.' I prised the offending piece of red plastic out of Jack's hand and pushed the other cookie-cutters across the table towards them, while an unfamiliar voice spoke into my ear.

'This is security at the Westin Mall, ma'am.'

'I'm sorry, who did you say?' I batted at the kids and the dog to be quiet and walked as far away from them as the extended cord would let me.

The woman repeated herself in a lazy, southern voice. Then she said, 'We have a Miz Marilyn Galen in custody here and she wants to know if you will come.'

'I'm sorry, I don't understand.'

The woman sighed. 'Is Miz Marilyn Galen known to you, ma'am?'

'Marilyn – yes. Of course. She's my neighbour.'

'And are you familiar with the Westin Mall?'

'Yes.'

'We have Miz Galen in custody, ma'am. Are you willing to come and collect her daughter?'

I said I would and hung up, dazed. I stared at my children, covered in a gloopy mess of cookie dough. I still couldn't believe what my brain told me I'd heard.

I tried everyone I could think of, but no one was free to mind the kids. In the end I had to bring them with me.

The security offices of the mall were behind a small door I had never noticed before. Inside, the lights were harsh on basic office furniture, lightweight partitions with see-through plastic panels. One of the fluorescent bulbs was about to blow. It fizzed and spat and the light sparked. Marilyn sat huddled on a plastic chair beneath it. Lucie sat beside her, swinging her legs and chewing her hair. A heavy-set security guard leaned against a desk near them, a truncheon obvious against his thigh.

Marilyn looked away when we came in, but Lucie stared at me, chewing hard on some kind of gum. She popped a bubble and waved.

The security guards were impassive. Some old tribal instinct of appeasement must have been at work in me. I smiled and introduced myself, tried to be pleasant. It was a waste of time. Those people were immune to any kind of charm.

I asked the desk clerk, a tiny, uniformed Hispanic woman, what was going on.

'Miz Galen is being arrested, ma'am.'

'What for?'

'Chequebook fraud.'

'What?'

The clerk sighed. 'Trying to pass a cheque with insufficient funds.'

'You can't be serious – you're arresting her for *that*?'

'It's not the first time, ma'am. She wants you to take her daughter until her husband comes home.'

'Of course.'

I left my own round-eyed children standing against the wall under a 'Most Wanted Criminals' poster, and went down to the far corner of the office where Marilyn was.

'Marilyn, I can't believe—'

Marilyn ducked her head and made her hair swing across her face.

'What can I do? Surely they can't—'

'Will you take Lucie? Byron will be home later tonight. He's at a sales convention in Chicago.'

'Sure I will.'

Lucie bounced off the chair and stood beside her mother.

'Go on, Lucie. I'll be home later.' Marilyn emerged to plant a quick kiss on Lucie's feathery hair and turned even further away from me, her body twisted into steep angles on the chair.

'How much was the cheque for? Can I get you the money from somewhere?'

'It's not that easy.'

The security guard who loomed over her pretended not to listen. I took Lucie's hand. 'Come on, sweetheart.'

I took a couple of steps away from Marilyn and stopped. 'Whatever it is, it's going to be okay,' I said.

When Byron got back, he asked if I could keep Lucie a little longer. 'I've got to go down and sort this out,' he said. 'Bail and all.'

'Sure.' He seemed familiar with the whole procedure, but I was determined not to ask any more questions than I had to.

'I want to go home,' Lucie wailed.

'Leave me a key, Byron. I can sit with her in your house when Dermot gets in.'

Lucie insisted on waiting up for her parents. We watched videos on the sofa until at last she fell asleep, her head on my lap. I stroked her hair and wondered what the hell was going on. It was nearly three in the morning when I heard Byron's car and saw the sweep of headlights across the window. I eased out from under Lucie and went outside.

Marilyn was still in the car. When she saw me, she ducked out of sight.

'She doesn't want to see you,' Byron said.

'But—'

'Thanks for your help. We can't thank you enough. She knows how shocked you must be.'

'Shocked? I don't understand. Honestly, Byron, I just don't think it's such a big deal.'

I thought back over a lifetime of cheques written against amounts that hadn't been lodged yet, fingers crossed that the timing would work in our favour. I knew, only too well, the embarrassment of bounced cheques, the mess of additional charges, phone calls from the bank. I couldn't see why it might be a criminal offence.

'Don't you? I'm afraid Marilyn makes a bit of a habit of it. Spending money we don't have.'

'Tell her it's okay. It's okay, Marilyn.' I turned back to Byron. 'For God's sake, tell her to come out. She can't hide for ever. It's crazy.'

He shrugged. 'She can't face you. She won't come out until you've gone.'

'Is she all right?'

'She's fine.'

'Okay. I'll go. But please tell her I don't care about this.'

I could see out of the corner of my eye that Marilyn had lifted her head to listen, but when I turned, she disappeared again.

'Lucie's on the sofa. She didn't want to go to bed.'

When I caught up with Marilyn the next day, I barely recognized her. She was wearing one of Byron's grey V-necked cotton sweaters over jeans that were too big for her. Her hair was dull and her speech was slower than usual.

'Thanks for taking Lucie,' she said, in that new, heavy voice.

'Any time.'

'I have chores to do. Catch you later.'

'Marilyn . . .'

'Byron told me what you said. You're kind. But I know what you think.'

'Don't talk to me as if I was a stranger! I really don't care! You think I've never bounced a cheque? Why didn't you ask me if you need money?'

'You never have any.'

I couldn't help laughing, but Marilyn was deadly serious.

'I'm sure I could find it. If you were in trouble.'

'Well, aren't you lucky.'

Marilyn went inside her house and slammed the door. I pressed my finger to the bell until the door opened again.

'What is it now?' Marilyn's fists were bunched on her hips, ready to punch something.

'Let me in. I have to talk to you.'

Marilyn stayed where she was, blocking the door, her chin jutting out. 'What do you want?'

'Look, do you think I've never done anything wrong?' She made a face.

'For fuck's sake!' I exploded. 'You think I never stole anything?'

She waved this away. 'Teenage stuff.' She took her hands off her hips and folded her arms. 'Okay, your holiness. What's the worst thing you ever did?'

Something reckless took hold of me. I wanted her to feel better. Or maybe I was tired of feeling like someone I wasn't, the matronly, respectable person I seemed to have become. 'I got paid to sleep with someone. A long time ago. I was desperate.'

Marilyn's face settled into a caricature of itself. She pursed her lips. 'Shoot,' she said. 'I wish I still smoked.' The air hummed between us. She looked at me again. 'Did you really?'

I could see from her face that this meant more to her than it ever had to me. If I could have, I'd have snatched those words back and stuffed them deep down inside myself, buried them so far they'd never be found again. But it was too late.

Marilyn whistled. 'Okay, so you're not perfect. But you sure as hell put up a good show. Everyone thinks you're wonderful.'

'It's not what you think, Marilyn. It was only the once . . .'

'Don't worry. I won't tell anyone. We've got dirt on each other now. That makes us safe.'

Safe was the opposite of what I felt. What the hell was I thinking?

'I'd be careful, if I was you,' Dermot said. 'There's something about that woman I don't trust. She spends too much time thinking about surfaces.'

In those days Dermot related everything to circuitry. He was working on a design for a new microchip. 'This one will change everything, wait and see. We're developing a sound card. When they're ready, computers will change completely.'

'Again?' I teased.

He didn't notice. 'You'll be able to play music, have voice-adapted software, everything. Moving images will be next.'

He was flushed with excitement. Just then, I felt Ben move inside me for the first time. I caught Dermot's hand and pressed it against my T-shirt. 'Ssh,' I told him. As if the baby was something we could hear.

There was Dermot, living with one eye on the future. The closest I could get to that was wondering if our next baby would be a boy or a girl.

That summer, Hannah joined the swim team, even though I couldn't imagine that a six-year-old wouldn't just jump in the water and drown, or flail around looking for her mother, going nowhere. I was surprised when the coach, a wiry woman called Sandy, waved me off.

'You mean – the mothers don't stay?'

'Lord, no. They'd just get in the way. Wouldn't they, Hannah?' Hannah squinted up at her and then at me, not sure. But she didn't flinch when I left and by the time Jack and I had got to the car, Hannah had already joined a small knot of girls her own age. Lucie was nowhere in sight.

When I came back, Hannah was struggling to finish a length of the pool with no armbands, while other children shouted encouragement from the side.

'See?' Sandy beamed at Hannah as she pulled herself, sleek and dripping, out of the water, pulled the tight cap from her head, shook her head like a wet puppy, grinning.

'Did you see me, Mommie? Did you see?' She turned back to look the length of the pool, checking with herself the extent of what she'd managed to do.

'She's a natural!' Sandy said. 'See you tomorrow, Hannah.'

At the first meet, I was amazed by the number of kids, their stamina, the apparent chaos resolving itself into a series of races, whistles blowing, splashing, cheers. The little ones ran around in tight little groups until it was their turn to swim, and then lined up, solemn, twitching with nerves, at the starter blocks. Grim-faced, they struggled from one end of the pool to the other, but the older ones launched themselves into the water like arrows. Elegant teenagers, smooth-skinned and confident, stood in groups around radios between races, their tight racing caps pulled off, eyes and teeth flashing.

There seemed to be medals for everyone. Hannah came third in two races and emerged from the water beaming. 'Next time, I'm going to win.'

Over that summer Hannah's puppy fat disappeared. She grew taller and muscular, her skin turned golden and her eyes shone. She was elegant in the water, as if she had gills. Graceful and languid in play, then suddenly darting out against some other child. Even Dermot was impressed when I finally managed to persuade him to come and watch.

'I'd just worry about the whole force-feeding aspect of it,' he said. But there was no denying Hannah's joy.

My brother Desmond and his wife, Jane, gave my mother a birthday present of a return ticket to visit us. I dreaded her arrival. I didn't know how our lives would stand up to her scrutiny. When she arrived that September, she came out of her room squinting, the light too much for her. We turned the ceiling fans on full and left them spinning violently all day, but the noise they made, the way they rocked on their bases, alarmed her. I could see her checking them out, shifting the children into the corners of the room to play.

'I don't know how you stand it,' she moaned, pressing a folded hankie to her neck, her armpits. Two scarlet circles of colour had appeared on her cheeks. When we went to the mall we circled the car park like sharks, looking for a spot near the door. I was afraid that Sylvia might keel over from heat exhaustion if she had to walk more than ten yards. She had packed all the wrong clothes. The Irish habit of packing for every eventuality brought her over with a coat, a woollen jacket, slacks and a heavy skirt, long-sleeved polyester blouses.

'I never imagined heat like this!' she gasped. Her hair stuck to her head in flat grey clumps.

I had to bully her out to the shops to buy short sleeves, cotton. I had rarely seen my mother's upper arms bare like that, the skin spongy and pale. I felt as if I was looking at something secret.

Sylvia bought sunglasses with lenses as big as plates. We drove around the expensive parts of town to look at money, but Sylvia wasn't impressed, not even by Diane's house, which surprised me. We went south along the freeway to the park where the alligators used to come up on the grass to bask, the one that had thrilled Pat and Conall, but Sylvia wouldn't get out of the car. So we turned north, took her for a fish fry in a shack at the side of a more glamorous lake. When the food came, Sylvia was suspicious. 'All that grease!' she said, scraping the beer batter off the fish with her plastic knife.

'It's the best part, Ma.'

She pressed her lips together, dabbed them with a paper towel, gripped her handbag and stared out over the water. Blackened tree branches broke the surface, but there were boats on the water. The woman who wiped our table told us about the flooding, the hydro-electric programme.

'This must be the only valley for miles around, and they had to fill it with water?' Sylvia said.

I was desperate to find something that would show the place in a good light. We drove out to Galveston, coasted up and down streets with imposing brick houses, turreted, with deep verandahs. Close to the sea, the buildings were on stilts, and further inland, on canals, were clusters of smaller houses, each with their own jetty.

'The very first time we drove down here these houses were in bits,' I said. 'Literally. After a hurricane. Trucks on their sides under water, boats up on porches, trees through roofs. As if nothing knew where it was supposed to be any more. Land and sea and sky all mixed up, barriers smashed.'

'Sounds about right.'

'What did you say?'

'Nothing.'

Dermot took the kids off to the beach so that we could go for a leisurely cup of coffee. I wasn't so sure this was a good idea. It was a long time since Sylvia and I had been alone together.

Sylvia leaned back into the slippery vinyl of our booth and fanned herself with the plastic menu card. 'How do you stand it? Even the air is fake!'

I could see she was uncomfortable, but right then I

didn't care. I was sick of her constant moaning. 'Just for once, do you think you could try to be positive about something?' I tried to keep my voice even. 'Because do you know what? I have to live here.'

'I didn't mean—'

'When this is over, you get to go back home and laugh. And where will I be? You remind me of Diane's friends. They sit around and moan all the time about everything they can't have here; how there's too much sun, too much light, too much heat, too much noise, traffic . . . the people are too loud, too big, too black, too brown, too American, too Latin, too greedy. They say you can't get a decent cup of tea in this town, or a sausage, or proper French cheese or good wine, a newspaper worth reading. They get food parcels sent out from home: bacon and sausages, ham, leaf tea . . .' I stopped for breath.

'What's your point?'

'You know what I think? If you live in a place long enough and still hate it, it says more about you than it does about the place you're in.'

'You always were a fantasist, Renée.'

'I believe in making the most of things.'

We were at a precipice. If we fell over the edge we would crash on the rocks of Sylvia's failings as a mother, my inadequacies as a daughter. I didn't care.

'Let's not fight,' Sylvia said. She bit her lip. 'I only have a few days left.'

We retreated behind our menus, placed our orders with a sweet young girl who had half a ton of metal stapled to her teeth. I watched her go, trying to figure out how much the braces had cost her. Our dentist had already suggested that Hannah might need them.

'It's only that I worry about you,' Sylvia said when the waitress had come back with our order and her cinnamon-flavoured coffee steamed in front of her. I had ordered mint tea, not sure whether temper or late pregnancy had upset my stomach.

'I'm fine.'

'We'll leave it, so.' She stirred her coffee. Then she looked straight at me. 'I'm sorry if I've upset you. I didn't mean to. You've done a wonderful job with those children,' she said, so quietly I had to strain to hear her. 'They're sweet.'

We stayed overnight in a raised apartment block on the beach, something we couldn't really afford. That night, Sylvia shocked me by offering to look after the children while Dermot and I went out alone. 'Give us a chance to get to know each other,' she said.

I looked at the children, who were plonked in front of the television set, and then at her. 'Okay,' I said. 'Thanks. We won't be long.'

All through dinner I imagined the worst. A return of Hannah's two-year-old tantrums and Sylvia locking her in the bathroom as a punishment. Jack dismantling a pipe and causing a flood, Sylvia not knowing who to call.

'She's an adult, for God's sake.' Dermot was impatient. 'They'll be fine.'

'You don't know her like I do. She's hopeless!'

But when we got back Jack was tucked up in the sofa bed, fast asleep, and Sylvia and Hannah were playing cards together, laughing like old friends.

'Time for bed, Hannah,' Dermot said.

'Can we play again tomorrow, Sylvia?' Hannah begged.

'Of course, darling.'

Hannah wrapped her arms around Sylvia's neck and gave her one of her strangler specials before slipping under the covers beside Jack. ''Night,' she said, sleepy.

'Hey, what about me?' I was at that awkward stage of pregnancy where I couldn't bend, so I had to sit on the bed and make Hannah sit up to meet me halfway to kiss her goodnight.

'Don't worry,' Sylvia said when she saw me wince. 'You won't know yourself in a few weeks' time.'

'She called you "Sylvia",' I said.

'That's right.' She gave me a shrewd look. 'Why not? Everyone else does.'

The next day when I woke up Dermot was cooking breakfast.

'Where is everyone?' I asked.

'On the beach.'

I went to the balcony. 'Good God. You have to come and look at this. They're burying my mother.'

Down on the sand, Sylvia was stretched out flat, her handbag prim beside her, while Hannah and Jack heaped sand on top of her. There was seaweed draped above her head. I could hear their voices, the children's high-pitched and excited, Sylvia's languid and droll. Behind them, the sea curled up and sank in tiny, harmless wavelets, making a sound like breathing.

In the end, the neighbours won Sylvia over. Ellen took her off for a whole day's shopping in Nieman Marcus and Sylvia came back entranced with the courtesy of the shop assistants, the luxury of air kept a couple of degrees too cold, the leisure of wandering around without children jumping at your hands wanting drinks, wanting to go home.

Laurie Franklin, who lived on Station Road, turned out to be a Catholic and brought her to church every day, a suggestion Sylvia dared not refuse. It gave her plenty to talk about. 'They have slide shows!' she said, indignant, the first time she came back. 'The priest, as you'd know if you ever went to church' – she gave me the evil eye – 'is known as Father Frank.'

But Father Frank was a nice man, who knew how to smooth the ruffled feathers of someone who was used to a more traditional approach to religion. He asked Sylvia questions about how things were done in Ireland and was respectful enough to make her feel better.

'It's a bit too modern for me,' she said in the end. 'But each to his own, I suppose.'

One day I came home from the supermarket and found Sylvia drinking beer, of all things, on our drive with a young man I hadn't seen before. Hunter was curled up on the stranger's foot, asleep.

'Come and meet Michael,' Sylvia beamed at me.

'I'm Stephen's brother,' Michael drawled. He had Stephen's sallow skin and blue-black hair, but he wore his in a ponytail. He had a dimple on either side of his mouth.

'Michael's from Midland. I told him you lived there. You'll have lots to talk about.' Sylvia had that Irish habit of thinking that just because you'd spent five minutes in the same city, you'd end up discovering at least five shared blood relations.

'Are you on holiday?' I asked Michael. I was surprised when he winked at me.

'Not ex-act-ly.' He dragged the second word out as thinly as possible, to make sure he had our full attention. 'I'm in disgrace. I'm the black sheep of the family and I've been sent into exile. My mother is not', he flashed a glowing look at Sylvia, 'anything like yours.'

'I bet he's been banished for being gay,' Sylvia said later that night. 'From what you told me about Midland, I don't imagine it's the easiest thing in the world to be a young gay man out there.' She looked around our messy living room from her position at the end of the sofa. 'Not that this would be easy, either. No offence.'

I was far too dazed to take offence. 'How do you know he's gay?' I said.

'He told me.' She stretched her legs out in front of her and reached for the remote control. 'Isn't it time for the news?' She flicked the TV on.

'What do you mean, he told you? Did he just come over and say, "Hi, I'm Michael, I'm gay"?'

'Don't be ridiculous, Renée. I asked him.'

'Mother!' I exploded. 'How could you?'

She dragged her attention away from the TV and looked at me instead. 'It's simple, really. I thought he might be – he's very camp, you might have noticed – and I wondered. He was dropping hints about being the black sheep of the family. I thought he wanted me to ask, actually. Yes, I got the definite impression that he was pleased.'

Camp? I wondered. Where had all of this come from?

'What's wrong?' she said.

'Nothing.'

'You think I don't know about gay people, is that it?' she sniffed. 'We're much more broad-minded than we used to be, you know.' Her pupils shrank to an almost invisible point. 'As you'd know, if you ever took the time to come home and see for yourself.'

For the rest of her stay, Sylvia was as good as gold. She never once remarked on how many hours the children spent in front of the television, or corrected the way they spoke. She stopped complaining about the heat, went out for short walks by herself and remarked, often, on how friendly people were, how hospitable. She came with us to the pool and admired Hannah's sleek body powering through the water, the way she muscled up and fired herself like a bullet from the low board. 'That child has real talent,' she said, with obvious pride.

Then she looked around the patio area, at the drinks machines, the wooden porch, the loungers. 'You've done well for yourself, Renée.'

'Because of the pool? You don't get it. It's the one thing they have everywhere in this city. Dermot says it's a kind of crowd control. It gets so hot, everyone needs to be able to get into water, fast. Otherwise, they'd have to drive round in those big fire trucks and hose everyone down. The really posh parts of town don't have public pools because everyone has their own.'

I sat on the edge of the water and let my legs swing under the heavy dome of my belly, watching Jack. He had none of Hannah's power in the water but he was comfortable there, clowning around, splashing with his friends, watched like a hawk by the lifeguard because of the racket they were making.

'This is wonderful,' Sylvia said and I was ready to forgive her everything.

'Come back again,' I said at the airport, and meant it.

17

When Ben was born he had no hair. Instead, his whole body was covered in a thick, waxy vernix that made him look like one of those cross-Channel swimmers who've been coated in lard to keep them warm. He was a plump, round baby and he stayed that way. His arms flailed out when he was asleep, and then he'd smile a buddha smile and relax, like a ball deflating. Hannah and Jack fought over who owned him, and that worked to my advantage, because I could send them running to find a nappy, or a clean towel, no matter what they were doing. We set up his car seat in the centre of the car so they could hold one hand each. I kept a wary eye on the mirror when I was driving, for when they started playing tug-of-war, or having windmill competitions, swinging one arm each. But all Ben ever did was cackle, in a grainy, dirty-old-man voice, as if he was enjoying himself. The more physical they got, the more Ben liked it. As he grew, he learned to settle things his own way, grabbing fistfuls of their hair and tugging, hard.

'No fair!' Jack complained.

'Baldy!' Hannah taunted.

But Ben grinned and blew raspberries and tugged harder. When I prised his fingers open, strands of

Hannah's coarse tawny hair or Jack's fine black wisps were usually embedded in their creases.

We had a street party for the kids and Michael helped out, making finger food and cutting vegetables into funny shapes. By the time we'd finished clearing away, I felt I'd found a friend. He was closer to our age than anyone else on the street and he made us laugh. Ellen made a point of frowning whenever she saw him, but everyone else accepted him as easily as they'd accepted us, once it looked as if he was there to stay. He soon got a job managing the deli counter at the local supermarket.

'Is that what you wanted to do?' I asked, when he came over to tell me.

'Sure.' He dodged out of the way of the kids, who were racing their tricycles around the circle, and skipped up onto the grass beside me. Ben was scrunched up on my lap and Michael made a face at him, then put out his finger for Ben to grab. 'It's what I do. Once they get used to me I can push a few new ideas their way. Broaden the range.'

'The range hardly needs to be broadened, Michael! I've never seen so much food on display as I've seen here. Believe me, I write letters home just about what's available in the supermarkets.'

He wagged his index finger at me. 'Don't mistake quantity for variety,' he said. 'And never mistake either of those for taste.'

'Is Michael lecturing you about food?' Stephen had come over to join us under the tree. 'I'm guessing this is a good sign. Did you get the job?'

'Sure did. I'll find a place of my own soon.'

'No hurry,' Stephen said.

Hannah's toy ponies began to disappear, one by one.

She had a favourite, a turquoise lump of plastic with a multicoloured mane and wings, called Puff. A vile thing, to tell the truth, but Hannah loved it. She carried it everywhere, like one of those security blankets some children have.

One day, I came into Hannah's room after putting Ben down for his nap and found Hannah holding Puff to her cheek, sobbing her heart out. 'I hurt her, I hurt her!'

I prised the toy loose from her fingers. Hannah had etched her initials, H.G., deep into the plastic, with my nail scissors.

A few days later, when Lucie went home after an afternoon spent indoors avoiding the heat, Hannah couldn't find Puff.

'Lucie took her,' she told me. Her green eyes were hard and dull, the way stones picked from a river-bed lose their magic when they dry in the sun.

'You don't know that, Hannah.'

'Yes, I do. I saw her.'

'Are you sure?'

She nodded.

It was the last thing I needed. Marilyn had been awkward, almost rude, the last time we met. But I couldn't let something like this go, even between seven-year-olds. I had had my own suspicions about Lucie for a while.

'Okay.' I strapped Ben into the baby-carrier on my chest and took Hannah's hand. 'Come on. Let's sort this out.'

Marilyn was kneeling on a towel beside her flower-bed, weeding. She didn't smile when we came onto her grass.

I held Hannah's sweaty hand. 'Marilyn, this is awk-ward, but . . . we think that Lucie might have taken Puff – one of Hannah's ponies – home. By mistake.'

A brightly painted, incredulous smile spread across Marilyn's face, as if she had never heard of My Little Ponies, had no idea how important they could be in the seven-year-old universe.

'Excuse me?'

I said it again.

Lucie came out of the house to listen. Her fingers slid into her mouth and she stood on one thin brown leg, leaning on the open screen door. She shook her head when Marilyn asked her about the toy.

'Are you sure, Lucie?' I asked.

'I'll look for it,' Marilyn said, in a voice as cool and neutral as water. She peeled off her gardening gloves and brushed her immaculate hands on the legs of her jeans. When she went into the house, Lucie slid in after her.

We hesitated and then went back to our own porch. I cracked open a cold beer and sat in the wicker chair with the broken seat and smoothed the hump Ben made on my chest while Hannah leaned against me. Hunter sat beside us, his ears cocked. Together we waited for the sun to go down or Dermot to come home, or something, anything, to happen.

Marilyn and Lucie appeared at the corner and Hannah edged closer to me. They came right onto our driveway and stood in front of us. Marilyn's hands were propped on her narrow denim hips. Lucie smirked and played with her hair. Hunter went over and sniffed her ankles. She moved away from him, closer to her mother.

'I want you to know that I've searched Lucie's room—' Marilyn said.

'You didn't have to go that far—'

'—to be sure of what I already knew. There's no sign of Hannah's pony.' There was a hard edge to Marilyn's smile. 'We are not stealing your stuff.' She swung around and walked away. Lucie skipped after her.

We watched them go.

'Hannah, are you very sure she took it?'

'Yes.'

'How sure?'

Silence. Hannah's eyes were screwed shut.

'Hannah, tell me now, before this gets any worse. Did you see her with Puff in her hands?'

'She was playing with her.'

Doubt was plain in Hannah's voice.

'Jesus!' I stood up and stared at Marilyn's shut front door. 'You mean, Puff could be somewhere in your room after all?'

We went in and took a look at the devastation on Hannah's floor, dress-up clothes mixed up with real clothes, toys and parts of games strewn everywhere. There was a full day's work in sorting through it all.

'You're not positive she took it?'

Hannah hunched her shoulders and squirmed, shook her head. Her face was scarlet.

'We've got to go over there and apologize.'

'No, Mommie! I don't want to.'

'Me either. But we have to. The sooner the better.'

'But—'

'Come on. Let's get it over with.'

I grabbed Hannah's shrinking hand, harder than I needed to, and hauled her down the street. Marilyn's front door opened as soon as we knocked. Marilyn and Lucie stood there with terrible smiles on their faces while I ground out an apology and made Hannah do the same. Hannah's face was a mask.

'I forgive you,' Lucie's voice was high and sweet.

'You should have checked before you did anything,' Dermot said.

'But I believed her.' I didn't say that I'd been afraid to accuse Marilyn too directly.

'I didn't lie, Mommie. I didn't.'

'You made a mistake, Hannah.' I looked at Hannah's closing face, worried. 'We both did. Daddy's right. I should have checked before I barged over there.'

She got up and slammed out of the room. Dermot went back to watching the news.

'I just – I've been half-expecting something like this,' I told his profile. 'So I jumped to conclusions. I feel really stupid.'

'I wouldn't worry.' He yawned, stretched his arms up over his head. 'It'll blow over.'

It was early in the morning, maybe half-past seven, and I was out on the front porch drawing chalk figures with Jack while Ben snored gently in his baby seat in the shade of the porch. Hannah was inside watching cartoons on TV. A strange car turned onto the street and parked at the kerb beside Michael and Stephen's house. I didn't pay much attention until a small woman got out wearing a silk kimono with a turquoise dragon on the back. It billowed and rippled over a pair of tanned legs and high-heeled gold sandals. The woman shimmied her shoulders and tossed her head so that the kimono fell into a scoop down her back and her waves of reddish-gold hair swung around it.

She sauntered up to Stephen's front door. The door opened and a low, musical voice sang out, 'Here I am!'

The door closed.

'Who's that?' Jack asked.

'I've no idea.' I stood up and dusted off my hands, brushed dirt from my reddened, grainy knees. 'D'you want to play hopscotch?'

'No, that.' Jack pointed at the car the woman had parked in the shade of Stephen's tree, each window open a crack. There were two boys in the back. One pointed an imaginary gun at Jack and squinted along the barrel. Jack shifted, uneasy. The other was intent on something on his lap. Reading, maybe, although it seemed to involve a lot of stabbing motions with his fingers.

Stephen's door opened again and the figure in the kimono waved at the boys in the car. 'Come on, boys. We're here!'

The two young teenagers got out of the car. Each one had a backpack. Their hair was long and curly. One was heavier than the other, but neither of them was slim.

'Hurry!' the woman called, in that musical southern voice. She held the screen door open for them. She waved cheerfully at me while they filed past her. It was only then that I realized that I'd been staring.

Before long, Michael hurried across the road.

'Thank God you're here. Let me in!'

He went straight to the fridge. He ignored Hunter, who danced around his feet, waving his tail.

'What are you looking for?'

'Crisis provisions. Have you any alcohol?'

'We're out of beer.' I didn't mention the wine. Michael shuddered every time one of Dermot's bargain boxes appeared at a party. 'Try the freezer.'

'Good girl.' He took the bottle of vodka out and poured himself a generous measure. 'You?'

'Michael, do you know what time it is?'

'The end of the world as we know it!'

'Why? Who was that?'

'*That*', Michael said, 'will be my undoing. Her name

is Judith. She's moving in with us, boys and all. She turns up just when Steve is wondering what to have for breakfast. "Have me," she purrs, so he does.'

'Come on, Michael. Be serious.'

'Scout's honour.' He poured himself another drink.

'Go easy on that.'

'Last one. Where was I? Oh yes. He spent the night with her a few weeks ago, at her apartment, in some nasty complex near the airport. Last weekend, more of the same. Then, last night, they met at a party and she told him she's not about to be anyone's casual one-night stand and he said he didn't see her like that at all and she said are you looking for a relationship, then? And the silly boy said yes. And she says, what about my boys? And he says he loves children. Children!' He rolled his eyes. 'Did you *see* the size of those boys? That woman has called Stephen's bluff. Doesn't she know this neighbourhood is a polyp on the colon of the city? Why would anyone choose to live here? Why drag teenagers into it? They asked me to leave while they sort it out.'

'We did. We chose to live here.'

'Well, you. Where else were you going to go?'

I let this pass. 'But ... are those her children, Michael? Where are they?'

'Those are teenagers,' he said. 'Sampling our movie channels. God only knows what their mother is up to. Did you see? They've brought *suitcases*. My dear, my days are numbered.'

*

And they were. Michael got into the habit of sitting on our porch to tell his side of the story. It wasn't that Stephen, or even Judith, asked him to leave, exactly. It was more that the combined effect of extra people and noise in the house, together with a few incidents involving Michael's more precious belongings and a remark from Judith about his social habits that went unchallenged by Stephen, sent him looking for another place to live.

'An adult community, I think. I'm suffering from over-exposure to children just now. Excepting yours, of course.'

He watched glumly as Jack trailed off down the street on his Big Wheel. I got up to go after him. 'I'll be back,' I said. But Michael put his hands in the pockets of his baggy jeans and headed for home.

Soon after that, Dermot helped Michael move to an apartment in a fancy development beside an artificial lake, way out in Sugarland. Hannah and Jack fell in love with the swimming pool as soon as they saw it. It had a trio of plaster flamingoes standing on a concrete lily pad at its centre. Colder water burst from their mouths in sudden jets. But children weren't allowed to swim there.

'You'll have to come to us in future, Michael,' I said. 'Or I'll have to spend the whole time chasing them out of that water. Anyway, it's too far away. Couldn't you find anything closer?'

'It's affordable,' Michael said. 'Being out in the boonies and all.'

'Come on, Michael. Admit it, the flamingoes got you!'

Michael fell into the habit of dropping in to see us when he had a split shift. I knew that he was killing time because it wasn't worth his while to drive all the way out to his apartment and back, but I didn't mind – he was good company. He always asked if there were any signs that a row might have developed across the road.

'I don't think that's likely to happen, Michael.'

'You don't think Michael fancies you, do you?' I teased Dermot one night.

Dermot made a face. 'No.'

'Are you sure?'

'Why do you ask?'

'Only that he comes around here so much. And you're so devastatingly gorgeous.'

'Don't you like him?'

'Of course I do. He makes me laugh.' The other thing about Michael was that he treated me like a person, rather than as anyone's mother. I was still thinking about that when I said, 'We all know that I'm not the attraction.'

'Is that right?' Dermot ran his fingers down my arm. 'I wouldn't be so sure.'

Stephen went around wearing the slightly stunned expression of a man who wasn't sure what had hit him. Every time I saw him, he was happily revealing the intricacies of his car engine to one of Judith's boys, or pitching to the other. Nick and Brandon settled in to the neighbourhood straight away. They used the climbing tree as a shortcut to the wasteground, where they spent hours kicking a football around with Eddie, from the middle house, and some other boys from Station Road. Hannah, being a girl and too young, didn't register with them at all, but they would just about tolerate Jack's hero-worship when he watched them play on the street.

Judith soon found herself a part-time job, so she was gone most of the day, while the boys were in school. I hardly ever saw her, except in the distance. Then, one day, she came striding out of Stephen's house straight towards me. Her auburn hair was scooped up on top of her head and held by a wooden clip. She wore a pair of cut-offs and a tank top, and looked carelessly pretty, in a Goldie Hawn kind of way. Goldie Hawn's older sister, I thought. She looked to be in her mid-forties. I wondered, meanly, how long it took her to create that girlish effect. Then I shook myself. Michael was getting to me more than I would have expected. A column of brightly coloured plastic bangles flashed on each slim, tanned wrist. She strode across the road. The cicadas shrilled out their tuneless racket.

'Hi there,' she said.

'Hi.'

'I'm Judith.'

I was thrown by this. We'd already met a few times; Stephen had invited us in for drinks the week after Michael moved out, we'd waved at each other in passing, all of the usual things you do with neighbours you're not in a hurry to get close to.

'I know. I'm Ray.'

'I know. I thought maybe we'd start over. Maybe.'

I was surprised by the firm grip of her outstretched hand. Her small hands were strong and dry, the veins prominent under her brown skin. Her nails were short and even and rimmed with black.

She caught me looking at them. 'I've been gardening,' she said. 'I need to ask you something.'

'Fire ahead.'

'Excuse me?'

'Sorry. I mean, what? What do you want to ask?'

'I know that Michael is y'all's friend. What I'm wondering is, is that going to be a problem for us? You and me.'

I was flustered. 'Stephen is our friend too,' I said, lamely.

Judith went on looking. I scuffed my toes on the drive, then looked straight back at her. 'I'm sorry Michael left,' I said. 'But I don't have a problem with you, if that's what you mean.'

'Good. I'm going to need a friend of my own in this godforsaken place. Someone to talk to. C'mon, sugar. Let's celebrate.'

She rounded up the children and herded them ahead of her across the street and into Steve's backyard. Square paving stones were stacked along the fence and some of them had been laid end to end at the back door.

'I thought I'd make us a patio.'

'I'm impressed.' I didn't say that she barely looked strong enough to open a can of beans by herself.

'I needed a break. I saw you and thought – now or never, girl. Go over there and sort this out before it drives you crazy.'

She ushered us into the kitchen, handed out juice boxes to the kids and busied herself filling a blue glass jug with ice, squeezing limes into it.

'Could you pass me that bottle of tequila?'

Surprised, I checked my watch.

'Sugar, a noonday drink is what gets me through the day. Come on. It won't do you any harm. This is a lightweight recipe. It's my sundowners you need to watch out for. They'll floor ya.'

She took two tall glasses out of the freezer and crusted the rims with salt before filling them with the pale-green drink and handing one to me.

'Besides, we're celebrating. To us!'

'I hear you and Judith are getting tight,' Michael pouted the next time I saw him.

'Not exactly tight, Michael. Just a little relaxed. And it was just the once.'

'He means friendly,' Dermot says.

I knew that. It was a joke. But I didn't tell them so. 'Sorry, Michael, I do like her. But don't worry – I still love you.'

'It's a pity he and Judith are so set against each other,' I said to Dermot after Michael had gone. 'They're so alike. They both love gossip. And drink. It would be much more fun if they both lived here.'

'This street isn't big enough for both of them,'

Dermot said. 'And I'd never see you. You'd be off gassing with one or other of them every minute.'

Julian had to fly east for a funeral and we invited Diane and the twins around. After dinner, we lit the fire.

'This is bliss,' Diane said. 'I wish I didn't have to go home.'

'Stay, then.'

'I can't.'

'Why not? The girls can sleep with Hannah. We'll take the boys in with us and you could have their room.'

'Are you sure?' She sighed, stretched her arms above her head and smiled at us. 'You two are terrific. I feel so at home here.'

We opened another bottle of the wine Diane had brought, now that she didn't have to worry about driving.

'This is really good wine,' Dermot said.

I swung my legs around and propped my feet on his legs. He began to rub them absent-mindedly. Hunter snored quietly on the floor beside us, just within reach of my arm.

'That looks like bliss,' Diane said. 'My feet are so sore.'

'Take off your shoes.' I didn't understand why Diane persisted in wearing narrow shoes with heels, why she didn't kick them off as soon as she could, the way everyone else did.

'I couldn't!'

'For God's sake, why not?'

Dermot squeezed my foot. 'Don't mind her, Di. It's late. She's always cranky late at night.'

I felt guilty then. What was I doing, rubbing her nose in the fact that Dermot and I were so easy together when her grumpy husband was out of town? 'Go on,' I said. 'Take them off. Let Dermot massage your feet for you. He's practically professional. He used to be famous for his foot rubs at home. He did it for everyone.'

'Even the men?' Diane laughed.

'Well – no, now you come to mention it. Why is that, Dermot?'

'I don't know many men who'd volunteer their feet to a mate for a bit of a rub,' Dermot muttered while Diane, her face flushed, eased off her shoes.

'I bet Michael would.' I lay back and hummed along to the record, one of the old nightclub songs, and played with Hunter's ears while Dermot rubbed Diane's feet.

Out of the corner of my eye I saw Diane's mouth loosen and her head tip back. I sat up and reached for the bottle, refilled everyone's glass.

'That's amazing,' Diane groaned. She curled her legs away from him. 'But I think', she said fuzzily, 'that's enough. I'm off to bed. 'Night everyone.'

She picked up the glass I'd just filled for her and walked unsteadily across the floor, as if she was so unused to walking in her bare feet that she had to learn the art of balance all over again from scratch.

18

No matter how hard we worked at it, life in that neighbourhood could be deadly. Sometimes when the temperature rose and swelled and ballooned out so that we were living in a bubble of bad-tempered heat, tempers would snap and the flat of a hand would meet the side of a face. Children would be yanked in and out of cars by women struggling with bags of groceries, babies, time, their own disappointments. I heard shouting after dark, some of it my own. I could never be sure that a sudden pop, like sound itself bursting, was a car backfiring and not a gun going off. Down by the bayou, spanish moss weighted the branches of the trees. Sometimes the stalled energy of too many women with their lives on hold would rise up and spill over onto the streets.

Still, when Judith said that a woman three streets over had killed herself with an overdose of toilet cleaner, I thought she was joking.

'I swear.'

'But – why toilet cleaner?'

'She drank it all the time.'

'Come on, Judith. You're lying.'

'Why would I lie, sugar? Everyone knew it. Her brand was almost pure alcohol. The woman was a lush. A flush lush!' Judith barked out a laugh.

'How do you hear these things?'

'I keep my ear to the ground, is all.'

But it wasn't Judith who told me about the rapist. She had gone out of town all of a sudden and taken Brandon and Nick with her. 'Some mysterious business of her own,' Michael said, still bitter about having been displaced.

'She's visiting her father in Atlanta,' I told him. 'He's ill.'

'How do you know?'

'Because she said so. Stop annoying me, Michael. Do you want another beer?'

'You're not as much fun as you used to be,' Michael sniffed. 'Oh look, heeeere's Marilyn!'

We both watched Marilyn bustle down the street. Her calves bulged over high heels under a lemon silk skirt. I didn't know how she could stand to wear those shoes in this weather, but she looked amazing.

'I thought you didn't like her?' I said under my breath, as Marilyn got closer.

'Any port in a storm. Marilyn! Hello!'

Marilyn frowned. 'Oh, it's you,' she said. 'Ray, have you heard the news?'

'What news?'

'A woman has been raped over by the swimming pool! This very afternoon. In her own house! Can you believe it?'

She sat down uninvited and looked back over her shoulder at the solid surface of her front door.

'She was expecting a repairman – for her washer. When this man turned up at her door she let him right on in. Her three-year-old daughter was there the whole time.'

'Oh, God.'

'I know. When the real repairman came, he found the front door open. She was wild. She told him if he took one step inside her house she'd shoot him dead. Pity she didn't get to use that gun sooner,' Marilyn said.

When Michael had gone, Marilyn wrinkled her nose. 'Well, at least *he* won't be a suspect,' she said. 'What you see in him, Ray, I just don't know.'

'I'm going in to start dinner, Marilyn. See you later.'

Sometimes I got exhausted balancing the currents of dislike that eddied around me.

'Could you try to come home early, until this rapist is caught?' I asked Dermot. There had been two more attacks and everyone was getting jumpy.

'I will if you really want me to, but don't get paranoid. We've got a reorganization coming up. It's not a good time for me to start leaving work early.'

Dermot had been headhunted by three different companies in as many months and he'd turned them all down. Partly because of the green card, but also because he'd been told, by J. P. Fischer himself, that he was in line for a promotion. They were on the verge of making a breakthrough with their latest chip and everyone was excited. The thing was to beat the big companies to it.

I couldn't blame him for the long hours he worked, or for his abstraction when he came home. He let the kids swarm all over him while he stretched out on the sofa in front of the TV, but he had no energy to play with them any more. He rarely took Hunter out to the wasteground the way he used to, no matter how often the dog came to nudge his foot while he sat staring at the screen.

'Look at this!' Judith ran across the street, waving the newspaper. She had it folded open to an article on page two about a woman on the other side of the freeway who had shot a maintenance man in the mistaken belief that he was the rapist.

Dermot took the paper from her and scanned the article.

'See?' I said. 'What did I tell you about guns, Judith? This whole town has gone mad. Did she kill him?'

Judith shook her head. 'Flesh wound. Pay attention, sugar. Look at the picture!' She tapped the paper with her blunt fingernail.

I took a closer look over Dermot's shoulder. Randall Marcus III, the caption read, under a blurred image of a fair-skinned man with a square jaw. 'What am I looking at?'

'It's Randy!' Judith whooped. 'Randy the roachman!' She took the paper back from Dermot and hurried off to show Ellen.

'I always wondered about that man,' Dermot said. 'He seemed too friendly to be true.'

'You've got it all wrong,' I said. 'Randy's not the rapist, it was a mistake. I wonder if he's okay?'

One afternoon, Mona Franks, the school secretary, was sleeping off a fever in her back bedroom when her dog Buster began to growl. By the time that Howie Spiers, from across the street, came bursting through her bedroom door, she had her shotgun ready. She shot him twice, and still he kept coming. She shot him again and he knelt down, suddenly, at her feet. She climbed out over her bed so as not to have to touch him, and ran for it, yelling for help. Buster stayed behind, snapping and baring his teeth, foaming at the mouth.

As it happened, the first person to come to Mona's aid was Lizzie Spiers, Howie's mother, so it was just as well that Beth's husband Curtis was in the neighbourhood and intervened, because who knew what might have happened otherwise. Curtis calmed the women down and called 911.

Michael told me all about it afterwards.

'It's wild,' I said.

'Which bit?'

I ticked them off on my fingers. 'First, that Mona had a gun and knew how to use it. She's so . . . frizzy. Second, that Howie was that crazed. How could he keep going after her with three bullets already lodged in his chest and more where that was coming from?'

'And Buster! Jeez!' Michael hooted.

We both roared laughing. That was the strangest thing of all, that loathsome little Buster, with his pointy snout and sharp little teeth and his habit of farting every three minutes, could turn out to be useful in a crisis.

'Poor Lizzie, though,' I said. 'Imagine how she feels? To think that it was her son . . .'

'Lizzie doesn't see it that way,' Michael said. 'As far as she's concerned, Mona is the one should be behind bars, for shooting her boy to ribbons.'

'How do you know all this?'

'Curtis told me. I saw his car and stopped in to visit – I didn't think you'd let me in with all this craziness going on.'

'Don't be stupid,' I said. 'How's Howie now?'

'It's touch and go.'

'Poor Lizzie.'

Judith snorted with derision when she heard this version of events. 'He's barely scratched,' she said. 'He'll live to stand trial in any case.'

'That's good,' I said.

Judith rolled her eyes.

'Isn't it?'

'She should have killed him while she had the chance.'

Howie was discharged from the hospital. Lizzie stood bail for him and the next thing he was sitting out on their porch, bare-chested, showing off his scars and collecting a tan while he drank beer and glared balefully down the street towards Mona's.

One morning Mona wasn't there any more. She'd moved out overnight, leaving no forwarding address. No one saw or heard a thing.

'Now, don't you wish she'd killed the bastard?' Judith said.

But there was a trial in the end and Howie was convicted and sent to jail. Everyone, except his mother, relaxed.

The next time I saw Randy, he seemed to have shrunk. When I answered the door to his ring, he stood halfway down our grass. His Astros cap had disappeared and his head looked naked and strange without it.

'Randy, come on in. What are you doing down there?'

'I wanted to let you see who it was.'

'I knew it was you. I was expecting you. And I can see your truck. Are you all right?'

'I guess. Thank you for the message you sent.'

'For nothing. I'm sorry you had to go through that.'

He shrugged, then winced. I'd heard from Judith that the bullet had damaged a nerve in his shoulder. Inside, I persuaded him to have a cup of tea, but he insisted on standing at the counter to drink it. I stood opposite him. Jack was dismantling a Lego tower on the living-room floor and Ben was picking up the bits and dragging them around in his Little Red Wagon.

'Hi, Randy.' Hannah came pirouetting through the kitchen in a shocking-pink skirt with a paper crown on her head.

'Well, howdy, Miss Hannah. Aren't you a picture?'

Her smile showed the new gaps in her front teeth. Randy pretended shock. 'What happened?'

'They fell out. Daddy says the tooth fairy is building a fence like Ellen's in her front yard.'

Randy caught my eye. We both looked out the window and studied the lowering sky. Hannah waltzed out again, humming. 'You'd better get dressed so we can go to the park!' I called after her.

'Can Lucie come?' she called back.

'You have your hands full there,' Randy said.

'Do you mean with Hannah? Or Dermot?'

Randy watched the boys, who were playing quietly, impersonating someone else's well-behaved children. 'I'm glad y'all were safe,' he said.

'I wish you were too.' I took his empty cup from him and carried it over to the sink with mine.

'See,' he said quietly, when my back was turned. 'That woman knows me as well as you or anyone else does. I've been treating her home at least five years. I've seen her children grow, just like yours. But she thought I could hurt her.'

'It was the time that was in it, Randy. Everyone was jumpy. I bet she didn't even recognize you until it was too late.'

'She saw me. She looked right at me and pulled that trigger anyhow. It's hard to feel the same about folks after a thing like that.' He coughed. 'I'd better get to work. You want to round those kids of yours up and take them out? I sure do appreciate the tea.'

*

252

Hannah turned moody. She took to hiding her toys, her favourite jewellery. She wrote KEEP OUT on a shoe-box and screamed with rage if anyone went near it. When we made our Christmas lists to burn in the fireplace, she asked for only one thing: a metal box with a lock on it.

One day, she came home furious. Jack and I were cleaning out the garage while Ben was asleep. I was getting ready for a sale. We'd sorted toys and swept behind the bicycles. I was hot, sweating beyond endur-ance, aware that I smelled sour. Hannah stamped in past me, her face flushed and tight.

'Hey!' I called.

Hannah ignored me.

'Hey, Hannah!'

Hannah stopped, her back rigid.

'What's wrong?'

'I was in Lucie's house.'

'What happened?'

She turned around slowly and held out a battered version of Puff.

'What is it?' I asked, but I already knew. I could see the awkward initials carved beneath the wing: H.G., with an overlay of scratches, as if someone had tried to cross them out. 'Oh, Hannah.' I remembered marching her over there to apologize, how furious I'd been because Hannah had put me in the wrong. I felt sick. 'Did you show Marilyn?'

Hannah shook her head.

'Why not?'

She shrugged. 'I didn't want to.'

'Hannah, I'm sorry. What do you want me to do? I'll go over there.'

'Don't.'

Hannah stroked the letters of her initials on Puff's discoloured back. Her fingers traced the jagged lines where Lucie had tried to etch over them. Then she dropped the pony in the trash bag with all the other old and broken toys that no one wanted any more.

'I'm going to watch TV.'

'What will I do?' I asked Dermot. 'I want to go over there and shake the thing in Marilyn's face, make her admit that she was wrong, that Hannah didn't lie.'

'What good will that do? I don't trust that woman, Ray. The less you have to do with her, the better.'

I went in to kiss Hannah goodnight. 'Hannah, I'm really sorry about Puff. About everything that happened.'

She sighed, a strange, elderly sigh. At last she said, 'I forgive you.'

'I know. That was the part I hated most too.'

'Isn't Daddy coming in?'

'Of course he is. He'll be in when his TV programme is over.'

One lovely morning, bright and clear, Ben and I walked Hannah and Jack around to school as usual. On the way back, we came across a small knot of people in front of Marilyn's house talking about Howie's conviction. Laurie Franklin was there, with her husband Bob beside her in his wheelchair. Ellen was talking, and Marilyn was listening with her head down. She pushed at a crack in the sidewalk with the toe of her runners, a stained pair that she used for gardening.

I stopped, to be sociable. Marilyn turned her face up at an angle and I was startled by the hollows under her eyes. There was no recognition in those eyes, either, when they passed over my face. There was no life in them that I could see.

Ben began to bounce on the balls of his feet. 'Want potty,' he whispered urgently.

'Take it easy, Ben.' I eyed the distance to our house and Marilyn's open door, right beside me. Then I looked at Ben's contorted face. He was still getting the hang of this potty-training business.

'Do you mind?' I asked Marilyn.

'Go ahead.'

The dark air of the interior of the house smelled. All of the curtains were still shut. I hurried through to the bathroom, but when I got there, I was shocked. I'm no advertisement for good housekeeping myself, but I had never seen anything like this. The shower curtain was half pulled off its runners, revealing flowers of mould on the walls. A small soft turd sat on the toilet seat and more filth stained the floor. I lifted Ben quickly to my hip and left, murmuring something unintelligible, even to myself, as I passed Marilyn on the step.

'I don't want you going into Lucie's house any more,' I told Hannah.

'Why not?'

'I just don't.'

Lucie stopped coming over. When I asked where she was, Hannah said, 'She's not my friend any more.'

'Oh? Why's that?'

'She says our house is boring and you're stupid.' Hannah darted a quick look at me. 'She says that's what her mom says.'

'Is it, now? And what do you think?'

'I don't care.'

In school, Lucie tormented Hannah with jokes about her clothes, her looks, her stupid mother.

One Friday night the phone rang at nine o'clock and Hannah answered it. I thought it would be Dermot, who had gone for a beer after work.

'Okay. Bye,' Hannah said and hung up. She sat with her shoulders hunched and stared at the phone.

'Who was it, Hannah?'

'It was Lucie. And Becca, Destiny and Efrat.'

'What, all of them?'

'They want me to know they're all over at Lucie's.'

I looked at my watch and frowned. 'Do they want you to go over? It's very late. And I told you I don't—'

'No. They just want me to know they're there.'

'Oh, Hannah.' I didn't know whether to cry or to go over there and commit murder.

I couldn't help wondering if Marilyn knew about that phone call. I stopped at her door on the way home from bringing the kids to school on Monday morning.

'So,' I said, when the door opened. 'Did Lucie enjoy her party the other night?'

'Yes she did, thank you.' Marilyn used her charming public voice, the oh-so-polite tones of the PTA. She had changed the colour of her hair to a reddish-brown. It didn't suit her; it made her skin look sickly pale. And she'd lost weight. I could see the sockets of her eyes. 'I'm so sorry Hannah couldn't come.'

'She could have.'

'Oh? Lucie tells me that Hannah is not allowed to come inside our house any more.'

So that was it. 'Marilyn—'

But Marilyn's door had already swung shut.

The next time I was called to go and collect Lucie from the mall, I was less forgiving. It was a Saturday, so I left the kids with Dermot, settled on the sofa, watching a video.

'I can't believe she has the nerve to call me for this again.'

'She must be desperate. You could say no.'

I was tempted. I watched Ben try to count the freckles on his father's face, lose count, start again. 'No. I can't.'

This time I knew exactly where to go. I went straight to the security office, marched up to the desk clerk. 'I'm here for Lucie Galen.'

'Sign, please.'

I filled out the form. 'What is it this time?'

'Shoplifting.'

'Jesus.'

The clerk frowned. 'Go through.'

I stood in the doorway of the inner office. 'Come on, Lucie. Time to go.'

'It's a mistake, Ray,' Marilyn said.

'Sure it is.'

'I swear.'

'You'll sort it out, Marilyn. You always do. Where's Byron?'

'New Jersey. On a buying trip.'

I avoided the security guard's eye while Marilyn rooted through her bag and produced a number for Byron.

'Can you keep Lucie tonight?'

'Do you have a key, Lucie?'

Lucie patted her pocket, her hooded eyes darting from one of us to the other. 'We have Twinkies in our house,' she said, in her high, irritating voice. 'Mom says I can bring them.'

'Great.'

'Could you post bail for me?'

'What?' I caught the eye of the clerk, who snorted and looked away. 'How much would it be?'

'I'm not sure. I'll let you know.'

'Do you know what her bail is likely to be?' I asked the clerk when we were out of earshot, at the main door.

'No, ma'am, I don't. And if you ask me, you'd have to be crazy to pay it.'

*

When I called Byron, he cursed and hung up. He called back straight away, curt, to ask if I would keep Lucie until the next day. When I said yes, he hung up a second time before I could ask if he'd talk to Lucie, who was in the next room, waiting.

'This is too much,' Dermot said. 'You can't keep doing this.'

'What else can we do?'

I told Lucie that her father had been called away from the phone, but that he'd come for her after school the next day.

Hannah scowled at the television.

Lucie was listless. 'Okay.'

Later, Marilyn called. 'Ray? What did Byron say?'

'Not much.'

'Is he coming home?'

'Tomorrow.'

'Will you post bail for me?'

I sat up straighter, looked over at Dermot, who was reading. 'How much?'

'Ten thousand.'

'Ten thousand *dollars*?' I had Dermot's full attention now. 'Marilyn, you know we don't have that kind of money.'

'You could do it on a credit card.'

'We don't have that kind of credit either.'

'You could do it if you wanted to. You could go ball some guy—'

I put the phone down.

'What happened?' Dermot asked.

'We were cut off.'

'That's it. You can't do this again, Ray. Make sure you tell them.'

I met Byron when I was on my way out to the supermarket and he was driving in. We pulled over and got out of our cars to talk. Byron leaned on the bonnet of my car.

'Byron, I don't know what's going on and I know it's none of my business, but you've got to do something.'

'I know. I will.'

'What would happen if I wasn't here? Who'd take Lucie?'

'I'll figure something out.'

'I can't keep doing this. Marilyn acts as if she hates me.'

Byron straightened up and stood away from my car, as if he'd been burned. 'There she is.'

I looked around and saw Marilyn's classic wagon slowed to a crawl. Marilyn and Lucie stared out at me. Lucie's face was masked. Marilyn's eyes burned into mine. She looked like a person who hadn't slept for a hundred years. Her pallor was shifting towards grey. My heart beat faster when I saw her. It had never occurred to me to be frightened of her before.

'What exactly is the problem?' I asked, when they'd passed. Byron was already on his way back to his car. 'What's wrong with her?'

'Thanks for all your help,' he said. 'I'll handle it from here.'

*

When I got back from the supermarket, Michael was waiting on the porch. I wanted to tell him to go away, that I wasn't in the mood for his company right now. But he looked wretched and I didn't have the heart. Maybe he'd be good for me. He usually made me laugh, so long as he wasn't moaning about Judith, so I asked him to stay and have dinner with us. He watched television with the children while I cooked, making them laugh by telling rude jokes about the puppets on *Sesame Street*. Sometimes I thought Ellen was right and that Michael was a bad influence. Then again, everything around here was so determinedly wholesome, up to and including Ellen's own silly little picket fence, that I figured a small dose of bad influence might be exactly what they needed.

The food was barely on our plates when there was a pounding on the front door. I went to answer it and found Marilyn, trembling with rage, on my doorstep.

'Marilyn—'

A hot weight crashed into my shoulder and I fell backwards. Marilyn's fist was up again and ready. 'Don't you dare discuss me with Byron!'

'I didn't—' I ducked another blow.

'Bitch! I know you did! Don't ever . . .' Marilyn's eyes were bloodshot, wild, her hair dishevelled. Behind her, across the street, I was dimly aware of Tyler turning in our direction, of Byron running up the road. Michael came out to see what was happening, and brought Hunter, who jumped around Marilyn's feet and barked furiously.

'Hey! Cut it out, Marilyn,' Michael said.

'Come on, Marilyn, come home,' Byron reached for her.

'Some friend!' Marilyn screamed, throwing her arms wildly around, as if she would punch me again if she could only make them do what she wanted. 'Leave us alone! Leave my husband alone!'

Byron pulled her away. Hunter barked after them.

Michael took my good arm and pulled me back inside. I hovered at the counter, dazed, rubbing my shoulder.

'Well,' Michael said. 'My goodness. What was that about?'

'Don't ask me,' I said, bewildered and sore. 'She's flipped or something.'

'I'll say. Are you all right?'

'I think so.'

'Come on,' Michael said, as gentle as any mother. 'Eat your food. Have another beer.'

Later, when we were stacking the plates at the sink, Michael asked in a dramatic whisper: 'Is there some-thing with you and Byron . . . ?'

'Jesus, Michael!'

'I thought not.' He sighed. 'This street always seemed so unpromising when I lived here. Now look.'

'It's not a joke, Michael. I'm worried.'

He stayed with me until Dermot came home.

'I hear y'all had a scene yesterday,' Judith said. 'Dang, I miss all the excitement around here!'

262

'Marilyn lost it,' I said. 'That's all. It's no big deal.'

'I heard she hit you—'

'Michael was here,' I said.

I got more than I'd bargained for in Judith's look. 'Well, shit, Ray, I already knew that.'

'Michael's my friend. He comes to see the kids.'

'Sure he does.'

'It's on his way home from work.'

'Sugar, this neighbourhood is on nobody's way anywhere.'

19

Brooke came flying around the corner and tugged at my arm. 'Please come,' she said. 'My mom's sick.'

'I'll watch the kids for you,' Judith said. She lifted Ben out of my arms. 'Go.'

I found Beth crumpled in a heap in the corner of her living room. When she saw me she groaned, a horrible, primitive sound. She turned her face away. I knelt beside her. 'What is it, Beth? Have you a pain? Where?'

Brooke stood behind me, chewing her nails.

Beth groaned again. Her body shook.

'Do you know what it is, Brooke?'

'Dad left.'

Beth started to cry.

Brooke cried, too. 'Please, Mom, don't.'

'Okay, Brooke. It's okay. Let her cry. Go and put on the kettle.'

'Don't!' Beth yelled. She sat up suddenly and turned her distorted, swollen face to us. 'Don't you start training her for that emergency TLC crap, Ray! You go outside in the sun and enjoy yourself, Brooke! Go find a party and have yourself a time!' She dried her eyes with the heels of her hands.

'What happened?' I asked, when I thought it was safe to speak again. 'Do you want to talk about it?'

'Don't give me that crap. You know. You *know*!'

'Know what? I'm sorry, Beth, I haven't a clue—'

'Your buddy, Michael.'

'What about him?'

'All this time, sniffing around my husband. And you gave him an alibi. Don't tell me you had no idea.'

'Do you mean – Curtis has left you for *Michael*?'

'That's exactly what I mean.' Beth's face creased again. 'Oh crap, I'm going to be sick.'

'This is what she does,' Brooke said, when Beth ran out of the room. 'She's done it all day. She pukes and cries, goes to bed and gets up again.'

I took a closer look at Beth when she came back. Now I could see that she had flecks of vomit on her cut-offs. I went into the bathroom and turned on the shower. 'Come on, Beth, love,' I said. 'Get in here and yell your head off.' I took Beth's clothes off as if she was a little girl, helped her into the shower stall, put a clean towel where she could reach it. Then I closed the lid of the toilet and sat on it.

'See if you can find something soft for her to wear when she gets out,' I said to Brooke. 'And then, could you ask Judith to come? And, Brooke, would you mind keeping an eye on my kids for me, just for a while?' I didn't want her to stay around with Beth like this.

Judith and I took turns staying with Beth for the first week after Curtis left. Brooke came and went. Sometimes she sat in my house and at other times she power-walked around the streets. She watched everyone from under hooded eyes and said very little.

'I worry about that girl,' Beth said at the end of the week.

Judith nudged me. Later she said, 'She's on the mend. What would women do without kids to keep us going?'

'That's a refreshing interpretation.'

'Sugar, it's the only interpretation I can stand to make.'

'Michael, how could you? Beth is a wreck! And you used me.' It was the third message I'd left on Michael's answering machine.

'You're wasting your time,' Dermot told me. 'He's moved. They've gone to live in Montrose. He got a new job at the wholefoods market.'

'How do you know?'

'I talked to Michael this afternoon. He called me at work. He said, "Tell Ray not to stay mad for ever."'

'Never mind me. What about Beth? And Brooke? When will Curtis see her? Do you have a number for them?'

'He wouldn't give me one.'

'Coward.'

I worried about Beth, who stopped eating, drank Coors beer for breakfast, Jack Daniel's for lunch, and both together for dinner. Brooke ate at our house. She stepped around her mother warily, jumped at shadows. 'Mom stomps around the house all night,' she told me. 'She sleeps in Dad's old chair in front of the TV.'

Judging by the shadowed skin under her own eyes, Brooke wasn't getting much sleep either.

*

'All men are bastards,' Joanne said when I'd finished telling her the story.

'Isn't that from a T-shirt or something?' I asked.

'It's still true.' Joanne was recovering from her affair with Tom. At the beginning he'd sworn that his marriage was over, but when it came down to it he discovered that he couldn't leave his wife. As Joanne said herself, it was the same old story. 'But what does that mean? You might have heard the story a million times over, but until it happens to you, you haven't a clue.'

'I think this is a little different,' I said.

'Why? At least this guy had the guts to make a clean break. It's all the lies that I can't stand. People who won't admit how unhappy they are.'

I went to find Dermot. He was working on his computer, tucked into the corner of the playroom. I brought him a mug of tea and sat down beside him.

'No one is who they seem to be!' I said. 'It's like I've read the signs all wrong. Am I stupid?'

'It's just life,' Dermot said. 'It's what happens.'

'What do you think, though? About Curtis going off like that . . . and with Michael? What a jerk!'

He stopped what he was doing to think about it. 'If he's gay, he's gay. Sooner or later he was going to leave. I'm sorry for Beth, but she's better off knowing. She can get on with her life now.'

I was stunned. 'Do you really think that? Aren't you angry?'

He took off his glasses and cleaned them on his sweater. 'Why? He hasn't done anything to us.'

'How can you be so bloody rational? Beth's our friend! And Michael used us.'

Dermot put his glasses back on and looked at me. 'This isn't about you, Ray.'

'I know, but . . . I'm furious with him.' I felt stupid and hurt and angry, and worst of all, I felt like I'd let Beth down. 'How could I have been so wrong about people I thought I knew?'

'I bet that's what Beth feels.'

For a second, there, I hated him. 'Oh, I'd imagine Beth feels a whole lot more than that!'

Dermot's attention was straying back to the computer. 'Damn!' He slammed his fist on the desk. 'It's frozen again.' He looked round at me. 'This isn't a good time, Ray. I have to get this problem sorted out before tomorrow. I'm sorry, but I need to concentrate.'

Beth came round the next day in a state. 'Curtis called. He put money in the bank yesterday. I don't know why, but that makes everything seem worse.'

'But you'll take it, won't you? How would you live, otherwise?'

'I'll take it for Brooke. No other reason. That man played me for a fool, Ray. He was my best friend. All my life, that's what I'd have told you, since I was thirteen years old. Curtis Knolls was my best friend in the whole world. And it wasn't just a lie, it was a *total* lie. Jerk!'

*

Beth found herself a cleaning job that started early in the mornings. She asked if she could leave Brooke with me before school. 'She'll have had her breakfast and all. Then she could walk to school with y'all. Would you mind?'

'No, but . . . what about your painting?'

'Painting doesn't pay the bills. I'll pay you to mind Brooke for me.'

'No.'

Beth sat me down. 'Now see here, Ray. You gotta let me give you money for this, or it'll go sour real quick. Trust me. This means a lot, for her to go somewhere she feels comfortable. And it means a lot that I pay my own way, starting now.'

In the mornings Brooke came and sat in front of our television and then walked with us to school. I hardly noticed she was there. She was sleepy, but pleasant. The shadows under her eyes were smoothing out. Beth paid me fifteen dollars a week.

'Is it worth it?' Dermot asked.

'She's no trouble.' It felt like a fortune to me. My very own money, the first I'd earned since we got here.

Before I had time to think about it, Shulamit asked me to take her toddler, Zara, who was the same age as Ben, on Fridays. Then Beth's friend Krista asked if Destiny could come home with Hannah after school every day and wait there for an hour and a half until Krista could collect her.

'Are you running a business here?' Dermot asked. 'You'd want to be careful. We could get into trouble.'

'These are my friends. I'm doing them a favour.'

'And they're paying you.'

'They're not going to report me, Dermot, if that's what you think!'

'Maybe not. But someone else might.'

'Don't you listen to him, sugar,' Judith said. 'You take that money, no matter what he says.'

Diane turned up unexpectedly one afternoon. It wasn't like her to come when the house was full of other people's children. She looked terrible. Her hair was greasy and her clothes looked as if she'd slept in them.

'What's the matter?' I asked.

She covered her face with her hands. 'I'm sorry. I shouldn't have come.' She looked back at the kitchen table, where the twins had joined my kids and the after-schoolers to make paper chains to decorate the house. Ben and Zara were ripping up scraps of paper too enthusiastically to be any use, but they were happy.

'What's happened? Is it Julian?'

Diane nodded behind her hands. 'I shouldn't talk to you. Dermot works with him. It's not fair.'

'Don't be stupid. You know I'll never tell a soul.'

'Swear?' She looked up suddenly, her eyes piercing. 'Do you swear?'

'I swear.'

'Not even Dermot?'

'Not even.'

She looked around and let her head fall into her

hands again. 'I feel so awful,' she said. 'I'm so un-happy.'

'What happened?'

'We had a fight last night. It was bad. I talked about leaving him. He said not to even think about it.' Her cardigan slid from her shoulders. I could see a nasty-looking, hook-shaped bruise on her left arm. She saw me looking and jerked the cardigan back up.

'Did Julian do that?'

She looked away. 'It's nothing.'

'Let me see.'

'No!' Her voice was sharp, but she wouldn't look at me. 'It's nothing,' she said again. Her eyes filled.

I let her cry, patted her arm, got up to find some tissues. 'The bastard,' I said, when I came back.

She took the tissues and blew her nose.

'Why do you stay with him?' I asked.

'I have to.'

'Why?'

'He'll take the girls. I can't stay in the country unless I'm married to him. And if I leave, he'll get a court to give him custody.'

'Diane, I'm sure that's not right. Have you talked to a lawyer?'

'Are you kidding? Julian has a lot of money. His lawyer is one of the toughest, meanest in town. They were in college together.'

'But you must have something. And if he hurts you . . .'

'I have nothing of my own, Ray. Julian controls

everything. My job has always been to keep everything just the way he likes it. The house, the girls . . . if I don't . . .' She shook her head.

'Why don't you take the girls and go, then?'

'Where? We'd have nothing. What would happen to us? How could I take them away from all this, everything they're used to, to end up in some damp, unheated flat in London? They'd hate me. They're the wrong age for it. It's too late.'

'Can your family not help?'

'No. My mother has gone into a nursing home. There's no one else.'

'What about Lorna and the others?'

'Ha!' Her laugh was a dry, bitter sound. 'That's unlikely.'

'Maybe you should give them a chance, Diane.'

'Oh, they'd help for a while. Just like you would. But don't be fooled by appearances, Ray. There's none of those women as well off as they pretend to be. And it's expensive, keeping up appearances.'

'There has to be a way.'

'Is that right?' Her red-rimmed eyes were furious. 'Well, when you figure out what it is, you come and tell me. And don't think I'd be the only one who wants to hear it. I'd say you'd draw quite a crowd.'

'There's a new temp at the office,' Diane told me over the phone. She'd called to reassure me that her outburst had been an aberration and that I was to forget it. 'Téa. You should see her. Her fingernails are at least nine inches long. I don't see how she can answer the phone, let alone use a keyboard.'

Téa was a car nut. Dermot told me that she drove a classic T-bird. 'How can she afford it?' I asked.

'God knows. It costs a fortune to keep a car like that on the road.'

'Is she pretty?'

'She's interesting, in a scary sort of way.'

'What's she like?'

He shrugged. 'Big nose. Big hair.'

'And her nails?'

'Don't get me started.'

I couldn't wait to see her. Diane said that she had all the men in the office eating out of her talon-like hand.

'Dermot doesn't like her much,' I said.

'Oh, well, Dermot.'

'What do you mean?' Why was she dismissing Dermot like that?

'Dermot is a little more subtle,' Diane said.

The next thing we knew, a middle-aged programmer called Fernando had left his wife Rosario and their four children to move in with Téa. Dermot said the first sure sign was when Fernando spent his Christmas bonus on a down-payment for a bright red Porsche.

'Rosario should have seen what was coming as soon as he showed up in that car,' Diane agreed. 'For a start, it meant that they'd always have to travel in separate cars. You can't put four kids in the back of a Porsche!'

*

One day, two children I'd never seen before came hammering on my front door. 'Our fire alarm is ringing!' the girl said. She was around Brooke's age, going on eleven. 'Will you come?'

I asked Eddie to keep an eye on the younger children for a minute and followed the girl and her little brother onto Station Road, to a house that had changed hands a few weeks ago. I went inside with them, checked everything out. I could smell smoke, but I saw no sign of fire. I stood up on a chair and pulled the battery out of the alarm. The sudden silence was a relief.

'We burned popcorn in the microwave,' the girl said, sheepish. 'I guess that was it. But Mom said if anything went wrong we should call you.'

'Open the windows,' I said. It took a while for them to figure out the catch.

'They've never been opened,' the boy said, his freckled face flushed. 'We use the air.'

'That won't help now,' I told him. 'We'll close them again in a few minutes.'

I put the battery back into the alarm and nothing happened. 'There we go.'

'I've never even seen their mother,' I complained to Judith. 'She took a bit of a risk, sending them round to me like that.'

'That's what you get,' Judith laughed. 'Everyone knows they can count on you.'

'You mean everyone knows I'm always here. I could do without it, to tell you the truth.'

'"Just say no,"' Judith mocked, but gently, as if she knew she was close to a raw nerve.

All around me, my friends were beginning to go back to work, picking up the threads of lives beyond the neighbourhood. And there I was, stuck. I had no qualifications, no work permit and, worst of all, I had a suspicion that I might be pregnant again. I was exhausted. I counted back fiercely, wishing I could undo the ear infection I'd picked up at the pool, the antibiotic that must have worked against the pill. I was sure that I was right – there was a quality to this exhaustion that could only come from one thing. It didn't help that Ben was sick and fretful just then, or that he pulled at me, whining, all day long. He was already too big to be carried, but that seemed to be all he wanted lately. I wondered how I'd break the news to Dermot. He was working long hours, coming home later and later in the evenings. He was irritable with the children, and if anyone else's kids were still in the house he went straight down to our room to watch TV.

'This is burnt!' he complained one evening, about his dinner.

'I never know when you're coming home. If you'd ring and let me know, it would be easier.'

'For God's sake!' He slammed his plate, food and all, into the sink and stormed off to the bedroom.

I watched crusts of potato and carrot rise to the surface and float on the scummy water. I wanted to scream, but instead I reached in for the plug, avoiding the two shrivelled chops which had sunk to the bottom, and tugged it loose. The horrible sucking sound of the water was like a comment on everything in my life. I tried not to think about what I was doing as I scraped the mess of food out of the drain and slopped it into the bin. This was not worth making a fuss about. Dermot was tired. It didn't mean anything.

Later that night, he started to make love to me. I moved away from him. 'Not tonight, Dermot.'

'Why not?'

'I'm tired.'

'Again?'

We lay there. The space between us was thick and charged.

'I have needs, you know,' he said.

When he reached for me again, I didn't pull away. Afterwards, I lay very still and quiet at the farthest edge of the bed and listened to his deep, satisfied breathing.

Dermot's promotion came through and he cheered right up again.

'That's great,' Joanne said. She'd called to tell me that she'd got a new job too, managing a medical clinic. 'At last I feel as if I'm doing something useful with my life,' she said. 'I was getting sick of feeding the rich and idle in the restaurant. So, what is he now, our Dermot?'

'A manager.'

'Terrific! Does that mean you'll get the green card?'

'It might help. We've a hearing coming up soon. We

got a new lawyer, she's all business. I'm a bit scared of her, to tell the truth.'

'So what does he manage, exactly?'

'A microchip.'

'A what, now?'

'A microchip,' I said. 'They've been developing this one for a while. Dermot wrote the code and now he has to see it through the design stage, market it, that sort of thing. He's excited about it.'

'Good news,' she said. 'If you get the card, you can come home, right? For a holiday, even?'

'Probably.'

'So long as you're not pregnant again.'

I didn't say anything.

'Don't tell me,' she said. 'Are you?'

'Maybe.'

At least the promotion meant that Dermot could be happy about this latest pregnancy. Our lives settled down again. Then the landlady wrote to say that she wanted to sell the house.

'Let's make an offer,' Dermot said. 'We can afford it now and it's a good time to buy. It might help our green-card application.'

So we did, and she accepted, and just like that we became homeowners, on the strength of Dermot's new salary. But before long, interest rates began to climb and we found it as hard to get by as we ever had before.

*

Within six months, Fernando had divorced Rosario and married Téa. At their wedding, anyone could see there was nothing but trouble ahead for portly Fernando, no matter how black and vigorous his moustache, or how proud the silken swell of his cummerbund. Téa was a good six inches taller than him, with eyes like a Disney-cartoon version of beauty, cheekbones that would slice silk. She danced with every single man at that wedding and wore them all out.

Three weeks later, Dermot came home and told me that Fernando had come into work looking pale and nervous. There had been bedlam at home, apparently, the day before. Rosario turned up mid-afternoon with the children and left them there to get to know their stepmother. After half an hour, Téa locked them in a bedroom and opened some of the celebratory bottles that still filled their liquor cabinet. By the time Fernando came home from work, she had sheathed herself in saran-wrap and draped herself along the banister. He came into his cramped new townhouse, which still smelled of fresh paint, to hear yelling and crying coming from upstairs, the sound of a door being kicked and shaken all at once, and the vision of his young wife wearing nothing but plastic and a pair of red stilettos, demanding sex to distract her from the noise.

'How come you never swathe yourself in clingfilm?' Dermot asked, a familiar smile on his face.

I moved out of his reach and smoothed my T-shirt over my swollen body. 'One of the children would probably choke on it.' I smiled, to soften what I'd said, but he'd already turned away.

Rosario declared all-out war. She maxed out all of Fernando's credit cards, opened accounts at every department store in town and ran those up to the limit as well. She reported him to the IRS for non-declaration of expenses. In no time, he was ruined. After that, Téa was to be seen in ordinary shorts and a T-shirt that strained over an obvious pregnancy, herding Fernando's children, the oldest almost the same age as she was, in and out of a modest two-door import. The flashy T-bird had gone and so had the red Porsche that had brought them together in the first place. I stopped laughing and started to feel sorry for Téa.

'Poor little bitch,' I told Diane. 'It gets all of us in the end.'

'What does? You've nothing to complain about, have you?'

I thought about the silent, growing unease between me and Dermot. The way I'd use any excuse to stay up late in the hope that he'd have fallen asleep by the time I got to bed. The way I stiffened, without ever intending to, when he touched me in the dark.

I'd laughed the first time I saw an ad in the TV guide for a fifty-dollar divorce. 'Look at this,' I told Dermot. 'Look how easily I could leave you.' But I wasn't laughing now. Not that we were anywhere close to that kind of trouble, but look at Beth. Look at poor Rosario. Just look at Diane.

'Whose side are you on, anyway?' Diane demanded. Being unhappy didn't suit her in the least.

Time passed and Lucie and Hannah sorted out their differences. They played together in the street and sometimes Lucie came into our house. I got used to having her around again, even if I didn't trust her. But she looked wary as well as defiant and I didn't have the heart to turn her away.

One day she came when I wasn't expecting her. The after-school kids made a noisy group when they turned onto the street. Hannah was in the centre, talking to Destiny. Lucie skipped along beside them. I frowned. Marilyn hadn't said anything about sending Lucie over. We were back on cautious speaking terms, even if we only ever spoke about arrangements for the girls.

'Lucie, are you meant to be here?'

'Mom said to come. She has an appointment. She says she hopes it's okay.'

Typical. I poured juice for everyone and got them settled with their homework. Even Lucie bent to her work, chewing her pencil.

When they'd finished, they went outside, down to the trees at the end of the street. When I went out to check on them, I thought I saw a shadow cross Marilyn's window.

My phone rang.

'Is Lucie with you?' Marilyn asked.

'Yes.'

Marilyn sighed, exasperated. 'I wish you'd checked

with me. I've been waiting for her. We have someplace to be.'

'But she said—'

'I'd hardly take you for granted that way.'

I tried to soften it by laughing. 'You wouldn't be the only one.'

'Please send her home.'

Lucie didn't even blink when I went out to tell her that her mother wanted her. It didn't seem to faze her that she'd been caught in a lie. She took her schoolbag from me and looked back at the others, still down by the trees. A strand of her fine, dark hair was caught between her teeth. 'I'll be back!' she called.

Don't count on it, I thought. Marilyn came out to stand on her porch, her hands fisted on her hips, waiting. When Lucie crossed the road, Marilyn turned and got into her car without a word.

'You should have told me if this is getting to be too much for you,' Beth said.

'What?'

'That's what I heard.'

I was startled. 'Where did this come from? Did Judith say something to you? Look, Beth, some of the neighbours have told their kids to come here if they run into trouble, without asking me first. And one day I had to go up to the school to collect a child I barely know because he was sick. That pissed me off. But it had nothing to do with you, or Brooke, or any of the kids who usually come here.'

'I don't like to think we're being talked about, especially by our friends.'

Beth was extra-sensitive just then. A journalist called Janey Carrera, who lived in the neighbourhood and sent her kids to the same school as ours, had written an article for the Sunday newspaper about gay partnerships. Curtis had featured in it, and been named.

'How did she find out so much?' I asked, after Beth had shown me the article.

'I told her. I was stupid. I forgot who she was. I met her and we got chatting and the next thing I knew – this.'

'She can't do that, can she?'

'Oh yes she can,' Ellen said. 'That woman is a viper, honey. Don't you pay no heed to her. No one ever does.'

'That's easy for you to say, Ellen, but what am I going to tell Brooke? She has to go into school tomorrow. And I'm going to have to talk to Curtis.'

'Why?' Ellen asked.

'I owe him an apology. Man, I should have been more careful.'

Brooke was the target of some vicious name-calling and rumours at school after that, and Beth had to put up with a lot of sly sympathy herself, from people who were more interested in knowing about her sex life with Curtis than in whether she was managing to pay her bills or keep her roof repaired without him.

So I forgave her when her smile didn't quite meet

her eyes. 'I've been thinking,' she said. 'Brooke is old enough to stay in the house that extra hour in the mornings now. She can walk herself to school. It's practice for next year, when she goes to middle school.'

'Are you *firing* me?'

Beth laughed and looked almost like her old self. 'I guess I am. But let's not say it that way.'

'I bet it was Marilyn,' Judith said.

'But I haven't been talking to her . . .'

'Anyone who's around you for more than five minutes could see what goes on here, sugar. People dump their kids on you all the time. I bet they don't even pay you, half of 'em.'

'I just lose track. It's my own fault.'

People started to talk about Marilyn. When they asked me if I'd noticed anything unusual about her, I said no.

'She's turned strange,' Shula said. 'You and she used to hang out together, didn't you? What happened?'

'Nothing.'

'I'm not a gossip either, Ray. But Laila plays over there. If you know something, you should tell me.'

I didn't know what to say to her. I didn't think Marilyn's arrests were anyone else's business. But I knew she was out of control, that things weren't right over there. What could I say? That I went into her house one time and found it filthy beyond carelessness? That Lucie had stolen from Hannah and bullied her in subtle ways that I'd never be able to explain? 'If you've concerns of your own,' I said in the end, 'why are you asking me?'

Shula pressed her lips together. 'I thought *we* were friends,' she said.

'I'm sorry.' I was miserable.

At that exact moment, Marilyn came out of her house and caught us standing on the kerb, looking in her direction. Her door banged shut and she clipped along the side path to her car. Every step she took, every fibre of her clothes and every rigid muscle in her body expressed her non-acknowledgement of our presence.

My heart sank. The way I felt, I might as well have told Shula the whole sorry story. 'If Marilyn and I are not friends any more, it's personal,' I said as we watched Marilyn reverse down her drive, check the road with exaggerated care and drive slowly away. 'She's angry with me, but I'm not sure why.'

'Well, honey, I don't know what y'all have fallen out about, but you should watch your back.' Ellen's voice was lazy, but her eyes were fixed on mine.

'Why, Ellen, what's she said to you?' I was standing at the base of the tree. I'd helped Ben up to sit on the lowest branch and I held on to his feet just in case he got it into his head to go any higher. Dermot had taken Hannah and Jack out shopping. I pretended not to know that they were looking for a present for me, for Mother's Day.

'Some nonsense about you and that husband of hers.'

'What kind of nonsense?'

'Honey, I didn't pay no attention. I know you. And that woman's brain is rotting in her head. You can almost smell it. Besides, look at you. You look like you could give birth any time. Do you want me to help Ben down out of that tree?'

'No thanks, Ellen, he's happy where he is.'

'You be careful now.' She wandered off again. I watched her go until Ben's swinging feet brought me back to where I was and I persuaded him to come down.

I had a cold, sick feeling in my stomach. I had never been aware that someone hated me before. It made me feel helpless and afraid.

'What should I do?' I asked Judith.

'Nothing you can do. Why do you care? She's not worth it.'

'What if she reports me?'

'For what?'

'Childminding.' This possibility had only just occurred to me. 'Without a licence. Dermot warned me, ages ago. I should have listened.'

A few days later, I answered the phone to a woman enquiring about a crèche. The voice was muffled, as if there was a problem with the line.

'I'm sorry,' I said. 'You have the wrong number.'

The woman recited our number.

'No,' I insisted. 'There's no crèche here.'

'After-school care, then?'

'Wrong number.' I hung up, my heart pounding. No one had ever contacted me blind like that before. Was it coincidence? Or had my sense of guilt somehow made this happen?

I did a quick head count of the kids at the kitchen table. Eddie was there. He often dropped in for company when Carla was working the late-afternoon shift at the hospital. It was me who suggested this when Carla said that she was worried about Eddie getting caught up with a gang after school.

'Not Eddie. He wouldn't.'

'You don't know.' Carla looked at my children. 'One, you're white. Two, Hannah is a girl. Wait and see when Jack gets to that age.'

'But Eddie's only thirteen.'

'You just wait,' Carla said, stubborn.

Jack was there, of course. And Carrie-Anne, Nancy Cartwright's daughter. Nancy had gone back to work full time when her husband left her for a girl who looked exactly like Nancy, only fifteen years younger. My Ben and Shula's Zara squabbled over blocks in front of the television. Hannah was back in her bedroom with Laila and Destiny. Even I would be hard-pressed to say who was supposed to pay me that day, who had turned up for company. There could have been more, but when Beth stopped sending Brooke, two other kids had dropped out. Maybe it was just as well. This latest pregnancy was tiring me out more than any of the others had done.

I drummed my fingers on the phone. Were the INS

checking up on us? I shivered. Dermot had warned me to be extra careful, not to screw everything up for us now.

When it finally happened, our green-card hearing was a simple formality. This time our lawyer, a striking Chinese-American in a neat grey suit, dark seamed stockings and high-heeled shoes, came with us. She carried a briefcase made of alligator skin. As soon as I saw it, I knew she'd have all the right documents with her.

Liz Wang was a miracle of efficiency. She spoke briskly to the officials, as if to warn them not to waste her valuable time, and found us somewhere to sit while we waited. This time I'd left the children with Beth, although I was so heavily pregnant that it wouldn't have surprised me if Grace had been born right there in the middle of that waiting room.

We went upstairs to a small, partitioned room and I was surprised by how nervous I was. Nothing we were going to say was a lie. It was all about how long we'd been married, Dermot's job, the births of our children. I was sure that something horrible would go wrong. But the question-and-answer session went smoothly. We had to swear our good faith, sign complex documents in several places, and then we were free to go.

'That's it?' I asked. 'We got it?'

'We got it!' Dermot grinned at me. His hair fell across his glasses and I had to smooth it away, and just for a second we might have been back in the Underground, our smiles were so big, so deeply felt.

*

I was as giddy with relief as Dermot when I described the visa application forms to the others that Sunday at the pool. I was there on my own because Dermot had taken the kids off to Astroworld. I was a week short of my due date and I couldn't face the crowds and the queues and the noise, so I'd begged off. There I was, for all the world like one of Diane's friends, childless and idle, lazing around a swimming pool.

'You have to sign a declaration to say that you're not a criminal, that you don't plan to pursue a career in drug-running or prostitution as soon as you get here,' I told them. 'Imagine! As if anyone would admit to *planning* any of those things.'

Marilyn's sunglasses swivelled in my direction. 'Did you say prostitution?' she drawled. She tipped her head and pulled the glasses down with her index finger and studied me, long enough for the others to notice.

My stomach heaved. I'd always known she'd use this against me somehow. 'Something on your mind, Marilyn?'

She slid her glasses back into position. 'Why, no,' she said. Her mouth twisted. 'Nothing at all.'

'Well, then,' I said. 'So long as you're sure. I'm going in the water to cool off.'

From the water, I watched Marilyn stretch and yawn and stroll languidly across the concrete to the Coke machine. She put money in, studied the display and pressed the button. Then she called Lucie over to her and they left. I stood, up to my chin in water, buffeted by waves as kids jumped off the boards. I rested my back against the wall of the pool and felt the smooth metal bar against my neck, let the sun burn down on the top of my head.

'What was that about?' Judith asked when I got back. Her face lit up the way it did when she was on the trail of a hot story.

'Nothing. Sorry to disappoint you, Judith. Marilyn has some twisted idea in her head that I have a sordid past.' My heart hammered against my ribs when I said it.

'Who cares about the past? She thinks you're after Byron.' Beth didn't even raise her head. She lay stretched out, half-asleep, in the shade. 'Man, that woman is strange.'

'Getting stranger.' Judith sounded hurt. She turned over on her stomach and lay face down, not looking at anyone.

'You're joking,' I said. 'Byron? That's crazy! Look at me, I'm like a whale!'

'We know.' Judith's freckled back told me that the subject was closed, for now at any rate. Any other time, she'd have pestered me for details.

'Some men find pregnant women a turn-on,' Beth teased.

I'd have to watch myself. Marilyn was starting to get to me. And what was this about Byron? Apart from the fact that I'd less than no interest in him, anyone could see that he was mad about Marilyn, even if it was hard to see why. It was in the way he always came to stand beside her if we were gathered outside, the way he brought her a drink before she even knew she needed it, the way he said her name, slowly, as if he liked the sound of it.

Grace was in no hurry to be born. I went two weeks overdue with her and my ankles got so swollen that I had to spend most of each day stretched out on the sofa with my legs propped up on cushions. Because it was summer, I didn't have to worry about the after-schoolers. Ellen and Norma brought food and Beth and Brooke took the other kids away as often as they could. Judith kept us supplied with videos and brought me trashy library books to read.

In the end, they brought me in to induce me. As soon as my waters broke I felt the first hard contraction, and within an hour Grace had stormed her way into our lives. She screwed up her face and bawled, indignant, a large, lobster-like baby.

'There can't have been much room in there,' the midwife told her. 'You're better off out here. More room to grow.'

But Grace wasn't interested in space. She loved to be wrapped and snug, close to my heart. Our sofa routine continued until I transferred her to the baby-carrier. I had to wear that baby strapped to my chest for almost four months, until she agreed to sit perched on my hip, facing outwards, like the figurehead of a ship. By then, school had started again and we were back to our old routine.

*

In Ireland, they were gearing up for a divorce refer-endum and this time Joanne was working for the campaign.

'The bastards broke the window of my car!' she said, when I asked her what had finally made her get involved.

'That was years ago – and wasn't it the anti-abortion crowd?'

'Same difference!'

'You sound as bad as them,' I said.

'You don't know what it's like.'

She wrote to me, sending quick bursts of information through the post. *You've no idea*, she wrote. *I've stood on street corners handing out leaflets in favour of divorce and people have spat in my face. The police look the other way. I was called a whore and a baby-killer outside a church on Sunday morning . . .*

'What's she doing handing out leaflets outside a church?' Dermot said. 'That's asking for trouble.'

'I wish you'd come home and vote in this election,' Joanne said on the phone.

'You know I can't yet. When Grace is older, we'll come. One vote won't change the outcome, anyway.'

'That's where you're wrong. If only everyone who's living abroad would come back for this, it would make a difference.'

'But you're going to win,' I said.

*

I tried to explain what was happening in Ireland to Judith and Beth. They laughed when I told them the story of the Taoiseach who'd crossed the floor of our parliament to vote against his own contraceptive bill.

Then Judith stopped laughing and looked at me with something like awe. 'You mean, even condoms are against the law?'

'I think they're legal for married people now, but I'm not sure.'

'Man!' Beth said. 'Sounds like something our boys in Austin would vote for if they thought they'd get away with it.'

'Ray?' The voice at the other end of the line was unrecognizable.

'Jo? Is that you?'

'It's not too late is it?'

'No.' I looked over at the clock. Half-past nine. Half-past three in the morning over there. 'What is it?'

'I've been . . . oh, it's so stupid! I've been mugged.'

On her way home from a meeting that night (midafternoon here, I reckoned, trying to remember what I was doing. Had I had any inkling?) Joanne was punched to the ground outside her flat. Her bag was stolen.

'Two guys. There were two of them.'

'Are you okay?'

'I've lost a tooth, it cracked on the pavement . . .'

I winced.

'. . . and a black eye. They thought my jaw was broken, but it wasn't. I've been in Casualty since.'

'Is anyone with you?'

'I made them go home. But I can't sleep. Is it still bright over there?'

I looked out the window. 'No.'

'Funny. I always think heat and light when I think of where you are. Everything larger than life.'

There was nothing to say to that.

'They were junkies, I think. Although . . . they could have been reacting to my badges. Any excuse.'

'Badges?'

'You know. Political badges. Things are pretty tense. Voting is tomorrow.'

'You'll win.'

'I'm not so sure.'

As it turned out, she was right.

Dermot was furious. 'She was mugged,' he said. 'It can't have been political. It's typical Joanne to say it was. Ireland's not like that.'

'How would we know?' I felt a sudden stab of regret for the streets I used to walk around with such confidence, at any time of the day or night. 'We've been away too long.'

20

It didn't make me feel any better when Norma and Bill put their house up for sale.

'But, where are you going?'

'Off to Dramamine Central,' Norma said, rueful. 'Y'all must come and see us, Ray. Y'hear?'

'But why?'

'Bill's taking early retirement. He says the writing's on the wall. He says next thing we know the property market's going to crash and we should all git out while we can.'

'But why would it crash?' I felt like Ben, asking 'Why? Why?' all the time. I wanted to stamp my foot. I didn't want them to go.

'The tide's turning in this town,' Bill warned. 'You just watch and see. Y'all should move somewhere else if you can.'

Dermot said that Bill's retirement was a sign of the times. There were lay-offs and rumours of lay-offs everywhere he turned. Most people's pensions had been wiped out in the Savings and Loan crash. The atmosphere on the streets was nervous.

A family from Hong Kong bought Bill and Norma's house. I knocked on their door to say hello, but got no answer. The house was eerily quiet. No one would know there were people living there if they didn't come out at weekends to go shopping in their rust-coloured Toyota. On Sunday mornings they came out of the house in their church clothes, got into the car and drove away without looking to the left or to the right.

'Those people travel in herds,' Ellen said. 'You git one family moving in, next thing the neighbourhood is full of them.'

'What about us, Ellen? We didn't bring a flood of Irish people behind us.'

'Y'all are different.'

'Why?'

'You know.'

'No, I don't know. Why? Because we're white?'

'I'm not prejudiced!' Ellen snapped. 'But I'm practical. You watch and see.'

Pete, the UPS man, who was in the habit of leaving parcels with me when the neighbours were out, came to me one day to say that there was no answer from the neighbours' house, although he'd swear on his own life he could hear someone breathing in there behind the door.

'I'll take it,' I said. I signed the docket.

'You're a lady.' Pete went over to push a notice under the neighbours' front door to say where the parcel could be collected. We both heard the notice being pulled through the other side. Pete shook his head at me and walked back to his truck, whistling. I waited to see if the woman would come out, but she didn't.

That night, a small thin man with glossy black hair came round to collect the parcel and introduced himself as Tony, our new next-door neighbour. He told us his wife's name was Angie and his little boy, Li, was eighteen months old.

'Why don't they ever come outside?' I asked. 'Lots of kids play on our street. They should come out and meet everyone.'

He drew his eyebrows together and shook his head, everything about him pointing downwards in a big disapproving frown. 'No good,' he said.

'Did he mean the wife or the world?' Judith said. 'Maybe she's not allowed to come out.'

'Judith, don't be crazy.'

'Maybe she's better off staying where she is,' Beth said. She looked at her watch. 'I should go. Curtis is coming for Brooke.'

'He is?'

'He's taking her out for dinner. If this works out, she might go to him for a weekend.'

'With Michael?' Judith couldn't keep the shock out of her voice.

'No!' Beth snapped. Then she said, 'Not yet. Maybe never. I don't know.' She looked young and lost. 'If it happens, he'll take her down to Corpus for a weekend. They need to spend time together again.'

'Good for you,' I said.

She shrugged. 'What else would I do? He's her dad.'

Sometimes, when I was out in the back garden, I could hear a rustle in the undergrowth next door and see the tips of canna leaves waving above the fence. I knew there was something moving, up close to the fence. If I listened hard enough, I could hear breathing. But when I called, 'Hello? Angie? Li? Are you there?' the rustling and the breathing stopped and the ticking of the cicadas swelled and mixed with the sound of my own heart.

Once a month, parcels were delivered for Tony. After a while, Pete gave up on trying to rouse Angie and brought them straight over to me.

'Sure you don't mind?' he always asked.

'What would you do if I said I did mind?' I asked one day. I didn't, really. After all, I was there, wasn't I? What was the harm in taking in a parcel for a neighbour from time to time? But it did bother me a little, to know that Angie was in her house and simply wouldn't answer her door to Pete because she knew I'd do this for her.

Pete stopped short, the parcel in mid-air between us. 'That's your privilege, ma'am,' he said. His face was a studied mask of courtesy. All his friendly ease evaporated into professional formality.

'I'm kidding, Pete.'

'Yes, ma'am.'

It took time to soften him. Time, and Ben's curiosity

about the truck, a storm of questions that ended up with Pete allowing him to sit in the driver's seat and blow the horn. Ben gloated about this all day and drove Jack crazy. Hannah was above it all.

Sometimes I saw Angie go out to their mailbox when there was no one around, but if I went outside she showed no interest in talking. She ducked her head gravely, and hurried straight back inside. She could have been Tony's twin sister. They were both small and thin, and walked with their heads down. They had the same glossy, thick black hair. Angie's was cut in a bob, Tony's was cut close to his head. The baby, Li, had spiky hair and crossed eyes. No matter how hot it got that summer, I never saw Angie without her cardigan, worn over a plain, knee-length skirt. Her legs were thick, out of proportion to the rest of her fine-boned frame.

But then, one evening, she came and banged on my door. In a clipped, high-pitched voice, she said, 'You come.'

'I'm sorry?'

'You come. Now.'

I found myself propelled inside her house, Grace on my hip. Angie thrust her phone into my hand. 'Talk. Is Tony, there.'

Hannah and Ben had trooped in after me and were staring around Angie's immaculate, empty kitchen with their mouths open. Grace knotted her fingers tightly into the neck of my T-shirt. When Bill and Norma lived here, the place was full of wooden furniture, bookshelves, chintzy pictures on the wall alternating with their son Mark's certificates for this and that on his way through school and Texas A&M. It had never been untidy, exactly, but it had been full.

I put the phone to my ear. 'Hello?' My voice echoed in all that emptiness.

'You have jump leads?'

It took a few seconds for me to adjust to the unexpected storm of Tony's heavily accented demand. He described the parking lot where his car had broken down.

'I don't think I can come,' I protested feebly. 'I have my children—'

'I keep,' Angie said.

I looked across her at Hannah's horrified face.

'No,' I said. 'I'll bring them with me.'

I strapped Ben into his car seat, hauled Jack out of the tree where he'd stopped to swing on the low branch, and set off with all four of my children into the worst of the rush hour, to find our strange neighbour in the Park-n-Ride lot. He looked cross when we pulled up beside him. His pale linen suit was crumpled.

'You took long time,' he said in his staccato, abrupt voice.

I could feel my blood pressure rise. 'There was a lot of traffic,' I said. 'I had to turn off the dinner, get my kids . . .'

He waved all this aside and pointed impatiently at my car. 'You have leads?'

I did. Despite his bossy tone, he didn't seem too

keen to use them or to get his suit dirty, so I ended up doing it myself. I connected the points and started my ignition, waited for his to fire. As he revved his engine it crossed my mind that if, for some strange reason, the power was to drain from our car, this strange man was as likely as not to drive off and leave us there. He probably wouldn't even notice.

'Cultural differences,' Ellen said. She slid her heavy gold collar around her neck and settled it into position.

'Those people are using you,' Judith said.

Li turned into a sweet little boy. He had a slight squint and a big square smile. He took to following big, red-haired Ben around with his uneven, side-to-side lope. Angie would come out and cluck, disapproving, and hurry him back inside. After a while, he stopped coming off his porch. Instead, he sat there and watched the other kids play. From time to time I saw his mother's shadow cross the window.

'I bet she's watching to make sure he doesn't play with the other kids,' Shula said.

'Why on earth would she do that?'

Shula looked embarrassed. 'Some people prefer to keep their children away from – other influences.'

'Do you mean me?' I looked around the toys scattered on my driveway. 'I'm not good enough?'

Judith hooted with laughter. 'She's quick enough to call on you in a crisis!'

But when I thought about it, I knew that Shula was right. I compared my noisy, chaotic garage to

Angie's immaculate house, the silence of her life to the chaos of mine. I blushed to think that I had ever felt sorry for her, that I had felt capable and secure in comparison.

'I'm as bad as Ellen,' I said.

'At least you know it,' Shula said.

Someone who worked with Dermot was married to a midwife at Hermann Hospital. She called me to say that she'd met a countrywoman of mine, a young woman who'd just had her first baby and knew no one. 'Would you go and see her?' she asked. 'She's real lonely.'

'Sure.' I took the phone number and dialled it straight away.

It turned out that Magda was Polish. She spoke English with a heavy accent.

'They told me you were Irish,' I told her. 'I guess all Europeans are the same to some people.'

'You sound American to me,' Magda said.

I wrote down the directions she gave me and told her I'd drive over to see her in the morning, when Jack and Hannah were in school.

Twenty minutes after leaving the main drag, I began to wonder if I'd taken down the wrong directions. This area was industrial, largely abandoned. Down in the shadow of the ship channel, with bayous, empty streets, dilapidated buildings, it reminded me of the INS building in Los Angeles. I soon found myself on a street where the weeds had almost completely overrun the concrete and five squat wooden shacks huddled at the edge of the pavement. Behind them the land fell into a steep concrete ditch.

The houses were unpainted, little more than sheds. They reminded me of the houses out the back road, except that at least these seemed to stand straight. The middle house, where Magda had told me she lived, had white curtains behind open windows. I could hear music, a clear flow of notes like a river swollen after rain. The air hummed under tall pylons, anchored somehow in a thin layer of dust. The grass was sparse, more like scrub than the glossy green growth I was used to.

I took Ben's hand and walked up to the screen door with Grace clamped to my other side. The houses were raised off the ground, but the crawl-space was hardly deep enough to make much difference to anything. Just deep enough for nasty things to hide.

I knocked on the screen. 'Hello?'

The music stopped. A young girl with her blonde hair swept up into a ponytail came running over to the door.

'Ray? Is that you? Thank you so much for coming.' She struggled with the latch of the screen and let us in.

'Magda?' She looked about seventeen. She wore jeans and a man's shirt. Up close, I could see that her skin was scarred by old acne. She smiled widely at Grace and hugged Ben as if she'd known him all his life, while I looked around the room.

'Where's your baby? Ben has something to give him, don't you, Ben?'

Shy, Ben held out a small package. He had painted a

brown lunch bag and stuck it down. Inside there was a packet of vests.

'It's not much,' I said.

'No, no, you shouldn't . . . it is great.' Magda had a wide smile but her teeth were bad. They were discoloured and uneven and they gave her away, instantly, as a recent arrival. 'He's over here. His name is Jael.'

Tucked away behind the single armchair was a moses basket with a baby asleep inside it. All I could see was a shock of fine black hair and sallow skin under a soft yellow blanket.

'He's sweet,' I said. The abandoned cello was at the foot of a music stand. 'Was that you playing when we arrived?'

'Yes.' Magda smiled again. 'I can only practise when he is asleep. And I want him to get used to music.'

'Should we go?'

'No, please.' Magda sprang across the room and gripped my wrist. 'Please, stay. It's so good to have you here.'

Behind us, the screen door made a sickening sound, like fingernails drawn across a blackboard. I turned around and saw a heavy-set man in a dirty string vest that hung loose under fleshy armpits, a lot of facial hair.

'What's goin' on?' His voice was like a growl. Deep and unpleasant.

'Clayton. This is my friend, Ray. From Ireland. I told you about her. That she was coming.'

'Is that y'all's vehicle out there? I'll keep an eye on it for ya. There ain't nothing happens down here I don't know about. Isn't that right, Miz Magda?'

'That's right.'

'You call me Clay.' His eyes made me feel hot. Sweat trickled down between my shoulder blades. A ceiling fan spun lazily over us but made little difference to the heat. I hadn't seen any air boxes outside.

When Clayton had gone, Magda released my hand.

'That's some grip you have there,' I said. 'Who was that?'

'He's our landlord,' Magda said. 'He looks out for me when my husband is at work. Lucca works nights, at a diner. But sometimes they make him stay in the daytime.'

I went to the window and watched Clay saunter over to my car and walk around it. He tugged a piece of paper out of his pocket and wrote something down.

'What do you know about him?' I asked. 'Is he okay?'

Magda shrugged, looked away. 'He's fine. Would you like water?' She poured drinks for all of us and gestured to the armchair.

The three of us piled into the chair and Ben rested his head on my shoulder, wide-eyed, listening to Magda play, while Grace rolled the skin of my forearm between her thumb and forefinger.

The baby slept on in the corner. This was the only room in the house. A tiny kitchenette took up one corner, a daybed filled one wall. The armchair and the music stand filled up the rest of the space. What looked like a corner cupboard was probably the toilet. There may or may not have been room for a shower in there. Outside there was nowhere to go except the concrete ditch and across the road the back of the abandoned warehouses. And, lurking somewhere, the vigilant, slightly threatening Clayton. There was a faint tang of ammonia in the air, even inside.

I had never seen anything that made me so glad to live in the Plains. I thought about how often I had run it down in letters to Joanne, how I'd mocked my neighbours, especially Ellen with her efforts to keep everything 'up', her petty snobberies and her six-inch picket fence, the time she'd left a note on the windscreen of the Volvo informing us that it was an eyesore and that it should be moved. The time she had mistakenly left a pile of old dog turd on our front porch, believing it to be Hunter's. I'd shovelled that turd into a plastic bag and carried it straight back to her.

'Ellen, you've gone too far this time.'

'I don't want excrement in my front yard. You clean up after your own dog.'

'I do,' I said. 'This is not Hunter's shit, if you must know.'

Ellen winced at the word and folded her arms across her impressive, glitter-endowed chest. 'Now, how can you possibly tell?'

'I happen to be intimate with my dog's bowel movements, being in the habit of cleaning up after him. But besides that, I can tell you that Hunter has not been out on the street for days, and that this comes from a much larger dog.'

Ellen opened her mouth to ask another question, but the logic of size and shape must have suddenly struck her because she closed it again.

'I believe this is yours,' I said. I put the bag down on the ground in front of her and walked away.

I nearly tripped over Judith, who was hiding behind her own car, listening, doubled up with laughter. 'Sugar, you are something else! "I happen to be intimate with my dog's bowel movements"! Oh! Oh! Wait until I tell Stephen this.'

When I wrote to Joanne, I saw my life through her eyes, and wrote accordingly. Even when I talked to Diane about life on our street, I probably shaped things so that she'd appreciate them better. But now, here, looking around Magda's room and thinking about the man lurking outside it, I felt a rush of gratitude and made up my mind never to run down my own neighbourhood again.

Magda continued to play, strange melancholy pieces in minor keys. 'You know music?' she asked.

'No. I wish I did. But don't stop.' Ben was enthralled. When we left he hugged Magda of his own accord. When I hugged her too, she looked as if she might cry. 'Come and eat with us on Sunday,' I urged. 'I want you to meet Dermot.'

'I don't know. Lucca might have to work.'

'Then I'll come and get you. Ring and let me know.'

'Where did you say it was?' Dermot was incredulous when I told him where we'd been. 'And you took the kids there? Are you mad?'

'It was fine.'

'That's a rough spot. You were lucky.'

'Magda has to live there.'

'But we don't.'

'What's the matter with you, Dermot? Is there something on your mind?'

'No. I'm tired.'

'You're very snappy lately.'

He didn't answer.

'You're going to love her. Wait and see.'

Sometimes I thought that Dermot and I only pretended to live in the same city. He worked in an air-conditioned, professional atmosphere where everything ran on schedule. I lived in a chaos of children, unruly emotions, flaring tempers, scattered toys. My friends and I were informal. Our lives were as messy and casual as his was regulated and well-dressed. It was as if we had moved to two different countries, and only occasionally met, in passing.

When Magda and Lucca turned up on Sunday, they had more on their minds than a social occasion. Everything they owned was stuffed into the trunk of their car and the cello was laid out on the back seat beside the baby, its neck across the top of his moses basket.

'What's happening?' I asked, although I took one look at Magda's swollen face, her eyes puffy from crying, and thought I could guess.

Lucca was a thin, sharp, dark young man with a narrow chin, a pointed black beard. He darted around the car to help Magda out, then folded himself protectively around the baby, eased him away from the cello, and stood holding him, awkward, in the shade of the tree. I shook his hand.

'Come on in,' I said. 'Dermot's in the back. We have cold drinks ready. You can tell us everything there.'

'Clayton, he come after me in the middle of the night,' Magda said in a rush, holding her beer as if she didn't trust it. 'I scare him off with a knife and call the police. When they come, he say it was lies, that we owe him rent, that he wants us to leave. When they go away again—'

'They went away?' I took another look at Magda's face. Something told me this might not have been the first time she'd had such a visit.

'He come back. He say I must pay him what he wants or he will put us on the street, call the INS, get Lucca fired.'

'Stay here until you find somewhere else to live,' I said at once. 'You can't go back.'

Lucca studied Dermot. 'Is a lot to ask.' His English was harder to understand than Magda's, but everything was in his face. Rage, disgust, pride, love. 'I should kill him,' he said suddenly. 'But then what? Where Magda and Jael then?'

'Stay,' Dermot said. 'We'll work something out.'

But later he told me that I should think twice before asking trouble like that into our home. 'We know nothing about them. Who they are, where they're from, what they're running from. Nothing.'

'They know nothing about us either.'

'That's different, and you know it!'

308

'Why?'

'They have nothing to lose, Ray. We have everything.'

'They have each other,' I said.

He slammed his fist against the wall. 'What the hell is that supposed to mean?'

The next morning, Magda told me that she'd heard what Dermot said. 'If we make trouble for you, we go,' she said.

'Don't be silly. We'll tell everyone we're related. So far as they're concerned, Europe is one country anyway. It's all "over there", to them. It's all "foreign". You be my cousin, Magda. And sit tight. We'll get you sorted somehow.'

I went out to the supermarket and left Magda watching the kids. When I came back, Lucie was there playing dress-up with Hannah. Magda had put make-up on the older girls. She sat in the old rocker and nursed Jael while the boys played outside in the sandbox.

'Life is good here,' she sighed. 'So quiet.'

'Lucie!' Marilyn called from the hall. She came into the room. 'Is Lucie here? The door was open and I . . . Oh.' She stopped when she saw Magda.

'This is Magda. A . . . cousin of mine. They're staying for a few days.'

'How nice.' Marilyn's voice sharpened. 'Lucie, is that make-up on your face?' She snapped a look at me.

'It was me.' Magda was quick to realize that something was wrong. 'Ray was not here.'

'Lucie knows the rules,' Marilyn said, her voice like velvet. 'Take that dress off, Lucie. Come on home.'

The white silk flapper dress with the red tassles snagged over Lucie's head and Marilyn tugged at it. We all heard the fabric rip. Marilyn's face went puce.

'It doesn't matter, Marilyn. It's a garage-sale dress. We'll fix it.'

'Mom!'

'Be quiet, Hannah.'

'That's my favourite dress!' Hannah complained, when Marilyn and Lucie had left.

'For God's sake, Hannah. We'll fix it!' Something in Marilyn's face had worried me. Magda had seen it too.

'That is an angry woman,' she said. 'I don't think she likes you.'

'No,' I said. 'I don't think she does.'

The incident with Marilyn and Lucie came back to me when I met Carrie-Anne's mother, Nancy, outside the school.

'I don't need you to take Carrie-Anne today.'

'Oh. Okay. We'll see her tomorrow then.'

'No, ma'am, you won't.' Nancy began to walk away.

I caught her arm. 'Nancy – why?'

Nancy stared over my left shoulder while she talked. 'I've heard things I'm not comfortable with.'

'What things? Tell me!'

Nancy looked around as if for help, then settled her gaze across my other shoulder. 'That you leave the children with some stranger none of us know.'

'I've never . . . once.' I didn't have time to explain that Lucie had come over uninvited, that it was only her.

'And', Nancy got braver, 'that there was nudity. The children dressed inappropriately. I don't know what-all else.'

'You're right,' I said quietly, after a few seconds of silence. 'Carrie-Anne had better not come back to us again.' I picked Grace up and pushed my way through the loose crowd of mothers waiting at the gate and went to stand further down the road while Hannah took Ben and rounded up the after-school kids.

'I've had enough,' I told each of the parents who came to collect their children later. Magda was sleeping with the baby in the boys' room, which she and Lucca had taken over. 'I can't do this any more. I'll mind your kids until the end of the week and that's it.' I wouldn't soften, not even for Shula. 'I'll take Zara when you need me to, for nothing. But I can't do it regularly any more.'

'Well, sure, if you say so. But why not?'

'I can't explain.'

The phone rang at odd hours and there was no one at the other end of the line. Magda and I were both jumpy. We didn't know which one of us was the target of this silent malice. I arranged to meet Diane's neighbour, Jilly, to see if she had any ideas of how we might help Magda and Lucca. I thought she'd have good contacts because of her work on the charity circuit. 'They need legal documentation, jobs, a place to live. It's more than I can handle.'

Jilly listened carefully, then she gave me a name and

number of someone Magda could call. 'It's an agency that works with illegals,' she said. 'But they don't guarantee confidentiality.'

'You mean they might get deported if they show up?'

'Eventually. If they're unlucky. Or they might get themselves sorted out. She's a musician?'

'She's really good.'

'Leave it with me for a few days,' Jilly said. 'I might be able to talk to someone. Now, what about you? How are things with you?'

'Oh, fine. You know, the usual. Hectic. I'm wrecked, actually. No one gets much sleep at our house just at the minute.'

'I bet. How's Dermot?'

'Fine. Busy. Tired.'

'You two should go out together more. Have fun.'

Jilly didn't have any children, she didn't understand. She didn't know the co-ordination it took to keep everything going; or the exhaustion; the effort to balance what everyone wanted and needed; the cost of baby-sitting. There was no point in trying to explain. Soon Brooke and her friends would be old enough to babysit for a couple of hours and things would get easier. Maybe.

Clayton turned up in Lucca's diner, drunk. He threw a chair through the plate-glass window and left before the police could be called. The cost would be deducted from Lucca's wages.

'That means no money for three weeks, or half-pay for six. My choice,' he told us.

'I'm afraid he'll find us here,' Magda said. 'We must go somewhere else.'

'We'll try California,' Lucca said. 'We might have more luck there.'

'Wait,' I said. 'We haven't heard from Jilly yet. She might have news for you, any day now.'

'We can't afford to wait any longer,' Lucca said.

Magda squeezed my arm. 'We can't afford the risk of being reported.'

We couldn't talk them out of it. They packed their things into the car that day. Before they left, Magda gave Grace a present of a rag doll. 'To remember us by.'

'Don't take the road through the desert,' Dermot warned. 'Go north instead.'

For days after they'd gone, I checked the street before opening my front door, hesitated before answering the phone. I didn't know exactly what I was afraid of – Clayton, or the INS, or strange women asking me to mind their children. Officials, following up on complaints.

'That Marilyn!' Judith swore when the rumours got back to her. 'You come on over here tonight, Ray. Stephen is out of town and Brandon and Nick have some dumb-ass party to go to. We'll have us a party too. Get that husband of yours to mind the kids.'

When I got there, Shula was already ensconced, glass in hand. Beth arrived soon afterwards.

'Ray, I'm so sorry.' She was nearly in tears. 'Did I

start this? I just heard about Nancy. That woman has the IQ of plankton. I swear, when I stopped Brooke coming, it wasn't out of badness. I wanted her to be more independent.' She chewed her nails. 'That's all it was. It had nothing to do with stupid Marilyn. I didn't know other people would take their kids away too!'

'Don't you hear anything?' Shula demanded. 'Two other people pulled their kids out right after you did.'

'I wasn't paying attention,' Beth wailed. 'That Carrera woman had me hiding under a sheet with my phone off! And then Curtis started coming round again and we all know what you', she glared at Judith, 'think about that. So I decided to lay low while I figured a few things out.'

'You were figuring out more than just Curtis, sugar. Didn't a certain eighth-grade math teacher start to call around to see you, in sympathy?'

I put my glass down in case I spilled my drink. 'Beth! Are you seeing someone?'

She cocked her head on one side and studied her toes. I looked at them too. I should have known. Beth isn't usually a nail-varnish kind of person. 'Who is he? Why didn't you tell us?'

'His name is Graham. And we're not an item. Exactly. He's Brooke's teacher.'

'Not next year, he won't be,' Judith said.

'Well.' Shula glared at both of them. Then she turned on me. 'You're worse! If you'd told me why you weren't taking the kids any more, I wouldn't have minded so much. I thought you'd flipped. Why do you never tell us anything?'

'It's because she's Irish.' Judith sucked stray tequila off her fingers and popped her lips in appreciation. 'You think I'm joking? Centuries of keeping secrets had to seep into the gene pool somehow.'

'Stop,' Shula said.

'Withholding information, then. Call it what you want. Refusing to co-operate with the authorities.'

I laughed outright. 'Since when are you the authorities?'

'When it comes to margaritas, I am.'

No one could argue with that. Before long they had filled me in on the versions of Marilyn's story that had come back to them. Luckily, Nancy had told people to ask Beth what went on in my house, since she was the first person to withdraw her child.

'I told them, sure, I know what's going on. She wants her life back! Is that a crime? I feel so bad!'

'All that stuff about you making a play for Byron!' Shula snorted. 'Where were all those children supposed to be when that happened? Where were you supposed to find the energy?'

'She sure acted like she had something on you.' An expression of hope dawned on Judith's face. 'Did she? Was there something . . . ?'

'Do you know, the only other person who ever asked me that was Michael,' I said.

'Yeah,' Beth said. 'You and Michael could have been real good buddies, Judith.'

It was the first time I'd heard her say Michael's name without bitterness. I raised my glass to her. Judith went into the kitchen and came out with a bowl of passion-fruit salad.

'Eat up girls. Let's get beautiful. You are what you eat, remember!'

'You are who you love,' Beth said. 'And who they love as well, like it or not!'

'No,' Shula said. 'You are what you do.'

'Ha!' Judith snapped to attention. 'So, who are we?' She settled on the sofa and plumped up the overstuffed cushions at her back.

'I'm a taxi service,' Shula began.

'I'm a cleaner. I clean. It was easy to find work that way once I started looking for it.' Beth was thoughtful. She looked at her reddened hands.

'A household sanitation expert,' Judith corrected her. 'You've got to talk it up. And Shula's a transport engineer.'

'What am I, then?' I asked.

'An educational facilitator!' Beth said.

Judith fell back on her scarlet cushions. Her shoulders began to shake, and then she laughed out loud. 'Girl, I tell you, when I was married to my ex, sex is what I did for a living. I didn't even like the guy and I had to ball him three, four times a week. As soon as I saw it, I got myself a real job and got the hell out of there.'

We all laughed, but I was uneasy. I couldn't remember the last time Dermot and I had made love and meant it.

21

I hated the way the radio alarm burrowed into my brain first thing in the morning, leaving no room for reverie. The day right there, other people's lives. But Dermot couldn't wake up without it. I shoved my head under the pillow, tried to pretend the distant noise was the sound of the sea, but the advertising jingles drove me out of bed every time.

'You see?' Dermot said. 'It works!'

One morning, though, we lay there and listened while the commentator described how the Berlin Wall had come down. Overnight, Europe had changed. I felt a strange mixture of excitement and loss. I wished I was there. The commentator's voice was high and excited, like someone reporting a football match. I went around in a daze that day. How could something so absolute have been dismantled so easily? Was that all it took, that enough people march up to it and pull it apart?

Later in that same week, there was horrific news. There'd been a grisly find in the desert outside El Paso. A container truck with several bodies, people who'd suffocated in intense heat, abandoned by the people they'd paid to smuggle them across the border from Mexico.

That day was a holiday, but Dermot went in to

work anyway to finalize a patent application. All morning I switched from channel to channel, riveted, only half paying attention to the children. This story was as compelling as a storm warning, as if it had something to do with me directly. The people who had died were women and children as well as men, all desperate for work.

When Beth showed up for coffee, we went outside to take a break from it. I needed to see the sky. First Judith and then Ellen drifted over to talk to us.

'Well, honey, they should've stayed where they belonged.'

'Ellen! They must have been desperate to get in that truck in the first place.'

'If they could pay that much to get here, why couldn't they live on that money where they were?'

'They probably borrowed it. Or sold everything they had to get it,' Judith said.

'Imagine the terror,' Beth said. She took Grace from me and held her close, as if for comfort. At last, she was painting again. Stains had begun to reappear on her fingers, to streak her clothes.

Hunter stood up from the drive, shook his dusty coat and came to join us in the shade of the porch. He lay under my chair, his tongue showing.

'Imagine the heat.' I shivered. No one said anything for a while. I put down my coffee cup. It seemed a travesty to drink it.

The others watched me sort out a row between Ben and Jack over a tricycle. I persuaded Ben onto the smaller one and steered them both off to the safe end of the street.

'We were there once,' I said when I came back. 'Not fifty miles away from where they found that truck. We were stopped by a border patrol, taken to a trailer in the middle of nowhere and kept there for hours while they phoned the whole world to see if we were legal. I knew we were, and I was still scared. No one else knew where we were. *I* didn't even know where we were. No trees, no landmarks. Just buzzards and hawks. And sun.'

Ellen went to say something but I held up my hand. 'You know what, Ellen? Whatever it is, please don't say it.'

'I was just—'

'I mean it,' I said. Although by then I was spoiling for a fight.

'—that Ben is headed straight for that tree.'

My ears burned while I hauled Ben out of the tree he was still too small to climb. I brought him back with me on a promise of juice and cookies. He ran ahead of me through the garage.

'Trust me', I said to Ellen, 'to put my foot in my mouth. I'm sorry.'

'Apology accepted,' Ellen said with her strange formality, bowing her head.

Hannah was growing up. She turned moody and secretive, blushed easily, spent hours on the phone. There was a boy who called her every night.

'Who is this Daniel?' I asked.

'A friend.'

'Well, Hannah, I know *that*. But how come he calls you so late? Next time he calls that late I'm going to tell him he can't speak to you.'

'Don't you *dare*!' Hannah yelled. Then she burst into a storm of crying. Alarmed, I backed down. But the next day I took it up again.

Daniel, it turned out, was a boy whose father had died the year before. His mother worked night shifts in a factory and he got lonely in the apartment on his own.

'She leaves him on his own and he's only ten?' I asked.

'Daniel's eleven,' Hannah said, and stalked away.

'Stay out of it,' Beth warned.

'But Beth, he shouldn't be on his own. Someone should know . . .'

Beth's face closed. 'There are things you'll never understand, Ray. The boy is still making it into school every day, isn't he? He's eating, he's got a home and a mother. She's doing just fine.'

'What does your friend Graham say about this sort of thing?'

'Graham is a smart man,' she said. 'He knows when to back off.' She stared off after Hannah. 'Sometimes that kid of yours has more sense than you do. You know what she said to Brooke the other day?' She looked sheepish all of a sudden. 'I probably shouldn't tell you. But she said, "I'm worried about Lucie. She needs a friend." Hannah's growing up, girl. Like it or not.'

*

Marilyn was taken off to hospital later that month. I saw her leave the house, clinging to Byron's arm. Her head was bent and her hair hung lank around her face. She wore an oversized T-shirt over baggy shorts, the kind of clothes I wore all the time, but on Marilyn they looked shocking, out of character. Her legs were stick thin. I pretended not to look as she folded herself into the car. Byron closed the door gently, as if she was a new baby or a very elderly lady. He never looked in my direction. There was no sign of Lucie. I went inside and watched the kids from there until they'd driven away.

Later, I heard from Ellen that Marilyn had gone to a psychiatric unit in the Medical Center. I brought a casserole over to Byron the next day, to add to the usual collection. It was getting so as I could recognize other people's dishes from this sympathy circuit. I'd been on the receiving end when I'd had Ben and then Grace. Beth had been looked after this way after Curtis left. When Bill had to go into hospital for minor surgery, we'd all brought food to Norma. Ellen always won out in the presentation department. She liked to finish things off with tartan covers, coloured ribbons around the necks of jars, that sort of thing. And she always brought something baked, for dessert. I'd forgotten dessert.

'Is she allowed visitors, Byron?'

He was absorbed in trying to remove a stain from the kitchen counter. I thought he was embarrassed because we hadn't spoken properly since the incident with Marilyn on my porch. I wondered if he knew what she'd said about him and me. I took a step away from him, just in case, and bent to pick Grace up from the armchair where I'd dumped her so as I could slide my casserole dish onto the table. I swung her up to my hip and she twined her fingers into the collar of my shirt and tugged hopefully.

'Not now, Gracie.' I prised her fingers loose.

'Uh, she won't be allowed visitors for a while.'

'Well, let us know,' I said. 'Can I help with Lucie?'

'Uh, no. Thanks. We're fine.'

'Are you sure? What about work?'

At last he looked at me. Just for a second, then he looked away again. He shoved his hands deep into the pockets of his trousers. 'Thing is, Ray, Marilyn doesn't want you to take Lucie. She has this – thing. That they'll take Lucie from her, and somehow she'll end up with you.'

'That's crazy!'

He shrugged. 'She figures you're this earth-mother type. You have babies so easily. See, we never could have another after Lucie.'

'I'm sorry, Byron. I didn't know.'

Ellen and Judith went down to the Medical Center to see Marilyn when she was finally allowed visitors. They said she seemed smaller than she was before, and that she spoke more slowly, her voice flattened out by drugs.

'Does she have to stay on them?' I asked. 'For how long?'

'They'll wean her off eventually,' Judith said. 'She'll come home first, and see how she gets on.'

'She wants to see you,' Ellen told me. 'She asked us to ask you to go in.'

Byron came with me because that's what Marilyn wanted. I couldn't help feeling nervous as we went up together in the wide hospital lift. What if they had planned some bizarre revenge for whatever damage I was meant to have done? I suddenly wished I'd insisted on a witness too, like seconds in an old-fashioned duel. Even Grace, but I'd left her with Dermot.

Marilyn was on the top floor of a seven-storey building and I wondered about the wisdom of having a psychiatric unit up that high, until we went into her room and I saw her windows. They were a bit like ours, only thinner – angled slits you couldn't put a fishing rod through, never mind a person.

Marilyn looked as if she was working on getting small enough to slip through the cracks. Her collarbones looked about ready to poke through her skin. I was shocked when I saw how grey her hair was. She wore the same big T-shirt and a pair of nondescript trousers. I would have walked past her on the street.

I'd brought a stack of magazines. *People* and *Vogue* and *Vanity Fair*. Byron stood by the window and looked out as if there was something fascinating happening in the car park, while Marilyn and I talked about celebrities for a while, the generalized, harmless gossip of the world that lets you talk to people for as long as you have to without saying anything at all.

But Marilyn was determined to have her say. 'I've

been weird,' she said at last, peering out through the narrow opening in the curtain of her straggly hair. 'I never meant you no harm, Ray.'

I could hear Byron turn behind me.

'Or, I did, but it wasn't me. I wasn't right. My head wasn't working right. I thought – strange things. Things that weren't real. About you.'

'Okay.' I didn't know what else to say.

'I know I was wrong. And it was me who made those stupid phone calls, to scare you. I'm sorry.'

'Forget it.'

She brightened a little. 'See? I even let Byron come in here with you. Shows how much better I am!'

We all laughed, the uncomfortable laugh of people who'd rather eat nails than be in the same room as each other ever again.

'I'll tell everyone I was sick, that none of it was true.'

She looked so small and fragile, sitting in an institutional armchair, knotting and unknotting her bony fingers on those cheap, ugly trousers. I could feel something pop in my chest, as if air was leaking from my lungs. If she was a child I'd have taken her on my knee and smoothed that tangled hair, told her everything was going to be all right.

'It really doesn't matter, Marilyn. I don't care. Most of our friends have figured it out by now anyway. No one blames you. You just think about getting better.'

I touched her hand before leaving. It was as dry and brittle as one of the silk flowers beside her bed.

Lilies. Why do people bring lilies to sick people, even fake ones?

'How is she?' Dermot asked.

I told him what Marilyn had said. 'But she looks awful. Not herself at all. As if all the colour has been drained out of her. It must be the drugs.'

'Good enough,' Dermot said. 'If they keep her quiet. Why are you looking at me like that? The woman is dangerous. She's never done you any favours, that's for sure.'

You don't always notice changes when they start to happen. It's only later, when you look back, that you can begin to sort out what was before, and what came after. Any fool could have seen the 'For Sale' signs that went up overnight in almost every second house in the neighbourhood and beyond, but somehow I'd missed it.

'The company's stock is sliding,' Dermot said. 'JP is introducing economy measures. People who leave aren't being replaced. It doesn't look good.'

'Do you think the company will fold?'

'We'll most likely file Chapter Eleven first. It's the first step – it buys us time, protects us from creditors for a while.'

'Should you look for another job?'

'Ray, this is happening all over town. Haven't you noticed? People are leaving.'

The expression on his face was one of impatience,

even outright dislike. I'd seen him look at Marilyn that way. It brought me up short. I tried to remember if I'd seen him look at me that way before. The trouble was, I wasn't aware of having looked at him properly for quite a while. When he came in from work, tired and irritable, ready to jump on the kids for the slightest thing, I was busy trying to keep the peace, trying to wind everyone down towards bed. In keeping the kids out of his way when he was moody, I'd stayed away from him myself.

And then, physically exhausted, raw from Grace's hugs, nervy from the constant high-stream chatter of other people's children as well as my own, all I wanted was silence and a little bit of space. I stayed up late until I knew that Dermot was asleep, and slid carefully into bed to avoid waking him. But even in sleep, his body found mine and pressed itself against me.

One day I ran into Diane at the mall and we went for coffee. I put Grace in a highchair, tucked Bat in beside her, and gave her a piece of bread to chew on to keep her busy.

Diane darted me a look, as if something was burning her up.

'What is it?'

At last she admitted that there was a man she fancied. 'I think he likes me too. What should I do?'

'Go for it,' I said. 'Julian treats you like shit, Diane. You deserve something good for yourself. Just do it.'

'Do you really think so?' She sat up straighter.

'What would you do, though,' she went on, 'if Dermot had an affair?'

'Sometimes I wish he would.'

'You can't be serious!'

'I feel touched-out,' I explained to Diane's shocked face. 'Maybe I've had too many children.'

Grace shrieked. The bread had broken into gooey crumbs and fallen to the tray. She wailed while I mopped it up and gave her a cup of milk to drink instead.

'I'm sorry, Diane. I know you have a rough time with Julian and that you think I'm lucky. This is just how I feel today. You've caught me at a bad time.'

Judith was called out of town again, to look after her elderly father. She and Steve came over to see us the night she got back.

'Daddy can't live on his own any more,' she said. 'We've talked about it. Steve's company is about to file. We're going to move to Atlanta.'

'No, Judith, you can't go! What'll I do without you?'

'It's only a matter of time before I lose my job,' Steve said.

'We may as well go now, get the boys into school,' Judith added. 'My dad needs me, and he has a house already. We can live on what we get for this one until we find something else.' She made a face. 'Not that we'll get much, from what I'm hearing.'

'Things'll turn around,' I argued.

'Not fast enough for me,' Steve said. 'Not for anyone

in the oil business. Who knows how long this downturn will last? I'm going to go back to college and get me an MBA, find me a more stable field to get into. It's what most people are doing.'

Even Ellen's eyes were red when we stood on Judith's drive and waved them off. 'It's so romantic,' she sighed. 'That girl set her sights on Stephen and moved right on in. I thought she'd walk all over him in those pretty little boots of hers, but look, they've got themselves a whole new life.'

'Yeah, in Atlanta,' Beth muttered. 'He won't be able to stand it. You wait and see. Texas is in that boy's blood. He'll be back.'

Beth and Ellen were like peas in a pod in those days. Some kind of latent Texan nationalism had been stirred in them. The more people who left, the more entrenched they became.

'It's a kind of self-defence,' Dermot said.

I didn't feel entitled to say that I felt it too, that the storm-cupboard mentality had broken out in me as well. All I wanted was to find a safe part of the house and burrow in deep, sit it out until it passed.

When the next big storm hit, I was ready for it. Ever since the first one, I kept a high shelf in the closet stocked with essentials. Canned food, water, batteries, candles, a pocket knife, matches. We'd had so many warnings and false alarms, storms that changed course at the last minute and vented their wrath on the coast to the south or east of us, that I was quite blasé about it by now.

I'd made up my mind to keep my distance from Angie, but all the same, I thought she might not be watching TV or listening to a radio. For all I knew, she'd never been through a storm like this before. I remembered how I'd felt before my first hurricane, years earlier. At the very least someone should warn her it was coming.

When the heavy rain started, I went to her door and knocked loudly. 'Angie!' I called. 'Just to let you know, there's a hurricane coming. Turn on your television.'

Tony had recently bought a new Ford sedan, and the rusting Toyota sat unused, day after day, out on the street. It caught my eye on the way back to my house and I wondered what to do about it. Later, when the first signs of flooding appeared at the corner, I ran across the rain-drenched space of our driveway onto Angie's porch. The wind roared up behind me.

'Angie, it's me! Can you hear me?'

At last the door swung open.

'The water.' I pointed at the corner. 'You should move the car.'

Angie shrugged. 'It no matter.'

'I'll move it for you, if you like. I mean, if you can't drive.'

'I drive.'

A gust of wind knocked me off balance and Angie had to catch her door and hold it.

'Okay,' I said and ran back for the shelter of my own

house. I called Dermot in his hotel in Denver, just to talk to someone normal.

'Maybe they're after an insurance deal,' he said. 'Where are the kids?'

I surveyed the wreck of our living room. 'They're playing desert island. Ben is dashing his ship on the rocks as we speak.'

Ben stood with his legs splayed across the hollow of the papasan chair, rocking it violently. Sofa cushions were scattered everywhere. Hannah and Jack were building a tent out of a sleeping bag. Grace was practising pulling herself up on the cushions and then pushing herself further, to stand. When she fell, she looked surprised and then offended, then she started all over again. Bat lay in a crumpled heap on the floor beside her. The TV was on in the background, with the volume down.

'Good. Stay dry. I'll call you later.'

When the phone eventually rang, just after the power went out, it was Joanne. 'I thought you'd be Dermot,' I said.

'I heard you'd a hurricane coming. Are you all right?'

'We're okay. The power just went, but the storm doesn't seem too bad.'

'Are the kids scared?'

I looked into the hallway where the children were camped out in sleeping bags, all asleep. 'No, they've conked out. They've turned the hall into a tent. And I've a torch set up in there.'

'Where's Dermot?'

'He's away, at a trade fair. He's promoting the chip. But it's okay. It's not a huge storm. We're fine.'

Dermot first said that we should go home on the night he came back from that business trip. He'd been in Denver for three nights, and I wanted to hear about the mountains. But he came in quiet and tired. When I told him the children were asleep already he didn't bother to check on them. I couldn't remember that ever happening before. No matter how late he came in from work, no matter how bitter an argument we were having, Dermot would never pass up an opportunity to go and watch the children sleep.

We sat up late that night, talking. Dermot stretched out along the sofa and propped his feet on the arm. I lifted his legs and slid under them, sat with his feet in my hands and held them while he told me about his trip.

'I nearly got a speeding ticket.'

'How did you get out of it?'

'The weirdest thing.' He took his feet out of my hands and sat up. 'I'd had a few beers. I was driving back to the motel and I heard a siren. The last thing I needed. The lights were changing. I stopped dead and so did the guy behind me. I was over the line, so I edged backwards and tipped his bumper.'

'Wow.'

'I know. So, I wait for the cop to come to the window. I watch him in the mirror. He stops at the car behind. If ever I prayed in my life, that was it. Then he comes along, looks at the back of my car, shakes his head, comes on over to me. I'm sweating bricks at this stage.'

'I bet you were. What happened?'

'He's as polite as you please. Asks for my licence, looks at it, nods, taps it off his notebook. "Is there a problem, officer?" I ask. And he says "No, sir, you can go. You won't believe it, but this character is under the influence. He claims that you backed into him." He shakes his head . . .' Dermot shook his head too, remembering. Then he went on with the story. 'The cop says, "There's no damage to either vehicle that I can see, sir. Would you care to check?" I smile and say no, I never felt a thing. Then I get out of there as fast as I can.'

I thought about this. 'The other guy was drunk, too?'

'I never said I was drunk. I just didn't know if I'd pass a test. But he sure as hell wouldn't. He was walking the line when I left. No point in both of us getting caught, was there?'

I got up and went to the fridge for more beer, just for something to do. My mind wouldn't be still.

'Where's your sense of humour, Ray?'

'I'm just tired.' I shrugged off my unease. I was glad that he was back. The house always seemed too quiet without him. 'And I can't help feeling sorry for the other guy.'

'What would you have me do? Confess? Spend the night in a cell? Lose my licence for definite and maybe the green cards? If he hadn't been pissed as a newt, he wouldn't have got into trouble in the first place.'

'No. No, of course not.' I bit down on the suggestion that if the other driver hadn't said that Dermot backed into him, the cop might have paid less attention to him.

'This is the real world we're talking about, Ray. There isn't always room for your precious principles.' Dermot sounded bitter. 'Everything's always black and white for you, isn't it? Things are one way or the other. Good or bad. Right or wrong.'

'What are you talking about?' Something new and dangerous had crept into the room and crouched, just out of sight, between us.

'What do you know about getting out there every day and dealing with the real world, real cases, hard facts?'

I was stung. Dermot often said that I lived in a cocoon of home, friends, neighbourhood. He said it was easy to have principles and ideals when they didn't cost you a thing. It was his way of winning an argument. It usually worked. I hated it.

'Have you ever stopped to ask yourself,' I said, my voice low and bitter, 'exactly why it is that I live like this?'

He marched past me to the fridge and tugged the door open, pulled out a can of beer and popped it open. 'Oh, here we go,' he said. 'My choices. My job. Your life on hold . . .'

'It's true!' I stamped my foot, willing myself not to cry or shriek or do anything he could sneer at.

He snapped his head around and stared at me. Up close, he could have been a stranger. I hadn't registered, until then, that he was getting older. His face was fleshier than it used to be and there were new lines around his eyes.

'I'll tell you what, then,' he said. 'We'll go home.'

'What?' I pulled back, startled. Then I laughed. It was so unexpected.

'Why are you laughing? That's what you want, isn't it? To go home?'

'*Wanted*, Dermot. It's what I *wanted*. Past tense. I don't know what the fuck I want any more.' I left the room, furious.

'Let me know when you find out,' he called after me. As if only my indecision stood between me and whatever I wanted.

The next morning we were cautious with each other. 'Did you mean what you said?' I asked. 'About going home?'

He put down his coffee. 'Yes.'

'But what about . . .' I swept my arm around in a gesture that included the house, the kids sprawled on the floor in front of the television, half asleep, the neighbourhood beyond the front door . . . 'your job?'

'Ray, the company is about to go down the tubes. We've talked about this. There's a recession coming in this state.' He corrected himself. 'No, wait, it's already here.'

'Is that why you've been so distant?' Relief washed

over me. Was that all? There I'd been, imagining that he hated me, that he was angry for some reason and all he'd been worried about was his job. I wanted to sing, or laugh. We'd weathered job trouble before, I knew we could do it again. I should have asked him sooner, but I'd been afraid of what I might hear. 'You'll find something else. You know you will. Everyone knows how good you are.'

'Eventually. If I'm lucky. I don't know that I have the stomach for it, Ray. There's nothing to hold us here.'

I opened my mouth to protest, but he was unstoppable. I shut my mouth again.

'I don't know why we've stayed so long. We should go home.'

'What about the kids?'

'That's why we should go now. Before it's too late.'

'Don't bully me, Dermot. Not about this.'

'We may not have an option, Ray. You must have seen . . . I *told* you.'

'Let's wait and see.' I thought he'd change his mind. It was too big a decision to make so casually.

As if there was a conspiracy to force our hand, Pat called one Friday afternoon while Dermot was still at work.

'I'm sorry to be so blunt about this,' she said, 'but we've been told that Conall has cancer. Bowel cancer. We heard today. They're not sure about the outcome.' Her words were brittle and sharp. 'There will be surgery, radiotherapy, chemotherapy, God knows what.'

Her voice broke then. 'I'm sorry, Ray. I promised Conall I wouldn't do this.'

'What – tell us?'

'No. Weep all over you. Will you tell Dermot? I don't know if I could bear to do it.'

Dermot didn't flinch when I told him. Calm, he stared off into space. 'You see?' he said. 'It's time to go back.'

I could have said that there had always been that danger of loss, illness, accident, death. Sooner or later we'd all die. The biggest cliché in the world and the most terrifying to look in the face. But I knew what he meant, all the same. Knowing in advance like this, an actual diagnosis, brought you up short. You had to decide, then, what to do. Stay or go. Live or die. I shook myself. What was I thinking?

'Come home!' Joanne sang down the phone. 'It'll be brilliant! And things have really changed, Ray. You won't know the place. You'll never guess – it looks as if Mary Robinson is going to run for president. Imagine!'

I vaguely remembered that Mary Robinson was a lawyer who'd taken on unpopular cases to do with civil and reproductive rights. A lot of people hated her for it. A lot of people loved her for it. Who'd win? 'Do you think she'll get it?'

'Don't sound so doubtful. Get over here and work on the campaign.'

'You know that's not my thing, Joanne.'

'You can lick an envelope, can't you? You can answer a phone? It'll give you something to do. A way to meet people. Come on, Ray. It'll be fun.'

'Maybe. Let's see what happens.'

It was later on that day, or maybe the next, that Brian Lacey, an old college friend of Dermot's, called from Ireland to say that he was setting up a business, that everything had changed, that things were opening up in a way that no one would ever have imagined. He wanted Dermot to go and work for him, with his design expertise and his knowledge of the American market. Afterwards I was never sure of the exact timing because it all began to blur, to take on a life of its own. Dermot went home by himself for a week, to visit Pat and Conall, to check out Brian's business plan. He came back beaming.

'Everything is going to be fine,' he told me.

'How's Conall?'

'Ready for the fight. They're excited about us going home.'

'Dermot – you told them? But we haven't decided yet.'

He looked confused. 'Yes we have. Don't you remember?'

When all the arguments had been exhausted, the work began on the freeway extension, out in the space beside our house, between the two halves of the neighbourhood. One morning we woke up to find that bulldozers, diggers, and cherrypickers had massed like an army along our borders overnight. A constant mechanical din began as the earth was laid bare. Trees and shrubs were torn up by the roots and tossed aside. Deep trenches of black mud appeared in the ground, with cylindrical pipes stacked alongside them.

And then the rats appeared.

I went out to the garage to take clothes out of the dryer one night. When I switched on the light I thought I saw a blur of shadow out of the corner of my eye. I definitely heard a faint rustle.

'Hello?' I called. 'Li? Is that you?'

No answer. I told myself it was nothing, filled the basket with clothes and brought them inside to fold them. But after a while I couldn't ignore it any more – every time I went out there, I was disturbing something.

'Rats,' Tyler said. He was on his way to buy traps from the hardware store. 'I'll get you some.'

He had gone before I could say I didn't want

them. Dermot insisted we should use them. 'Even you couldn't possibly want to tolerate rats.'

Local boys came out like a gang of vigilantes. They carried sticks and baseball bats and crept around garages and sheds. I was afraid that one of those boys would lose his fingers to our traps. As soon as they were primed and Dermot came back inside, we could hear the staccato *Rap! Ratatat!* of the traps closing. I made him go out to empty them. After a week or so the traps, still making their sudden music, turned up empty.

'They're too smart for us,' Dermot said. 'We'll have to get an exterminator.'

I called Randy, but all I got was a message on his machine to say that he'd left town. The company sent someone else out to poison the rats, but he was dour and unfriendly, nothing like Randy. When I asked, he said that he'd no idea where Randy had gone.

Even though the company was in trouble, the office party went ahead that year, early in the summer. The party had been booked and paid for a year before, so they decided to honour the bookings, with a few changes, like having a cash bar instead of free beer. The children weren't included. It felt like a leaving party, and not just for us. Everyone knew that Chapter Eleven was just around the corner.

The party was held in the back room of a motel south of the county line. There was a faux pond outside, faux wooden piers. A model pirate ship drifted on shallow water. Inside, stuffed parrots were glued to perches over gangplanks, papier-mâché cutlasses drooped on the walls. There was an irritating sound-track, the sound of a ticking clock. The waiters wore patches over their eyes and had hooks dangling from their sleeves. The waitresses wore low-cut blouses and short skirts under frilly aprons.

'Good God,' I said.

'The kids would love it.' Dermot was defensive.

'So would Michael.' For the first time in ages, I felt a pang of loss for Michael's irreverence.

Pitchers of Cap'n Hook's Revenge, a drink the colour of blood, were set up on tall caskets around the room. A real stuffed alligator, whose glassy eye I preferred not to meet, was mounted on the bar.

As the evening wore on, things broke down. Janelle from accounts told J. P. Fischer exactly what she thought of him and his stupid economy measures. 'I mean, is this for real?' she squeaked. 'You seriously plan to take out every second lightbulb in the building? Are you nuts?'

JP walked off to join a small knot of men gathered in a corner under a sad-looking rigging with gangrenous starfish glued to its sides. The men's ties were loosened or stuffed into their pockets, their faces flushed and shining.

Diane and I tried to reassure Janelle that she would still have a job on Monday, that JP would forget all about it. 'He's pretty relaxed,' I told her. 'And anyway this kind of thing happens at office parties all the time. It's expected. It's practically what they're for!'

'Like that lot over there.' Diane stared over at the rowdy group in the corner. Julian was in the middle of it. We could hear his voice booming out a punchline and there was a roar of appreciation from the crowd.

'Is Dermot somewhere in there?' I craned to see. I was bored and I wanted to go home.

'Dermot is such a sweetheart,' Janelle sighed into my ear. 'A real sweetie. You're so lucky.'

I caught Diane's eye. She stood up. 'I'll see if I can find him,' she said, nodding at Janelle's head, settled comfortably on my shoulder. 'I'm on my way to the restroom anyway.'

She was gone a long time. I left Janelle in the capable hands of her friends, Debbie and Linda, and went looking for Diane. I found her sitting beside Julian in the centre of that loud group who were having too good a time. There was no sign of Dermot, but Genie, his secretary, was there and she made room for me at the table. 'He said he'd be back in a minute,' she told me. 'Pit stop, I think. Or maybe he was looking for you.'

I squashed in beside her.

'Diane is the only person I know who's ever talked her way out of anything with the Highway Patrol,' Julian was saying. His face was flushed and his no-crease polo shirt looked slightly the worse for wear.

I listened while Julian told a story that mimicked a degree of simpering and exaggerated eye movements, a flick of imaginary perfect hair. I looked at Diane to see how she was taking it. It was hard to tell whether this story was meant to show her in a good or a bad light. Diane's reaction gave nothing away. Her eyes were veiled and she rolled a glass of wine between the palms of her hands, stared at its shadow on the wooden surface of the table. Afterwards, I remembered the feeling that washed over me, like a smell. *These two people really do hate each other.* No one else seemed to notice.

'. . . and she got off with a warning.' Julian sat back, pleased with himself. I wondered whether to go and look for Dermot and drag him home. I'd had about enough. I got ready to stand up, but Diane had started telling a story of her own.

'I'm not the only one,' she said. 'Listen to this one.'

She leaned forward, looked into everyone's face in turn. Her eyes rested on mine for a second too long and my stomach turned. Was she going to tell a story about the man she'd told me about? Surely she wasn't about to get her revenge on Julian right here, in front of everyone?

I sat still, to listen.

Directly across the table from me, Julian's face was slightly damp, out of focus, flushed from too much beer.

'. . . So there we are, stopped at the light. And we hear the sirens. And he looks in his mirror,' Diane was saying.

'Who?' I asked.

Diane gave me a look from under her fringe. Did I imagine it or did she flush a little? She certainly hesitated. 'This guy I know. He was . . . giving me a ride.'

I smiled to myself. Did she say that deliberately? It was hard to tell with Diane, she was such a chameleon. There were words that were innocuous in one place that could be explosive in another. I'd tripped over most of them through the years that I'd been here. Crack. Rubber. Republican. Ride. I looked at Julian's rubbery lips, listened to the edge in Diane's voice.

'. . . and he reversed a little, just to get back over the line. And we heard glass breaking. And we waited. I didn't dare look around. He was staring in his mirror and he told me what he saw. *Here they come. No, wait. They're talking to the other guy.*'

I shook my head. There seemed to be water in my ears. I couldn't be hearing her properly.

'. . . and then they come over to us. He opens his window, gets ready with his excuse, but we don't need it.'

'What happened?' someone asked.

I lurched to my feet. My drink spilled across the table. I ignored it. I let it spread while people shuffled out of the way, trying to protect their clothes. Genie pounded at the mess with a pile of paper napkins.

'They told him to drive on,' I said, in a trance. I could feel that Dermot had come up behind me. I turned around to include him. 'What was it, Dermot? "Drive on, sir. This man is so drunk he claims you backed into him." That's right, isn't it?' I turned back to Diane. 'Isn't it? Only you got one thing wrong, Diane. There was no glass. Nothing got broken.'

Just my life. Just my stupid heart. I shook so hard I had to sit down again.

Someone laughed.

'What's going on?' Genie asked.

Julian's eyes flashed from me to Diane and back again. 'Is this some kind of urban legend?' he asked.

'Why are you telling that story?' Dermot asked, not getting it yet. He frowned. 'Didn't I ask you to keep it to yourself?'

'You should have told her that.' I stabbed the air in Diane's direction. Diane flinched, as if she thought I might hit her.

Dermot looked from me to Diane and then over at Julian, whose eyes had closed.

For the longest time, all I could hear was the beat of my own heart and the sound of Genie pounding at the table with that stack of paper towels, as if cleaning up had any relevance to the knowledge that was opening like a poisoned flower between us all.

At last I was able to stand up again. 'I'm going home.' I pushed past Dermot.

'Ray, wait—'

I shook my head again, trying to clear it. 'No, Dermot. I'm done with waiting for you.'

Dermot looked so pale and shaken when I saw him again that I could almost pity him.

'I'm sorry,' he said.

'Sorry's not going to fix this, Dermot. It's too big. How could you?'

'Don't talk to me as if I'm one of your bloody children!'

We stared at each other, shocked.

'Don't do that,' he said, more quietly. 'I've had enough of that.'

I started to cry, hated crying, turned it into a shout instead. 'How could I have been so fucking stupid? It's such a cliché! I can't bear it.'

He let me scream until there was nothing left to say. 'Can I talk now?'

'No! Just get out. Leave me alone.'

'If that's what you want. But I just want you to know that I didn't sleep with her.'

He took down his travelling bag and started to pack.

'What's that supposed to mean? Do you think I'm thick?'

'No, I don't think you're thick.'

He walked past me to take socks from his drawer and I shrank back so that no part of him could touch me.

'I admit that I nearly slept with her. I was going to. But when it came down to it, I couldn't. I booked her a separate room. She left the next day, got an early flight back. I haven't seen her alone since.'

'I don't believe you.'

But, against my better judgement, I did. I thought that if he had slept with Diane, I'd have known somehow. Then again, what does anyone know? Look at poor Beth, who still swore blind she had no clue that Curtis was seeing anyone else, let alone a man.

'But you meant to,' I said.

He went on packing.

'This is easy for you,' I said. 'We're going home anyway. Our whole lives are about to change. You've had plenty of time to get used to the idea of you and Diane, but I have to adjust in about five seconds flat?'

'There is no "me and Diane".'

'Did it ever occur to you that I might not go with you?'

'Don't be ridiculous. Of course you'll come with me!'

'What's ridiculous? I have the green card now. I can stay if I want.'

'And what would you do for money? What about the children?'

'I'd think of something! Other people do.'

'You wouldn't leave me. You promised . . .'

'I used to think you'd never cheat on me.' I made my voice sickly sweet. 'You promised.'

Loathing and the need for violence were heavy in the air between us. One more word, one move in the wrong direction, would have tipped the balance.

Dermot took a deep breath. 'I'll go to a motel for a night,' he said. 'I'll ring you tomorrow and see what you want to do.'

I stared at the door for a long time after it shut behind him.

'We had a deal,' I said, my voice swollen and loose from crying, when he called. 'You promised you'd tell me if something like this was going to happen.'

'It will never happen again. I swear.'
I hung up.

'I wouldn't cross the road with you, the way I feel right now,' I told him the next time.

Then I called him in the middle of the night to tell him to go back alone, and that I hoped his plane would crash.

'What about the other 250 or so people on board?' He was only half awake and spoke as calmly as if this was a dream and it was the most normal thing in the world to hear so much hatred coming his way.

'They'd all survive, except for you.' I hung up.

Two minutes later I called back. 'I didn't mean it.'

'Why her? What did you see in her?'

'Ray, you can't keep phoning me in the middle of the night.'

'Why the hell not? I've nothing else to do! Tell me what you saw in her.'

'This won't help.'

'I want to know.'

'I thought she needed me.'

'And I didn't?'

'No.'

What the hell did he mean by that? Visions of Diane's bent head crossed my mind, her fine blonde hair sliding down the narrow stalk of her neck. Her way of breaking off her sentences as if she couldn't bear to finish them. Her brave, solitary air of holding herself together at all costs. She'd taken me in that way too. I'd always felt inferior when she was around, as if I could never aspire to her standards. Now I saw that she had cultivated that. I'd allowed it, yes, but she'd encouraged it.

I wondered why she'd set her sights on Dermot. Beth said it would probably hurt Julian more, to know that she'd been running round with one of his colleagues, and a junior one at that.

I wasn't so sure. I thought about, but didn't mention, the magic of Dermot's hands. The velvety texture of his skin and his sweet, musky smell. The way his face opened when he took his glasses off. How the sound of his voice could travel straight to the depths of a person, if that person was only open enough to receive it. I remembered the night when I had sat there and watched Dermot with her feet in his hands. How could I have been so stupid?

Pat phoned to see how the arrangements for our return were going. She listened to me drone on about our options with Hunter, as if our dog could possibly matter to her when her husband was dying. 'I'm sorry.' I stopped myself when I realized what I was doing. 'How's Conall?'

'It's so good for him to have the children to look forward to. I swear there's a difference in him already.'

I accused Dermot of putting his mother on to me, to make me feel guilty, but he swore he hadn't.

'I would have thought you knew her better than that, whatever about me,' he said.

'I'm not naïve enough to think I know anyone any more!' I shot back at him.

Sylvia kept phoning to say how pleased she was. Not that she'd say it quite like that. The things she said sounded more like warnings.

'It's not as easy over here as you think.'

'Have you looked into schools, yet?'

'House prices are going up. You'd want to get a move on.'

But I knew what she meant. At last, I was beginning to understand the furious, helpless rage of motherhood.

When Diane rang, I almost hung up on her. 'What do you want?' I snapped at last.

'Just to tell you that we never slept together.'

I tried to control my breathing.

'You know, it didn't bother you until you found it was Dermot,' she said.

'What the hell are you talking about?'

'You encouraged me. "Go ahead," you said, "you deserve something good in your life." Or words to that effect.'

'Not Dermot. I didn't mean Dermot.' I felt my voice snag on his name, like skin on barbed wire.

'It's always someone's Dermot,' she said.

'Julian never hit you, did he?' I'd been thinking about

this, about her wounded looks, her suggestive silences. About how she'd been upset that I didn't pass my suspicions on to Dermot.

'I never said he did. You know, if it had been some other woman's husband, you wouldn't have cared. You said it'd be a relief to you if—'

'Fuck off, Diane.' I slammed the phone down so hard that tears came to my eyes and all the small bones in my hand stung.

'She has some nerve.' Beth had come over with her new man, Graham, and they'd found me squeezing my own hand to bits, not able to see them properly.

'She's right, though. That's what's killing me.' I glared at Graham. 'What do you think?'

He threw his hands up, palms out, fingers wide. 'I don't have an opinion,' he said.

'I bet you do!'

'Easy, girl,' Beth said. 'This isn't Graham's fault.'

'I'll bet your husband is having a hard time at work, is what I think,' Graham said.

'Good!' I snapped.

'Man, I hadn't thought about that!' Beth puffed up her cheeks and tilted her head from side to side, imitating Julian as I'd described him to her.

I couldn't help laughing, but not for long. 'Beth, I'm losing my mind!' I wailed.

'Tell me about it,' she said. 'Graham, baby, didn't you say something about checking the oil levels in your car?'

'Sure.' Graham ambled out. I had never once seen him act as if he was in a hurry.

I swivelled around to look at Beth. 'You're not leaving town, are you?'

'No, Ray, that'd be you.' She peeled paint from around her nails, not looking at me.

'I haven't made up my mind yet. I might not go.'

That made her look up. 'Sure you will.'

'You think I should. I don't belong here.'

'Girl, that's crazy. What are you saying?'

'I don't know.' I could feel my face turn to rubber, as if I was going to cry. 'It's like, all these years I've sat out there and watched people come and go and I thought I had a handle on things, you know? And it turns out I got everything wrong. Every single thing. I didn't have a clue what was really going on. I was wrong about Michael, and about Diane – I was down-right stupid about Marilyn – and now Dermot.' I had to stop talking or I'd choke.

'You weren't wrong about me,' Beth said quietly. 'Or Judith. Or Ellen.' She caught my eye. 'Maybe Ellen, but just a little.'

I tried to smile. She came over and took my hand between her broad, capable ones. I looked at the stains around her nails, a long gash of crimson across her knuckles.

'I think I win in the getting-it-wrong stakes,' she said. 'It's not because of where you're from, it's how you are. You're out there, for everyone to see. More than most people.' She shook my hand a little. 'You think other people should be the same. But no one ever knows what's going on in someone else's head, or what's waiting for them around the next corner. None of us do. Don't hate yourself because you didn't see this coming.' She dropped my hands and stood up. 'Believe me, it's a waste of time. It's what you do now that matters.'

'What do you think I should do?'

'Think, Ray. What do you want most?'

'For none of this to have happened.'

'Well, did it? The way I see it, Dermot nearly cheated on you, but when it came right to it, he backed off.'

I shook my head.

Beth's voice slowed to a crawl. 'If I could have done anything to get Curtis back and keep our family together, I would have. But that was too big for us to fix, and I lost my best friend. You can still have yours, if you want him. Your kids can still have their daddy. You just think about that.'

I told Dermot to come home. The children missed him and so did I. I missed the sound of his voice, and his smell, and after the first few nights I even missed the feel of his body beside mine. 'Surly fucker that you are,' I said, angry because I missed him. Every little thing made me angry now. 'We have too much to talk about. We can't do it over the phone.'

In the end, I agreed to go back to Ireland with him because it was a chance for a completely fresh start, back where things had been best between us.

'I'll go home with you,' I told him. 'But I'm not promising that I'll stay with you once we get there.'

'You can't do that,' he said, red-faced with anger. 'You can't jerk me around like that. Make up your mind, one way or the other.'

All my philosophizing deserted me. 'Take it or leave it,' I said. 'There's no guarantee.'

We went to the swim-team parents' night to mark the end of the season, even though I wasn't sure I could face it.

'We have to do it. For Hannah,' Dermot said.

It would be a test. To be out in public as a couple again, to tell everyone our plans. I dreaded it.

'The end of an era, it feels like,' Beth said. 'How many of these people will be here again next year?'

All around us, people were talking about the changes. They named families who had left the area since the year before, remembered the swimming stars of last year, the promising kids and the awkward ones, wondered how they would have fared this year if they'd stayed. It struck me that next year, this is how they'd talk about us. I began to feel as if we'd already left, and now we were just going through the motions.

Everyone was talking about the new road and what it meant. 'Is there no way to stop them?' someone asked.

Sandy complained about losing her most talented swimmers. 'I hope Hannah will swim over there, in Ireland?'

'I'm not sure she can. Swimming isn't all that big over there.' I couldn't deal with her horror. I turned away to listen to the conversation about the road instead.

'We've always known it was coming,' Sandy's husband said.

'But why now?'

No one could explain it. The foreclosures had begun. Dermot told a story about a man who went to a city auction and bought a house on his credit card. 'Imagine. A house. For five thousand dollars.'

'I know someone who bought a condo for cash,' somebody else volunteered. 'One thousand.'

People shook their heads over the rising price of oil, interest rates, unemployment figures.

'Where will it end?' Sandy asked.

'It's like the end of the world,' someone said. No one contradicted her.

PART FIVE

Leaving

(Houston, 1990)

The gathering dark reminds me that I have no time to waste. The cicadas are frantic now, their last shrill roar before the night. And I still have no idea where Hannah might be. I should have noticed months ago that she's been practising how to hide from me, and not just physically. I know it's a cliché, but I really thought I'd get away with it, that we'd be able to reason our way through the changes in our lives. Even when I saw Brooke, the sweetest, most placid child I had ever known, flash her eyes at her mother and slam doors. Even when Shula told me about the antics of her oldest daughter, Riza, who was given to climbing out of her bedroom window after midnight to go walking through the neighbourhood with her boyfriend. Secretly I'd thought that Hannah and I would manage to avoid all that. I certainly never expected it to start so soon.

'Everything starts so early now,' Shula warned me. 'There's a girl in the sixth grade who had a baby last month.'

'Are you sure? She'd only be . . .'

'Twelve. And I've heard worse. A ten-year-old, down in Sugarland.'

'It's all those hormones in the meat,' Beth said.

Hannah's body has begun to change, but slowly. It's her mind that worries me.

I could stay here all night, in the soft, electric air. I suddenly know that I'll miss the cicadas when we leave. It's not only Hannah who'll have adjustments to make when we go back.

All the same, sitting on this park swing is not about to bring her out of hiding. I leave the park slowly, and the gate creaks shut behind me. For once, it doesn't snag my fingers.

'Ray? Any news?' Beth leans out of her car.

I'm so far lost in my own thoughts that I'm startled to find myself here, where I am, in the small car park with Beth calling out to me.

'Beth! Where did you get to?'

'I went home to get the car.'

'No news at home either, then?' I have trouble making my legs move. They seem to want to turn to some gelatinous substance that never heard of bearing weight.

'We could drive around some, if you like.'

I get into the passenger seat and it seems to me that I have never felt such luxury as the way that Beth's perfectly ordinary Dodge supports me and carries me along.

'Have you tried the pool?' Beth asks quietly.

'She wouldn't be able to get in there, would she?'

We look at each other. Dread pokes a finger down my throat, clutches my stomach.

Beth turns the car and we roar off towards the pool, two streets away.

The pool closes early on a Saturday, but the arc-lights are on in the car park. They throw shadows around the patio area, the maintenance hut, the lifeguard's stand, make it seem darker than it is. The water makes a sucking sound around the drains.

'I can't see anything,' I say.

'Nor can I. Wait here. I know someone who has a key.'

Beth disappears. I twist my fingers through the looped wire of the fence and strain to see the water. The half of the pool that I can see looks clear, undisturbed. But what if something is trapped at the bottom, or just around the corner? I tug at the fence and wonder if I'd be able to climb it. If I could, then Hannah could too. I walk around the perimeter, looking for holes in the wire, craning my neck to judge how high it is, what it would take to get through it. When I get back to the gate, Beth is there with Keri Summers, one of the lifeguards.

'I'm real sorry about Hannah, Miz Graves.'

I nod. I'm surprised that this teenager with her perfect teeth, her smooth brown skin and her velvety drawl knows my name.

Keri keeps talking as she unlocks the gate, but I don't listen. I rush over to the water while Keri flips a switch and light floods across the concrete and spills along the surface of the water. The navy-blue tiled lines waver at the bottom. No matter how hard I stare, I can see that there is nothing in that water. If not for the apparent movement of those dark tiles and the sound of the drains, there could be nothing there at all.

'. . . y'all are leaving,' Keri is still talking. 'Hannah could have swum for the middle-school team next year. I help coach 'em. I've been watching her. She's real talented.'

I pull myself away from the winking tiles. Of course. Keri is talking about Hannah's swimming. That's how she knows who I am. If she's been paying attention to Hannah in the water, she'd know who her mother was.

'Thanks for letting us in,' I say.

There's nothing else to do here. Keri turns off the light and locks the gate after us. We stand around, awkward.

'Hannah talks about you a lot, Keri,' I blurt out all of a sudden. 'She'd love to be like you. When she's older.' I step back, horrified by my own loose tongue. Hannah wouldn't forgive such a betrayal easily. But it's true. When Keri is on duty Hannah spends more time flipping off the low boards, racing her friends across the width of the pool and back down by the deep end, under the lifeguard's stand, diving for pennies.

Not that she'll be doing that any more. Now that we're leaving. First Hunter, now this. I can't bear to think any more about what Hannah is losing. I don't know why I haven't thought about it properly before. Going home seemed too natural for us to have to think about all the implications.

Blindly, I tug the heavy door of Beth's car open and get in. Beth touches Keri's arm in thanks and comes after me. She sits with her back against the driver's door, plays with her keys and waits for me to say something. I turn my head away and look at the darkening water.

'I knew she wouldn't be in there.'

I stare straight ahead of me on the drive home, as if I can make Hannah appear from the shadows between the houses, uncoil from a low-hanging tree branch, slide out from under a car, just by the force of looking. I'll prise her loose from anywhere and carry her home, no matter what. And if my own legs won't carry me, I'll fold myself up around her and hold her, right there on the street, until morning comes.

Don't be ridiculous, I tell myself. Hannah's all right. She's going to be all right. Don't let yourself think otherwise.

'. . . idea?'

'Hmm?'

'I said, we could do a house-to-house check along here? People might have seen her walk by.'

We're on Station Road. There's a fence at the end of this road, too, that will come down on Monday. The day we're due to leave, so long as we find Hannah.

I ignore the sprinklers at work on a perfectly kept lawn, and stride across it, so that when Bob Franklin wheels himself up to his front door and opens it to my knock, I drip water onto his porch.

'I'm so sorry, Ray,' he says, his hands spread on the

arms of his wheelchair. 'We heard about Hannah. Did you find her?'

Laurie appears at his shoulder. Laurie is a large woman. When she walks, she rolls a little from side to side. 'Oh, honey,' she says, when she sees me. She reaches into their guest bathroom beside the door and hands me a scented towel to dry myself with. I press my face into the rough fabric of the towel and rub, hard. When I put the towel back into Laurie's big, soft hands the skin on my face smarts and there are traces of lavender and lime under my nails.

'I wish I could get out there and look.' The knotted veins on the backs of Bob's strong hands bulge.

'Please come in,' Laurie says, but I refuse. I accept their hugs and their concern, their promises to call if they hear anything. Anything at all.

We knock on every door of that street and the small one that connects to the rest of the subdivision. Most times, it's a woman who answers. Some of them say that Dermot has been there before us and their men are already out looking. The women have been on the phone, spreading the word, asking for news. They tell me what they've heard, press my hands, pat my face. But I notice that they avoid meeting Beth's eye.

There's no answer at Marilyn's house. The front of the house is in darkness and the garage is closed. We peer over the side gate. The garden is shadowed but we can see that the wrought-iron chairs on the patio are angled down against the surface of the round table, so as not to trap water.

'I wonder when they'll be back?' I was surprised, this morning, by how hurt I felt when I heard that they had gone away without saying goodbye. Even after all the trouble there has been between us. Still, maybe it was just as well, to avoid one last scene. Now I wanted them back, if only so I could ask Lucie if she knew where Hannah could be.

'What time is it?' I ask Beth.

'A quarter of nine.'

Hannah has been missing for an hour and three-quarters.

'We should go back.' Suddenly, I know that she's at home, eating her pizza and waiting, sullen, for me to come in and give out to her. How could I have stayed away so long?

Brooke gives us a string of messages when we get in, but none of them is about Hannah. She says that Dermot called the police right after we left, and they said not to worry yet, to keep looking for her, that they'll send someone over as soon as possible. No, there's been no sign of them yet. Ben and Grace are already asleep. Jack has been restless. Dermot has gone out again, but not for long. He wants me to stay put when I get in. Ellen has dropped around a casserole and a loaf of banana bread from her freezer, because we need to eat something more substantial than pizza. Brooke is to make sure that I eat the casserole. The banana bread is for Hannah.

I play with the tinfoil covering of Ellen's casserole. When all else fails, women will still turn up with gifts of food.

'You go on in and get Jack settled,' Beth says. 'I'll stay out here by the phone.'

I don't know if I'll have the strength to leave Jack once I rest my head against the top bunk, where he's breathing heavily, his eyes closed. I'm not sure I'll be brave enough to straighten up from the sight of his small fists, knotted at his neck, the musky smell of his skin.

'Did you find her?' he asks.

I turn my face so that it's level with his. 'I thought you were asleep.'

He shakes his head violently from side to side but keeps his eyes closed.

'Do you have any idea where she might be, Jack? Where would you go, if you wanted to hide?'

'If I tell you, you'll always know where to find me.'

I catch my breath. 'That's exactly what I need, lovey.'

'There's the fort, in the park.'

'I've looked there.'

'And the glory hole.'

'I've looked there too.'

'And there's that kind of hut out on the Parkway.

The other side of the playground. Where the old man used to live.'

'Where?'

He tries to explain, but I can't think of the place.

'I've never seen it, Jack. Come out and tell the others.'

Dermot has come in while I was in the back of the house. When Jack has finished describing the hut, Dermot takes a torch and goes out to look. Beth flicks channels on the TV.

'I hear a car,' Brooke says.

We all go to the window, but it's only Shula pulling onto the drive. She lifts a cardboard box out of her trunk and carries it carefully in through the garage. 'I've brought food,' she says. She looks at Ellen's casserole and the remains of the pizza. 'Are you swamped?'

Beth puts on the kettle while Shula sits down and I tell her what's happened, where we've looked, who we've spoken to. Beth makes the tea Irish-style. She even remembers to warm the pot. We sit around the kitchen table to drink it.

'Ray, what will you do if she doesn't come back before you're due to leave?'

'Shula!' Beth is indignant.

'Do? What do you mean?' I'm confused. 'We'll stay here.'

'Yes, but where? Won't the new people be here? You'll have no furniture, nothing.'

'They'll stay with us,' Beth says.

'They can't do that for ever.'

I push back from the table. 'It won't be for ever. That's not going to happen. She'll come back. Dermot will walk through that door any minute and she'll be with him.'

'Yes, but . . .' Shula is insistent. 'What if she planned this? What if she means to make you stay? Laila says Hannah is beyond upset about leaving.'

'Why didn't you tell me?'

'I did, remember? You said she'd come round. But what if—'

'No. You're wrong. This is because of Hunter. He was the last straw.' I begin to tell her about the garage sale, but Beth interrupts.

'What if she's right, Ray? What if Hannah had a plan, and the dog was just an excuse?'

'It's too devious. Hannah's not like that!'

The room is suddenly quiet. Shula, whose teenager, Riza, is becoming notorious for her midnight sorties with her boyfriend, looks quickly at Beth, and then away again. I think about all the times they've teased me about what's ahead of me with Hannah. Canned laughter comes from the flickering glow of the TV.

We hear heavy footsteps in the garage. Like someone who might be carrying the weight of a tired child. I run to pull the door open.

'Oh. It's only you.'

'There was no sign of her.' Dermot anchors the bridge of his glasses to his face with his index finger, as if they are trying to slide away.

'Did you find the right place, are you sure?'

'It was the right place, Ray. But there's no sign of Hannah.'

Dermot is tired. I can hear it in his voice. I can see it in the slope of his shoulders and the way he holds his glasses to his face, the way he scowls at everyone. It's not like him.

I sit down again, defeated. 'What do we do now?' I know, but I don't want to be the one to say it.

'We should call the police again,' he says. 'It's coming up to two hours since we saw her. That's too long.'

The air condenses around me. I'd swear the humidity went up ten per cent right there, and that I heard it happen as well as feeling the extra pressure in my lungs.

Beth comes in from the TV. 'Uh, I'm not sure I should tell you all this, but—'

'But what, Beth? Say it!'

'There's a storm warning. There've been tornadoes over Galveston way. And there's a tropical depression in the Gulf, headed this way . . .'

'Oh, no! That's all we need!'

'But if it rains,' I say, 'she'll come in. Surely.'

We all troop in to look at the weather map. The familiar icon of a cyclonic storm swoops in a dipped circular pattern on the screen, a blot on the Gulf of Mexico. It's alarmingly close to the coast, but south of here.

'That looks more like Brownsville to me,' I say.

'No, Corpus.' Dermot and I have never once agreed about anything to do with a map, but I don't have the energy to argue with him now.

We wait for the announcer to settle it. Somewhere between the two, it turns out, but the trajectory of the storm is northwards and it's moving fast. There is a chance that it could hit the city before morning.

I haven't let myself think about what might happen if Hannah isn't back by midnight, let alone tomorrow morning. I stare at the map.

'It was a storm that helped us settle here,' I say, to no one in particular. I look over at Dermot. 'Do you remember?'

The phone rings. Dermot snatches it up. It's Laurie Franklin, wondering if we've had any news. 'No, nothing yet,' he says. 'Thanks for calling.' He hangs up and turns to me. 'I've been thinking,' he says. 'About the plane tickets. I'm wondering what we can do about a refund, if—'

I know he doesn't mean what he's saying. But I punch him anyway, full in the chest, with both fists, driving in hard. 'Stop talking about money!' I yell. 'Stop going on about leaving. Can't we just forget all that for one minute and concentrate on finding Hannah?'

He's knocked backwards by the force of my blow or by surprise or maybe both. His hands are up and clenched, ready to come back at me. He shakes his head and lets them fall by his sides again. 'This won't help,' he warns.

We're quiet, then. We avoid looking at each other, or at anyone else. I find myself staring at Dermot's feet. He's wearing sandals made from inner tubes or some such ridiculous thing, and his toes are curled in a tight grip, as if he's fighting to keep his balance on the deck of a heaving ship.

'You must call the police again,' Shula says.

'I'll do it,' Dermot says.

I walk past him, down the hall to our bedroom and curl up on the bed. How has everything we ever meant to each other come to this? I can't remember why it ever seemed like a good idea to marry Dermot, to follow him across the world. I used to think we shared everything, that I could anticipate his every thought or need and he could do the same for me. And here we are, strangers. Our daughter missing. Calling the police. It can't be real.

They all stop talking when I go back out to the kitchen.

'What did they say?'

'They took it more seriously this time. They said they'll be here as soon as they can.'

'I'm going out to check that hut myself,' I say.

'Oh, what's this now?' Dermot sounds bitter. 'You don't believe I could do that properly?'

'Stop fighting, you two.' Shula is impatient. 'It's just the strain talking. I'm sure Hannah will be okay. We just have to find her.'

I go to the window and look out. Long fingers of light stretch across the grass from our windows, deepening the shadows under the trees. A sudden power surge makes the lights dim and then brighten behind me. I don't know what to hope for, whether I want the storm to stay away, or to break right over our heads, shake everything loose. If Hannah is outdoors, maybe rain will drive her in. I try to think of all the things that might have that effect: rain, lightning, loud thunder, snakes. Cold, fear, hunger. Regret or loneliness. Love. Why hasn't she come home yet? What's keeping her?

I turn back into the room. It looks unfamiliar, like some place I've never been before. Dermot is making noises with his mouth, trying to tell me something I don't want to hear. I wish he'd stop. I want them all to go away now. Maybe then Hannah will come home.

24

I know that I'm the one who was reluctant to call the police before, but now I wish they'd got here hours ago. Preferably before Hannah even left. I've run out of ideas. I pace nervously around the house, which has filled up with people. Beth and Brooke are still here, and Nancy Cartwright has turned up with Laurie Franklin. Ellen and Tyler talk to Shula in low voices. Curtis has been on the phone to see if there's anything he can do. Brooke called him, apparently. She calls him about everything these days, relieved that he and Beth have declared a truce and might even see their way to being friends again, if only for her sake.

Tony comes in from next door, with little Li in tow. Tony's face is creased with distress as he asks if we've found Hannah. He tells us that he has searched their house and back garden twice, just in case. Dermot promises to let him know as soon as she turns up.

'How's Angie?' he remembers to ask.

Tony smiles and ducks his head. 'She resting, still. She pray, for Hannah.'

'Thank you.' Dermot walks them to the door.

We make more tea and have a council of war. We go through the whole list again. The park, the pool, Beth's house, Shula's house. The hut in the wasteground. We go through the list of Hannah's friends. When I mention Daniel, Beth offers to ask Graham to trace his number through the new school secretary. Ten minutes later, Graham calls.

'Daniel's mother is home tonight. She hasn't seen Hannah, and neither has Daniel, but if they hear anything they'll call.'

'Oh.'

'Is it okay if I come over?' Graham asks. 'I don't want to intrude.'

'You won't be intruding,' I say. I hang up and turn back to the others. Everyone had stopped talking while Graham was on the phone. 'The most obvious place is Lucie's house.'

'Let's check it out again,' Dermot says. Tyler goes with him.

They come back alone. 'The place is deserted,' Tyler says. 'All the lights are off. Even the motion-detector is blown.'

'The garage isn't locked,' Dermot says. 'But there's no one there.'

I sit in the corner. My head feels too heavy on my neck. The weight of it presses down through my shoulders, tightens my lungs, makes my legs ache.

Nancy is standing with her back to me, talking to Laurie, who looks at her as if she might recently have crawled out of a drain.

When I come up behind them, Laurie is spitting words at Nancy, low and angry. She stops when she sees me and tries to get Nancy's attention, but she's in mid-sentence.

'I tell you, now,' I hear Nancy say. 'No matter what you say. It turns out to be the husband. Nine times out of ten.'

'Ray,' Laurie says to me, more loudly than she needs to. 'Come and join us.'

Nancy snaps around, spreads her lips apart in a wide smile. That giggle of hers erupts from somewhere behind her nose.

'Get the hell out of my house,' I say.

'Why, Ray, honey . . .' Nancy's mouth gapes open, foolish, while colour runs across her face and down her neck.

'Get out. And don't ever come back.'

I watch her tug at the front door and leave. My heart feels like it's flown up to my mouth and is throbbing there, trying to escape. I'm glad that Laurie has the sense to stay quiet.

'What did she say that upset you so much?' Dermot asks.

I can't tell him. I watch the slump of his shoulders as he walks off across the room, the defeated tilt of his head. I know that if there is one thing in the world I can be sure of, it is that Dermot would never hurt any of our children, or any child. For all that I've been bleating about how you never know anyone, for all that I know that such things can and do happen, I know that Dermot is not capable of that kind of harm. I'd stake my own life on it.

What I feel then is so overpowering that I have to go outside. It's like a surge of tidal water, all the rage and resentment that I've felt, the wounded indignation, receding. I couldn't hold on to it if I tried, which I consider doing just for a second. All that bitterness rushes out of me like water through a drain and I let it go. I don't want it. I have nothing to hold it with.

Outside, the air is sweetening, the way it can in this town. It has become scented velvet, inky and rich. There are too many people in our house and I'm in no hurry to go back to it. I cross to the gap in the fence and look out at the sea of grass. A few dark shapes with flashlights move around the diggers and my heart sinks. They are looking for Hannah, but I know that if she could see all this activity, she'd be terrified. I worry about when the police get here, the lights and the sirens and the noise. Big men in uniforms and heavy boots tramping around all the places we've already been.

Think, I tell myself again. Go back to the beginning. And it's Lucie whose face comes to haunt me. Lucie, the time she ran away and hid behind our air-conditioner for three-quarters of an hour and Marilyn thought I knew where she was the whole time. Lucie's eyes sliding away from mine. Lucie planning parties just to make Hannah jealous.

Why was their garage unlocked? I wander down the street and across the road and, almost casually, I walk up Marilyn's driveway, try the garage door. It opens and I slip inside.

Byron's precious TransAm fills half the space. Tools are hung on orderly racks around the walls. The washer and dryer stand empty and free of clutter. I turn to go and for a split second I think I see a shadow move across an upstairs window of the house. I stop dead. Stare hard into the blackness. Nothing.

I creep through Marilyn's side gate into her backyard and up to the back door. I put my face against the glass of the kitchen window. 'Hannah?' I call, but quietly. Just above a whisper. 'Are you there?'

There's no answer. But I'm sure, now.

Marilyn used to keep a spare key on the shelf above the washer. I go back inside the garage to look, but there's no key there. Nor on any of the other shelves, or in the toolbox. Of course, she would have found a different hiding place once things turned bad between us.

I sit on the patio, on one of Marilyn's wrought-iron chairs, like a beggar. Moonlight washes over the grass and Marilyn's well-tended plants, her ornamental pond. Where would she hide a key? I stare at the house. Hanging baskets full of flowers are suspended from plastic hooks and a pair of Marilyn's gardening gloves hang from the nail under the eaves. I remember Marilyn confiding, once, that she used to hide chocolate from Lucie in the oven-mitt.

I get up slowly and walk into the shadow of the house. I pull down the gloves, put my hands into them as if I want to wear them. The fingers are tight, but I push my way in until I find what I'm looking for. I turn the glove upside down and shake it and the key strikes a metallic note on the concrete.

I'm past caring about the alarm, I'm going in there. I won't go back for the others and I certainly won't wait for the police. The last thing I want is for a crowd of strangers to come barging over here, scaring Hannah out of her wits.

If she's in there.

I ease the key into the lock and open the door. Moonlight makes squares on the kitchen floor. Streetlights finger their way into the hall through the tall narrow panes of glass on either side of the door. The stairwell rises, dark, in front of me.

I turn on the light. I have butterflies in my stomach, cramps in my gut, everything knotted and tightening. Sweat runs down my back. I take the stairs two at a time, talking in a level voice: 'Hannah? It's okay, sweetie. It's only me.'

I hear something knock against a wall somewhere. I jump with fright, catch myself, start moving again. At the top of the stairs I push open the door of the inner room, the one they use as a storm shelter. It's pitch black in there and for an instant I falter. What if I'm wrong?

I turn on the light. A sleeping bag is heaped on the floor, with some of Lucie's toys spread around it. An unopened box of fruit rolls. A bowl of cereal spilled, soggy cornflakes and a puddle of milk on the carpet. I touch it and find it still cool and wet.

'Hannah,' I say, as calmly as I can. 'I know you're

here. You're not in trouble, sweetheart. No one is angry with you. Please come out.'

I sit down and wait. I'll give it the count of ten and then I will slam open the door of every closet in this house, I'll empty every drawer, I'll turn everything inside out until I find her. My foot begins to twitch. *Three, four.* Will I be able to hold myself down until ten? Why bother? *Seven, eight.* There's no one here.

The closet door slides open and Hannah is there, looking out at me. Her eyes are wide and her face is streaked with tears.

'Oh, baby.'

I hold out my arms but she stands still, holding on to the door, working the wood with her hands.

'Hannah. Please. I'm so sorry.'

And then she's in my arms, there's a storm of sobbing at my neck. I pull her tighter and closer. If I could pull her right back into myself, I would. I'd keep her there for ever.

She wriggles free. 'I can't breathe, Mom.'

'Sorry.' I let her go.

We look at each other. I don't know what to do, or say, next. This girl in front of me is someone I don't know anything like as well as I thought I did.

'I don't want to go,' Hannah says.

'I know you don't.'

'I want Hunter back.'

'I know, lovey. I do, too. But he's gone. And we have to give this a try.'

'If I hate it there, can we come back?'

I catch my breath. It's exactly what I asked Dermot ten years ago. 'We'll have to see what happens.'

'But we might?'

'Maybe.'

'What about vacations?'

'Definitely.'

'Promise?'

'I promise.'

'We can, right? You got that visa thing.'

'Hannah, you have a passport. You're a citizen. You'll always be able to come back.'

We go into Lucie's bathroom and I help Hannah to wash and dry her face.

'There. Better?'

She nods. We hold hands on the way back down the stairs, let ourselves out the back door. I lock it and put the key back where I found it.

'I'm glad you left it there,' I say.

'I didn't.'

'Then how did you get in?'

'Lucie left the door open for me.'

I shudder to think what might have happened if someone else had found that door unlocked first, if someone else had been waiting for Hannah when she got into the house. I squeeze her hand, hard. But none of those things happened, I remind myself. Nothing happened. Hannah is safe.

*

When we get to our own front door, it's open. Dermot is already on his way through it.

'Oh!' he says, when he sees Hannah. He scoops her up onto his shoulder, buries his face in her neck and bursts into tears. 'I'm so glad,' he says. 'So glad. Oh, God.'

It turns out that he was on his way back over to get her. Marilyn had called and told him where Hannah was as soon as she'd found out what the girls had done. She went away, she told Dermot, crying down the phone, because she didn't want to be around for the whole fuss of our departure. But all along she'd planned to come back and say goodbye before we left.

'She wanted to let you get all steamed up and ready to believe she didn't care you're leaving,' Beth says. 'She's still playing games with you.'

'Sssh, Beth. I don't care.' I squeeze Hannah's hand again. I can't take my eyes off her. 'Go on, Dermot.'

'But then Lucie started making phone calls from the motel room. And they checked with the desk and discovered she was calling home. So Marilyn checked her messages and heard yours, and one from Beth, to say that Hannah was missing. And at last she got it out of Lucie. How she had left the door open for Hannah, and how Hannah would stay in the storm room at the top of the stairs, where no light shows on the street.'

'Is Lucie in trouble?' Hannah asks in a small, sleepy voice.

'No,' I say.

'I helped her to hide the food in the closet,' Hannah

379

says. 'And the flashlight. All the things you do, Mom. It was fun.'

'But what were you thinking, Hannah? How long would you have stayed there?'

'It was just so as we'd miss the plane. Lucie was going to hide too, when they were supposed to leave the motel. So they wouldn't get back until it was too late.'

We call the police to tell them that Hannah has turned up. Wouldn't you know it, we're still on the phone when the doorbell rings and a burly blonde officer, with shoulders as wide as our front door, stands there looking solemn. We have a bit of explaining to do. He comes in to speak to Hannah, to make sure she's all right.

He frowns at me when I explain how I found her. He says he'd better go over there to check the premises. Dermot goes with him.

Hannah is bug-eyed but I tell her I don't care. 'Marilyn isn't going to make any trouble for us, Hannah. I promise you that.'

'But I spilled milk on their carpet. Marilyn will be mad.'

'No she won't, lovey.'

When all the explanations are over and Hannah has finished two mugs of hot chocolate and is tucked up and fast asleep in our bed, when everyone else has wished us well and gone away again, we're left with nothing to shield us from each other.

*

We sit, exhausted, in front of the TV and watch the distant storm as it spends itself in the Gulf and makes landfall just south of the border as a tropical storm.

'What a relief, to have her back,' Dermot says. 'Do you think she'll run again?'

'She says no. She was pretty stunned by all the activity. She heard the traffic-watch helicopter and thought there was a criminal on the loose, so she was extra scared. I'd say she'll stay pretty close to us now.'

'What about you? Are you going to run?'

'Me? No.' I'm tired of the effort it takes to keep my distance from him. I move closer so that our bodies are touching, but lightly. He takes my hand between his and rubs the base of my thumb, the way he rubs his own thumbs when they're sore from work.

My heart is still beating harder and faster than normal. While Hannah was missing, all the terror in the world gaped open at my feet. Now that she's back, that pit has closed over again, as if it doesn't exist. But I know it does. Already I feel a little foolish, as if we overreacted. Somewhere, someone else is out searching for a daughter who won't ever come home. Just because ours did is no reason to be complacent.

We sit there, holding hands, staring at the vanishing storm. After a while I pull myself up to face him. 'Don't you feel as if we've got away with something? As if we were careless and now we've been given a second chance?' Of all the things that are going through my head, this is the safest one to say out loud.

'How do you mean?'

'Losing Hannah made me see everything – differently. If I'm really honest, I have to say that I understand why that thing happened, with you and Diane. Almost.'

He starts to say something but I put my hand up to stop him.

'I wish it had been someone else. But at least you pulled back from it in the end. So, what I want to say is, let's leave all this shit behind us when we go. Let's really make a new start.'

He looks puzzled. 'Okay.'

I sit back, exhausted. I don't know where to go from here.

'Do you really think I make all the decisions without consulting you?' he asks later.

'You do! But maybe this time there really was no choice. I don't know. And hey, it could be fun, going home. Joanne says—'

'Oh God,' Dermot groans. 'Joanne.'

I smile to myself. 'You love her really, Dermot. She's like a sister.'

'How's that, now?'

'She keeps you in line. It's good for you.'

'That's that, then,' he says, after a silence.

'I wish I was so sure.'

'But you just said—'

'I mean Hannah. I have a feeling we're only getting started with her.' If today's performance is anything to go by, I'm going to need all the help I can get with Hannah. Looking back on myself as a teenager, I can see that it's no more than I deserve. 'What'll we do?' I ask.

Dermot misses the point. 'We'll finish clearing out the house tomorrow. We'll hand the furniture over to Beth's cousin the next day. Then we'll get a taxi to the airport. And we'll go home.'

'No.'

'What do you mean, no?'

'I vote we ask the kids what they want to do tomorrow. Let's take a break from all this. We'll spend the whole day at McDonald's if we have to.'

'But we don't have time. There's too much to do.'

'We've been packing and leaving for days. What the hell does it matter if the house isn't ready when we go? It's not the end of the world.'

'But . . .'

'Come on, Dermot. It's only fair. Let's just ask them what they want. For once.'

25

'The beach,' Hannah says. 'Please.'

Dermot begins to object. He mentions sand and dirt and wet towels and swimsuits and all the gear we don't have any more, like buckets and spades, or the kite, but when he catches my eye he stops. We drive down to Galveston and we take turns to bury everyone in the sand, the way the children once buried Sylvia. That makes it easy to talk about her, and about Pat and Conall and all the other people who are waiting to meet them on the other side of the ocean.

'This ocean?' Hannah stares out past the oil platforms at the horizon.

'Further out, beyond the Gulf.'

'But is it all the same water?' She looks down at her feet. We've moved into the sea now, to clean ourselves of the oily sand.

'Yes,' I say. 'I suppose it is.'

'Could we swim there?'

'No. It's too far.' I see Hannah looking into the distance, her chin at an angle I don't like. 'Leave it, Hannah. Until you're older, anyway. Put in some practice, first.'

'Granny says there's a swimming club near her. She says she's going to make enquiries. That means she'll ask if I can join, right?'

'We'll see. It depends where we'll live. But we'll find something.'

'What about me?' Ben asks.

'There'll be loads of things for everyone to do. You'll love it,' Dermot says.

Just then Grace loses her balance and slips under water. She comes up screaming, her eyes screwed shut, her hands making frantic windmills. I lift her out of the water to calm her down.

'Bat! Bat! I dropped her!' Grace yells.

Hannah rushes over to rescue Bat and squeezes her out over the sand.

'She's okay, Gracie. Hannah saved her.'

Hannah takes Grace onto her lap. Together, they tease the tangles out of Bat's hair with their fingers.

'Look, look!' Jack calls, excited. 'A jellyfish!'

'It's a man-o'-war,' Dermot says.

He chases the boys, laughing, along the beach until at last they come and flop down beside me, Grace and Hannah on our single, soggy Garfield beach towel. It doesn't seem to matter at all that we're wet, in that warm, murky air.

Later, we join the traffic on the freeway, moving slowly towards home.

'When we come back that new road will be finished, won't it?' Hannah says. 'That means we'll be able to get here faster.'

My eyes sting. We're on the raised part of the road, coming up to the bend that swerves away above our neighbourhood. I stare out of my window over the level of the trees, over the apartment complexes and shopping malls, the arc-lights of sports centres and parking lots and wonder what we'll find if we ever come back. What we'll imagine we're looking for.

Worn out and cranky, I begin to wish we'd stuck with the original plan. We should have stayed at home and cleaned the house.

'Tomorrow's going to be murder,' I say quietly to Dermot.

'We'll get through it.'

We jump out of bed as soon as we're awake, throw the sheets in the washer. We have barely boiled the kettle when the doorbell rings.

'It's only us!' Beth says. 'We've brought breakfast.' Brooke holds a giant box of Dunkin' Donuts. The children squeal their delight and sweep her off to the kitchen table.

'We'll never eat all those,' I say.

'Yes we will!' Hannah's eyes shine with excitement. I wonder if she fully understands what's going on around her. It's as if all that trouble never happened.

At nine o'clock Beth's cousin comes to take the furniture, as promised. When it's gone, I look at the marks on the floor, at mounds of discarded rubbish from drawers. 'We'll never get through all of this.'

'Ellen said she was coming to help.'

'Ellen? I couldn't have her wash my floors!'

'Why not? A floor is a floor!' Ellen sounds offended.

'I hope y'all don't mind. The garage was open, so I came right on in.'

And before long, everyone is here. Tyler hooks up the trailer Bill left behind and makes a trip to the Goodwill store at the mall with bags full of cutlery, clothes, old toys. Beth and Ellen set to work scrubbing down the tiles in the bathroom.

'I don't see why you want to leave the place so clean,' Dermot says.

Ellen, Beth and I exchange a look. 'We do,' Ellen and Beth say at the same time. And off they go, armed with Comet and scraps of rag. Shula gets to work with the hoover. We empty one room at a time, then Shula goes in with the hoover while I wash the windows and then, when each room is clean and empty, we close the door.

Brooke plays with the kids down at the end of the street, by the live oak tree. They're playing 'What time is it, Mr Wolf?' It brings a lump to my throat, but there's a lot of happy screaming going on.

'Does someone need to watch them?' Dermot asks uneasily.

'Brooke is on it,' Beth says. 'And Laila's there too.'

'But ... the work has started again, out on the Parkway.'

We all know that's not what he means.

'Brooke is on it,' I repeat. 'It'll be okay.'

The next time I look up, Marilyn is standing there. She is thinner and paler, but I'm glad to see she's wearing her burnt-orange sundress and a matching ribbon in her hair. Byron stands just behind her. He could be holding her up, but he's not. She steps forward all by herself.

'I came to say goodbye,' she says. 'And I'm sorry about what Lucie did.'

'There was a pair of them in it. Where is she?'

'Down in the tree, with the others.'

When I hug Marilyn, she feels as if she could easily break in two under my hands. 'You were my first friend here,' I remind her. 'I won't forget you. How are you doing?'

'They've begun to reduce my medication.'

'Good for you! Good luck with it. Let me know how you get on.'

'Okay,' she says. 'I will. And you – write me.'

'I will.'

There's an awkward silence. Then she says, 'I won't stay for the goodbyes.'

'No.' I let her go. 'That colour suits you,' I say. 'I'm glad to see you wearing it again.'

'You don't think it's too strong?'

'That's your style, Marilyn. I'll miss it.'

Byron waves and they go out through the garage door. Before I have time to think about the fact that they've gone, Shula is beside me with the hoover. 'What's next?' she wants to know.

We urge people to take anything they might want. The coffee pot, the teapot, the mugs we've used right up until the end. Whatever's left in our fridge, the cans and sauces from the press that other people have passed on to us.

Time blurs. Someone takes the kids off for one last swim. People I thought had left already turn up to say goodbye. Curtis drives right across town from his trendy new apartment just to say, 'Don't y'all forget us now, y'hear?'

'How could we?' I say. 'Where's Michael?'

'He wanted to come. But then he thought y'all'd drive him out with y'all's shotgun.'

'Curtis. You know we've never owned a gun.'

'We should've thought of that sooner.' He grins over at Dermot.

'Well, if you're ever in Ireland, come and look us up,' I say. 'I'll have forgiven him by then. Maybe.'

'Beth already has.'

'Beth is a better person than I am.'

There's only one room left to clear, the living room. Suddenly, there's no one there except for me and Beth.

'I don't think I can do this.'

A horn blows outside.

'Sheey-it,' Beth says. 'The taxi.'

'Oh God, what time is it? I'm not ready!' I look around. There are still bags of stuff for recycling stacked against the walls.

'Don't you worry, girl,' Beth says. 'I'll deal with it.'

'There's still the kitchen . . .'

Dermot sticks his head in the door. 'Ray, it's time to go.'

'But there's a whole—'

'I know, but it's too late. Come on. The kids are already in the car.' He goes out again before I can ask who had managed to arrange that. I know I could spend the rest of my life trying to piece together how this day has passed and I will never be able to figure it out.

He sticks his head back in the door. 'We'll miss our flight if you don't come now.'

'I don't care!' I mutter when he's gone again.

'You don't mean that. This is what you said you wanted. Remember?'

'When?'

'Way back. When I first knew you. You said you wanted to go home.'

'This is home.'

'I know. But there is home, too.'

Rueful, we try to smile. I wish I'd known sooner what it would cost me to leave this place. These people. It's not just the children who are being uprooted after all.

Beth hauls two tissues out of the pockets of her tracksuit and hands one to me, using the other one herself.

'Better?' she asks, when I've blown my nose.

'Better.'

'You don't want those beautiful children of yours to get upset. You take care of them, y'hear?'

'Don't!' I can't even say Brooke's name.

'Best stop talking, then.'

'Okay. We can do this.'

Arm in arm, we go out to where everyone else is grouped around the grass, the path, my driveway.

Even Angie and Tony have come out of their house to say goodbye. They stand on the street with everyone else, close together. I can see now that Angie is pregnant. Her folded arms rest lightly on the swollen curve of her belly. Li has one hand tucked into Brooke's, but his parents don't seem to notice.

'This is just like one of your after-school days, Ray,' Ellen says.

'Y'all have been wonderful,' I say. 'I'm going to miss you.'

Someone whoops. 'Did you hear what she said?'

'Y'all,' they chorus back to me, cheering.

I duck my head and get into the front of the taxi. Dermot asks the driver to do a loop around the central circle three times before leaving the street, for old times' sake. The driver rises to the occasion, driving faster with each turn, making the children laugh and fall over on top of each other.

Outside on the street our friends are waving. Their mouths are open, calling farewells that I can't hear. It's like a fairground ride, the kind I love and hate, the false starts that get your adrenaline pumping before the ultimate freefall sends you spinning out of control, not knowing where or when it's going to stop. All I can do is hope that someone, somewhere, knows what they are doing, that this fall won't last for ever and we'll find solid ground. That I'll survive, in one piece, to start again.

Acknowledgements

Special thanks to my agent, Shirley Stewart, and to her assistant, Julia Forster; to Patricia Deevy and Michael McLoughlin and everyone at Penguin Ireland; to Christie Hickman at Michael Joseph, and to Eugenie Todd.

Through their sponsorship of public art and artists (including writers), Ballymun Regeneration Ltd helped to make it possible to write this novel. Thanks to everyone at Breaking Ground, especially Aisling Prior and Sheena Barrett.

Parts of the novel were written at the Tyrone Guthrie Centre, Annaghmakerrig. Thanks to Sheila Pratschke, to my fellow residents, and to everyone who works at the centre, for their hospitality and encouragement.

For their comments and suggestions, thanks to members of the Women Writers' Web and members of the Tierney Writing Group (Karen Brady, Maura Clancy, Ray Corcoran, Eileen Dennan, Anthony Furlong, Eric Lalor, Joan McDonnell, Joe Morelli, Margaret Moriarty, Victoria Sargent, Daniel Seery and Andre Venchard); also to Sheila Barrett, Susan Connolly, Celia de Fréine, Catherine Dunne, Janet Hampshire, Ann Marie Hourihane, Felicity Hogan, Aisling Kearney, Eithne McGuinness, Belinda Martin,

Jackie Mills, Ger Philpott, Zita Reihill, Prue and David Rudd, Sheila Vance; and to Trudi, Clair and Joe.

As always, the biggest thanks go to Simon, Zita, Emma, Nessa, Eoin and Ryan, who had to live with it.